Seven Laurels

Seven Laurels

A Novel

by
Linda Busby Parker

Southeast Missouri State University Press • 2004

First published in the United States of America, 2004
by Southeast Missouri State University Press
One University Plaza
Cape Girardeau, MO 63701
All rights reserved
Printed in the United States of America

First edition
ISBN: 0972430474 (paper)
ISBN: 0972430482 (cloth)

Seven Laurels is a work of historical fiction. Other than the occasional use of historical public figures, events, and quotations of
historical record, the characters, events, and dialogue herein are
fictional and are not intended to represent, refer to, or disparage any
known person or entity, living or dead.

We gratefully acknowledge:
Sections from *Invisible Man* by Ralph Ellison, courtesy of Mrs.
    Fanny Ellison
Poem, "Little Brown Baby" by Paul Laurence Dunbar
Excerpt from Lars Gustafsson's "Greatness Strikes Where It
    Pleases," courtesy of Lars Gustafsson

Cover and dustjacket art and design by Liz Lester

For Donald—my love,
and for my father, Louie Barton Busby

Acknowledgments

A writer writes in isolation, and any affirmation that the words are traveling from the writer's heart to the heart of another is sustenance for the continued journey. In writing *Seven Laurels*, I have partaken of manna along the way that kept me writing. In 2001, early chapters of this novel won the Heartland Fellowship at the Indiana University summer writing conference; that small fellowship encouraged me. In 2002 *Seven Laurels* (under the title *The Sum of Augusts)* won the James Jones First Novel Fellowship. That recognition was sustenance to complete the novel. I am grateful to the scholars and the writers and readers at the James Jones Foundation—especially Kaylie Jones and Michael Lennon.

In the MFA program at Spalding University, I learned to write— really learned to write. Many thanks to Sena Jeter Naslund for starting and directing the program and to Karen Mann for making everything work at residencies and all the times in between. Many heartfelt thanks to my mentors: Roy Hoffman, Wesley Brown, Mary Yukari Waters, and Julie Brickman. And thanks to the novel goddesses: Charlotte Rains Dixon, Maryann Lesert, Katy Yocom and Deidre Woollard. I am also grateful to the Novel Circle at Spalding. These people read my book and gave me much needed feedback: Anne Axton, Katherine Danner, M. Kay Miller, and Mary Popham. Other excellent readers included Sister Mary Ellen Doyle, Joseph Crow, Holly Compton, Susan Storm, and Orin Harvey Parker Jr. Thanks to each one of you—you made this novel possible.

For bringing the novel to life, I owe Susan Swartwout at Southeast Missouri State University Press. Susan is the driving force. She is the publisher, the editor, the copy-reader and the promoter. She is one of those women who can spin five plates at once—and not one falls. She also remains calm and encouraging through the entire publication process. I have tremendous admiration for Susan.

Finally, but certainly not last, a special thanks to my family. To my husband, Donald, and to our daughters Amanda Leigh, Allison Ann and Kiran—you tolerated all the times I was in Low Ridge instead of being present in our moment in Mobile. And thank you to my mother, Betty Busby, for filling in for me when I was off earning my MFA or attending a writing conference. I love you all.

The hourglass-shaped ribbon of light moved across the surface of the planet, dawn line and dusk line rushing forward like great wings across distant plains and mountains. Slowly or swiftly, depending on how you chose to measure it, the earth moved in its orbit and would never return to the same point where it had once been. Slowly or swiftly, the solar system moved in its orbit, and with silent, dizzying speed; like a disk or light, the galaxy moved in its mysterious rotation around itself.

—Lars Gustafsson
"Greatness Strikes Where It Pleases"

Part One

The Promise of Land

September 1956
Low Ridge, Alabama

A boy becomes a man when he has his own house—leased or paying notes doesn't matter; the tangible property anchors one corner of manhood. Even heaven is defined by property—*in my father's house are many mansions.* When he was a boy, his father Tom took Brewster's small hand in his own and forced it to rub the old wound, thick as molten plastic. "This house cost me," he had said when he guided the tips of Brewster's short fingers over the sealed cut—raised, clear and shiny. Brewster hated the feel of it, waxy under the pads of his fingers. Tom had won the money for the little house on Perry Street in a game of cards that went from accusations to flashing knives; Tom placed his right hand over his hip pocket, protected the cash and shielded his chest with his left arm, which suffered a jagged gash from his elbow to his wrist, leaving Tom's left arm and hand drawn and worthless for all but balancing and lifting.

"Whip tails, kick butts out on that street. You know this my house!" Tom said.

"We know this is your house," Brewster's grandmother, Mama Tee, consoled her son. "We live in Tom's house."

In the small front room, Tom staggered and cursed. Spit flew with his angry broad-tongued words, "Whip butts to that street!" He circled the couch, bumping against it.

"This is Tom's house," Mama Tee repeated over and over again from the kitchen. Tom staggered, slamming into a tall end table that stood on three delicate feet, and a lamp went down, the one Brewster's brother TeeBoy had given Mama Tee, one of the last things TeeBoy held. Brewster brought to mind a clear picture of TeeBoy, a grin on his face, holding out the lamp to their grandmother. When Tom's loose left hand hit the lamp, it landed on the floor and the base of it shattered. Mama Tee gasped. Something ran through Brewster like electric current. He snapped from his chair in the kitchen, ducked through the low doorframe, and grabbed the front of his father's shirt, lifting him. His open palm slapped Tom's left jaw, and he fell back on the couch.

Brewster wanted to lift Tom, carry him to the front door, throw him outside, and kick him until he rolled into the ditch. If he grabbed a knot of Tom's shirt and whiffed the stench of stale liquor on Tom's breath, his fist would start on the wiry stubble over Tom's jaw, and he would not stop. With his own knuckles, he would hammer and smash and crush.

He went out the front door, slamming it.

He walked down Perry Street toward Paulette's Café where the air wasn't so still because Paulette kept the doors and windows open and had a couple of electric fans on six-foot legs that made half-circles, giving the place some breath. The floors in Paulette's were raw wood, darkened by years of feet—working feet in mud-caked brogans, Friday night feet in three-inch heels, wing-tipped feet of door-to-door insurance men, and worn-soled feet of traveling men. The air in Paulette's smelled of fried eggs and sausage, boiled eggs and coffee, fried chicken and turnip greens cooked with peppers and bacon. On a table in front of the bar, Brewster spotted an abandoned Sunday paper. He sat, facing one of the fans that stirred the air in front of him.

He ordered himself a cup of coffee, and he folded the paper at the real estate ads. He had exactly three hundred, thirty-five dollars and fifty-two cents in the bank. This might be enough to find him some kind of little place. He held steady work and he knew he could not live in the house of his father. If he did not get out, he would kill Tom because he would not be able to stop his hands when they met Tom's flesh. A man must leave his father's house and the time was past ripe.

He held the coffee cup at his lips with the steam drifting up his nose and the ad for Ole Summit rose to his eyes. *Sixty acres. Ole Summit Highway, twelve miles south of Low Ridge. Attractive Price.* A telephone number. The ad was not under "Colored Property," but the way the letters came off the page and up to his eyes was a sign. Mama Tee taught him to be alert for signs.

He ambled back to Perry Street with the paper tucked under his arm. Mama Tee had a three-way party line that Mary Lee Luce put in so she could reach Mama Tee whenever she wanted her house cleaned, and Mary Lee would not have to walk on the colored streets to find her.

Mama Tee sat at the dinette, her Bible open on the Formica top, and she looked at Brewster when he stood in front of her. He raised the folded paper. "Going to call about some property."

"Property?"

But Brewster didn't answer her. He went to the front room and dialed the number. The voice on the other end was thin, no thicker than an alto. "Sixty acres," the man said. "Sixty dollars an acre. Inherited the land from my uncle and I have no reason to hold it."

Three thousand and six hundred dollars. No one Brewster knew had that kind of money. He was sorry he called the man because his mouth smacked dry from speaking with him, and his hand was damp where he held the telephone against his ear. He did not tell Mama Tee about the sign, and he dismissed the land as quickly as he had embraced it.

Brewster was at the Three Brothers shed early next morning, before Deak Armbrecht opened the barn-like doors. Old Deak and his brothers had come from Holland at the close of World War I, establishing Three Brothers, manufacturers of hand-made cabinets and furniture. They positioned their shop between Montgomery and Birmingham, maintaining steady business. Deak was the last remaining of the brothers, and this circumstance brought Brewster McAtee and Deak Armbrecht together. Before Brewster graduated from high school, Deak employed him to cut lengths of lumber, stack boards, and sweep wood shavings, but Brewster stayed past the time his wages covered, and Deak taught him how to rout bedpost mortises, lathe a table leg, and reed a column with a scratch stock. For over four years they had worked side-by-side and they talked little, which suited both of them. They observed each other and each man thought he understood something about the nature of the other.

Brewster took pleasure in arriving early and sitting on the stump to the left of the barn-like shed, waiting for Mr. Deak to spot him. When the old man looked out his kitchen window and saw Brewster, he came running, apologetic, as if he had been caught with his pants down. He didn't like a hired man waiting to work. It was worth getting to the shed early to watch Mr. Deak run out like a bow-legged chicken, his feet skittering in the dust, racing to open the shed doors, switch on the lights, and throw the strap of his leather apron over his neck. A jump-start like that and the old man wouldn't settle down until mid-morning.

After lunch on this Monday, they knocked off in the shed long enough to deliver a walnut serving-board to Mrs. Mertle Scruggs. Brewster did all the work on the sideboard, which had pencil-post legs and was plain and ordinary until Mr. Deak carved sunflower tambours on rosewood and joined these to the tops of the square-faced legs, then set brass pulls on the drawers. Mrs. Scruggs paid Deak in cash, and when he returned to the shed, he put his back to Brewster and counted his money. He walked across the raw-board floor and put a twenty-dollar bill on Brewster's workbench. Generally, Mr. Armbrecht wouldn't part with a dime unless he had studied it before his short, flat thumb delivered it to his index finger, but here he was giving a twenty away.

"You do t'at work, you earn t'at money," he said, but the "m" on money carried more weight than "m's" should.

Brewster would put his money in the bank. This would give him three hundred, fifty-five dollars and fifty-two cents. Deak Armbrecht had taken him to the bank for the first time. "You need to put some of t'at money in ta bank, boy. You know how to do t'at?"

He had followed Deak Armbrecht to the Bank of Low Ridge where Mr. Armbrecht told the woman behind the window to open Mr. McAtee an account. Brewster enjoyed the importance of doing business in the bank. He liked the thick front doors, tall ceilings, heavy beams, and marble floors. He put in five dollars on his first visit, and on most Fridays, he walked to the same window and made a deposit. The women called him by name, and he knew exactly how much money he had earning interest in the Bank of Low Ridge. If he had hidden his money on Perry Street, Tom would have found it and spent it on liquor and dice.

With an extra twenty in his pocket, Brewster again thought about the land. After work he drove out Ole Summit Highway just as the sun was setting. He spotted a stake with a red strip of canvas tied to it and he knew this was the beginning of the land he had read about in the ad. Through the open window of his truck he smelled the weeds and thick grasses drying in the heat of September. Pines, oaks, and scrub trees grew almost to the road. The cicadas drilled their circular chant and a solitary mockingbird yelled through the trees. Brewster wanted this land.

Until he fell asleep that night, he lay in bed thinking of schemes to increase his cash. TeeBoy broke into his rest, showing his wound, blood pouring from his heart, his eyes round and wild, his mouth a silent circle, but his face giving voice to shock. TeeBoy danced in heavy, wide-weighted steps, a folded newspaper in his hand. Brewster sat up in bed, arms outstretched, but TeeBoy vanished as quickly as he had come. Brewster rolled from his side to his back, freeing his chest of weight and keeping his nose in open space, allowing himself to breathe while he worked through the vision—TeeBoy's broad, blunt dance. He held the folded *Gazette*.

When Brewster eased back into sleep, TeeBoy came again, showing him scenes that bound the two as brothers, playing out his last hours. Brewster had not wanted to go to DuBose. The place was too dark. You couldn't see trouble coming. DuBose himself shot two boys who flashed knives and drew blood that looked like liquid gold in the dim amber lights strung on black cords across the center of the room. But he went to watch out for TeeBoy because he was younger and he was hotheaded, always had been. It was Saturday night, and DuBose had the blues sliding like hot, sweet syrup, with the High Steps playing. The man on the trombone blew notes slick, curvy, and smooth. Brewster had three whiskies, no ice, and he had Antonette, whose shoulders were thick, but soft as butter.

Mr. Trombone slid easy notes that sounded like Charlie Patton's blues, easy moving tones. TeeBoy was with the jivers from Happy Landing, the flophouse off Limrick Road that had a red neon sign out front, but the "d" in Landing burned out as soon as the red-lettered sign went up.

"That a place for rovin' niggers," Mama Tee said. "Steer clear 'round that place."

But TeeBoy was at DuBose with the Happy Landing crowd and a couple of discharged military boys who still wore uniforms. Brewster told TeeBoy not to play pool with the soldier-boys because they thought they were something in those uniforms, though the outfits didn't have any merit because they were old enough to have moth holes eaten clean through the wool, but there he was, playing pool with the Happy Landing boys and the would-be soldiers. When the piano player started with short, free and easy notes, TeeBoy headed for the platform. His body moved to the fast beat; he looked like he was in the air, not on the floor. His feet lifted short steps, clean as glass.

TeeBoy laughed with his head back, and his eyes looked into the soft gold lights. Three girls tapped their feet and twisted their hips at the edge of the raised floor, waiting for their chance to glide into the yellow light with TeeBoy. Brewster went outside to get some air and let the breeze wash the smoke out of his eyes. He sat on the fender of his truck, lit a cigarette, and listened to the music drift past the rafters. He slapped the beat against his thigh, and he thought about going back inside, sliding in alongside Antonette, tasting her sweet neck and pressing his fingers into the full, soft flesh at her hips. That's when the door shattered—pieces flew in the air. The pack from Happy Landing erupted through the opening with TeeBoy struggling in the middle of the circle. Brewster saw TeeBoy pinned against the wall by two of the Happy Landing boys. He jumped from the truck, but his legs moved in slow motion. With weighted legs, he ran toward TeeBoy, and he could see himself running, like he hovered above, watching himself. He ran and ran, and made no sound. He ran toward TeeBoy. One of the boys drew a knife, the blade burnishing a silver streak in the dim light of the bare bulb over the door. The boy's elbow pulled back, the hand flew out, the fist held tight around the handle. Brewster saw the thrust, but he didn't see the blood yet because he was running and watching himself. He saw TeeBoy stagger, fall to his knees, and lean backward at an awful angle.

"Shit, man, shit," were the first sounds Brewster heard when he was knocked off balance by the military boys running in a pack. A path cleared before him, and he saw TeeBoy on the concrete, hunched on his elbow, looking down at the blood that flowed from his chest so fast there was nothing that could stop it. TeeBoy didn't scream; he laid his head back and his eyes glazed like liquid glass was poured over them, and they froze in place. Brewster knelt beside TeeBoy, trying to catch his blood, putting his hands on TeeBoy's shirt, over TeeBoy's heart, pushing the wound together, but the blood came up over his fingers, warm and red-orchid in the light of the naked bulb. The blood soaked TeeBoy's shirt, ran down on the concrete slab, ran behind TeeBoy's head, and off into the dirt. The crowd fleeing DuBose stepped in the dark orchid flow, making bloody footprints on the concrete and on the dirt, and all the time Brewster tried to push the slit together to hold life inside TeeBoy's body.

Three men wrapped TeeBoy in a tablecloth. Brewster climbed on the truck bed of his pickup, put his arms out, and the men handed TeeBoy to him, wrapped tightly in the white linen. Old Man Malone drove. Brewster cradled his brother in his lap, holding him like a child, cupping his hand around his brother's hand, feeling the coolness in TeeBoy's fingers, watching the red stain grow in an uneven circle on the white cloth. Old Man Malone slowed at the traffic light on State Street and Brewster shouted toward the cab,

"Don't stop, Malone. Ain't nobody on the road. Don't stop, man."
Malone stepped on the pedal. Brewster's head jerked, hitting the back
window of the cab, but he held TeeBoy, cushioned him like a baby.

"Hold on! I'm holding on TeeBoy. You hold on! Hold on!"
Brewster's voice crashed through darkness, then murmured in dull
chant, and all the while he felt the coolness of TeeBoy's hand.

Old Man Malone pulled Brewster's truck to the colored door of
Low Ridge County Hospital. He hopped out of the cab, leaving the
door of the truck standing open. "We got a man been cut," he
shouted into the hallway of the hospital, and he rushed back to help
Brewster unload his brother.

A woman in a tall nurse's cap stuck her head out the door.
"You'll have to wait for a colored orderly. I'll call for one." She
pulled her head in and closed the door.

Old Man Malone looked almost comic now. He ran back to the
door, his feet lifting high, his thin legs almost dancing, his red
suspenders marking his path. He opened the door to the waiting
room. "We got a dying man here. Needs a doctor right away." Old
Malone jigged back to the truck, but the woman in the cap put her
head out again.

"I can't let you in. The colored orderly will be here in a minute."
She said this sharply. "I've called Dr. Hamilton." She pulled the door
shut with a thumping force.

Josiah Hamilton, the only Negro doctor in the county, had his
office in his house, not a great distance from the hospital. Brewster
lifted his brother's head, cradling it close to his chest.

"The doctor's coming, TeeBoy, but it don't matter. Don't you
worry. Whatever's going to happen is going to happen anyhow.
Don't you worry." He wrapped his arms around his brother, giving
TeeBoy's body some warmth, but all the while feeling the coolness
of TeeBoy and the wetness of the blood that soaked his own shirt and
pants. He rocked his brother back and forth as a mother does a small
child. He felt the smallness of TeeBoy's shoulder and the heaviness
of TeeBoy's head, which he cradled in the bend of his elbow, and he
felt also the chasm that opened up inside himself, a bottomless, dark
gorge. He longed for TeeBoy even while he held him.

Old Man Malone paced wildly by the truck, cursing and spitting,
but Brewster rested his shoulders against the back of the cab and
pulled TeeBoy's head up under his chin. He closed his eyes and
pressed TeeBoy's body against his own. He felt no rush. He wanted
to hold TeeBoy. He wanted TeeBoy to feel his arms tight around him,

but when he took TeeBoy's hand, there was no grip in it. It held the coolness of death.

"What time you got, Malone?"

"What you say?"

"Time, what time, Malone?"

"Don't know the time."

"Find out from that nurse."

"Hell, don't matter. Doctor be here soon. Don't matter." Malone paced by the truck.

"Damn, Malone, find out from that nurse what time it is." The old man jigged a path to the door again, summoning the nurse.

Forty-five minutes past one, Sunday morning, October 7, 1954, three days before his sixteenth birthday, TeeBoy slipped away. Brewster left the hospital walking in darkness too thick for breathing, too deep even for weeping.

The denseness of night Brewster walked in suffocated him. He woke with a tightness around his lungs and heat on his shoulders. He threw his legs to the side of the bed and sat up, letting the darkness ease. When his lungs took air easy, he rose and walked to the kitchen where he turned on the light and steadied himself.

Since Low Ridge had not spread south of town, thick timber woods were on both sides of Ole Summit Highway. Just before Brewster reached the stake with the red canvas strip on it, he passed a small tarpaper covered house, close to the road, where an old white woman sat on her porch, shelling beans into a bowl in her lap. She waved when he slowed his truck, then realizing he was a Negro, she rose quickly and went inside. An old stove rested on its back in the yard, and a faded truck stood on blocks to the right of the house, weeds tall around it. Low whites, Brewster thought and drove on.

When he reached the midpoint of the property, he parked his truck by the side of the road. He jumped a ditch and pulled himself clear of vines, dodging bare limbs jutting into his path. His heavy steps beat down the wiregrass. He found a natural clearing where the bramble was low and the sky visible in a beautiful uneven oval. He had seen the sign when the ad rose to his eyes and TeeBoy had come in the night carrying the *Gazette* with the telephone number. This land was meant to be his. He knew this. He stood in the center of the clearing and breathed in as much of the air as his lungs would hold.

2

"Think I've sold it," the man said in a thin voice, barely audible over the telephone. "Give me your number. If the deal falls through, I'll call."

In the shed, Brewster worked in silence. He polished woods as silky as pieces of satin fabric. He chiseled a claw foot, not marring it, smoothing it with the finest sandpaper, and hand-rubbing linseed oil into the grain, running the pads of his fingers across the wood, feeling the effect of his labor. He was a man in a tunnel. He licked his wounds like a hurt dog, tasting blood, curling up and licking his hind parts. He lost the land. No, it was never his to lose. A Negro could not own rich land like that. He looked for signs and had found them, but they had not led to the land.

Mama Tee stepped into the doorframe separating the kitchen from the front room. "Some man call you. Left his number. Baby, you not into nothing you not supposed to be into, are you?"

The aluminum bowl she held was pressed against her belly, circled by her left arm. She placed her right hand on her broad hip, studying him. She made an imposing silhouette leaning against the door, her gray hair in bunches around her face, her glasses at an angle over the bridge of her nose, her bib-apron untied at her waist, hanging loose and forgotten. Her tennis shoes were unlaced with the tongues angled up.

Brewster called the number. The previous deal had fallen through. The land was for sale, but the man would not take payments. "Cash only," he said.

Deak did not want to sign the loan papers. When Brewster sat on his bench at noon in the middle of the barn-like doors, eating a can of deviled ham that he spread on saltine crackers, he heard Deak and his wife Gretta in their kitchen, which was fifty feet across the yard from the shed. "You an old fool to be signing a loan for t'at boy. You pay t'at boy on Friday. Let him save his money, then he buy t'at land."

"Bank won't give ta boy a loan," Deak said. "I need t'at boy. I'm old man."

21

In the afternoon Deak came to Brewster's workbench with a pained expression in the loose folds of his hollowed face. "I sign t'at loan, boy," he said. "You work in t'is shed 'til t'at loan is paid. You don't pay, I get t'at land."

"Yes sir," Brewster said.

When they went to the bank, a sharp-nosed man in a black suit said to Deak Armbrecht, "I'd think long and hard before I put my John Hancock on papers for this boy, but it's your business entirely, Mr. Armbrecht."

He passed the papers to Deak without ever looking at Brewster. The land rested in Deak Armbrecht's balance. The old man lowered his glasses on his nose. He glanced over the pages again. With his lips pressed tightly together, he signed at the bottom. Brewster made a decision not to dwell on old Deak's agonized face.

The morning was cool and clear. Brewster watched for Deak to come around the corner with the car. When Deak's Buick turned the corner at the light, Brewster could see only four inches of his head, a little ball directly behind the wheel, not above it, and when the car pulled alongside him, Brewster pondered for a moment where he should sit, but got in on the back passenger side.

"Goot morning," Deak said, with a thick "g" hanging in his throat.

Brewster sat deep into the back seat, but his knees pressed into the fabric of the front, and when he leaned forward, putting his elbows on his thighs, his head was nearly beside Deak Armbrecht's. "Mr. Deak, you think he's going to sell me that land?"

"Why would t'at man come t'is day if he not going to sell you t'at land?" The words sounded angry, coming with a twang from the old man's nose.

"I'm colored."

"You got ta money, Brewster. Money ta same."

I could sit here in this Buick and name you a hundred ways the colored man's money don't spend the same as the white man's money, Brewster thought, but he didn't say it. He directed his mind to the sixty acres off Ole Summit Highway, pushed his back against the seat, and spread his legs to give them more room.

Deak Armbrecht's Buick made a right at the light in front of the law office of McBride and Sweeney, a flat, red brick rectangle of a building—squatty, but two storied with a dark green painted slab of concrete for a porch. The stubby building was partially shaded by a scrub oak, and two yellow, metal, high-backed chairs were on the front porch. Deak Armbrecht pulled his car onto the gravel-covered drive and parked alongside the building. He led the way to the front door where Mr. McBride's secretary held the screened door open for them and smiled when Deak Armbrecht stepped onto the concrete porch.

"Come on in, Mr. Armbrecht. Mr. McBride will be ready in a minute." Her voice was friendly, but when she looked up at Brewster, she bit her lower lip, and her face strained. "Sorry, but we don't have a colored waitin' room."

Brewster backed away from the door and sat in one of the metal chairs, which had a seat that dropped off in the back and gave his legs an extra inch.

This was another example of where the colored man's money didn't spend the same as the white man's money. He was buying the land, spending his savings. He would pay the loan, and he sat on the porch, not in the building. He wouldn't think about it because thinking about why he sat outside would make his insides stir, and there was no reason to whip himself.

Deak Armbrecht had already walked the acres with him, identifying the trees—pine, oak, hickory, and walnut. Brewster would sell some of the timber for pulp, and some of the pine and oak he would mill for lumber. The sun fell full across his chest and angled half over his face, and he closed his eyes, pushing the crown of his head against the wall.

After a while, Deak Armbrecht came to the porch, letting the screened door pop to a snapping close behind him. He sat in the other high-backed chair. "T'ey waiting for some of t'ose papers to come from t'at bank. Seems to me t'ey would be ready. T'ey know what we be here for." Deak inhaled air in a swishing sound through his long nose. "I drink me some coffee. You want some of t'at?"

"No, Mr. Deak."

Deak walked in easy steps back to the screened door, but again he let the door pop loudly against the casing. Brewster knew this was Deak's protest: The old man loathed wasting time. Brewster knew too what he was thinking: *Those papers should have been here. I'll let them know I'm annoyed.* Outside of Deak Armbrecht, no one had given Brewster a report on what was happening.

Brewster pushed his legs hard against the concrete porch and leaned his chair to the wall again. When he heard a door open and close on the side of the building, he knew the bank papers had arrived. Maybe it was best that he had sat on the porch, because the man who owned the land had not seen his face and still might not know he was colored. Besides, he would have felt awkward in the building with the white men. Where would he sit? What would he say? It was best he had stayed here. He had the porch to himself.

"Mr. McAtee, you can come on in now." The secretary didn't come to the door, but summoned him with a raised voice from where she sat behind her desk. When he entered the screened door, she did not rise, but pointed to a room across a narrow hall where Deak Armbrecht and the sharp-nosed man from the bank sat with two other men. When Brewster entered the room, he took his seat beside Deak Armbrecht. Sweat dampened his shirt under his arms, and a mist settled on his upper lip. The man who owned the land rose, leaned across the table, extended his hand and said his name, but it did not stick in Brewster's mind because sweat was on his right brow about to drip into his eye. The man had not said one word about his being colored and that fact did register with him.

Parts of long papers were passed before Brewster to sign, and minutes were given in silence for him to read the rules of lending. With each paper, he read a word here and a word there and signed the document, passing it back across the table to the man from the bank. He felt sweat bullets gather on his forehead, his tongue stuck to the roof of his mouth, and his head floated on his shoulders. He wanted to sign the last paper and leave.

"You want to read from here to here," McBride said and drew a line in the margin down the page. Brewster reached for his handkerchief in his back pocket and wiped his forehead. "This is the last one," McBride said. After Brewster signed his name, he collected the documents that were passed to him and placed them in the folder they gave him. He stood when they rose and he walked toward the door when Mr. Armbrecht moved in that direction.

Deak and Brewster made their way to the Buick, Brewster carrying the papers. He sat slack-legged in the back of the car with the brown folder pressed to his stomach. He would take the papers to the courthouse to register his property, and when he left Three Brothers he would drive to Ole Summit. He hoped to find a convenient stopping place in his work before the day grew too dark to see his acres.

In the shed, he worked quietly. Figures in the wood were more beautiful; the walnut was softer, the purple-brown of the grain, more

intense. At three o'clock Deak walked across the shed and stood by
Brewster's workbench. "You young man to own t'at land."

"Twenty-three," Brewster said.

"Go to t'at land. You be studying it all ta day if you not go."
Deak shuffled to the cabinet and pulled out a small black notebook
with fine-lined paper sewn into the side of it. He used these notebooks for recording quantities of wood, various supplies, and the
progress of projects in the shed. He handed the notebook to Brewster,
a symbol of his status—a holder of timbered land.

In the afternoons Brewster went to his land, driving his truck
back and forth, again and again, beating a path into his woods,
crushing the wild grass into submission. It was nearly dark when he
pulled the cab of his truck onto the grass, took his ax from the truck
bed, and began hacking at vines as thick as fists clinging to the trees
like old men's fingers holding on to life. Brewster had a vision for
his land. He had seen curving paths on other property and that was
what he wanted. With every blow of the ax, he dictated how his lane
would bend. He hacked and swung, clearing another twenty feet. The
muscles in his arm froze and refused to lift and swing wide. Brewster
stepped to the track he had already cleared and sat on the edge of a
flattened cardboard box, easing his head down on the flap of the
carton, his knees in the air.

This land was meant to be his; there was no question in his mind
about it. Tom had said not one word about Brewster's land. Tom
owned the little house on Perry Street, and it had cost him his left
hand; Brewster owned sixty acres on Ole Summit Highway, and he
knew he had been smiled upon. He did not know why, but Brewster
Thomas McAtee had been favored.

He opened and closed his hands, feeling the ache from gripping
the ax and the slingblade. His shirt stuck to his shoulders from his
sweat. He decided to knock-off for the night. He stepped into the
bramble to gather his blade and ax. When he turned to throw his
tools into the back of his truck, he saw a man standing in the lane. He
focused narrowly to be certain it was not a shadow drawn by the low
afternoon sun. A man, an old white man—unmistakably. Brewster's
blood surged past his eardrums. He dropped the slingblade, but
gripped the ax firmly, keeping his eyes on the man who walked
toward him.

"Whatcha doin' here?"

What the hell, Brewster thought. He held the ax handle and surveyed the man, who was short and nearly bald and wore a deep green jacket, too small for him. The man stuffed his hands in his pockets, and he spit a stream of rust-colored tobacco on Brewster's land, running his tongue across his lower lip lapping the residue.

"Whatcha doin' here, boy?"

Brewster decided he could take the man out easily enough if the man wanted to fight.

"I'm Brewster McAtee. I'm cutting a path into my property." He said this as a concession to the man. Knowing white men did not often shake hands with a Negro, but knowing this man was on his land, he extended his hand. The man spewed a stream of rusty spit. The flow sputtered onto the side of Brewster's hand, dripping into his palm.

"Travis Peets," the man said, giving no recognition that he had fouled Brewster's hand—his own hands still stuffed thick into his pockets.

Brewster drew his hand to the back of his hip and wiped. Current flowed through him. He wanted to kick Travis Peets down and see his eyes bulge when he hit the ground. If TeeBoy had lived, TeeBoy would have slashed through this green coat finding skin and blood, muscles and organs, lashing and hewing, and he would have paid for it when the time came. The ax was in Brewster's hand and he could swing it, cutting the man into two pieces.

"Keep that head low," Mama Tee had said. *A Negro keeps his head low,* echoed in Brewster. His grip was steady on the ax handle. The man had to see that.

Travis Peets spit again. "Knew they was tryin' to sell this land. Didn't know they sold to a nigger."

Old man, Brewster thought, *I'm holding this ax.*

"This is my land," Brewster said in an even tone.

"Whatcha gonna do out here?" The man narrowed his eyes on Brewster while his lower jaw worked in circles on the plug of tobacco.

"Build a house back there," Brewster said, nodding in the direction that was yet to be cleared. He didn't take his eyes off the man, refusing to give Peets an advantage.

Travis Peets' mouth rotated several more circles against the tobacco, his tongue pushed the wad past his front teeth, copper saliva showed on his lower lip. "Guess we better steer clear of the other," he said. Without taking his hands from his pockets, he turned and walked into the woods, taking one of the paths that led toward the tarpaper house.

Brewster watched him—a short man, balding on the top of his head, thin, and showing age; when he entered the path, a vine wrapped around his right leg, nearly pulling him down. Travis Peets struggled to free himself, snatching at the dried twine. When he pulled his leg free, he looked toward Brewster. He established his feet on the path and disappeared into the coming night.

Feeling he might be ambushed, Brewster looked around as he threw the slingblade, the ax, and shovel in the back of his truck. He eased out onto Ole Summit Highway, and at Travis Peets' house he stopped his truck in the road to examine the place. Through an uncovered window, he saw light in a back room. *Too bad Travis Peets lives here*, he thought, *but Peets is not going to spoil my land.*

Brewster recorded in one of his fine-ruled notebooks every penny of the money he received from selling his timber. Deak Armbrecht took great interest in drafting the plans for his house. "You got to build timber-frame house," Deak said. "Solid construc-tion," but the word sounded, "Sawled." He nodded his head, affirm-ing his own words, and the slack skin under his neck shook like the thick, red skin under a rooster's beak. "Sawled," he repeated and the word was firm and made the plans valid.

"I want a porch," Brewster said. "A wide porch."

"You use t'at lumber for porch?" Deak asked, and Brewster knew the old man disapproved of a wide porch as waste, but Brewster held firm and did not flinch.

"I'll draw ta porch. You don't pay t'at note, I'll sit on t'at porch." Deak shrugged his thin shoulders.

Beams were milled from timbers on the property, and the house was sited to get the morning sun in the kitchen and the afternoon sun in the big room with the house facing south. Mortise-and-tenon joints, locking the principal framing members, were crafted in the shed. The house would be a story-and-a-half, supported by multiple H-frames, with a four-foot kneewall above the second story. The construction would be easy because the house was simple—one big room downstairs with a kitchen to the north end, a hearth on the east side, and one bedroom and bathroom upstairs. Although the house was small, a porch would wrap around two sides, the east and south.

Brewster examined Deak Armbrecht's drawings and was pleased to see that Deak had drawn a spindle-posted porch, a white man's porch. The house would be unlike any that lined Limrick Road or Perry Street, where the houses were built from discarded lumber and had uneven floors, cinder blocks for steps, and short door frames. The house Deak had drawn stood tall with a wide porch and high ceilings. It had an uneven look to it, the porch being too big for the small house, but the lane would come into the property at an angle, lending the house more breadth and more nearly balancing the narrow house against the wide porch.

Deak brought a dining room chair to the property to sit, watch, and ensure that his plans were followed—three-foot square footings, sill timbers and first-floor joists leveled and squared, floor joints spaced twelve inches, girders placed in midsections, corner braces snug. With his hands on his hips, old Deak inspected every stage, stepping back and gazing at the symmetry of the floor frame, placing the level on flat surfaces, peering at the mercury. He ran his hands over nail heads, pulled against supports, hammered a little here and placed a few planks there, and he sat in his dining chair watching the house rise, one board at a time.

Through the spring and summer months, Brewster did not see Travis Peets on his land, but he saw Peets and his old woman on their own place. Brewster did not give up looking around and peering into the woods because Travis Peets could watch him from any of the paths, and he would not know it. Peets would know when he was at Ole Summit because the pounding of Brewster's hammer ricocheted from the trees and bounced through the woods. Some of Brewster's lumber came up missing, as did sacks of nails, pipes for the kitchen, and a handsaw. He attributed these losses to Travis Peets, but he had no proof.

The first Saturday in August, Brewster finished priming the beaded porch posts and went inside to rub cottonseed oil on the bottom cabinets, which he did with his bare hands, the warmth causing the oil to penetrate deep into the wood. He rubbed and wiped until his muscles strained.

When he pulled his truck into the yard at Perry Street, he yearned for nothing more than sleep. In bed he counted the spots of pain on his body, identifying and measuring each soreness. Long after he had fallen asleep, he heard the telephone ring, but he could not come through sleep into wake.

Mama Tee's hands were on his shoulders. "Get on up, Brewster. We got to go get Tom."

He pulled himself through the fog. "Get Tom? Where's Tom?"

"Sheriff done called. Put your pants on."

Brewster sat on the side of the bed and watched Mama Tee. From her black patent-leather purse she withdrew the white envelope that held her pay. She took out a five, and then she counted out five ones.

"Come on, Brewster. We need to go on and get your daddy."

"Let him stay in jail." He rolled into bed and pulled the cover up to his chest.

"Come on, son."

Brewster closed his eyes.

"I'm walking on then," she said, and she went out the door into the night. Brewster got out of bed and pulled his pants on. He tugged his brogans on his bare feet, tied them, and went out the front door. He started his truck, rolled down Perry Street, turned onto Limrick Road. He caught up with Mama Tee before she reached State Street.

"I'm sorry," he said when she got in the truck beside him. He wanted to say, *I'm sorry, but you know it makes me angry for you to bail Tom out every time he gets himself into trouble,* but he let "I'm sorry" carry its own weight. Mama Tee put the money in her lap and began folding it into a tight triangle.

"Sheriff Tate must take in four hundred a month, arresting niggers and letting them go." Brewster said this even and flat, letting the words hang.

"You know what happens if they don't be let go," Mama Tee said, matching him with equal flat and low.

Brewster knew. The guards at the work farm made sport of them, feeding them salt-cured pork and giving them no water. Dr. Hamilton had gone to the newspaper about the number of bodies carried off the county farm, but nothing came of it. Ten dollars rolled tight and slipped into Slim Tate's hand could spare a man, and there would be no record of an arrest.

At the jail, Brewster leaned against the wall, his arms folded across his chest. Slim Tate sat at an old wooden desk in the center of the room, with richly finished oak floors and high ceilings.

"Howdy do, Miz Teelda. Good thing I was on duty tonight," he said. He looked at Brewster and then past him, and Brewster knew Slim Tate dismissed him in the process.

"I 'preciate your callin' me," Mama Tee said and slid the green wedge on the desk within Slim Tate's vision. Slim Tate stood and put the triangle in his pocket.

"I'll go on and get Tom for you." He stopped before he went through the door he had unlocked. "He got a woman with him. Take her on too."

Mama Tee walked over and stood in front of Brewster.

"What they put him in for?" Brewster asked her.

"Didn't ask. Sometimes it's best not to," Mama Tee said and stood clutching her black patent-leather purse with both hands.

The sheriff came through the door again, followed by a deputy bringing Tom, with his right wrist cuffed to the feeble bend of his left wrist.

"Get on back and get that woman," the sheriff said.

The deputy unlocked the cuffs, and when Tom took a step forward, his knees buckled. His left eye was swollen, as was his lower lip.

Mama Tee went to him. She took him by the elbow, easing him into a straightbacked chair. The deputy brought a Negro woman through the door; her white blouse was opened three buttons down the front, and her red brassiere showed. The blouse had a rip under the sleeve and when she raised her hands for the deputy to remove the cuffs, hair showed in the pit of her arm, hanging like sprung wire.

"Says she lives over in Hurley," the sheriff said.

Tom pushed himself out of the chair with his right hand.

"You stay out of trouble now," the sheriff said.

"Thank you, sheriff," Mama Tee said, putting her hand under Tom's arm. Brewster had said nothing to the sheriff and the sheriff had said nothing to him.

"Not taking that whore home," Brewster said when they stepped outside and the door to the sheriff's office closed behind them. "I won't have them in my truck."

"You got to take her on home," Tom said, his speech thick.

"Got no way home," the woman said. She slid sideways when the back of her foot slipped off her open-heeled shoe. "I could stay on with Tom," she said and her lips couldn't stop the o's, making Tooooom.

"Hell if I'm gon' drive all the way to Hurley," Brewster said.

"She can sit in Tom's lap," Mama Tee said. "We got to get her home."

Tom rested his head on the seat back and the woman sat in his lap, leaning her body against his chest. Brewster rolled his window down because a sour smell filled his truck. He focused on the coolness of the night air, breathed and drove. He was doing this for Mama Tee because if she had not been beside him, Tom would have been ripped from the truck and left in darkness beside the road. When the woman turned her head, her breath was heavy with the sharp odor of sun-spoiled fruit. Brewster exhaled the foul air before it reached his lungs.

"I done forgot Hurley was so far," Mama Tee said. The woman's thigh slipped on top of Mama Tee's knee, and Brewster could feel Mama Tee's shoulder pressed tightly against his.

When he left Mama Tee and Tom at Perry Street, he went to his own property in the darkness before dawn. When he pulled onto his curved lane, he drove up to his house, and the light from his truck reflected off the whiteness of fresh paint. He parked and leaned his head against the seat in the truck and closed his eyes, waiting for dawn before starting work again. He was in half-sleep when light flashed past his closed lids; he sat upright and TeeBoy stood in front of the truck, laughing and dancing. When TeeBoy had come before, his head was down and blood was on his chest. Now TeeBoy moved in wide, heavy-weighted steps, a grin on his face. He laughed and danced, strutting in front of the truck, throwing his head back, rocking his shoulders, moving his legs in rhythm. Then he was gone.

When the sun fell this night, Brewster would sleep at Ole Summit because TeeBoy had danced on the land. This land, his land, set him apart, separated him from the Negroes off Limrick Road. He had timber and acres and a house with a spindle-post porch. He was a man rising past all that held him down.

3

Travis Peets, in his undershirt and overalls, stood barefoot in the dirt before a large tub in his side yard. Brewster slowed his truck to watch as the old man splashed water toward his face and upper body. *He's got no bathroom inside*, Brewster thought. When he stood in his own shower, allowing hot water to run down his back, he would think of Travis Peets in the cool of autumn and the cold of winter splashing frigid water toward his face. Brewster wondered how much land Peets owned. He would like to buy him out, get the old man off the perimeter of his land. If Travis Peets didn't own but a few acres, he could sell enough timber to buy his land. The idea pleased him, and he drove on to Low Ridge.

After Mama Tee cleared the dishes from Sunday dinner, she brought the triple-layer coconut cake to the table and placed it in front of Brewster. "A happy twenty-three to you," she said, and she rotated the cake a quarter turn for his inspection.

"Yes indeed," Tom said, and Brewster ignored him. There was not one word in him to be wasted on his father. When he spoke to him, he addressed him as Tom, but he rarely talked to him. Tom sat at the table in a tee shirt with a dirty baseball cap set at an angle on his head.

"Know how you got that name?" Tom asked. Before Brewster could answer, Tom began the story Brewster knew already.

"See, I wanted to name you Rooster. The day you was born, I crowed like a rooster, struttin' 'round the room." Tom laughed hard. His right hand had an alcoholic's quiver when he took the plate Mama Tee held in front of him. Tom could pass for a man at least ten years older.

"Thought that gal gon' call you Rooster. Tricked me. Wrote down Brewster." He slapped the table with a limp, flat thud. "Bess sure 'nough tricked me. Never stable you know." He shook his head. "Your mother was never stable."

"Let's take our cake to the back porch," Brewster said to Mama Tee, because it angered him when Tom spoke of Bess. Tom had taken Bess down the road to her death, and while Brewster had never said this, he knew it, and he didn't want to be in the same room with his father. Tom would not go with them to the back porch because September had turned cool and Tom didn't like even the hint of cold air.

"Should be ashamed of yourself," Mama Tee said when she settled in her chair. "Birthday back in August and don't have time to eat a birthday dinner 'til the fifteenth day of September."

"He was not going to argue with Mama Tee on this point. She would shower him with swift and snapping words if he countered her.

"You right," he said, and he pushed his chair back, balancing it on two legs, resting it against the washing machine that was housed on the small screened-in back porch. Mama Tee accepted his contrition by patting his knee with her large knuckled hand, and they ate coconut cake in the silence that settled between them.

"I got to go with Tom to the doctor," Mama Tee said when she broke the quiet. "His stomach hurt him all the time. I done told him, and the doctor told him too, it's all that liquor he puts in his belly." She shook her head and rubbed the knuckle of her index finger at the corners of her mouth. "I told him to go on. I don't have time to go and sit with him at the doctor, but he won't go 'less I go with him."

"Tom's a grown man," Brewster said.

"Tom can't take care of hisself, never could," Mama Tee said. "Tom's my burden to bear."

"Bear him then," Brewster said, and he regretted his words as soon as he had spoken them.

They sat in silence again until Mama Tee spoke. "Marlenna Mixon's back in Low Ridge. You know her mama passed, let's see, been several months back."

"I haven't seen Marlenna Mixon since high school. Don't think I've seen her since she went off to Raleigh."

"Ladies from the church made supper when her mother passed. None of her bunch went to the church. We made the supper because we love the Lord," Mama Tee said. She tilted her head, drew her lips in and looked almost dainty. "I made my sour cream pound cake, but I didn't take it. Sister Sampson picked it up. So these eyes haven't laid on that Mixon girl yet." Brewster finished his cake and placed the plate on the floor beside his chair.

"You still going with Eunice McKnight?"

"I never was going with her, Mama Tee. Never was and never will. What makes you think I'm going with Eunice McKnight?"

"Because I know from Eunice mother, Pearlee, that Eunice wants to go with you. I know they done invited you over for dinner after church two Sundays ago. That's what I know," Mama Tee said with some annoyance in her voice. "I know they invited you back again on Friday. You ate at least two times at Pearlee's and I know it for a fact."

"I did go over for Sunday dinner and they asked me to come on Friday night. Before I could think what to say, those two women had me coming. So, I have been two times with Eunice McKnight and I'm not going back."

"I don't see one thing wrong with Eunice. She's a good girl. A little plain. Her voice not quite as sweet as some, but she manages with what she's got. She sang in that trio Sunday week and was pretty good too, when she stayed in the middle and the other two covered her on both sides."

"I'm not worried about her voice, Mama Tee. She's not the woman for me and I know it for a solid fact." He decided to give Mama Tee the news she wanted about Eunice, because he knew if he did not she would pick it from him, piece by piece.

"Eunice and her mother are two of the most peculiar women I've ever met, and Pearlee's daddy lives there too, and he must be about a hundred and sixty years old. He smells like it anyway."

"Don't talk like that," Mama Tee said.

"That house, they clean out just enough to walk through the middle, but on all sides they got everything shoved up everywhere. I started to sit down and peanut shells were in the chair. Eunice took her arm and shoved those shells off on the floor, like her arm was a sweeper. 'Pappie,' that's what they call him, 'Pappie must have just eaten these,' Eunice said.

"Pappie, he sits there and he says, 'Eunice, I eat those 'bout Wednesday week, maybe Tuesday.'

"'Don't pay him no mind,' Eunice says, and when I got up to go to the table, peanut shells were sticking to the bottoms of my shoes, and I'm sure my butt was carrying a load of those shells."

Mama Tee laughed. "Lord, I always thought Pearlee could cook, though. She does her part for church suppers."

"There wasn't much wrong with the dinner those two set. My appetite got curbed before I got the first bite to my lips. We no sooner sat down than a roach came walking across that table, not a giant fellow, and not a baby neither, a junior roach I'd say. Well, before you could bat an eye, Pearlee took that big hand of hers and mashed it there on the table. Eunice shouted, 'Mother please!' Pearlee said 'I'm sorry, I'm sorry.' She took her napkin and scooped that fellow into it and passed me the mashed potatoes, still holding the napkin in her hand."

Water rose to the corner of Mama Tee's eyes from her laughter. She took her handkerchief from the belt of her dress and wiped at the rims of her eyelids.

"Pearlee's not as good in the kitchen as you think. She left the skin on her chicken, and the grease oozed every time I even thought about taking a bite."

When he left Perry Street, he drove slowly past Albert Mixon's house, hoping to see Marlenna. He was not sure why he wanted to see her, but he had some curiosity about Albert Mixon's daughter, who had been sent off to boarding school in Raleigh, North Carolina, when she was fourteen or fifteen, and a few years later her sister, Carmella, had been sent to the same school. He wanted to see how Marlenna had changed, see what kind of woman she had become.

He had gotten reports from Anvil Thomas, his friend and the grandson of Herbert Thomas, principal of County Training School For The Colored. After Anvil graduated, he had gone off to Fisk, and now he worked on a law degree at some university in Washington, DC. Brewster could not remember which one.

Brewster had never been invited to Albert Mixon's house at the corner of State Street and Limrick Road, and he never expected to be. Anvil Thomas got invited there because his grandfather was the principal, and because he was nearly white—a white man slipped in there, somewhere. Both of these factors fit well with Albert Mixon, who was the only Negro who had a house that fronted on State Street, the white folks' street, although the side of his house ran along Limrick Road, the Negroes' street. Albert Mixon had one leg on the white street and one leg on the colored street, but he was still colored, no matter how hard he tried to be white.

"She's a knock out," Anvil had said. "Quiet though. I like me a girl who's a little raunchy. Not easy, I'm saying. But easy enough and you can't tell with Marlenna. She's too quiet. That scares beejesus out of any man. Know what I mean, Brewster?"

Brewster slowed his truck at the corner of Limrick and State and peered into Albert Mixon's backyard. Seeing no sign of Marlenna or anyone else, he turned his truck onto State Street and headed for the Three Brothers shed. Deak Armbrecht didn't mind if he worked on his own projects on a Sunday afternoon, and he wanted to work on a swing for his porch at Ole Summit. He had fashioned his swing after a fan-back settee, band-sawed and sanded the slats. He had turned the posts with the sixteen-tooth saw, sanded and stored them, and he was ready to begin assembling the swing, which he planned to paint white to match the house. The porch looked heavy, stretched out in front of the tiny house, and it needed to hold something to balance itself. He was thinking about putting two swings on his front porch, one on the east end and one on the south.

"Brewster, you going ta build t'at swing before you build ta table ta eat on?" Deak had asked. "Never saw a man what build a swing to sit on before he build ta table ta eat on."

"I know what I want for the swing, Mr. Deak," Brewster answered, "but I don't know what I want for the table." Deak snickered through his nose, and Brewster knew Deak thought it was strange to build a thing of pleasure before constructing principal furnishings. But he reflected on his answer and was certain he spoke the truth. He wouldn't allow one thing to come onto Ole Summit unless it was what he wanted. In most cases, he had not made up his mind exactly what he did want. That was why he had a mattress on the floor in the upstairs room, no sheets, two blankets, a pillow without a case, three plates, one cup, a saucer, one bowl, several forks, spoons, knives, a dishtowel, several bath towels, and a small quantity of cupboard food. He did not want to clutter his place with useless things.

To the house on Perry Street, Mama Tee had brought armloads of brown bags stuffed with things white families didn't want. A cracked lamp with a raveled shade, a quilt with cigarette holes burned through the fabric, cups with no handles, an ice cream churn without a crank, two wise men, the third one having been broken. Mama Tee stored these things in open closets, mountains of riffraff. He would not have this at Ole Summit and would do without until he determined what he wanted and what he wanted was a white swing on his porch.

Albert Mixon was the only Negro in Low Ridge to have a wide front porch with a white swing. "What it feel like to be rich and sit up there on that porch?" TeeBoy had asked when the boys had walked shirtless and bare-foot up State Street, past Mixon's house to meet their mother who worked for Mrs. Carl Beaudreux. Mixon's two daughters, Marlenna and Carmella, ten and seven, the same ages as Brewster and TeeBoy, were on the front porch, always in portrait dress with satin bows in their hair.

"We should go up there and play with those girls," TeeBoy said. But Brewster knew going up on Albert Mixon's front porch was a challenge even TeeBoy couldn't face.

"Don't come up to the door," Bess told the boys when she said they could meet her at the Beaudreux house. "Sit across the street on the curb. A weed lot over there. Nobody mind if you sit there," Bess had said. "I'll be out soon as I can be. You sit and don't get yourselves into any trouble. I'll get the belt to you when I get home, if there's trouble." They sat on the curb at the weed lot. Sometimes their wait was short, but often it stretched an eternity with the afternoon sun blazing and the gnats swarming in front of their eyes.

"What you boys doin' over there?" an old woman asked from her porch where she sat in her swing, peering over the opened afternoon newspaper.

"We waiting for our Mama," Brewster shouted. "She works there at the Beaudreux house."

"You boys don't have business over there," she said. "No business on this street."

She came off her porch, got the hose, and watered the elephant ears in the bed closest to the house. She turned off the water, put her hand on her bony hip, and turned back to Brewster and TeeBoy. "You boys go on home. Don't need niggra boys sitting on the street."

Brewster stood up to leave, but TeeBoy shielded his eyes from the direct afternoon sun and sat. "We not gon' go," he said. "Our Mama said we could stay over here." The old woman in her thin duster that barely concealed her loose teats hanging to her waist made a beeline for the Beaudreux house.

That night Bess followed through on her words and whipped the back of TeeBoy's legs with her belt; she banished the boys from the Beaudreux's street, but she allowed them to wait in front of Bernard's Grocery, across from the Mixon house, where white Low Ridge ended and Negro Low Ridge began. To pass the time, they walked early to the concrete post in front of Bernard's Grocery, and that spot was a good vantage from which to watch what went on at Mixon Domestics and Laborers where colored folks in Low Ridge and Hurley County were connected with white families who needed maids, yard men, day laborers, or domestics to sit with children or the elderly. Mixon even found jobs for colored in New York City. He posted signs on power poles on unpaved streets.

Domestics Needed. New York City. Good Pay.
Free Transportation. Room and Board.
Albert Mixon Domestics and Laborers, 32 State Street

There was no need for him to put his address on his posters because every Negro in Low Ridge knew where he lived. His was the only colored property that fronted State Street, which rested fine with the white folks because Mixon's house was ideally situated for linking Negroes to white families. To the right side of Mixon's front porch was an office, a small building, low to the ground, but with a gabled entry and a black, curved, wrought-iron sign, *MIXON DOMESTICS AND LABORERS*. White folks came to the office, walked inside, spoke with Mr. Mixon, and didn't pay a penny. Colored paid a fee, then ten percent of their pay every week for seven weeks.

White women came to 32 State Street, walked through Mixon's office door, and visited like he was a white man. Mixon was always full-suited—white shirt, coat, vest and tie. He was short and portly with his rounded abdomen preceding him. The gold chain of his watch hung from his right vest pocket to his left. White folks called him "Mr. Mixon," and Negroes didn't speak to him directly unless involving employment. With the exception of Herbert Thomas, Anvil Thomas's grandfather and the principal of County Training School, Mixon didn't have one friend in the Negro community, and this fact appeared to be of no concern to him. He strutted between his office and his front porch, and on several occasions, he crossed the street, put his short, thick hand deep into his trouser pocket, and pulled out change, giving Brewster and TeeBoy three pennies each to buy Tootsie Rolls or Peanut Butter Logs. The investment was sound because the boys were future revenue.

Every Negro in Low Ridge or Hurley who wanted to work came to Mixon's back porch where, with clipboard in his hand, Albert Mixon himself filled out the application. The curb at the corner of State Street and Limrick Road was a good spot for any boy to sit and watch what happened in Low Ridge because this was the location where the Negro community and the white community came closest to convergence.

Brewster saw his mother as soon as she turned onto State Street, a full three blocks from the curb at Bernard's Grocery. She wore flowered dresses, and she smiled when she saw her boys. Brewster watched her, a small figure, who by magic grew larger and larger as she walked closer to them with her arms outstretched. But the magic melted as soon as they turned into the direct afternoon heat on Limrick Road where all the shade trees had been cut and there were no sidewalks for easy walking. On good days, scorched, orange dust stuck to the bottoms of their feet and to their ankles; on bad days they walked in mud, thick and oozy as potter's clay. The magic ended entirely the afternoon the boys found Bess in the kitchen at the dinette, still wearing one of the Beaudreux's aprons.

"I should kill him," Tom shouted from the front room. "This hand knows to manage a knife," and Tom raised his right hand in front of his face, turning it.

"Hush!" Mama Tee said.

"Ain't nobody gon' touch my woman," Tom said, his left hand swinging loose.

"Walked into the kitchen, grabbed me round the shoulders, put his hands on my breasts," Bess told Mama Tee who placed a glass of cold sweet tea in front of her. "Put his face close. Smelled his liquor. Would have fallen out straight on the floor but my mind froze. Froze solid."

"You go on to see Albert Mixon. He'll find you work," Mama Tee told Bess. But when Bess went to see him, she returned with an unexpected report.

"That ole chair of his creak when he rock, back and forth, back and forth. Can't get you work in Low Ridge. Now if you interested in going to New York City, I might be able to make a placement there. Go on now. That's what he told me, and then old Mixon got up out of that chair and went in his door. Left me standing in his backyard."

At County Training School, in the afternoon shade of a maple on the east side of the building, Mrs. Mixon waited for her daughters, Marlenna and Carmella. If it rained, Albert Mixon himself pulled his '52 Dodge to the front door, cutting muddy tracks through the grass, never offering any other child a ride, with the exception of Anvil Thomas.

TeeBoy pointed at Marlenna. "When she get off to herself, gon' go over there, grab that girl and tell her real loud, her Daddy ought to get Mama a job."

"Don't do that, TeeBoy," Brewster said, but at the same time, he wanted TeeBoy to plead the case for Bess.

TeeBoy couldn't get to Marlenna on the playground, but he grabbed her shoulders one afternoon before she went out the door to meet her mother. "Didn't shout," he told Brewster. "I was nice. Told her my Mama needs work. Tell your Daddy, get my Mama a job."

On the walk home, TeeBoy stopped, threw his arm up, cutting the air in anger. "Brewster, I done forgot to tell that girl Mama's name."

Albert Mixon was at County Training School next morning
before the first bell rang. TeeBoy's punishment was to spend a day
with Mr. Thomas, doing his arithmetic outside Herman Thomas's
office, reciting the multiplication tables as they walked the halls,
listening to Mr. Thomas's stories about Sojourner Truth, or spelling
whatever word Mr. Thomas might call out.

"He told me if I speak to Marlenna Mixon anymore, he'll use the
paddle," TeeBoy told Brewster.

Brewster and TeeBoy began to watch the Mixon house. After
dark, they hid in the low shrubs at the east end of Mixon's office,
watching, observing the family and stealing their privacy. One
evening Marlenna came into the parlor and sat on the piano bench.
Mrs. Mixon sat on a wine-colored settee that curved like a thick
bean, bowed at each end, and Marlenna played the piano.

"Look at that," TeeBoy whispered. The faint sound of notes
could be heard where the boys hunched behind the shrubbery. The
parlor, the hall, and the first few steps of the stairs were the only
territories their vantage allowed.

One evening while the boys watched, Albert Mixon came into
the parlor, his shoulders back, forming an arch large enough to
support his rounded stomach. He sat on the wine-colored settee, put
his feet on the low table in front of him, read the newspaper, and fell
asleep with the paper across his chest.

"Thinks he's important," TeeBoy said. "Somebody need to
knock him on the head." With those words, TeeBoy threw a rock,
hitting the parlor window with a sound that clanged in the night air.
Albert Mixon sat upright, dogs barked, and the boys fled, running
down Limrick Road. If Tom found out, he would hold a belt in his
tight fist and whip them until welts raised on their legs and backs,
but worse, Mama Tee would read to them from the Bible—*Exodus* or
Lamentations—and her hand would slap against their thighs, stinging
and snapping them to attention if they drifted. She would make them
sit by her in church, and she would pinch them when they wiggled.
She would make them kneel beside her, praying for their deliverance
from the devil.

When weeks passed, the fear of discovery waned. Mama Tee got
washing and ironing for Bess, who wore flannel shirts instead of
flower-print dresses; she ran clothes through a wringer washing
machine on the back porch, hanging the clothes on lines stretched

across the backyard like silks of a spider's web. The skin on Bess's hands cracked in rough saw-tooth lines. Her back stooped over the wringer or over the ironing board, and her hair circled her face— wild and tangled. Tom brought her liquor wrapped in brown paper twisted up to the bottle lip.

"Take a taste." Tom offered the bottle to Bess, who pulled a shirt between rubber rollers. Bess pushed him away, but at night when they sat outside on the hard-packed dirt by the front door, Brewster saw his mother take small drinks from Tom's brown bag.

When the weather turned to rain, Bess laid other people's wet clothes in the house. A slip placed over the back of a chair and a child's dress over the arm. A shirt laid to dry on the back of the sofa and towels hung from clothes hangers hooked to tops of doorways. Sheets thrown over two dinette chairs, strung together to carry the load.

"Goddamn clothes live in this house. Man owns the house don't," Tom fussed. "My house," he said. "Those clothes got to go." He held Bess's wrist tight with the fingers of his right hand.

"We got to have money," Bess hissed and stretched another sheet across two chairs. Tom snatched at the wet cloth, grabbed a corner, and threw the clean linen on the kitchen floor, overturning a chair with the end of the wet sheet.

Rain came in buckets, and Mama Tee's vegetables rotted in the garden at the side of the house. Mildew grew up the front of the gray wood at 20 Perry Street. Wet clothes took days to dry, thrown over furniture. Bess ironed clothes that were wet, let them dry some, and ironed them again.

"I been a whole lot of little places, but I never been to a big place like New York City. Bet I could make lot of money there. Enough money to help Mama Tee and buy nice things for my boys," she pulled Brewster close to her, rubbing the side of his head. He could smell the sharp sour odor of fruit liquor.

"That New York sounds good, don't it, Brewster?" TeeBoy asked when the boys played in the side yard.

"She'll be gone and we won't see her for a long time."

At night, TeeBoy curled in his mother's lap and put his head against her breasts. "Don't go, Mama," he said. "We won't see you for a long time."

"Time goes fast," and she kissed him on the top of his head. "Before you hardly know, I'll go and be back."

"It'll be cold there," Brewster said. "You know how you don't like cold."

41

"Probably make B-I-G money there," Tom said. "Bet they got cards you could clean up on. Take the pot. Come back the richest nigger in Low Ridge."

"You ask Mr. Mixon all kinds of questions before you say you want to go," Mama Tee said. "How much you gon' be paid? Who you gon' work for? When you gon' be back?"

Summer came, hot and sticky with more rain. "I got to see Albert Mixon," Bess said. "My back don't want to stand straight. It aches when I stand and it aches when I sit down."

With an umbrella tucked under her arm, Bess went to see Albert Mixon.

She smiled when she returned home. "I be with a good family. Watch the children. Some little housework—helping, you know. Some rich family, live in a big house up in New York City." Bess spun around like somebody in the movies that got good news.

"What you be paid for helping this rich family?" Mama Tee asked.

"Don't know, but Mr. Mixon, he says I maybe make twenty-five dollars a week. I'll send most all that back here."

Tom picked at his teeth with the end of a chewed-off match. "Sounds great to me, baby. Might come too. We'll come back here and buy Albert Mixon's house. Sit on that front porch and watch the poor niggers doing the Low Ridge shuffle, back and forth, workin' for peanuts." Albert Mixon placed Bess with the Madison Powell family. Mr. Powell owned movie theaters, lived in the Harlem section of New York, had five children, would meet Bess at the bus station, and he paid Albert Mixon's fee, which Bess took as a sign of his wealth and his goodness.

Bess ironed her clothes, folded them, and placed them in a flowered cardboard box, which she tied with cord.

"Buy yourself some kind of coat with the first money you get. Don't you be sending any money here until you get you a coat. Hear me, girl? Wouldn't hurt to have a sweater, too," Mama Tee told her.

"Can't believe you gon' work for some rich nigger," Tom said. "Tell him you got a man in need of work."

The Greyhound pulled away from the Low Ridge station at 6:30 on Sunday mornings, headed for New York. The day Bess left she wore a green dress with white spots, a green between dark and light, a green the color of a lime leaf on a cloudy day, the color promising fair skies, but the clouds saying otherwise. The dress was unsettling, but everything was out of balance because Bess kept the family awake getting ready for her trip, and everybody was up by four-thirty to be sure she got off on time. She giggled about this and about that, and when she held Brewster's hand, her fingers trembled. Brewster felt uneven, sharing a little of Tom's excitement, but feeling something dark, something that dragged him down. Mama Tee gave Bess a string of quarters rolled and tied in a handkerchief; she gave her some lunch packed in a metal box and some drinking water in a Mason jar, wrapped in a cloth and placed in a paper bag.

"Not every place gon' have a colored drinking fountain," Mama Tee told her. "Drink that water, but don't drink too much because the bus don't stay still long. When it stops, you get off quick-like and look for the colored bathroom. If the place don't have no colored room, you make a trip to the bushes, but don't you tarry. The driver won't think twice about leaving a colored girl. You don't want to be stranded in some place you don't even know the name of. If your water runs out, you ask can you fill your jar at the spigot."

Brewster stood with TeeBoy and Mama Tee at the bus station, huddled together passing time, and then everything happened too quickly. The Negroes boarded first so they would not disturb white passengers who would sit in the front. Bess picked Brewster up off the ground. At eleven years old, he weighed as much as she did. Her face glistened in the incandescent light, but Brewster could not tell whether with tears or sweat. She held him, his body pressed tightly to her, his feet dangling at her calves.

"You be thinking 'bout what you want. I'm gon' write and you tell me what you want from New York."

Brewster held his mother's thin body, feeling like he would die from the hollowness that opened him like a cave. Bess's whole body trembled in quick repetitions, like heartbeat gone wild, then she was on the bus, her face pressed to the window, her nose flat against the glass, her eyes visible, watching her boys when the bus pulled out of the station.

TeeBoy cried and wiped his nose on the sleeve of his shirt until his right arm was as wet as if a spigot had drained on it. Late in the afternoon, TeeBoy climbed a tree and jumped onto the roof of the house where he sat, his thin knees under his chin, his bare arms wrapped around his legs. Not even Mama Tee could make him come down until the sun had set.

Brewster test-fitted the joints of his swing and drew an X to be certain that the spots were marked where the glue would be applied and the wedges drilled for final assembly. The sun was going down, and he decided to clear his workbench, put the posts back in their buckets, and wait for an afternoon when he finished his work early and the sun, coming through the west window of the shed, was strong and direct. Then he would put the swing together, fitting, gluing, and tapping. He was in no rush.

There was a room behind a little store over in Hurley where he could get a beer or a whiskey, even on Sunday night. He wouldn't stay long, but a whiskey would be good and would help him close Sunday down. The next time he drove past the Mixon house, he planned to slow his truck and study the front porch swing, comparing it to his own. He had no interest in driving past the Mixon house again this night because he had whiskey on his mind, and Mixon's swing would be there when he got around to observing it.

He cranked the engine several times before his truck started. He turned on his radio and heard Chuck Berry's voice beat the words hard and fast, *Maybellene.* He dipped his head with the guitar riff and tapped his thumb against the wheel, accelerated, and headed toward Hurley.

4

Mid-afternoon on Monday, a large Negro woman with hair dyed a shocking orange, came from Mixon Domestics and Laborers to clean the Three Brothers showroom because Deak's wife, Gretta, who usually did the cleaning, was sick. The woman came through the shed to get her instructions from Deak. Brewster had not seen her before. She was not from Limrick Road, but probably lived west of County Training School.

Deak and Brewster worked quietly through the afternoon because each man had his project that engaged him in solitary labor. Brewster worked on a Sheraton bed, a special order for a man in Greensboro. The posts had been turned in the ten-foot lathe from a single piece of wood. Three-quarters up the shaft, on a squared pedestal, he had carved an urn from which a sheath of wheat spread, the center gathered by a half-inch band. Brewster carried two of the posts back to his workbench as a young Negro woman entered the shed. She was slender, her hair pulled to the back of her head and caught in a lavender ribbon. Deak walked toward her, but she spoke before he reached the doorway.

"I'm waiting for Evangeline. She's cleaning for you this afternoon. I'll wait until she's done."

"I check and see how long she be," Deak said and moved toward the showroom.

The young woman came closer to Brewster, near enough that he could smell the unmistakable fragrance of rosewater. She stopped and watched him. Brewster didn't turn and look straight at her, but he watched her with indirect vision. She wore black patent high-heeled shoes and a black skirt with a cream-colored blouse. When she stood in place for some seconds, he turned to her. "Let me get you a chair."

"I'm fine," she said, and she put one hand on the post, feeling the edges of the carved urn. Her voice was soft and sibilant, but had a lilt to it. Brewster rubbed his hand against his canvas apron and extended it toward her.

"I'm Brewster McAtee.'"

She put her hand out, and he could feel the small bones encased in soft flesh. She smiled. "I know who you are. You probably don't remember me. I haven't been in Low Ridge for quite some time. I'm Marlenna Mixon." She took a step closer to him, and he released her hand when Deak charged into the shed.

"She coming. She coming. Won't be but a few minutes now. Brewster, get t'at nice lady some chair ta sit on," he said, almost breathless.

"No, don't bother with that. I was admiring Brewster's work. This is lovely." She extended her hand toward one of the urns on its pediment. "Brewster and I went to school together," she said.

"I've finished, Mr. Armbrecht," Evangeline shouted. "But I can't find some of those light switches and I don't know what you want left on."

"I coming," Deak took off in a fast shuffle toward the showroom floor.

"How long you been back in Low Ridge?" Brewster asked.

"Two weeks. You probably know my mother passed away several months back, and my father hasn't recovered. Herman Thomas gave me a job at County Training School. I'm teaching English and literature. Had to finish a job in Raleigh before I could come, so I'm getting a late start on the school year. That will keep me hopping."

Hopping? Brewster thought. She moved in a gliding motion when she walked, smooth and erect.

"We done," Deak shouted.

Marlenna turned and moved toward the door, and Brewster followed her.

"This here's Marlenna Mixon, my cousin," Evangeline said to Deak Armbrecht when they reached the door. "She come on to pick me up because my battery's busted. Tires are slick, too, like drivin' on cellophane. Don't know what to do first, fix the battery or dump the tires. Don't matter," she shrugged her shoulders. "Don't have money for none of it anyway. Uncle Albert said your wife might need me to clean the house later this week. You know about that?"

"We go ask her," Deak said. The two trotted off toward the back door of the house.

Brewster and Marlenna walked to the driver's side of her car, a two-toned blue '57 Chevrolet that looked like it should be on a showroom floor instead of parked at the curb beside the shed.

"You going to stay in Low Ridge?"

Marlenna tilted her head at an angle and furrowed her brows when she looked into the low afternoon sun. "Don't know about that, but for now, I'm here. My father hasn't gotten himself established since my mother's death. My sister, Carmella, couldn't come because she has her son to take care of. So, I was the chosen one," she turned toward Brewster. "My plan is to get my father back to where he can take care of himself, and then I'll see what I'm going to do."

"I'll be doin' the house, too." Evangeline charged toward the car holding in her fist the cash she'd been paid for cleaning the show-room. "Thanks, baby, for waitin' on me." Her large hand cuffed the back of Marlenna's neck in a friendly gesture before she walked around to the passenger side and slid in the front seat. The two-toned blue Chevrolet pulled away from the curb, headed for the light at the corner.

When he left the Three Brothers shed, Brewster decided to go to Paulette's Café for supper. He slowed his truck in front of the Mixon house, but didn't see the blue Chevrolet. He peered at the front porch swing and saw that it had plain flat slats, probably rough-hewed. He was pleased by the quick comparison he made between this common swing and his white, fan-back settee that would hang on the east porch at Ole Summit.

At Paulette's Café he sat by himself, ordered his meal, then he pushed his chair back from the table, and folded his arms across his chest. He watched and listened to the talk around him, but he also thought back on his conversation with Marlenna Mixon. You probably don't know me, she had said, but I know you. I was admiring Brewster's work, she had said to Deak Armbrecht. She called Brewster by his first name, giving him license to call her Marlenna. We went to school together, she had said. In that simple sentence she established a connection. Although they had been in the same space, they had never been together, but that was not discernable from what she said.

Paulette's daughter, Kenisha, brought Brewster's plate, and when she put it in front of him, she sat down in the chair opposite his. Kenisha propped her chin on her hands, which she connected by extended fingers and she watched him. Not yet twenty years old, Kenisha was Paulette's youngest. There was no question that Paulette welcomed his attention for Kenisha, and when she passed by the table, she studied them. "Kenisha, honey, get Brewster some pepper sauce," Paulette said, balancing a tray on the palm of one hand.

He was four or five years older than Kenisha and had not yet decided whether he would pursue a courtship. Though Kenisha was attractive, there were a number of oppositional forces at work, keeping him from moving in her direction. For one, Mama Tee and Paulette served as ushers at Limrick Road Baptist, and talking was their sport. Brewster knew if he eased one inch in Kenisha's direction, Mama Tee and Paulette would follow the move and their tongues would waggle.

Brewster knew if he pursued Kenisha, their courtship would take place largely in the café under scrutiny of all who came and went. And besides, Kenisha had never uttered one word to him that he had not solicited. She giggled and watched him eat. She answered his questions in single words, and otherwise she smiled and looked appealing. She was a mantrap that, for now, he had decided to avoid.

Paulette would not let him pay for his meal. "Put that on my account for some nice piece of furniture. You come on back in here every day and I'll build me a lot of credit." She threw her head back and laughed. "Then I'll tell you what I want," she said with her right hand resting on her hip.

When he left the café, his truck started with a loud roar, which reminded him that he needed to replace the muffler. He rumbled up Limrick Road to State Street and at the corner saw Marlenna's car parked close to the back porch. He turned and headed west away from the Mixon's house, but then he eased his truck onto the grassy shoulder near the corner. He parked, got out, crossed the street, and walked past Marlenna's house, but saw nothing beyond a light coming from a back room. After pacing a block down State Street, he turned and started back. Before he reached the Mixon house again, a sheriff's car cruised beside him, slowed down, and then stopped. Brewster recognized Ken McBride, one of the sheriff's deputies.

"Brewster, what you doing walking 'round here like this? You know some folks stirred up about all that integration stuff over in Arkansas. You don't need to be walking on State Street after dark. Get yourself into some trouble we couldn't get you out of."

Brewster walked around to the driver's side of the car. "I ate over at Paulette's, and that food was mighty heavy. Decided to work it off."

Brewster knew the deputy would understand this because on a regular basis he stopped at Paulette's to listen to the conversation, keep a thumb on the Negro community, and eat a free lunch. He knew the food was plentiful and cooked sparing no grease.

"You want to go for a walk," McBride said, "go on Limrick Road there. Nobody's gonna mind if you walk there. You know, some these old women look out, see a colored man on State Street and they think they got themselves a Peeping Tom. Then we got ourselves big trouble. Go on home now."

"I will," Brewster said. "Thank you."

McBride rolled up his window and slipped the cruiser into first gear. When Brewster got back to his truck, he raised his foot and kicked a dent in the side panel. He reasoned that this was better than kicking McBride in his teeth. He got into his truck, cranked the engine and heard the roar. Making a u-turn on State Street, he headed toward Ole Summit Highway. There was not a question in his mind that he would see Marlenna again. He wanted to see her—even though her father was a link to his mother's death because he wouldn't give Bess a toehold once she started to slip.

Bess had sent back to Low Ridge only one package from New York. The box held a small plastic model of the Empire State Building for Brewster, and a metal bust of the Statue of Liberty for TeeBoy. She included a tablecloth for Mama Tee, but it was too long for the dinette, and she sent a shirt with yellow dots on it for Tom. He balled it up and threw it on the couch like a football.

"Shit! What that girl do with her money?"

"That job prob'ly not near as nice as Albert Mixon let on," Mama Tee said. "Not near the money." Tom left the yellow-spotted shirt on the couch, but TeeBoy kept the Statue of Liberty on his pillow by day and on the floor beside him at night.

Bess returned to Low Ridge on the late bus, with the rain coming down thick as a dense screen. She arrived with no presents and no money. Brewster thought she would return on a cloudless day, wearing a flowered dress, and she would smile when she saw her boys. She would hold a suitcase in her white-gloved hand, and a small hat would be pinned on her neat hair. She would laugh and grab them, spinning them around so hard their feet would come off the ground. But when she got off the bus, she wore a beige dress, no color to it, and flat shoes. Her hair was pulled tight to the back of her head with a rubber band around it. She looked weary. She pressed TeeBoy to her, but didn't laugh, and she didn't try to lift him.

By the time they walked home from the station, they were wet down to their skin, and the rain made squishing sounds on the insides of their shoes. Bess shivered from the cold. She paced in the kitchen, holding her elbows. She was thinner than when she left, her eyes larger, but sunk into her head. Brewster and TeeBoy watched from their living room bed as Bess lit a cigarette and drank from a bottle with a paper bag twisted around it, and she didn't go to bed until the sky was visible in the gray light of morning.

"Tell us about New York," he begged his mother on the first days after she returned.

"Don't want to talk about that town. Thought I would never get back. Never would get back!" She shook her head and pursed her lips tight.

When Mama Tee asked about the Powell family, Bess wrapped her arms around her body, holding the sides of her waist. "That was not what Mixon said it was. I got stories to tell. Plenty stories." She held her sides with her hands and her eyes rolled, but Bess never told her stories.

Some months after Bess came home to Low Ridge, TeeBoy sat on the concrete banister at the back of County Training School where he waited to walk home with Brewster. He studied a small figure at the farthest end of the playground, almost over at the weed lot.

"That's Mama," TeeBoy said.

Brewster put his hand above his eyes, shielding them from the blinding afternoon sun, and he too studied the small figure sitting on a tree stump under the giant oak. The woman wore a purple skirt and a pink blouse. When she stood and looked toward the school, Brewster knew it was his mother. Both boys shot down the steps, racing to meet her. Like Helen Mixon, Bess McAtee had come to escort her children home. They raced, cutting the air, wind rushing past their ears, but when they reached her, she was barefooted. Her purple skirt was turned with the zipper in front, the pink blouse was out on one side, and her hair exploded around her face—full and wild. Her eyes were large and bright, but her speech was nonsense.

"You find me." She spun in a circle, losing her balance and touching the ground with her hands. "I hide and you find me." She rested on her haunches, over the roots of the giant oak, staying there as if ordained that she remain on the ground in this position of supplication.

"Get up, Mama," Brewster said, but Bess did not move.

"My boys done find me, all the way out here," she said.

Two kids ran past them to the weed lot, but they didn't stop to look at Bess. Brewster lifted her by the elbows, and TeeBoy tucked her blouse and straightened her skirt.

"What we gon' do?" TeeBoy asked.

"Let her sit here awhile," Brewster said, directing Bess back to

50

the stump where she had been sitting. "Most people be gone soon. Then we get her on home."

"Been drinking again. Mama Tee told her not to drink that stuff."

"I want to go to this school. Think they let me go here? Never did go to no school even whole year. Always goin' from one place to the 'nother. Few months and my daddy move on someplace. Travelin' man," Bess laughed and rested her chin in her hands but the points of her elbows against her knees shook. "Think I start here. Think I be in class with you, Brewster?" She laughed again, loud this time, and two boys over in the weed lot looked at them.

"Let's get her on home," Brewster said.

There was no other way to get Bess home than to cross the schoolyard. The boys held Bess, each supporting an elbow. When they reached the east corner of school, they came face to face with the Mixons, a moment Brewster would have given almost anything to erase. Mrs. Mixon, standing tall and straight with her hair pulled tightly in a bun, nodded her long neck, indicating the boys should pass ahead of her.

Brewster had planned to walk up State Street until they reached the first of the houses, then take a short cut and risk being caught when they cut through white property without permission. With the Mixon women behind them, they couldn't take an unauthorized shortcut. They had to stay on State Street, supporting Bess and trying to look ordinary, although Bess had no shoes and sputtered nonsense, sometimes subdued, sometimes loud. Her lips blabbered half sentences and her bare ankles wobbled, and all rational thought flew from Brewster's mind. He wanted to run because a violent current shot through him but, supporting Bess, he moved in slow motion. Brewster walked up State Street inchmeal while Bess jabbered and staggered. There was not one thought in his head. Disgrace had taken the place of every idea.

TeeBoy turned his head to look at the Mixons. Brewster heard them snicker, but he turned his head only once and he saw Mrs. Mixon, her dark eyes looking straight ahead as if the boys were not there struggling with their burden. He saw Carmella with her hand over her mouth, suppressing laughter. Marlenna glared at her sister, and she put her finger to her lips and hissed the universal language of *quiet.*

This was the only time Marlenna Mixon ever saw Bess McAtee. Brewster wondered if Marlenna remembered that day when he walked on State Street with weights around his ankles, supporting his

mother—he, a mental mute, his reason silenced. He had borne his
burden that day because there was nothing else to do.

On Sunday, the anniversary of his mother's death, Brewster
made his annual pilgrimage to Hope Hill Cemetery with Mama Tee
to place bought flowers on Bess's grave. Slabs of rock brought from
north Alabama told the truncated stories of Negroes with one name,
privileged in death by headstones.

JOLANTA
FAITHFUL SERVANT OF THE MCBRIDE FAMILY
DIED MAY 3rd 1825
R.I.P.

Letters from other pillars, stolen by stealth of wind and rain,
"ABDA, BORN 18—," had become indentations in stone—numbers
and letters erased by time. On several graves, African masks carved in
dark wood watched with hollow eyes, embodying spirit and life that,
with the odor of moss and lichen, gave the Negro cemetery an earthi-
ness that caught in Brewster's throat and lingered in his mind. Many
graves had no markers and, after a century, the earth was collapsing
in an elongated rectangle above the bodies of the deceased. Newer
sections were claimed from the woods as the Negro cemetery grew.

BESS CLARK MCATEE
BORN 1915
DEPARTED THIS LIFE SEPTEMBER 23, 1945
GOD WATCHES THE SPARROW
AND HE WATCHES ME

The words Mama Tee chose for the marker were etched in gray
granite. "That child was like a bird," Mama Tee said when she filled
the bottom of a coffee can with dirt, poured water over the dirt, and
stuck the gladiolas in the boggy soil.

"Not meant for this life," Mama Tee said. "Such a tiny thing.
And life pickin' her apart, piece by piece. Didn't weigh nothin' when
she passed. Her box look like a child done died." Mama Tee stood
back and shaded her eyes to see the full effect of the purple gladiolas
on the grave.

When he was thirteen, Brewster thought Mama Tee's epitaph was right for his mother, but now the inscription was ironic. Bess was bird-like in her size—small boned with a dainty face, fine-drawn features, delicate, and in need of a bolster insulating her from the roughness of life. But there had been nothing to shore her up, nothing to lessen the jabs that shattered her into pieces. When Brewster read the marker, he thought again that God might have been too busy watching the sparrow and taken his eye off Bess, who was pulled down by Tom, a rock around her neck. The sparrow could soar, but Bess had died on the ground, coiled in a bundle, poisoned by rotgut Tom brought her, home brews from back porches or uncovered vats concealed in Alabama thicket. Concoctions even Tom wouldn't drink, but gave to Bess.

Brewster remembered once holding a bird, shot from a tree by white boys. The shot was meant to kill the bird, but missed its mark and only wounded. The tiny body trembled, and like the bird, Bess was almost always vibrating in fear or worry or habit, even before she poisoned her nerves. Over the years, Brewster weighed the accuracy of the emblem Mama Tee had chosen for Bess's stone, and he had not settled the issue with himself, but it was comforting to think that the very eye of God now watched his mother.

Mama Tee went forward, bent, and ran her index finger in the scored letters. "These letters gon' be here a hundred years from now. Bess got a good marker. Wanted her to have that. The sparrow was supposed to be carved right here." Mama Tee tapped her index finger on the spot above the letters where she wanted the bird to sit on an olive branch. "That money was all used up before the bird got carved. Didn't know how long before I'd have more money like that, so I decided to go ahead and put the stone at her head."

Brewster had every intention of having the tombstone lifted, the bird carved, and the stone replaced. He wouldn't tell Mama Tee. The two would walk to the grave and he would wait for her to see it. The thought made him smile, and he put his arm around her shoulder. "It's a beautiful stone even without the bird."

"It's a miracle stone, anyway," Mama Tee said. "That money came from Alfred Luce Jr. You remember?"

"I remember."

"I took care of old Mrs. Luce until the day that woman died."

Brewster remembered it all. Mama Tee had told him how she combed the old woman's hair, brushed her teeth, bathed her, held her hand, and read to her from the Bible. When she had stayed by the old woman's bed late into the night, there was no supper at 20 Perry Street. When the sun went down and he realized Mama Tee would not be coming home, he and TeeBoy spread butter on bread and poured honey over it. This was their supper while old Mrs. Luce was dying. Yes, he remembered it.

"Alfred Luce Jr. drove his La Salle to the house, parked, jumped the ditch, and knocked on my door. Handed me that envelope. You remember that Brewster?"

"I remember that too, Mama Tee."

He did not tell her that he remembered how the man stood awkwardly at the door, rotating his hat between his hands. And he remembered the sound of Alfred Luce's slow speech, and his voice, no higher than an alto. "My family wants you to have this. You took such good care of Mama."

Mama Tee hid twenty-five dollars, emergency money, in a cup shoved deep in the cabinet under the sink, and with the rest of the money still in the envelope, she went to the stone-maker where she picked the headstone that marked Bess's grave. Her only regret was that the money did not stretch far enough to cover the sparrow that should have stood above the letters, with feet wrapped around an olive branch.

Overnight rain had left moisture, thick and clinging to the air in the old cemetery. Brewster and Mama Tee walked through the denseness of sodden fall morning and found the gravesites of each of the other family members. On these graves Mama Tee placed flowers grown in her own garden. She put the blooms of the gold and red zinnias on TeeBoy's grave. On Daddy Divine's, she placed a single rose in a slim olive jar she had brought from the home of Mrs. Alfred Luce Jr., where she had worked since the death of old Mrs. Luce.

"Not a day goes by I don't miss him," Mama Tee said. Daddy Divine had died not a full year after TeeBoy. He had collapsed in July heat on the loading dock behind Gwin's Department Store where he had hauled and unloaded, unboxed and toted for twenty years. "My sweet man," Mama Tee said, and she stepped back, surveying the carefully placed tribute. There was oneness, an unbroken line connecting past to present, a union of caring, thwarting even death.

On Monday afternoon, Brewster was eating his lunch in the cool breeze of the doorway at Three Brothers when his friend, Matthew

James, the new pastor at Limrick Road Baptist, walked to the shed to speak with him. Deak saw Matthew coming with his hat in his hand. "I need to see Brewster for a minute, sir," he said. Deak didn't speak, because he didn't like visitors at work, but he lifted his hand, palm open in a gesture signifying *okay, go ahead.*

Matthew James was only six years older than Brewster, but his stocky build and receding hairline made him appear considerably more mature. "Brewster, come on by the parsonage when you get off work today. I have a little information for you."

"I'll do it," Brewster said and didn't stop to talk with Matthew because Deak Armbrecht was watching.

Matthew James looked directly at Deak and walked over where he was standing, ankle-deep in wood shavings. "Mr. Armbrecht," he said in his deep voice, "I have an interest in that large chair in the Three Brothers' window. May I see it?"

"T'at big chair and you big man. You sit in t'at chair fine."

Deak put his hand on Matthew's back and pushed him gently toward the door that connected the showroom to the shed. Brewster knew the unexpected visit from Matthew James meant that he had discovered something about Travis Peets. He had asked Matthew to find out how much land Peets owned and to get some information about the man. If anyone could do this, Matthew James could, because he came and went at the courthouse where he married Negro couples, and he heard news through his congregation. Brewster didn't like the presence of Travis Peets at the edge of his land. He had seen the man on his property despite the fact that he had nailed **NO TRESPASSING** signs to the trees closest to Peets' house.

After a while, Deak and Matthew came back into the shed. Matthew had purchased the chair without ever walking through the front doors of Three Brothers.

"We load t'at chair in ta truck and you take t'at to Preacher James t'is afternoon," Deak said. Deak and Matthew shook hands at the back door, and Deak watched him walk away. Then Deak came over to Brewster and, without saying a word, he slapped him on the back. Brewster understood this to mean that Deak Armbrecht liked a purchase no matter whether it came through the front door or through the shed.

When Brewster was done with his work, he loaded the chair in the back of his truck, and when he pulled onto the hard clay at the side of Limrick Road Baptist, Matthew James stepped out on a small metal platform that was at the top of narrow steps at the side of the church. Matthew wanted the chair hoisted up the steep metal steps that led to his tiny office. The steps were too narrow for the chair, so the two men leaned the chair against the metal tube that served as a stair rail, and eased the chair up.

June James, followed by two of her three young children, came out of the parsonage to help. When they got the chair into the tiny office, both of the children sat in the big seat. June folded her arms across her chest. "That's the finest piece of furniture we own, and you going to put it here in this place?"

"I spend most of my waking hours here."

"Well, I'm next," June said. "We need a new couch bad. The springs are popping up through the fabric on that awful thing we got inside." Her brows furrowed. Matthew rubbed her shoulders that rounded forward.

"The next thing will be a new couch," he said, and he kissed her on the cheek. After June left with the children, Matthew James sat in his chair, resting his hands on the over-stuffed arms of the burgundy brocade. He looked like an African king, except for the fact that the chair was out of place in the small office with dingy walls that were painted an indistinguishable color, something between a green and a gray. With the exception of a small chair, the only other piece of furniture in the office was a metal desk that had been abused severely before it was salvaged. The light in the office was dim, and papers littered the desk. Nonetheless, Matthew James sat like a king in his brocade chair.

Brewster sat on the edge of the desk and Matthew stood abruptly. "Here, Brewster, you take the chair."

"I refuse. It would take pleasure from me to see you get out of that chair." Matthew eased himself back down into the softness of the chair's cushion.

"Told you I had some news."

Brewster raised his foot to the ledge of the desk and wrapped his arm around his leg.

"Took me three trips to the Deed Office," Matthew said, "but I found out Travis Peets owns three acres. That's all, three acres. If I was walking in those shoes of yours, I would buy him out. Find out what he wants for that land and get him out of there."

"Assuming I could get the money to buy him out, how am I going to get close enough to discuss the issue?"

"Thought about that, too," Matthew said. "I'll go to Sheriff Tate and ask him to talk to Peets first, then we'll set a time when he can go with us to visit Peets. Slim Tate's not a friend to the Negro. I don't mistake that, but he wants to keep order around here and he likes to be in the middle of things. One Tate or another has run things around here for as long as I can remember." Matthew ran the pads of his fingers across his forehead. "Slim intends to hold the reins. Guess we got that going for us.'"

"That's not a lot."

"You right about that, Brewster, but I have seen it worse. You want me to go ahead and talk with Sheriff Tate?"

Brewster nodded and eased off the desk.

"Stop by after you get off work tomorrow afternoon, and see what I know," Matthew said, and Brewster left him sitting in his chair, rubbing his hands over the silk brocade.

Brewster didn't want to sell more of his timber to buy Travis Peets out. He had stripped his south acres and the land was bald, cracked and rutted, with the rain washing over it like a swift bandit stealing the best of the topsoil. But Peets owned only three acres and he could buy him out with little additional damage to his land. He wouldn't own much when he bought Peets' miserable three acres. He would tear down the house and salvage the lumber. The ground in front of Peets' house looked hard as concrete. Peets would, no doubt, leave all the junk in his front yard, and Brewster would have to haul that off, too. It was bad when a man had to cut beautiful timber to buy a gouged and shoddy place like that, but maybe he would level the old house and turn the soil for crops.

Late Wednesday afternoon Evangeline came through the shed and shouted at Deak. "I finished up in the house, but I'm gonna dust a little more in the showroom. Still got the bedroom section to do."

"Marlenna Mixon going to pick you up?" Brewster shouted at her before she went through the back door.

"Shore is. Got to have a ride 'cause my battery's still busted. Won't hold a charge." She shrugged her shoulders and went into the showroom.

Brewster kept a careful eye on his watch, and at fifteen minutes past five, Marlenna came through the barn-like double doors.

"You doing fine t'is nice day?" Deak asked.

"Fine," Marlenna said, and Deak hobbled toward the back entry of the showroom to call Evangeline. Marlenna walked toward Brewster's workbench.

"How's your third week back in Low Ridge?" Brewster asked before she reached the area where he worked.

"I'm torn between an honest answer and a nice answer." Marlenna ran her index finger across a piece of sanded mahogany on the workbench.

"Give me the honest answer."

"I won't go into details. You wouldn't want to hear that, but my Father isn't the easiest man to care for, and I started the school year late. On top of all that, Low Ridge is as small and provincial as I remembered."

Brewster didn't know what provincial meant and he didn't want to solicit her dislike for Low Ridge, so he turned the conversation in a different direction. "I would like to take your mind off your trouble. Would you go someplace with me on Friday night?" Before she could answer, he continued talking. "We could have some supper at Paulette's or we could go out to Club Troubadour." Thinking the crowd at Troubadour would not suit Marlenna, he hurried on. "We could drive over to Hurley and go to the drive-in movie. They're showing that Elvis Presley movie, *Jailhouse Rock*. He's supposed to have new songs in that. They have a café over there that's not as busy as Paulette's. We could go out to my place on Ole Summit Highway, or we could . . ."

Marlenna interrupted him. "Why don't you come to our house Friday night. We can have dinner with my father. I'll have a chance to get Mama's good dishes down, set the table, and it will give both me and my father something to look forward to."

Before Marlenna left, it was settled. Brewster would arrive at the Mixon house at seven o'clock on Friday evening.

5

When Brewster pulled up in front of Limrick Road Baptist and looked up the stairs to the east of the church, he saw Matthew step out of his office onto the metal platform. Matthew waited for him at the top of the steps. When they entered the tiny office, he motioned for Brewster to sit in the brocade chair, but Brewster backed up to the metal desk. Matthew eased himself into his burgundy brocade, which looked like a red dress on an old woman because he had placed a wooden crate in front of it for a makeshift table, and he had stacks of papers on the wooden box and on the floor beside him.

"Sheriff Tate's got a meeting set for next week. Don't have any idea what Peets wants for his three acres." Matthew rubbed the pads of his fingers in circles on the brocade. "We'll know soon enough. Sheriff's going with us when we meet with him."

Brewster didn't tell Matthew about the weight he felt on his chest. He already had the burden of going to Albert Mixon's house and, added to that, he now had to think about meeting with Travis Peets. He stayed long enough to ask about each of Matthew's children. Matthew walked with Brewster down the narrow metal steps. They exchanged some talk about Little Rock, Arkansas and the school integration that was taking place there. Little Rock was the talk everywhere, on everyone's minds, headlines in the newspaper, and the first story on the television news. As Brewster backed his truck off the hard orange clay of the church driveway, he vowed to himself to build a small table to go in front of Matthew's brocade chair. It was a crying shame to see a man with a fine chair like that couple it to a crate.

When Brewster arrived at the Three Brothers shed, Deak was observing his first ritual, reading the *Low Ridge Gazette*. He sat on his stool positioned between the doublewide doors. Brewster walked in front of Deak, carrying two clothes hangers, one holding his Sunday jacket and on the other, a shirt that he had ironed the night before, careful to get the creases straight in the sleeves and all the twists out of the collar. He carried a grocery sack containing a tooth-brush, toothpaste, deodorant, dress shoes, and a tie. He had also remembered to pack his aftershave. Deak Armbrecht studied him, and Brewster felt obliged to offer an explanation. "I'm having supper with Marlenna Mixon tonight."

"Oh, t'at Mixon gal," Deak said. Brewster hung his shirt and jacket in the back of the shed so they would not call attention to themselves. He went to his own workbench and threw the strap of his leather apron over his neck.

Brewster knew the routine. Deak would finish reading the news, then sharpen his pencil with his pocketknife, and work a full thirty minutes on the crossword puzzle. If he completed it, he would strut through the shed slapping the workbenches with the rolled newspaper. He would cut the puzzle from the paper with his knife and post it on the corkboard with an upholstery tack. Without uttering a word, Deak would pass the remainder of the newspaper, folded in quarters, to Brewster, who would read it at noon, sitting on his own bench in the middle of the opened barn doors.

This morning Deak slipped off his stool without working the puzzle. He folded the newspaper in half, not quarters, and walked to Brewster's workbench, where he placed the paper in front of him.

VIOLENCE ERUPTS IN LITTLE ROCK, ARKANSAS: NATIONAL GUARD SWORN INTO FEDERAL SERVICE

Deak, wearing his red plaid shirt, looked like a bantam rooster, standing on pencil thin legs. He watched Brewster lift the folded newspaper and crack it across the crease, holding it at full size. Brewster saw the pictures of angry mobs and federal troops outside Central High School, and he read the first paragraph out loud.

> *Little Rock, this once peaceful city in central Arkansas, has now become the battleground for school integration. Yesterday Army paratroopers from the celebrated 101 Airborne Division took off from Fort Campbell, Kentucky, en route to Arkansas. Convoys of soldiers rolled onto the highways in trucks and jeeps and all manner of military transports. The more than 500 soldiers, federalized on orders from President Dwight D. Eisenhower, were all battle equipped. The men will face angry mobs determined to block nine Negro students from entering Central High*

*School. The eyes of the nation are turned to Little Rock
where the U.S. military confronts its own citizens.*

Brewster was not going to discuss this stuff with any white man,
not even Deak Armbrecht. He decided to acknowledge what was
happening without giving any of himself away. "Umm," he sounded
through his nose. He pushed his lips out and shook his head. He
placed the newspaper on his workbench and continued to screw a
wing head into a piece of beige canvas on the underside of the chair.

"T'at one big mess," Deak said, blew air out his mouth, and
ambled across the shed.

Brewster was fortunate to be working at Three Brothers and he
knew it. He didn't like to think about his good luck for very long
because somebody might read his mind and tell old Deak that he
needed a white man for this job, but everybody allowed Deak
Armbrecht some range for peculiar ways because he was a foreigner.
Brewster knew he would not discuss Little Rock with Deak. He would
keep his head low and his opinions close to his own chest.

At noon, Brewster took the newspaper and sat on his stool in the
wide opening of the barn-like doors. Another bench was beside him,
and on its hardwood seat was an opened can of deviled ham, a knife,
a jar of dill pickles, and a box of saltine crackers. He lifted a dill
pickle from the jar with the point of the steak knife, sliced it into thin
green ribbons and dropped them back into the jar. He spread deviled
ham on a cracker, fished the end of the knife into the jar and impaled
a pickle slice, which he placed on top of the ham spread. He unfolded
the newspaper and looked again at the photographs from Little Rock.
Soldiers were sitting in an open wagon, helmets on, bayonets jutting
beyond rifle barrels, but what held his eyes was the picture of the
Negro girls, dressed like the white girls, with loafers and bobby socks,
patent leather belts tight around their waists, and full plaid skirts.
They could have been the white girls except for the shade of their
skin, the tightness in their jaws, and their eyes looking straight ahead,
not at the mob.

Brewster read on. The senator from South Carolina said, "If I
were governor of Arkansas, I'd give the President a fight such as he's
never been in before. I'd proclaim a state of insurrection and call out
the National Guard. The President would find out who's running
things in my state."

"Shit," Brewster mouthed. "S-h-i-t."

But the next paragraph read, "NAACP officials disclosed that the nine students will return to Central High School when the Army secures the building."

Brewster closed his eyes and tilted his head toward the sun. At church on Sunday, he had heard at least two opinions. Old Aunt Laney, her little gray head nodding, had said, "We gon' hurt ourselves if we start doing this kind of stuff. We moving along fine now. Things better than they was when I was a girl."

Matthew cut into her words, "Auntie," he said, "we haven't gone far." Brewster didn't want to see a stir of trouble, but at the same time, he knew what Matthew was saying. Just last week he bought a hat in Gwin's Department Store and had to line it with tissue paper before trying it on. Although it was not exactly what he had wanted, he purchased it because the white clerk would have created a scene if he placed it back on the shelf once he had put it on his head, even though it was lined with tissue.

Brewster folded the newspaper and went back to his workbench, leaving the paper behind. He walked to the Low Ridge Flower Shop, two blocks up State Street. As soon as he opened the door, the two women arranging flowers stopped their work and watched him. "I want to buy roses," he said, "a dozen roses."

The women looked at each other, and for a moment Brewster thought he would be told to leave the shop. But one of the women slid off her stool and took a step closer to the counter.

"What color?"

"I don't know."

"We got these," she said pointing at a bucket of deep red roses, "these, and these," she said, pointing at pink roses and yellow ones.

"Yellow," Brewster said. "A dozen yellow roses."

The clerk lifted twelve roses from the metal bucket, each one dripping water onto the floor; she dried the ends with a white, gauze rag and put them in a long, narrow box that had a cellophane panel on the lid, and she tied a white ribbon over the plastic window on the box. Brewster's forehead was wet and his shirt stuck to him under his arms before he left the flower shop. On State Street, he felt clumsy with the box tucked under his damp arm. When he entered the shed, he put the roses in the short rusty refrigerator that stood by the door leading to the showroom. He worked in solitude during the afternoon, envisioning dining at 32 State Street, Albert Mixon at the head of the table.

At quarter of six, Deak untied his leather apron and hung it on the peg by the doors. "You close t'is shop up when you leave," he said and turned his back on the shed.

"Mr. Deak, I'm going to leave my truck here by the curb tonight. No need to drive," Brewster said, but the truth was he didn't want to park his loud and rusted-out truck in front of Albert Mixon's house.

Deak Armbrecht shrugged his shoulders and walked through the double-door opening, then he stopped and turned back to Brewster, "You have good supper," he said. "Young man should have good time." And with that he walked to his back porch.

At seven minutes past six, Brewster put on the clean shirt he had brought and went to the chipped and rusty sink where he brushed his teeth with the Ipana that was in the brown grocery sack. He reached into the bag and withdrew his Sunday shoes, and his navy and light blue Sunday tie. He put these on and then slipped his arms into his jacket, adjusting the sleeves and cuffs. When he was dressed, he looked at his face in the small, cloudy mirror that hung at the back of the shed. He walked to his workbench and sat on his stool, holding the box of roses tied with the white ribbon. He watched the clock that hung over the barn doors, and at exactly twelve minutes of seven, he rose like a man anointed, and he began his walk to the corner of State Street and Limrick Road.

When he reached the white house with the dark green porch, he went up the concrete steps, walked across the painted floorboards past the white swing, and rang the doorbell. The parlors were illuminated, as was the hallway in front of the stairs—the vista that belonged to him and TeeBoy when they watched the house years earlier, hidden in the shrubbery. When Marlenna opened the door, he handed her the yellow roses. She wore a cream-colored blouse and a dark skirt, giving her the appearance of a student at County Training School. The heels of her shoes clicked on the hardwood floors when she led him through the passage between the parlors and into the kitchen where she had set their table.

"We're going to eat in here," she said. "I thought it would be nicer for just the three of us."

The kitchen was warm and bright and smelled of roasted meat. He stood with his back against the counter and watched her remove the roses from their box. "These are beautiful," and she brought the entire bundle to her nose. "Brewster, there's a vase up there," she said, pointing to the cabinet behind him. "Can you reach it? It's good to have a tall man in the house." She filled the vase with water and placed the roses at the end of the table.

When she offered him wine or whiskey, he chose whiskey and settled himself on a kitchen stool, feeling comfortable, though he knew that in the Mixon house, he was in alien territory. Albert Mixon entered the kitchen and Brewster stood. Mixon wore a navy-blue suit with tiny pin stripes, and his stomach pushed hard against the buttons where the chain of his watch hung from one vest pocket to the other. His hair had gray mixed with black, and his lower jaw protruded even more than Brewster remembered. When Marlenna stood beside him, she was at least an inch taller than her father who had settled with age.

"Father, do you remember Brewster McAtee?" Marlenna asked and, in this question, Brewster heard a domestic formality with which he was unaccustomed.

"Certainly, certainly," Albert Mixon said and extended his hand. Brewster knew if Albert Mixon remembered him it was in some general sense—another young man who might have come to the back porch in need of work.

Marlenna employed her father in carving the meat, and Brewster held the bowls for her while she scooped rice and vegetables into them. When Albert Mixon had carved the meat, Marlenna gave Brewster a plate. "Please go first," she said. "You are our guest."

Albert Mixon sat at the head of the table, Marlenna and Brewster on either side of him, and they exchanged pleasant talk about Brewster's projects at Three Brothers and Marlenna's return to Low Ridge. Then Marlenna shifted the flow of their conversation.

"Brewster, the other day, you said you had a place out Ole Summit Highway, tell us about that."

Brewster was a little cautious, not wanting to sound over-proud, but he desired to do justice to his land. "I have sixty acres, beautiful land, at least by my reckoning," he said to soften any sound of arrogance. "My grandmother looks for wildflowers out there and she's found just about everything—lady's slippers, buttercups, violets, and black-eyed Susans by the armloads. I built a small house, but it's got wide porches that wrap around two sides." He could have told them about the beautiful spindle-posts, but he fell silent, not wanting to appear vain. He could have told them that his house was not like the poor and pitiful places that lined Limrick Road, and he could have told them that his land would sustain him with corn and soy beans, pulpwood and timber, but he allowed the silence to stand in place of these remarks.

He was afraid the conversation would stop, but Albert Mixon stepped in, "And how are the students at County Training School?" he asked, looking at his daughter.

"They're fine and I'm working hard trying to keep up with them. I'm staying a couple of jumps in front of my students, but with a little time, I'll pull ahead."

She looked at Brewster when she continued, "I have two English classes and three literature. Right now, the students are caught up in what's happening in Arkansas, and some of them are reading the newspaper for the first time. It's pushing them to think about where they are here in Low Ridge and where their lives are headed."

She paused as if she thought about her own words. "On the radio this afternoon, they said the government won't prosecute anybody from the mob that nearly killed the students the other day."

"I have one thing to say about that," Albert Mixon said and raised his chin, with his lower lip pushing hard against his top lip. "Some people like to suffer."

"What does that mean?" Marlenna asked.

"Means exactly what I said. Some people like to suffer. Those nine students knew they were not wanted in that school, but they went on anyway, and now they face the consequences." He said this slowly, still chewing his meat, looking like an old owl with his head fitted tightly to his shoulders, his short gray hair wiry around his face and his glasses resting almost on the end of his nose.

"If they waited to be invited, they wouldn't ever go inside that school, Father," Marlenna said.

"All things in good time," Albert Mixon said.

Brewster listened, but he was not going to involve himself between Albert Mixon and his daughter. He looked down to cut his meat.

"It's time to move forward," Marlenna said.

"Negro and white can get along, can even work together. I'm the example of that, Daughter," Albert Mixon said and wiped at his mouth with his napkin. "One group needs to respect the other and not go where they are not invited." Brewster looked up to see him fork a red-skinned potato and put the whole thing into his mouth.

"I'd like to be with them in Little Rock," Marlenna said, facing her father.

"Then I'm glad you're back here in Low Ridge and not getting into trouble," he said, and Brewster could see the red skin of the potato in his mouth.

Marlenna turned her head from her father and addressed Brewster. "Tell me what you intend to do on your sixty acres."

"I've harvested some of the timber, and I'm thinking of turning that land for crops—corn, soy beans. I'd like to buy some more land as time goes on and plant cotton. Eventually, I'd like to buy all the land on my side of the road from Low Ridge out to where my property begins."

Albert Mixon chuckled. "Ambitious," he said.

Marlenna ignored her father. Brewster hoped he had not said too much, but he had left no doubt that he loved his land and took pride in it. He suspected he was the only Negro in Low Ridge to own so many acres, and he liked the idea. He told Marlenna and her father about the trucks that pulled onto his land to load pulpwood, and he told them about tapping some acres for turpentine. The conversation at the table eased along smoothly, until Albert Mixon placed his fork in the middle of his plate, and Marlenna stood and pushed her chair away from the table.

"Let me clear the dishes and we'll have our dessert in the parlor," she said. Albert Mixon excused himself, and Brewster heard him go up the stairs.

Brewster helped Marlenna put the dishes in soapy water. Then she took a lemon meringue pie from the refrigerator, cut through the browned top, and placed three slices on small plates. Brewster carried two plates, and Marlenna carried the third one. At the stairs, she stopped and called to her father, "Join us for dessert. We're in the parlor." Marlenna led Brewster into the room to the east of the stairs, the one with the wine-colored settee that was twisted in the center like a giant purple hull bean.

Albert Mixon came down the stairs and settled himself into a deep green chair beside the burgundy settee while Brewster and Marlenna brought the coffee, the cups, cream, and sugar. After Brewster and Marlenna sat on the twisted settee, Albert Mixon was the first to raise his fork and break the meringue on his pie. He brought a nearly translucent gold bite to his mouth. He closed his eyes and held his fork in the air like a wand.

"Oh my," he said. "This is just like your mother used to make." He grunted and forked another bite. While they ate lemon meringue pie, Albert Mixon recited lists of his favorite foods, meals his mother had cooked, dishes his sisters, who lived over in Hurley, still prepared for him, and he ended with a roster of favorites from his deceased wife, Helen. He completed his food docket and his pie, placing his dish on the coffee table.

"Play something on the piano, Marlenna," he said. "I always loved hearing your mother play."

"Mother could play almost anything. She could hear something and play it. She could put chords together and make music for hours. I can't do that. I have to remember a piece to play it." But Marlenna moved to the piano bench and struck a few notes, listening to the tones. Then she played the most beautiful music Brewster had ever heard. Old Albert Mixon closed his eyes, folded his hands across his chest and listened. Brewster didn't want to close his eyes; he wanted to watch Marlenna as she sat at the piano with her body leaning toward the keys. When she finished, her father opened his eyes. "Splendid, daughter. Absolutely splendid. What piece was that?"

"One of the Chopin waltzes. I can't remember which one." She looked at Brewster. "I learned that in my senior year in Raleigh." She turned toward the piano again and played another piece, and then another. Albert Mixon breathed heavily, the music having soothed him into sleep.

Marlenna spun around on the bench. "I don't know whether to wake him or let him sleep," she whispered. "He sleeps so poorly since mother passed away. Sometimes he's up for the day at three in the morning. I think I'll let him sleep. Let me get a sweater, and we'll sit on the porch for a while if it isn't too cool."

When Brewster sat in the white swing on Albert Mixon's front porch, he rubbed his fingers on the armrest and felt the roughness of the inferior wood. He knew he would be proud to show Marlenna his own swing, which was sanded as smooth as polished marble.

"You and your sister played up here on the porch with your dolls lined up in this swing. You had a little table, and I guess you had dishes and probably food on that table. My little brother, TeeBoy, wanted to come up on this porch. We would have played any role you gave us."

"We didn't play with anybody but occasionally Anvil Thomas," Marlenna said. "There were lots of reasons for that." She pushed her small foot against the floor of the porch and the swing moved. "We were lonesome."

"There wasn't any reason to be lonesome. Plenty of children wanted to come on this porch and play."

"Mother and Father wouldn't allow it. There was considerable resentment toward my father, and there still is. Some of our own people thought Father should provide his services for free. And there were the white folks to consider. Mother thought if we had Negro children come on the porch or in the yard to play, the white folks on State Street wouldn't like it. They tolerated us because of father's business, but if we had other Negro children in the yard, they wouldn't tolerate that."

Marlenna leaned forward, pulling at the sweater that was around her shoulders. She shivered, and Brewster helped her slip her hands through the armholes. "We may have to go inside," she said.

Brewster wrapped his arm around Marlenna's shoulder and placed his other arm across the front of her, pulling her to him. She rested her back against the side of his chest. He could have sat for hours, feeling the warmth of Marlenna's body and her sweater, which was the softest wool, the fibers raised and plush under his fingers.

"Until I went to Raleigh, this house and County Training School were my entire worlds. We didn't go to church. Mama took us twice, but the ladies didn't talk to her. We sat on a pew by ourselves. After that, Mama listened to a radio preacher on Sundays. I would have loved going to Sunday school with the other girls."

"You could have taken my place. Mama Tee made us go every Sunday. Scrubbed and dressed," he said and leaned his head closer to her, smelling the fragrance of roses. He closed his eyes and concentrated on the feel and the smell of Marlenna.

"We hardly ventured from this house. It was and still is a splendid refuge, but I think I crave solitude because we were raised on it. This was it. This house on State Street was all there was."

The screech of the screened door startled both of them. "I'm going to bed now, Daughter." Albert Mixon crossed the porch and extended his hand toward Brewster. "Good evening to you."

"I'll turn the bed back for you." Marlenna rose to follow her father.

"I'm fine," Brewster said, shoving his hands into his pockets and stepping to the edge of the porch. Across the street, the building that had been Bernard's Grocery Store didn't look at all like it did when he was a child. A young couple had purchased the building, expanding the front, adding more plate glass and more lights. Unlike Mr. Bernard, who had lived upstairs, the young couple lived in a row of new houses west of town. Everybody still called it Bernard's old place, although the sign above the door read Fisher Shoes. He lit his cigarette, went down two steps and seated himself on the concrete pillar. *Lonely*, Marlenna had said. But lonely was better than hopeless at 20 Perry Street. *Hopeless*, that was it. There was no hope for

68

TeeBoy or Bess or Tom either, but he had turned hopeless into a future with sixty acres and his job at Three Brothers. He drew hard on his cigarette, pleased with his own thinking.

"That didn't take long," Marlenna said when she opened the screened door. "Mother always turned back the sheets at night. I've tried to do that to give my father a sense that some things have stayed the same."

She sat on the banister beside Brewster and hunched forward, wrapping one arm around the other. She spoke in a soft voice, straightening her back and leaning against him, not facing him.

"Because they didn't have many friends, Mother and Father depended on each other. He's always done well until she died. He's smart. When he moved to Low Ridge from the country, he had absolutely nothing but the clothes on his back and the head on his shoulders. For a Negro to have established a successful business, especially one that's dependent on white patrons, is nothing short of a miracle. Mixon Domestics and Laborers provided for us well."

But the money came from poor folks who needed to work, Brewster wanted to say, but he held his words. Marlenna was the miracle, he thought. Albert Mixon's daughter had turned into this beautiful woman.

I've been working with my students on rhythm," Marlenna said. "We've been writing songs. Old songs, new songs, our own songs." She snapped her fingers.

> *Nothing's a nothing,*
> *Five's a figger.*
> *The white man got it all*
> *And none for the nigger.*
>
> *Amen for number ten,*
> *But listen here honey,*
> *You can't count good*
> *And you don't get no money.*

Brewster laughed out loud. "Tricks," Marlenna said. "I have all kinds of tricks to show my students they can write. Teaching is part what you know and part magic. So, we write songs. Silly songs, sad songs, around-the-town songs."

"I like that," Brewster said. He felt his own magic in the moment, a spell that bound them on a clear-star night with a nip in the air. A night when Low Ridge sat quiet and waited for Brewster McAtee and Marlenna Mixon to get acquainted.

Marlenna brought her knees up in her skirt and wrapped her arms around them. They sat in silence. Brewster locked both his arms around her and held her in the pocket they created.

She pulled away. "I've got to go in now. Father will have me up at six tomorrow. I've promised to take him to visit family over in Hurley County. He has two sisters over there, nieces and nephews, and so many cousins I couldn't count them. We'll be on the road by seven."

They both stood. "I've sat here and gotten so cold, I can hardly move," Marlenna said.

"I want to see you tomorrow night."

"I don't have any idea when we'll be back. It may be early evening or it may be late. If you're in town, check to see if we're home." She touched his face with her fingers. "Good night." She went up the steps quickly and inside the screened door. The lights went off in the foyer.

Brewster walked back to the curb beside the Three Brothers shed where he had left his truck. The night was cool and clear and he was certain he wanted Marlenna. He wanted her as much as he had wanted his land. He wanted her more that he had wanted any woman, and he could not imagine what pleasure lay there for him under the thin white blouse and the black skirt.

When he reached his truck at the curb beside the Three Brothers shed, he didn't want to start the engine because it would make a terrible roar and would probably wake Deak Armbrecht and his wife Gretta. Having no choice, he started the motor, turned around in the driveway of the shed, and rumbled off toward Ole Summit Highway.

6

Midday on Saturday, when Brewster turned out of his lane headed toward Low Ridge, he was surprised to see a large sign standing at the edge of Travis Peets' property. IMPEACH EARL WARREN. The sign must have been added on Friday, but when he came home, it was too dark to see it. He stopped in front of the sign and studied it. Printed, not handwritten, the sign was nailed to new two-by-fours that had been driven into the soft dirt at the edge of the road. The wood was fresh and yellow in the midday sun.

Peets has spoken, Brewster thought, and it angered him that Travis Peets had placed the sign at the very edge of his property. When he got into town, he would tell Matthew about the sign. He wanted to buy out Travis Peets, if for no other reason than to dig up the two-by-fours and burn the sign. When he passed the tarpaper-covered house, old Mrs. Peets sat on her porch, watching the road. He accelerated and drove on toward Low Ridge, headed for Big Eddie's Motors on Highway 9, close to the Hot Dog Diner.

The sign for Big Eddie's had a red heart painted on it and inside the heart were the words, BIG EDDIE LOVES YOU! Under the slogan, a large cartoon man in a small car extended his head out the window and grinned. Brewster drove his truck onto Big Eddie's lot, parked, and walked between the rows of new and used cars. He had decided to be cautious with his money and buy a used car, a classy car, but one that would leave him enough to buy Travis Peets' three acres. He looked first at a '53 Chevrolet with a sticker in the window: 4-DR. POWERGLIDE SPECIAL TODAY $395.

"Not bad for a car only four years old. I'm Ernie Ladd. Can I interest you in a car?" The salesman extended his hand to Brewster, who noted that a white man grasps firmly when selling a car to a Negro. Ernie Ladd was tall, middle-aged, with thinning hair. He wore a plaid shirt and a navy-blue sports coat that was tight across his bulky shoulders.

"That one looks good," Brewster said.

"A fine car, a one-owner car. Can't find a car of that quality at such a low price." Ernie Ladd rocked back on his heels.

71

Brewster spotted a '54 Ford station wagon. He hadn't considered a station wagon, but it had some appeal. He could carry lumber in the back. He could keep his old truck for heavy hauling. FORDOMATIC, POWER STEERING, THE CLEANEST IN THE SOUTH—EDSEL TRADE IN.

Then he spotted it. A '56 Buick Riviera. Low to the ground with fins front and back. Two-toned, light blue and white. He walked around it slowly. He stepped back to look at the rear of the car. He walked to the front of the car admiring it. He read the sticker, '56 BUICK RIVIERA COUPE, DYNAFLOW, R&H, EDSEL TRADE-IN, LIKE-NEW CONDITION $875. His hands sweated. He could see himself in this car. But would he have enough money after he bought-out Travis Peets? The timber men gutted his land, and he hated to see that. But his land was meant to sustain him and he needed a car.

"Can I drive this one?'"

Ernie Ladd trotted off toward the showroom to get the key. Brewster wanted a car that would park itself nicely at 32 State Street. Dress the house, not bring it down.

When Ernie Ladd came out, he climbed in the passenger seat beside Brewster, but he didn't surrender the key; he explained every indicator on the dash. "You'll look mighty fine in your neighborhood in this thing," he said, and then he leaned across the seat and put the key in the ignition. Brewster started the Riviera and eased out on the highway. He didn't say a word at the traffic light at the corner of State Street and Highway 9. The Buick engine was so quiet and the idle so steady that he was not sure the car was still running until he put his foot on the gas pedal and eased onto State Street. Brewster headed west toward the Mixon house. This was the test. How would the car feel when it passed 32 State Street? Ernie Ladd maintained a constant chatter, but Brewster kept his mind on the car—the feel of the cloth interior, which was a shade darker than the outside paint, the ride of the car, which was smooth, and the smell of the car, which was new, like it came straight from the factory.

"I see what you want to do," Ernie Ladd said. "You gonna turn on Limrick Road here and let all your people see you in this car." He chuckled. "That'll be fine. Don't go too far down Limrick. Road's real bad. May get the tires out of alignment."

Brewster passed the Mixon house and observed to himself that the Riviera had just the right feel. A fine car. He passed Limrick

Road and continued on to County Training School where he turned the Buick around in the front driveway.

"You not going down Limrick there and let your folks see how you look?" Ernie Ladd asked.

"I'll take this one," Brewster said, making a commitment to sell the full fifteen acres, even twenty acres, if necessary, to have this car.

"You made a good decision, but how you gonna pay for it? We can take some down and put the rest on weekly payment, but we gotta talk to your boss man before we do that. You don't make those payments and Big Eddie'll come get this car fast as lightning. I drove Big Eddie over to get a car that a colored man off Limrick there had stopped making payments on. That man didn't get the keys right away, and Big Eddie reached through that screened door and had both his hands around that man's throat. He lifted him straight off the floor. I never seen a man put his hand through wire mesh like that, but that's what Big Eddie done and his knuckles was bleeding. When Eddie let him down, that man went flying to get those keys." Ernie laughed. "See what I mean? You make those payments every week and on time." He put a beefy finger in the air.

"I'll write a check next week," Brewster said, listening to the soft purr of the engine.

"How much you gonna write that check for?"

"What did it say on the sticker? It was eight hundred, seventy-five, I think."

Ernie stopped talking. He studied Brewster. "That's big money. You got that kinda money?" Brewster ignored the question. Ernie Ladd was quiet on the drive back to Big Eddie's lot.

"I'll come next week and bring a check," Brewster said, when they parked the car.

"You bring that check on in and I'll talk to Big Eddie about it," Ernie Ladd said. He nodded toward Brewster, but didn't extend his hand.

Brewster drove out of the lot and headed toward Low Ridge. He decided to park his truck at the curb beside the shed, walk to the Mixon house, and see if Marlenna had returned from Hurley. He regretted not being able to write the check today and drive the Buick off the lot. If he had the Riviera, he would park in front of 32 State Street and wait for Marlenna. Instead, he parked by the shed and walked down State Street on the opposite side from the Mixon house. When he reached Fisher Shoes, which had been old Bernard's

Grocery Store, he stopped and studied the Mixon house. There was no sign of Marlenna or her father. He crossed the street and walked down Limrick Road, stopping at the Mixon driveway and peering into the backyard. Marlenna's car wasn't there.

He walked back to his truck, got into the ragged cab, started the rumbling engine, turned around in Deak Armbrecht's driveway, and headed toward Ole Summit Highway. He would use the last sunlight to examine his trees and decide which acres to clear. After he walked through the timber woods, he would make a quick stop at his house, put on a little aftershave, and drive back into Low Ridge to see Marlenna. The sun was going down quickly. He had just enough time to examine the south acres before he lost daylight.

On Ole Summit, the woods grew thick and close to the road, and several of the yellowing trees caught the last rays of September sun, glowing like lighted zinc. When he passed Travis Peets' place he always looked toward the house to examine the confusion in the yard. He had memorized some of the clutter—a rusted '39 truck on blocks, weeds tall around it, an old refrigerator with the door standing open, and the porch burdened with junk that rested against the rails and pushed through the bottom slats. It had become a game for Brewster to identify as much stuff on the porch as he could while the truck was still moving. He had spotted a washtub, piles of old clothes, lard cans, what appeared to be a car battery, an old sofa, and a stack of firewood. But these were only the beginnings. The porch was loaded with junk.

As he neared Peets' place, he saw several trucks and cars parked in the yard, and he was surprised that Travis Peets had company. He slowed his truck to examine the gathering, and he saw by the nearest truck two men, wearing white robes, looking at him through square-cut eyeholes in pointed hoods. A dizzy wave washed through Brewster's head. His truck ran onto the gravel at the edge of the road. His heart pelted his chest, hitting rapidly against the wall of bone that kept it from erupting past its cavity. One of the hooded men put his hand to his white-screened forehead in mock salute. Heat rose through Brewster's body; hellish, white-hot heat encased him.

The limb of a tree cracked hard against the windshield, scrapping heavy across the truck roof. Brewster eased back onto the highway driving toward his lane. Sweat popped up on his forehead. His stomach squeezed into long, tight knots. He wanted to turn his truck around and head back into Low Ridge, but to do that he would have to face them again and he dared not. How many of the hooded men were there? Should he go on toward Hurley County? Bulah was the first little town he would come to.

While these questions rose in his head, a car came from the opposite direction, and Brewster saw two of them in it. The points of their hoods stood up past the window rim, making their heads appear flat and squared, like solid white rocks. The driver turned toward Brewster, and the eyes looking through those square-cut holes horrified him. Death, not the grim reaper shrouded in black, death wore solid white, a white devil in a white robe. Sweat ran down the sides of his ribs. He leaned forward on the steering wheel, his breath tight. They had come from the direction of Bulah. How many of them were on the highway? He had a shotgun in the house, if he could get inside.

He slowed the truck almost to a stop to turn onto his lane. He did this while looking in his rearview mirror. When the wheels of his truck were on his own land, his own territory, he felt a moment of relief. But he was isolated, and this flashed through him too. He peered into the woods on both sides as he pulled his truck to the front porch, bumping it. He gazed around, then in one movement, he made a dart for his unlocked door.

He moved through his house, focused on finding his shotgun and shells. He did this without turning on any lights. He found the gun in the bedroom closet and the shells on the top shelf in the kitchen. Then he loaded the gun in near darkness, shoved the box of shells in his pocket and stood by the door. He could hear his own breath loud and urgent in the silence. Holding the shotgun like a flag bearer, he paced to the far north corner of the kitchen, looking out the window into the woods in the direction of Travis Peets' place. He inhaled deeply, hearing his breath like a distant siren. He had no telephone. He couldn't summon help and he dared not go out. A caged animal. He paced sentinel-style between the door and the north window of the kitchen with both hands on the stock of his gun. He could get in his truck and drive toward Hurley County, but there were likely to be more of them on the road, and there were not many houses between here and there, making it easy to be ambushed.

He saw himself forced from the road, jumping from his truck, making a run for the woods. That would be his only hope. He had looked at the picture of Emmett Till killed over in Mississippi. *Jet* showed the boy with one eye gouged, his head crushed, and his face swollen from where they had beaten him. Not even his own mother could recognize what was left. What would they do to him? His size would justify a Klan army mutilating him into submission.

They would drag his body into the woods, put it under some light ground cover, and nobody would find it. Sheriff Tate wouldn't organize a search because he would reason it was best to leave the situation alone. If no one could find Brewster McAtee, then he was a missing person. "Maybe he up and left," Sheriff Tate would say, and he would not create a problem for himself by locating a corpse. No, he would not try to drive toward Bulah because that would give them an open opportunity.

Sweat ran into the corner of his right eye, stinging it. He wiped his eye with the back of his hand. He needed to hide himself, but he wanted a vantage so he could see them when they came. He could at least get off a few good shots. He would go to the roof. That would allow him to see them and it would give him a good range, but he needed to hide himself and keep his range at the same time. He had a giant oak to the South of the house, just into the woods. If he climbed the tree he would be hidden, and he could do considerable damage to them before they ever got to him. This was what he should do. He would go out the back. Darkness would cover him. He crossed the kitchen, moving toward the door, keeping his face toward the windows. When he reached the edge of the door, he stood beside it and took a deep breath. As if on orders, he opened the door and slipped through it, pressing himself against the house with the gun held in both of his hands. He surveyed as far as his eyes could see into the darkness, and then in one jerk, he darted toward the woods.

When he reached the tree, he secured the gun in his left armpit, reaching for a branch and pulling with his right hand. He grasped the branch with both hands, still pressing the gun under his arm, and using his feet, he pushed to the lowest branch. From there his climb was easy. He went up three more branches and stood in a fork of the tree, pressing his back against the bark and easing himself down on his haunches. He breathed deep and felt sweat run down the side of his face. By morning he might be dead, but from here he would take some of the hooded men with him, and he wanted to do that. He wanted to take them with him. He would stand at God's great judgment and see justice roll forth from the bench of the Almighty. *The ungodly shall not stand in the judgment. The ungodly shall perish before the seat of God.* There would be some consolation, standing beside them at the great bar of justice, their hoods removed.

Another idea flooded his mind, rushing on top of the last one. If he lived, he would be taken to jail, and he would not survive there. He knew this. If he shot them and if he could get away, he had better jump in his truck and drive out of town, past Hurley, and keep on going. He might have a chance to run, get to another town, find some place like Happy Landing, and sleep for a day until he could run some more. He would go south and then west, and maybe go on to Texas. This thinking settled him. For now the woods were quiet.

He had planned to meet Travis Peets next week and buy his miserable three acres, but that would be too late. Time had outrun him. Matthew James would be stung with remorse because Travis Peets had played his hand before they could fully study their own. Matthew would know what happened here and would not let it rest, even though Sheriff Tate would deny what was obvious. In the quiet, Brewster wondered also about Marlenna. Was she back from Hurley? Was she safe inside the white house on State Street?

Maybe he should come down, get in his truck, and drive past Travis Peets' place with his headlights off, easing back into town, but with the cracked muffler, his truck would roar and he would give himself away. Surely Marlenna was back on State Street, tucked inside the house with the green porch and the white swing.

He eased himself down on the branch and spread his legs on either side. He was up this tree because what was happening in Little Rock had stirred the devil out of hiding, and he was up this tree because he was colored, and he would likely die for that very reason. Before he was six-years-old he had learned the boundaries of dark skin.

He had been with his daddy at the Luce house where Tom cut the grass with a push mower, and he picked up twigs and light branches that had fallen from the giant oaks, putting these in a pile to the side of the yard. When they had finished, Tom knocked at the back door, and when Mrs. Luce gave him his pay, Brewster had asked for water.

"I'm thirsty, Miz Luce. Can I have me a glass of water?" To this day, he remembered the look that slid over her face. Tom grabbed him by the collar.

"We going on home, boy. We got plenty water there. Don't you bother Miz Luce about that."

"I'm thirsty now," he had said.

Tom snatched him off the porch. "I'll check with you in about two weeks and see if this grass need to be cut again, Miz Luce."

When they reached the sidewalk, Tom had said, "I'm gon' tan your hide like leather, boy."

"What did I do, Daddy?"

"You don't never ask no white for water, nor nothin' else. You smart enough to know that. If you not, you gon' know after I put a strap on you. White folks don't want to drink after you put your lips on their glass."

"I didn't know, Daddy. I didn't know."

Tom whipped him until blood oozed from the raised edges of welts. When Mama Tee came home, Tom made him stand in the kitchen and show her the red welts.

Mama Tee stooped to embrace him and pulled him to her. "This is my boy," she said. "You ought to be ashamed to whip him so hard."

"He got to know he a nigger," Tom said. "That whippin's easy in consideration of what gon' happen if he don't learn that lesson. Don't 'spect he forget that now. I got more to give him if he do."

If Tom could have seen his feet run up this tree like a flying squirrel, he would have laughed. "You know you a nigger now, boy." But the afternoon when Tom had whipped him, Mama Tee lifted him and set him on the table. She wiped his face with a cool cloth, and he could still feel the coolness of that cloth on his skin.

A thud on the tree limb, quick and flat, sent a small wave of movement along the branch. Blood raced past Brewster's ears. He snapped the gun at ready. By the light from the half moon he saw a possum stretched at full length on the branch, frozen, hissing low and steady. He snapped the safety on his gun and watched the possum. The scared animal could come at him anytime. He rotated the stock-end of the gun out, slow with his movements so as not to alarm the animal and not to undo his balance. Holding the gun with both hands, he pulled back. He hit the possum's head, shattering it with the blow. The possum fell from the tree, and Brewster heard its body knocking branches and thumping to the ground. There might be others around him, but he couldn't see them in the thickness of the tree.

He heard a voice in the distance carried by the wind, and he strained to make it out, but there was no sense to it. The lone voice blended with the others. There would be a number of them when they came because he could hear their howling. They would go into the house and hunt for him and probably set fire to smoke him out like a rabid bat, but he would stay quiet, and if they found him, he would shoot them because he hated them for hunting him. He would not surrender himself to them, but at the back of his mind was the question: Would he turn the gun to his own head? His stomach knotted hard. Air, thick with dread, came heavy into his chest—air as thick as dark molasses cloying over the lining of his lungs. When he heard them coming, he would stand, because the fork of the tree was wide and stout enough to rest his back against the giant trunk. He would not give them the pleasure of ending his life. He would do that himself before they had a chance.

For now he sat straddle-legged on the branch and rested his head against the bark. He needed to be calm when he looked into their oddly squared eyes. He had read about soldiers surviving hopeless situations because they remained cool-headed. Be still, wait, and think. He was not ready to die, but when they came, they would bring death.

"Help me Jeee-sus." He had heard Mama Tee whisper this a thousand times through clinched teeth as she stood at the kitchen sink or when she lay in her bed at night, her words uttered in relinquishment, cutting through the darkness. He whispered these words and thought how strange that the mind of man is a solitary link to God. He thought of Mama Tee's prayer when she made him and TeeBoy kneel, and she placed large, fleshy hands on their heads praying for their souls, "Keep us through this night, and splendor the morning, Oh Lord with your light." When these words passed through him, he pressed the crown of his head against the bark, surveying the night sky brightened by the light of a half moon.

He encountered the hooded men only once in Low Ridge. He had been eight and TeeBoy not yet in school. Word spread that a Negro had come in the house of a white woman over in Hurley. The story rolled down State Street, turned the corner at Limrick Road, rumbled through every dirt lane, and by dusk there was not one soul visible on any of the Negro streets.

Inside 20 Perry Street, all the lights were out. Mama Tee, Daddy Divine, Brewster, and TeeBoy huddled with their heads together at the base of the front window, peeking out at pick-up trucks where white robes flapped from raised arms. "They kill the first man be out," Daddy Divine had whispered. Bess sat in a dinette chair behind the others, and she moaned a deep sound that rose from the middle of her neck. Tom stood over the four who hunched their backs, peeking out the bottom of the window. Fear wrapped tightly around Brewster's chest, threatening to cut off his air. TeeBoy cried when he heard the men howling. In a flash, the heel of Tom's right hand slammed down on the back of TeeBoy's head, hitting him solidly, smashing his nose against the window ledge. Blood spurted a dark wetness onto the floor. Mama Tee put her apron over TeeBoy's nose, wrapped her arm around him, and took him to the kitchen where she chipped ice with a pick and placed it in a dishtowel without turning on a single light.

When the Klan wheeled off Limrick Road, the family remained in darkness, listening to the trucks roll down the side streets. TeeBoy fell asleep in Mama Tee's lap, nested against her broad chest with the ice pressed to his nose. Daddy Divine rested on the sofa, and Brewster sat on the floor, his head against the couch. Bess curled herself into a small heap under the dinette table. Tom paced back and forth.

"Goddamn! Don't nobody hear me! Got to get out of here. Can't stand to be huddled up like this."

"Don't go nowhere tonight," Daddy Divine had said. "Done seen what they did to a man. Seen it when I was a boy. Dragged him behind a wagon, hung what was left of him to a tree. Took his shirt off and hung it on a post up in town. That shirt stayed there 'til the blood turned purple. I walked past that shirt going into town." The words rumbled up from Daddy Divine's chest. He didn't need to tell the story again. He had told it before, and Brewster had a clear vision of the bloodstained shirt, flannel, red-and-blue checked, hanging on the post in town, the blood fading to a deep purple in the sun.

"Shit, we packed in here like rats! This man not 'fraid of the old guts on those trucks. This man not 'fraid." Tom slapped his chest. "Shit those guts!" he shouted. Brewster came in and out of sleep that night with *shit those guts, shit those guts* drifting through his brain. Tom broke dishes in the kitchen before he found a bottle to wrap his lips around. Sucking the whiskey calmed him, but still he whispered, *shit those guts, shit those guts*. The echo of it was in Brewster's ears now, *shit those guts*.

He brought his feet up to the limb, changing his position. He needed to urinate. It would be best to do that before they came. He didn't want to pee in his pants while devils watched. He stood, leaned the side of his body against the tree, and pissed, feeling good to do something so ordinary in this extraordinary position, waiting for death, up a tree in the half-moon of September. He needed to keep the circulation going in his legs. He crouched, resting the butt of his gun on the limb. They had a fire going because he could smell smoke. It drifted up to him, as did the sounds of their voices around their fire.

They couldn't be fools enough to set fire to the forest. He leaned forward sniffing like an animal hunting food. Only a half-witted man would torch the forest because the trees would burn like kindling in this dry weather. If they burned the woods, there would be mayhem. He could flee ahead of the fire. He thought he saw a faint glow of orange in the distance. A sudden flicker of hope like an urge or craving swept through him. Maybe he should jump down. He surveyed the distance, but couldn't convince himself that he saw fire. He could smell the smoke, though—timber smoke.

He straddled the branch again and leaned against the giant oak. If he turned the gun on himself, where would he position it? To his temple and he would feel no pain, but he would leave a stump, no eyes, no nose to identify. He could put the metal to his chest and blow his heart out. This would be kinder to Mama Tee who would identify his body, but his brain would continue to work for some seconds. God forbid it would work past one long minute. He could endure one long minute after his heart exploded, a blood parachute coming out of his back. He would start counting at sixty and go backwards, hoping he would not make it to the final number—One. He would not give himself to them and he knew this. He was certain. He leaned against the giant oak and breathed more thick dread.

The night the Klan rode in Low Ridge, he had fallen asleep on the floor, and when he woke, Daddy Divine sat at the table, his pants held up by wide suspenders over his tee-strapped undershirt.

"Didn't hear him leave?"

"Done told you I didn't," Mama Tee had said, irritation in her voice. "Dozed some. When I woke up, I thought Tom had settled down, but when I got up I knowed then Tom was gone."

"Not one thing I can do if he get caught by the crowd that doing the riding. Tom got to know that," Daddy Divine had said.

Mama Tee and Daddy Divine went to work, but Brewster remembered the world out of balance. They hid in darkness, peeked out the window, slept on the floor. The world couldn't be positioned the same after a night like that. But people went about their own business. Laundry hung on clotheslines and cars rested in the air on the rack at Stanley's Service Station. Men in suits came and went from the courthouse and no one spoke of the white-robed riders, not even on Limrick Road. Brewster wedged his fear and his knowledge inside himself, swallowed and held it.

"Best not to talk about things like that," Mama Tee had said.

He had to keep the blood flowing in his legs. He eased himself up and stood slowly, trying to dodge the suckers sticking out from the main branch. He shifted his weight from foot to foot. His head caught the silk of a spider's web; he jerked, nearly losing his balance. Brewster steadied himself by pressing his back against the trunk and pushing the crown of his head hard against the wood. He slapped his hand against his face to remove the filament clinging to him. He had seen tree spiders, two-inch disks in the center of intricate webs. He did not want one of these to crawl across him, but the night belonged to them, and to the white-robed men who worked themselves into frenzy. Tom was the nigger-man who made himself crazy—mean crazy. Why couldn't they have found him? Sacrificed him as the nigger-man. But Mama Tee had prayed for Tom when she woke in the night, pacing through the house.

TeeBoy blew blood from his nose and spoke with a hollow voice. "Hate him. Gon' whup his butt, when I get big. Be easy. Get me a strap and whup his butt."

"He won't be coming back," Brewster had told TeeBoy. "His shirt'll be up on the post at Bernard's Grocery."

"Turnin' purple," Teeboy jumped to the end of the story.

Three afternoons they walked by the concrete post at Bernard's, waiting to see Tom's shirt, but Tom found his way home like a dumped cat. On the fourth afternoon, Tom stood in the kitchen on unsteady feet, unshaven, his eyes red, and he carried with him the stale odor of liquor and time. Mama Tee stood in front of the kitchen sink, the muscles of her jaw as tight as they had been when Tom was gone.

"Give yo Daddy a big kiss," Tom said when the boys came in the door. He went toward TeeBoy, who fled, but Tom caught him, encircling him in his right elbow. TeeBoy turned his face squirming from the vise created by his father's arm, but Tom's loose left hand dropped in the waist of TeeBoy's pants and yanked, in one movement exposing him.

"Stop it! Stop it!" TeeBoy hit at Tom's face.

"Stop that!" Mama Tee shouted with her wet hands on her hips. "You two get out of here." She waved her arms at Brewster and TeeBoy. "Tom, you get those filthy clothes off." Brewster lifted

TeeBoy, carrying him from the kitchen, feeling TeeBoy's nakedness against his arm.

The half moon had climbed from the eastern sky and glowed straight over him with a cool color like the reflection off a newly minted coin. He could see his land stretched before him in the light from the moon. Travis Peets and the hoodlums with him had not taken that from him—could not take that from him. This was still his land and would be even after he was gone.

His teeth ached from the tightness in his face, and his eyes had a tiredness that he fought against, but he knew he would not surrender. Then he heard it, the car engine. Distant, but easing down his lane. He snapped to attention like a shot was fired up his butt. His legs scrambled to get steady on the tree limb. He was calm. Remarkably calm, a calm that passed all understanding. The very peace of God. He put his left foot in front of his right and checked his balance. Two cars. They pulled behind his truck. Brewster gripped the shotgun.

One door slammed and then the second one.

"Brewster, it's Matthew James. You can come on out if you're in there. I don't want to come in on you." The words made no sense.

"I got the Sheriff with me. Come on out now. That mess down the road's been busted up."

The words passed through his head, but he had been on alert too long to let go. What was Matthew James doing here?

"Probably ain't here," Brewster heard Slim Tate say.

"He's 'round somewhere," Matthew said. "His truck's still here."

"Matthew?" Brewster lowered himself two branches and jumped from the tree. "Matthew?"

Was he already dead? If this was death, there was no pain. He moved toward the clearing with the gun tight in his hands. There stood Matthew James.

Brewster walked out on the lane and put his arms around Matthew. He felt his friend's flesh—skin, muscles, ribs, *a body*, and the spiciness of Matthew's aftershave. The strap of the gun was over Brewster's shoulder and its stock and barrel flapped like oars out of water. Brewster and Matthew made one complete circle, holding each other.

Slim Tate stood back from this, leaning against his car. "Where the devil you come from, Brewster? What you doin' with that gun?"

Brewster laughed. He was alive, and the feel of it, the smell of it, the seeing of it, made his head as light as when Anvil Thomas used to slam down on the gas pedal of his '51 Chevrolet, going from stop to fifty in a minute flat, leaving parts of head and heart at the start position. It would take minutes for his body to catch up with itself, but it had felt good flying down the highway, airy as a feather. He had not had that feeling in years, but now his head had a light, swimmy feeling, and he laughed, feeling the mellowness of his own laugh in his chest.

"Where were you, Brewster?" Slim Tate asked again, still leaning on his car.

"Up a tree," Brewster said, and he spewed laughter because he was alive and he felt good.

"You mean you been up a tree this whole night?" Slim Tate laughed for the first time. "Guess you was scared," he said. "But I had this situation under control fast as the Preacher here come got me. Can't believe you spent the night up no tree," he laughed again, but Brewster stopped laughing.

"He was prepared to save his life," Matthew said. "When one man's up against a mob, Sheriff Tate, the best place for that man to be is out of sight like a jaguar concealed."

"Up a tree," Slim Tate said. "There wasn't anything to this 'cept what's happening over in Arkansas got them all stirred up. Reading the paper these past few days made them want to get together and burn themselves a little bonfire. It's Saturday night. They could burn themselves a fire, drink some, and sleep late on Sunday. Wasn't nothin' to it." He walked around to the front of his car. "Brewster, you stay out of trees now, you hear."

Brewster and Matthew watched the patrol car turn around and head down the lane toward Ole Summit. "Let's put ourselves on a pot of coffee. Done lost this night," Matthew said.

Brewster made it strong and they drank it black, elbows on the table, cups held in both hands. Brewster felt his tiredness, flat and dull, but he also felt anger stirring in his stomach. "I never should have said I was up a tree. That story'll go around to every shit-headed cracker in Low Ridge. A nigger run up a tree out Ole Summit Highway. This nigger didn't circle that tree like black Sambo, he run clean up it. That story'll be told in the Low Ridge Diner Monday morning and he'll say some county boys got out of control out Ole Summit Highway, he had to bust it up, and he found a nigger up a tree."

"How many times you eat in the Low Ridge Diner?" Matthew asked.
"None."

"Then whatever Slim Tate tells don't make a bit of difference. You won't ever hear it, and I won't ever hear it, and not many folks we know will ever hear it." Brewster didn't argue because he knew what had happened was done and what would happen was done too.

"I doubt things was as easy as Slim Tate let on. I expect he was doing some scrambling to keep that bunch under control," Matthew said.

"How'd you get involved?"

"Saw them coming from across town, two of them riding down State Street, turning at the light. Had those hoods on, big as you please, like they could ride on the main street and nobody was going to stop them. I went on to Sheriff Tate's office and told him I saw two of them in a car headed out Ole Summit Highway. With what's happening over in Arkansas, we don't want trouble here too, I said. Told him I knew you had a place out this way. He said he would find out what was happening and I asked him to come get me. When he came by the parsonage, I followed him on out here. Grace was walking with us tonight," Matthew said.

"Grace was a fine woman," Brewster said, and Matthew slapped his shoulder.

The sun was coming up when they stepped out on the porch and Brewster saw his woods in an orange-pink mist that had yellow shot through it. Matthew James looked around. "Could be the Garden of Eden. Need to get that serpent gone, though." He went down the steps to his car, started the engine, backed up and waved.

Brewster shouted at him, "You still gon' preach today?"

"Sunday morning," Matthew shouted back. "I'm going to preach."

"I'm coming on," Brewster said.

"Should be quiet now. Slim Tate has things under control for a while. I'm going home to work on my sermon. Got a few things I want to add to it." The engine of Matthew's car made a steady clacking sound as it moved down the lane to the highway.

Brewster sat on his steps and watched the sun rising. He had not expected to see this sight, and the way the rose-orange cut into the gray-blue and purple bands filled him with satisfaction. He would not go to bed because it was contrary to his nature to sleep in the daylight, and the coffee was working on him. He would get his day going, doing what he intended to do. He remembered reading a story about a woman who lost her husband and children in a Nazi war camp. The woman survived, but had no will to live until she realized that walking through her day in a regular pattern was her victory. He thought of Mama Tee's prayer, "Splendor the morning, Oh Lord."

Travis Peets was probably sleeping now, his head resting at the edge of Brewster's property. But Brewster would not let Travis Peets have this morning—seeing it and walking through it would be his victory.

When the sun shone fully above the trees, he went inside and poured himself another cup of coffee. He had brought yesterday's newspaper from the shed, and he put it in front of him, reading again the story about Little Rock. He looked at the picture of the nine students who could not hide in the tree. He studied their faces, looking for signs they were ordained to face the fire that consumed Little Rock, but in their faces he saw nothing that set them apart. There was enough trouble for everybody, he thought. He folded the newspaper and stepped to the sink to wash up.

7

When he drove past Travis Peets' place, there were no signs of the night before. Peets had demonstrated his pedigree in the hellhounds who whooped on his property, and now he could sleep. He had sent Brewster a warning: *Move back into town. Limrick Road is where you belong.* But what Peets didn't know, Brewster thought, was that this land was ordained for him—for Brewster Thomas McAtee. He had seen the signs, he had secured the loan, and TeeBoy had danced on the lane. Travis Peets would go before he would.

The tarpaper-covered house was mottled in sunlight and shade by the trees that grew close to the porch. Everything and everybody appeared to be at rest. He was driving to church after spending a night up a tree with no sleep, and he was also reclaiming himself. He wouldn't give himself away. He thought about the morning after the Klan rode on Perry Street, when Mama Tee and Daddy Divine had gone to work. That was right, and he knew it now. To be pulled off his own center would be to give himself to them. Travis Peets would not have Brewster McAtee or his land.

He drove into Low Ridge and slowed his truck in front of Marlenna's house, but 32 State Street also appeared to be resting. When he turned onto Limrick Road, he looked into Albert Mixon's backyard, but Marlenna's car was not parked by the porch. He didn't know Albert Mixon's relatives, but if Marlenna was not at home by early afternoon, he resolved to drive to Hurley and find her.

Amazing grace, how sweet the sound that saved a wretch like me! I once was lost, but now am found, was blind, but now I see. The words rolled through the door when the deacon opened it. Brewster slipped in on the back row because there he would have greater freedom to think and doze. Mama Tee turned her head at the beginning of the second verse and spotted him.

'Twas grace that taught my heart to fear, and grace my fears relieved; how precious did that grace appear the hour I first believed! She glanced at him and adjusted her glasses. *Through many dangers, toils and snares, I have already come; 'tis grace has brought me safe thus far, and grace will lead me home.* She rotated

her neck on the fourth verse and stared at him. *The Lord has promised good to me, His word my hope secures; He will my shield and portion be as long as life endures.* She took another peek at him and he gave in. He walked forward to the fifth pew from the front and stood beside her. *When we've been there ten thousand years, bright shining as the sun, we've no less days to sing God's praise than when we've first begun.* She patted his hand.

After the hymn settled through the rafters and drifted out to the edges of the sanctuary, Matthew James walked to the lectern. "I've thrown everything out today," he said. "I'm picking the songs I want to hear and I'm going to say what's in my heart. I'm going to speak as God directs," he said. "There is no text."

"Amen. Tell it, brother," echoed from the back of the church.

"Grace. Now that's the same thing as mercy, forgiveness, kindness, and love," he said. "It could also mean a stay of execution, or a benediction, or the knowledge of right and wrong, or a thankful heart. How many of us have seen grace lately? How many of us know grace personally? How many of us walk in grace every day?" There were answers and rejoinders that stepped all over each other, but Matthew James didn't slow down to untangle them or let them settle.

"You may not know it," he said, "but grace paid us a visit last night. You see, there were some white-robed men and their garments were not lucent, and they were not sent from on high. Did you see them? Did anyone see the men of ill-will?"

Brewster wondered how much Matthew would say. For himself, he had decided to say little. Nothing had come of it, and he would protect himself and his land, and he didn't want to engage in conversation about spending a night up a tree in fear.

"Up there on State Street," old man Jeeter said from the side.

"What you talking about, Brother James?" a woman's voice shot from the front row.

"I know what the preacher's saying," another said.

"I seen them too." There was another voice, and then another.

"What I'm saying is that the Klan gathered outside Low Ridge last night. They cut through town, riding on our streets."

"Sweet Jesus! Sweeeeet Jesus!"

"I can testify," old man Jeeter called out. "These eyes saw them."

Matthew James continued. "What I'm saying is we're in troubling times. A little over a year ago, Martin King's house was bombed right here in Alabama, but grace was walking that night too.

His wife and children were spared. Martin and his family held tight in Montgomery, and God's grace was with them. You know that story, same as I do."

"Yes, yes. We know it."

"Miss Rosa Parks was tired after working all day. When they told her to give up her seat on the bus so a white man could sit down, she said, No. She said it politely, but she said, No. They organized in Montgomery and you all know the results."

"Yes. Yes."

"Segregation on public buses is wrong. Not just wrong," he added, "it's illegal."

"Yes! Yes!"

"Now, to our west, over in Arkansas, we got nine young people who want an education, and every day they walk through the mob going to school. Grace has been with them too. They have not been injured, and they can attend school another day and then another."

"Yessssss! Yessssss!"

"And what I'm saying is we're going to need more courage and more prayer right here in Low Ridge. If we've got the courage, and keep the prayer lines linked up, God will supply the grace. You know the state has done banned the NAACP here in Alabama, so Martin King started something he calls the Montgomery Improvement Association. I'm proposing that we start some kind of group here at Limrick Road Baptist, and that we devote our Wednesday nights to organizing and to praying for this country, this state, this city. We need to pray for the nine over in Arkansas, and for Martin King, and Ralph Abernathy, and for ourselves here in Low Ridge. And yes, we need to pray for the men who put on those white robes last night."

The congregation was alive with responses. "This church will become a prayer stronghold," he said. "We'll be the arsenal of heavenly entreaty, the storehouse of supplication. This is not a time to be angry. This is a time to petition the Almighty." The congregation responded to his calls, one voice succeeding another, erupting into potency ready to be refined. Before the congregation filed out to their Sunday dinners, Matthew James led the last song, "Leaning on the Everlasting Arm."

"Come on," Mama Tee said, when they walked through the church door and into the sunlight. "I got chicken ready to fry." He wanted to check on Marlenna, but Mama Tee locked her arm inside his elbow. They walked to the truck and drove to 20 Perry Street, where Mama Tee heated oil in a cast-iron skillet, and she placed a bowl of cubed potatoes in front of him after he seated himself at the dinette. She put an apron over her Sunday dress, tied it in the back, and she maneuvered between the stove and the table, putting ingredients into the bowl on every pass—diced dill pickle, minced egg, paprika, salt, pepper, mayonnaise. He stirred in each new ingredient.

"Tom's been up the country with Trumpet Eyes Sam. Gone all week," she said on a final pass with a tablespoon of mustard. "Trumpet Eyes got family up there, making shiney, no doubt. Don't do Tom one bit of good to go off with Trumpet Eyes, but they big buddies." Mama Tee rubbed her nose with the backside of her hand. She looked at Brewster. "That brings me to you, son," she said. "Too much carousing give you a heavy look like you wearing today. That's all I'll say about it." She put both hands on her hips, looking at him.

He wasn't going to tell her about his night up the tree, and he decided to give the score to Mama Tee. He groaned and affirmed her. "I know about that," he said.

She was satisfied and turned to inspect the chicken, frying in the hot oil. From the cabinet she removed two plates, which she pressed against her stomach with her arm around them. She placed silverware, paper napkins, and two tall, pink plastic tumblers on the plates. She brought her load to the table, and Brewster distributed it while Mama Tee delivered the chicken and the tea.

"I'm glad Reverend James will be starting some kind of organization here, but if there was stuff going on last night, I don't know one thing about it. I slept, and I'm glad of it," she added.

She forked a piece of chicken and put it on Brewster's plate. He had begun eating it before Mama Tee settled herself in her chair. The chicken was crisp on the outside, but the meat was warm and tender inside. He had eaten a bowl of cornflakes before he drove into Low Ridge, and his stomach was on empty. He shoveled in potato salad with his chicken.

"When Reverend James talked about that bus stuff in Montgomery, I was thinking about TeeBoy. Brewster, you remember when we went on the bus to Birmingham to see my brother before he passed?"

"I do," he said, holding the bone of a chicken thigh in his right hand.

"Took both of you boys with me. You was easy to manage, but TeeBoy wanted to sit on that front seat and watch the driver. TeeBoy couldn't have been but six or seven. 'I'm gonna sit here, Mama Tee,' he told me. He pretended he drove that bus, but I couldn't let him do that. 'Gon' talk to the driver,' he told me. That driver grinned and watched what I was gon' do. I went on to the back and I put my things in the seat. Then I went to the front. I got TeeBoy under the arms and carried him to the back. I pulled his pants down and I wore him out, right there on that bus. That was what I had to do." She inhaled a deep breath, causing her breasts to rise.

"That was over a dozen years ago."

"I remember it like yesterday." She folded her arms under her chest and watched Brewster eat.

The sky had turned gray and there was an unseasonable chill in the air when he left Mama Tee's. He drove to Marlenna's, determined to hunt for her if the two-toned Chevrolet was not parked by the back porch. He slowed his truck on Limrick and saw her car in the driveway. He turned onto State Street and parked in front of her house. A night with no sleep had given him immunity from embarrassment over his rumbling and battered truck. Marlenna saw him, or heard the roar of his truck, and she opened the door before he reached the green floorboards of the porch. She stood in the doorway with her cranberry sweater draped over her shoulders and she held the sweater in place by crossing her arms over her chest.

"We just got home," she said when he stepped into the passage. She took his jacket, hung it on the hat tree and led the way to the kitchen where Albert Mixon sat at the table with a sandwich in front of him. "I'll make you a sandwich," Marlenna said. "We had an early lunch with my father's sisters."

"No. I ate with Mama Tee. But I would like some coffee if you have that."

Marlenna removed the coffee pot from the stove, poured two cups, placed one in front of Brewster, and the other she set next to her father's plate. "We stayed the night in Hurley. Hadn't planned on that, but late yesterday a neighbor came to my aunt's and said she saw Klan on the road, headed toward Low Ridge. I didn't believe a word of it, but my aunt wouldn't let us leave."

"I don't think there was one thing to it," Albert Mixon said. With his thumb and index finger, he slid his glasses up the bridge of his nose.

"I saw them," Brewster said. "They were on the road out by my place last night." This was more than he intended to disclose. He took a drink of his coffee, and he could hear his own swallow in the hush.

Marlenna watched him. "Was there trouble?"

"Anytime there's Klan, there's trouble," Brewster answered.

"Was there trouble here in Low Ridge?"

"I didn't come back into Low Ridge. Didn't sleep much either."

"I'm sorry," she said.

"Matthew James said today he wants to have some meetings at Limrick Road Baptist. He wants to organize a group, something like the Montgomery Improvement Association," Brewster said.

"Don't know of any organization that can get rid of the Klan," Albert Mixon said. "We don't have city buses here like they do in Montgomery, and I'm not sure we need that kind of organization."

"I'm sure we do," Marlenna said, walking on the heels of her father's words. "Brewster, do you know Anvil Thomas?"

"We were friends in school."

"That's right," she said. "Anvil spoke of you. After Anvil graduated from Fisk, he went to Georgetown for his law degree, and he's clerking at one of the federal courts. Can you believe that? I can't even imagine. He does some organizing for the NAACP. He's someone your minister should contact."

"If Anvil Thomas has anything to do with a matter, it's going to be done right," Albert Mixon said and took a bite of his sandwich. He raised his eyebrows, and the glasses on the bridge of his nose slid down again.

Brewster was tired, and he didn't like the sound of Marlenna's and her father's confidence in Anvil. But he was a guest at Albert Mixon's table and he said nothing against Anvil.

"Well, if they put Anvil in charge that will be saving grace," Albert Mixon said. He took another bite of his sandwich and wiped mayonnaise from the corner of his lower lip.

"Whatever group is organized, I'm going to be a member," Marlenna said.

"Well," Albert Mixon said, "that may be okay."

When her father finished eating, Marlenna removed the dishes from the table. "We're going to make a fire in the parlor. Why don't you join us?"

"No," Albert Mixon said and took his watch out of his vest pocket, reading the time. "Going on up to my room. I want to listen to the Series. The Yankees have two and the Braves have one. Warren Spahn and Whitey Ford are pitching, Yogi's catching, Hank and Mickey are hitting. I'm surprised you're not home listening," he said to Brewster, and Brewster knew Albert Mixon was encouraging his departure.

Brewster brought firewood from a stack on the back porch, and Marlenna made a bed of shredded newspaper and wood chips for the logs. He wanted to unload some of the baggage he assumed when Marlenna and her father spoke of Anvil. He wanted to tell her that Anvil Thomas had a foul mouth and he planned to give her a few specific examples, but when the fire was started he stood with his hands outstretched toward it and maintained his silence. He knew a woodworker in Low Ridge didn't equal a lawyer in Washington and this troubled him. He pulled his hands back from the fire, crossed his arms, and put his hands under his armpits. Marlenna studied him for a moment. "Brewster, have you read *Invisible Man*?"

"The what?"

"*Invisible Man*. You know, Ralph Ellison's book? It stayed on the bestseller list for weeks and weeks a few years back. He's black, and he writes about a young man going off to college and into the world and trying to find out who he is."

Brewster felt stupid. He had never heard of Ralph Ellison. She was showing him that because he didn't go to college, he didn't know important writers. But he felt defiant. "Never heard of him or that book," he said, and he was careful to maintain a tone that didn't bespeak his embarrassment.

"That's fine because I'm going to read it to you. I need to reread it because I have several seniors who are studying it." With that, she went upstairs to locate her book. He didn't have much interest in reading because people who had time to sit and read had too much easy time, but if Marlenna wanted to read to him, he was more than willing to listen. When she returned to the parlor, they settled on the floor, leaning their backs against the wine-colored settee and Marlenna began.

> *I am an invisible man. No, I am not a spook like those who haunted Edgar Allan Poe, nor am I one of your Hollywood movie ectoplasms. I am a man of sub-stance, of flesh and bone, fiber and liquids—and I might even be said to possess a mind. I am invisible, understand, simply because people refuse to see me. Like the bodiless heads you see sometimes in circus sideshows, it is as though I have been surrounded by*

*mirrors of hard, distorting glass. When they approach
me they see only my surroundings, themselves, or
figments of their imagination—indeed, everything and
anything except me.*

Only a few pages into the book, it turned ugly. Brewster didn't
like the battle royal where the Negro boys engaged in a savage fight
for the amusement of the drunk white men, and the naked white
dancer undulated for the pleasure of the white men and the humiliation of the black boys, and just past that was the wretched Trueblood.
If Marlenna read this stuff, she would not be shocked by the foulness
of Anvil Thomas's mouth.

They read until the sun set, and Brewster's eyes closed from their
own weight. When the doorbell rang, it startled both of them. When
Marlenna opened the door, Brewster heard a familiar voice. "I saw
Brewster McAtee's truck parked out front here, and I wanted to bring
him this dog." Brewster stepped to the door and saw Matthew, rain
soaked, and holding a rope, which was attached to a large dog.

Matthew looked at Brewster. "When Aunt Laney's sister died, I
took Valiant here. But I think you need him more than I do." He
paused while Brewster and Marlenna looked at the dog whose fur
stuck close to its skin, wet and matted. The dog looked up at them
with calm and curious eyes.

Matthew addressed himself to Marlenna, "Maybe the name made
me think this dog should belong to Brewster. I'm not going to tell the
story, but he was stalwart last night, valiant in his own way. It's his
story, but Brewster needs a dog out on Ole Summit."

Brewster was amused and annoyed that Matthew James stood at
this grand door with an old mongrel that looked like a wet and docile
wolf, but the humor of the situation overtook him, and he laughed.

Marlenna extended her hand, "Won't you come in?"

"No. I just wanted Brewster to know I had this dog for him."

Brewster stepped out onto the front porch. "I'm about to leave
because I'm asleep on my feet."

"I'm not trying to rush you. I can take Valiant back to the parsonage and you can come get him."

Brewster took the rope from Matthew's hand. The rain left a
thick mist in the air and when he walked into it, he felt as if he were
in a dream. Nearly everything had felt like that for the past forty-eight
hours, and he was too tired to unscramble it. "I'm going on," he said.

"Brewster, I want to hear your story tomorrow," Marlenna shouted.

He tugged on the rope, and Valiant jumped into the cab of the pickup. When Brewster got in and closed the door, Valiant shook, splattering him. "Shit!" he said. He started his truck and headed for the light at the corner.

At Ole Summit, he tied Valiant's rope around the porch banister, but then, on impulse, he untied it and opened the door. He extended his arm in a cordial gesture. Valiant walked through the front door. Brewster dragged the mattress down the stairs from where it rested on the floor of the upstairs bedroom, and he positioned it close to the door in the big room. He placed his loaded shotgun on the right side of his bedding. Then he and Valiant stretched out on the mattress and slept.

On Monday the rain was gone, and the day was cool and bright blue. Autumn was showing itself. Looking out his kitchen window, Brewster saw red and brown mixed with the deep greens of his forest. He had slept from sheer exhaustion, and the rest renewed him. He would not be driven off of his land. He planned to work through the winter getting the soil in his cleared acres ready for cotton and corn. Travis Peets was not going to take his land from him. A telephone at Ole Summit would give him some added protection. Maybe things would settle down over in Little Rock, and the Klan would not show itself in Low Ridge, but if you lived in Low Ridge, you lived with it. No, that was not true, a black man lived despite it.

He sat on his porch in his white swing when he drank his coffee, and Valiant lay on the floor close to his feet. Before he left for Three Brothers, he put a rope around Valiant's neck and tied the rope to a porch post. He emptied a box of cornflakes into a bowl and poured the last of his milk over it.

"I'll bring you something better for supper." He patted the dog's head and went down the steps headed for Low Ridge and the Three Brothers shed. When he passed Travis Peets' place, he spotted the man standing at the side of his house, splashing water from a large tub onto his face. Peets gave no indication that he noticed the truck, and Brewster drove on toward Low Ridge.

He hadn't gone through the double barn doors at Three Brothers before Matthew James' old Cadillac pulled up by the curb. Brewster walked to the open window of the car and squatted. "Slim Tate came by the parsonage early this morning. The meeting with Peets is set for this afternoon. I think Sheriff Tate hurried the meeting because of what was going on out there Saturday. I'll come on at four and ride out there with you."

Brewster stood with his hands on his hips. "When you showed up at Marlenna's with that mangy dog, I was thinking about whipping your ass. I've kind of taken a liking to that old hound, though."

"Similar personalities," Matthew said. "A preacher has a way of seeing things others can't see." He had a grin on his face when he rolled up his window and eased away from the curb.

Brewster did not want to speak with Travis Peets, no question about that, but he wanted the man off the edge of his property. He did not want to ever see white-robed men out Ole Summit, not so close to his curved lane, the path on which TeeBoy danced and he himself had felled every tree, every shrub, every blade of wire grass. This was his property, and never again did he want to be afraid on his own land. He hated all that Travis Peets stood for. What he wanted to do was buy the old man out and hope he would leave the county, would leave the state—would go somewhere, maybe to a desert, a place where he could do little harm. Off and on through the day, Brewster saw Travis Peets, his little tarpaper-covered house in a vast desert surrounded by miles and miles of barren sand—orange-tan sand—devoid of vegetation and people. In this vast desert Peets would have his own hate for comfort, and it would transform into a rattlesnake and slide its cool, moist skin around Peets' neck.

At four o'clock, Slim Tate drove his patrol car ahead of Brewster and Matthew, who rode in Brewster's old truck. Brewster swallowed hard, with his tongue nearly stuck to the roof of his dry mouth; he smelled acid on his own breath, bitter from the necessity of speaking with Travis Peets. Out Ole Summit Highway, the woods showed their beauty where pines mingled with thick-leafed, deep green magnolias and a few massive oaks. By the road, little spruce trees thrived in the afternoon sun.

When they reached Travis Peets' place, they pulled onto the rutted dirt and parked alongside the Sheriff's car. Travis Peets and his wife sat in faded metal chairs that backed against the outside wall of their house. Slim Tate leaned his butt on the grayed porch rail. Brewster and Matthew walked to the cinder-block steps and stood there. They were not invited to come any closer, and to stand on the porch would have been awkward because it was cluttered with an old table, bottles, plants in lard cans, a wringer washing machine, and an old sofa that, even at a distance, gave off an odor of mildew.

Peets wore overalls and the same green jacket he had worn the first time Brewster saw him. The small coat exposed his denim bib and the white of his undershirt. Mrs. Peets wore a red and gray flannel man's shirt over a gray print dress. Her braided hair wrapped around her head, and her hands held each other with the thumb of her left hand rubbing the rounded knuckles of her right hand. She glanced at Brewster, and when she met his eyes, she raised her chin looking into the distance beyond his head. Her lips continued to work out and back.

With everyone settled, Slim Tate spoke. "Miz Peets, Travis, this here is Brewster McAtee and Preacher Matthew James. Brewster here is interested in buying you out. I'm here to see if we can come up with a deal. That is, if you're interested."

Travis Peets looked up at Slim Tate and said nothing. Mrs. Peets stared straight ahead, her only movement being her lower lip that pushed against her upper lip, causing both of them to flair out, and then in again, like a fish out of water, trying desperately to suction something.

"You take your time, Travis. We done talked about this, but you take your time. We not gonna rush you."

Travis Peets sat quiet, his eyes fixed on the distance, and Brewster thought the afternoon's effort would be wasted because the man would not speak, not with two Negroes present. There was something not right about the man, and this thought amused Brewster. *Funny old man, not dangerous.* Brewster looked directly at the little ball of the man's head that rested against the back of the faded metal chair. *Pitiful old man. Something's wrong with his mind. Crazy old man. Generations of soft-minded men—Peets lineage. Won't speak. Won't speak with Negroes present.*

But then, not speaking in the direction of any of the three men present, Peets said, "This whole thang got me stirred up. I been up most two nights thinkin' on it. Been here more than twenty years." Then he stopped. He raised his shoulders several times as if he were checking the weight of his jacket. *Up and back,* Brewster observed, and he noted the peculiarity of the old man's movements.

"That's okay, Travis, maybe you want to think on it some more. A man ought not to think too fast," Slim Tate said and eased his butt off the rail, putting full weight on his feet.

Travis Peets looked away from the Sheriff and raised his stubby chin. The words came flat and hoarse, "Ten thousand," he said. "I take me ten thousand for this place."

"Travis, you willing to sell this place for ten thousand? That's what you telling us? You willing to sell for ten thousand?"

The number lodged in Brewster's head like a cannon ball, dropping, too heavy to explode. *Ten thousand dollars.* He had paid three thousand and six hundred dollars for sixty acres. Why would he pay ten thousand for Peets' pitiful three acres of littered and cracked soil? A thousand dollars would be an outrageous figure, and he had prepared himself for that awful sum, but this was beyond anything he had thought about or could imagine.

"You willing to sell for ten thousand?" Slim Tate asked again.

Travis Peets turned his head toward Slim Tate. "Ten thousand," he said.

"There you go, Brewster. You got yourself an answer. You got something to say?"

Brewster ran his tongue across the roof of his mouth to the edge of his lips to lubricate them. "I paid three thousand and six hundred dollars for the sixty acres I own. I don't see how I could pay that kind of money for three."

"Maybe a little steep, Travis," Slim Tate said, "You fixed on that price?"

Silence again. Travis Peets and his wife stared out past the parked cars to some place beyond clear focus. "Ten thousand," Peets said. "I got a house, a shed in the back, good timber on the north here, and ground broke." He leaned to his side, picked up a coffee can, and spit into it. "Ten thousand," he said.

With this Slim Tate rose. "We got ourselves an answer."

Matthew, who held his hat in his hand, put his free hand on Brewster's back.

"We have to have some time and we get back with you, Travis," Slim Tate said, and he led the way to the cars, but Brewster did not move. *Ten thousand.* He wanted to bolt for the porch, grab the little dark green jacket, lift Travis Peets, throw him in the back of the pickup, and haul him outside the county. Matthew James pressed a solid palm on Brewster's back, pushing him, nudging him gently toward the truck.

"Thank you, Sheriff," Matthew said. He looked at Slim Tate, but did not extend his hand.

"I do whatever I can to keep peace 'round these parts, Reverend. It does seem to me Travis Peets and Brewster McAtee would be best separated, but I guess Travis don't want to sell his land. You let me know if there's another thing I can do." With that, he got in his car, turned around in the yard, and headed back to Low Ridge.

Brewster turned his truck around behind the sheriff's car and followed it.

"You want to come on back to the parsonage? We can discuss this some further. June was baking pies when I left. Come on and we'll have us some hot pie and coffee."

"No," Brewster said. "I'm going to Marlenna's house. There's not much to talk about anyway."

"Maybe we'll think of another way to get the serpent from the garden," Matthew paused, "or at least keep him off the paths."

Brewster didn't want to think about it anymore because he intended to push Travis Peets out of his mind, and he was not going to sit around the table with June and Matthew James discussing some shit-headed honkey. There was no point in discussing things that were done—over with! He reached forward, turned the knob on his radio. Johnny Mathis crooned clear and strong, gliding the truck on a stream of floating velvet—royal blue. *Chances Are. Chances Are. Chances Are.* Brewster accelerated and his truck shot a cloud of thick gray smoke out the rear. He laughed and pumped the accelerator again.

8

On Saturday morning, when Marlenna took several senior girls to visit Stillman College in Tuscaloosa, Matthew drove Brewster to Big Eddie's. Brewster didn't tell Marlenna about the Riviera because he wanted to surprise her by parking in front of her house without her hearing the roar of his truck.

When he and Matthew pulled onto Big Eddie's lot, they spotted the Buick. They saw Ernie Ladd across the lot and headed toward him. "I'm here to get that Buick," Brewster said when they were within easy earshot.

"I remember. The Riviera," Ernie Ladd said. They walked over to the Riviera, and Matthew circled it while Brewster ran his hand over the back fin, feeling the sheen of the blue finish. "We got to take care of the paperwork in the office," Ernie Ladd said. "How you gonna pay for that car?"

"Got a check," Brewster said, and he patted his shirt pocket.

Ernie Ladd tilted his head to the left and eyed Brewster. "That's a big figure."

"Sold timber off my land."

"Come on," Ernie Ladd said and led the way to the showroom. Inside, he knocked on a half-opened door. He walked into it and left Brewster and Matthew standing between a new '58 Edsel and a '57 Bel Air Sport Coupe. Matthew occupied himself inspecting the Edsel, and Brewster sat on the rim of the plate-glass window, waiting.

"I've heard all about these on the radio. This is that new Ford car. I like the blue," Matthew said, "baby blue." He stood back to admire it. "I like those white walls too—extra wide." He put his fingers together, forming a box and brought the square up to his face, looking at the Edsel as if he were looking into the lens of a camera.

A man as tall as Brewster but larger, his belly lapping over his belt, came from the side room with Ernie Ladd. "I'm Big Eddie," he said. "You go ahead and write that check, but we'll have to make a few calls. I'll see if I can catch one of the bank fellas at home." Big Eddie smiled and his face was as broad as a Saint Bernard. "We're proud to have your business, don't get me wrong about that, but we got to know the money's in the bank."

"Fine," Brewster said and wrote his check on the trunk of the Edsel. Big Eddie took it and went into his office. Brewster walked around the showroom looking at the displays, thinking his '56 looked every bit as good as any of these '57s and '58s.

"Can't reach my man at the bank," Big Eddie said when he came out of his room. "Where you work?"

Eddie went back into his office, pushing the door nearly closed. Brewster walked to the sticker on the window of the Edsel and bent to study it when he heard Big Eddie's voice.

"Mr. Armbrecht, this here is Eddie McGhee at Big Eddie's Motors. I got me a colored man done wrote me a check for over eight-hundred dollars. Says he works for you. Says his name is Brewster McAtee."

Big Eddie fell silent. "Yes, sir," he said. "Yes, sir. Well, we'd have to do some investigation on just about anybody write a check this size. Don't many folks got this kind of money," Big Eddie chuckled. "Yes, sir," he said again. Big Eddie got out of the conversation with Deak Armbrecht. He dialed another number.

"Sam, this is Eddie McGhee. Got me a nigger here just gave me a check for over eight-hundred dollars. Works for that crazy Dutchman owns that furniture store. Dutchman says he got plenty of money. What you know about that?"

Brewster felt sweat in the palms of his hands. "Never have seen a nigger come in here and write a check like this," Big Eddie said. "Name's Brewster McAtee."

Eddie fell silent again. "Don't say. Well, never have seen it before, a colored man wheeling around with money like that," Eddie laughed. "Don't make no matter to me. I put the check in the bank come Monday. Don't make no matter to me at all. Just never have seen it before, that's all. Thank you, my man." Big Eddie came out of his office, a grin on his face.

"Check's good." He folded his arms across his chest, picking at the skin on his elbows with the tips of his fingernails. "Finally reached Sam Dann. My man at the bank, knows you. Said to give you his regards." Big Eddie put his hand on the back of Brewster's shoulder, prodding him into the office. Within an hour, the paperwork was completed and Big Eddie shook Brewster's hand, bestowing the keys on him, as a coach would present a trophy. At nearly two o'clock Brewster drove his Buick Riviera off Big Eddie's lot with Matthew James following him to the parsonage.

When Brewster left the James' house, he decided to show his car to Mama Tee because he knew Marlenna would not be back from Tuscaloosa until late afternoon. Mama Tee would want to ride in his new vehicle, but as soon as Tom found out about the car, he would present himself with his hand outstretched, wanting cash, and Brewster planned to avoid showing Tom the car for as long as possible. Tom and Trumpet Eyes rode around in an old DeSoto. If Brewster found it parked in front of the house, he would cruise on and see Mama Tee at church on Sunday.

He eased his new Buick by the house slowly, looking for signs of Tom. The DeSoto was not in the yard. He parked and jumped the ditch. He went inside the house and called for Mama Tee, but when she didn't answer, he walked into the kitchen and saw her through the open window, cutting limbs off of her shrubs, shaping the bushes with a butcher knife. He stepped onto the back porch, shouting at her.

Mama Tee threw her hand over her heart, and the butcher knife hung there. "Lord Jesus! You scared me!"

"Come on. I got something I want you to see."

Mama Tee shifted the knife to her left hand and put her right hand above her eyes, shielding them from the low afternoon sun. "How you doing, baby?"

"Come on. I want you to see something."

She wiped her face with the back of her hand. "I hope this something's not company, because I'm not presentable."

"Come on. You're fine for what I want you to see."

Brewster met her in the yard, and they walked around the side of the house. When she saw the blue Buick parked in front, she stopped.

"That's my new car. How you like it?"

"S-w-e-e-t Jesus! It makes this whole street look rich."

"Come on. I'm going to take you for a ride."

"I been working in the yard all afternoon. I need to clean myself up before I get into a fine car like this."

"That car doesn't know whether you're clean or dirty, and I want you to be my first passenger."

They cruised past County Training School and out on the highway where Brewster took the engine up to 60. The motor purred. He knew this car would assure Mama Tee he was doing well, because the Buick elevated him to distinction and announced that Brewster McAtee was a man to be regarded.

"You slow this thing down." Mama Tee put her hand above her rounded belly, but she laughed and her hair flew loose from the knot at the back of her neck, whipping freely in the wind blasting through the window. They glided on the highway with feed corn drying on stalks on one side and the spotty-white of harvested cotton fields on the other. On the way back into town, Brewster stopped and bought them cones of vanilla from the colored window at the Country Churn Ice Cream Shack.

"I want to bring somebody for Sunday dinner, Mama Tee, and this is somebody special," he told her when he pulled the Buick into the yard at 20 Perry Street.

"Special as in f-e-m-a-l-e special?"

"Special as in female special," he answered.

Mama Tee rolled her eyes and tilted her head, "Who is this Miss Special?"

"You'll find out tomorrow." He had not asked Marlenna about Sunday dinner, and if Mama Tee knew this, she would accuse him of counting chickens still in their shells.

"I'm going to have me a guest at my table and you not going to tell me who?"

"A special guest and you'll know WHO tomorrow."

"It's time you find yourself Miss Special," she said when she got out of the car and claimed her butcher knife, which she had placed on the back floorboard.

It was nearly dark when Brewster drove past the Mixon house. He saw no sign of Marlenna, and he headed toward the Three Brothers shed to work a little and wait. But before he turned the corner at the light, he saw the Chevrolet in his rearview mirror. He made a u-turn, went back to the Mixon house, and parked at the curb. Marlenna got out of her car carrying an armload of papers.

"Well, look at that! Does that belong to you?" she shouted at Brewster.

"Bought it today."

He met her in the yard and they walked to the curb. "Oh my, this is beautiful," she said and paced around the car, rubbing her hand across the wide fin, then she stepped back for a long view.

Albert Mixon came out on the porch and shouted, "Whose car you got there, Brewster?"

"Mine. Got it this afternoon."

Albert Mixon headed for the curb to inspect the car. "This is fine," he said. "I thought about getting one like this when I bought that Chevrolet. I like it," he said. "But it's low to the ground and I didn't know if I could get used to that."

Brewster walked Marlenna to the porch, while her father continued to admire the Buick. When they were inside, and Marlenna had placed her papers on the dining room table, she went into the kitchen and shook two aspirin into her hand. "I have a splitting headache," she said. "I was with four senior girls all day. Every one of those girls was so excited. About to pop, just thinking about going to Stillman."

Albert Mixon came into the kitchen. "That's a fine car," he said and leaned his back against the cabinet. "You did well for yourself."

Despite his resolve not to woo Albert Mixon's favor, Brewster felt the flush of pride rise in him.

Marlenna rubbed the pads of her fingers in a circular pattern against her temples. "I had a long day," she said. "I now have four senior girls who want to go to college. I hope the girls have had an education sufficient for college. It would be a shame to create a desire that can't be fulfilled."

"Herman Thomas provides good education at County Training School," Albert Mixon said.

"You felt I needed to go away for education."

"Low Ridge didn't have the opportunities Raleigh had," Albert Mixon said.

"I shouldn't have had to go off to Raleigh. That's why the struggle for education over in Arkansas stirs my heart."

"Heart?" Albert Mixon let loose. "We need to use our heads, not our hearts. There never was a man, or woman either, who got ahead using a heart. That's what heads are for. My head tells me there's no cause for stirring up trouble."

"There's every cause," Marlenna said with an edge in her voice.

Albert Mixon spoke calmly, "I count many white friends in this town. They come in my office and visit, same as they would if I was a white man."

"Personal friends?" Marlenna countered. "Father, when have you ever been invited to any white person's house? When has a white person ever come through these doors?" Marlenna's arm extended toward the front door. "And when have you ever sat at the table and had a meal with one of your white friends?"

"That will be enough!" Albert Mixon said, his voice raised and his words deliberate.

"It's true that white people come to your office because they don't want to go down Limrick Road knocking on pitiful doors looking for somebody to clean their house or haul their trash."

"Marlenna!" Albert Mixon said, anger in his voice. "I've gotten along fine." He took a breath as if he would add another thought, but let the air go without spending it. "I'm going up to my room." He left with a paper napkin in his hand, wiping his forehead.

Marlenna pulled a chair out from the table and sat down. She formed an arch with her elbows on the wood and her hands locked together and she rested her chin on her interlocked fingers. "I apologize. I shouldn't have taken my father on like that. This headache has set my nerves on edge." She rubbed her forehead again with the tips of her fingers.

Brewster had not involved himself in the conversation because he had distanced himself from the integration stuff going on over in Little Rock. He had no intention of working in Matthew's organization. He had explained this to Matthew by telling him that he arrived at the shed before eight in the morning and didn't leave until nearly dark. On weekends there was plenty of work at Ole Summit, and sometimes on Saturdays he went back to the shed to work. He was not going to attend any meetings because he could not occupy himself by sitting. What he didn't tell Matthew was that he was not going to be drawn into arguments about integration. He was fortunate to have a good job and to be driving his new car, and he would keep his own counsel.

"My head feels like it's splitting. I was up before six this morning. I'm going on to bed early," Marlenna said, rising from the table. Brewster felt disappointment descend on him; the evening was closing before it had gotten a good start.

"Get some rest," Brewster said and rubbed the back of her neck. "I want you to go to Limrick Baptist tomorrow. Then we'll have lunch at Mama Tee's and go out to Ole Summit because I want you to see my land."

Marlenna put her arm around his waist and held it there as they walked through the passage to the front door.

"I want to do all of that."

"I'll be here at ten-thirty," he said when she opened the door at the porch.

"I'll be ready."

He wanted to take Marlenna for a ride in his Buick and show her how smoothly the gears shifted, how quiet the car ran, how luxurious the velvet on the seats felt to an open hand. But he was leaving early without Marlenna even sitting in his car. The moon had come out and it was big and fire-orange, an autumn moon. This would make a fine evening for a drive, but the screened door closed behind him.

The door opened again. "Brewster, you don't mind if I ask Father to join us, do you?"

"Of course not." At the very moment he uttered the words, he hoped that old Albert Mixon would have no interest in Limrick Road Baptist Church or in Ole Summit because his presence would spoil the picture Brewster had created in his head of squiring Marlenna Mixon through Sunday.

Driving to Ole Summit by himself in his new Buick was not right. He would go to Hurley, find the room behind the little store, drink a whiskey or two, and play a few hands of cards. A new car needed to be driven, especially on a night like this when the moon hung rose-orange, favoring Low Ridge like it was a town as big as Montgomery or Birmingham.

On Sunday morning, Albert Mixon decided to drive himself to Hurley to visit his sisters, promising Marlenna he would be home before dark, and Brewster was relieved. When Marlenna got in the Buick, she admired the velvet on the seats and ran her hand over the dashboard. Her appreciation of its easy ride and rich interior soothed Brewster from his disappointment of the night before.

"This is luxury. I wanted a Buick, but father decided on that Chevrolet. At least I get to ride in this grand car." Her voice had the impact of a warm iron smoothing wrinkles from his brain, still creased from last night's whisky.

They pulled up in front of Limrick Road Baptist while the Sunday school crowd milled around the front steps, using the minutes before the service for socializing. All eyes turned to see the blue Riviera. Mama Tee talked with two of the ladies from her Sunday school class when she spotted Brewster's car. When Brewster parked and walked around to the passenger side, opening the door for Marlenna Mixon, Mama Tee's mouth came open a full inch.

"Ladies," Brewster said, "Marlenna Mixon."

Six eyes circled Brewster and Marlenna. The ladies juggled Bibles, gloves, and Sunday school papers, freeing hands to extend toward Marlenna. A heavy-set woman in a purple dress spoke first. "It's a pleasure to meet you," she said awkwardly and looked at Mama Tee.

"Certainly is. Certainly is," Mama Tee said.

A deacon put his head out the door. "Ladies, Brother James is about ready to begin."

Mama Tee locked her elbow inside Marlenna's. "Come on, honey, let's get down to my pew."

Several times during the service Brewster caught Mama Tee studying Marlenna, and she looked directly into Brewster's eyes, asking in words unspoken, *When did this happen?*

After church, in Mama Tee's kitchen, the two women conversed politely about the death of Marlenna's mother and about Marlenna's return to Low Ridge to care for her father. They talked about Marlenna's teaching at County Training School, but the conversation became animated when they spoke about Matthew's new organization.

"I asked the preacher what I could do to help," Mama Tee said, "and he gave me this great big stack of papers to file. I got letters from people all over the place. There's one from Dr. King there. They done banned the NAACP here in Alabama, and Dr. King was writing a letter about some new group they formed in Montgomery. I got letters from everybody, but I don't know what to do with all that stuff."

"I want to do something," Marlenna said. "Maybe I can help you organize and file the correspondence."

"Sure would be nice," Mama Tee said. "I even got letters about what's happening over there in Arkansas. Some woman named Daisy Bates sent Reverend James her newspaper where she wrote down all about what's going on." Mama Tee poured the gravy into a bowl. "We keep the prayers going at church. We got us prayer teams that meet every day at five o'clock. Honey, we get down on our knees and we pray," Mama Tee said. "I'm glad we got ourselves a speaker coming. It's Brewster's friend, Anvil Thomas. He's a lawyer now, you know."

"Anvil's coming?" Marlenna asked.

"He's been asked to come," Mama Tee said. "That's why Reverend James didn't mention it this morning. We don't have a definite yes. But he's been asked."

"Anvil's one of my best friends," Marlenna said.

"That boy knows this house too," Mama Tee said. "I can't tell you the number of times he sat with Brewster at this table for supper or ate himself a hot biscuit with my blackberry jelly."

After lunch, Mama Tee got her papers, sat on the couch, and spread them in front of her on the living room floor. "I guess I don't know how to go about putting these papers in some kind of order. I keep on stacking them up."

Mama Tee and Marlenna examined one paper and then another, turning each sheet over and placing it face down on the floor.

"I can help you," Marlenna said. "I want to go to the meetings with you too, if you don't mind."

"Yes and yes," Mama Tee said. "Yes, I would be very happy for you to help me get this stuff in some kind of order. I got about three times more papers in my bedroom. How about coming over tomorrow?" Mama Tee was still rifling through the papers while Marlenna read the page she held in her hand.

Brewster hurried the women, encouraging them to leave the paperwork. This day he desired Marlenna to see his land.

Mama Tee wrapped three china cups in one towel and china plates in another. She put the towel-covered china in a cardboard box, placing the box beside her on the back seat of Brewster's car. Marlenna held a coconut cake covered by a glass-domed top; Mama Tee had baked the cake on Saturday, especially for her Sunday company.

When they passed Travis Peet's place, Brewster wanted to say to Marlenna, *Don't look over there. That place will ruin your eyes for what I've got to show you.* But he kept quiet and he slowed near his lane at the sign that read IMPEACH EARL WARREN. This was an embarrassment to him, taking Marlenna past a shoddy place like Travis Peets' and then her seeing the sign posted at the very edge of his property. One way or another he had to get Travis Peets off of Ole Summit. Marlenna remained quiet about the sign, but she studied it.

He pulled onto the curving lane, and he began to watch Marlenna. The late afternoon sun glazed the land, bringing forth the richness of October colors. He was glad the path came to his house at an angle, making his house look wider and better balancing the porches. He drove slowly, stopping when the grounds were in full view revealing a panorama of woods, house, porches, his white swings, and his deep green joiner's chairs on the front porch.

"This is yours, Brewster?"

"Sixty acres. I want to own all the land on this side of the road from Low Ridge to beyond my house."

"Built this whole place with his two hands," Mama Tee patted Brewster's back as they got out of the car and walked up to the porch.

"I haven't finished my furniture yet. I make a piece when I know what I want and when I have time."

Marlenna examined one of the swings and the deep green chairs in which Brewster had placed cushions Mama Tee made from a piece of brown plaid fabric. The swing and the chairs looked elegant on the porch in the late afternoon sun.

Inside, the big room was nearly bare, but the floors glistened, the pine reflecting like jewels. He had gotten on his hands and knees, wiping the floorboards before he left for church, even though a pain shot between his eyes when he bent down—last night's whisky striking a bull's-eye above his nose. He had wiped in every corner and across the counters, and when Marlenna stood in the center of the big room absorbing the beauty, he felt proud. He decided it was better that he didn't have too much furniture because Marlenna could envision placing things in the house her own way.

Mama Tee sliced the cake and poured coffee in the three china cups. They made two trips to the porch, carrying plates, cups, cream, sugar, and Brewster's sketches. Marlenna and Mama Tee sat in the swing, and when they were settled, Brewster showed Marlenna a drawing of the table and chairs he planned to build for dining in the big room and a draft of his plans for bedroom furniture. They sat on the front porch talking and blending into the stillness that was Sunday afternoon. Darkness overtook the day and night birds sounded in the woods.

"I done missed Sunday night service," Mama Tee said. "I don't do that very often." She breathed in and blew air out between her parted lips, causing her upper lip to flutter. "But this is a special day and the Lord makes allowances for special days."

Even old Albert Mixon seemed to accept Brewster's comings at 32 State Street as the ritual of afternoons. "I hear Anvil's coming to Low Ridge to give a talk," he said when they sat on the screened back porch.

"That's right," Marlenna said. "I went to the meeting with Mama Tee, and Anvil has confirmed he will come. I wrote him a letter and mailed it today. I told him he would have to have supper with us when he's here."

"That boy used to spend as much time at this house as he did at his own house. Now that's a man making something important of himself," Albert Mixon said, and Brewster thought he had made a point of saying this to demonstrate that Anvil Thomas left Low Ridge and had transformed himself into someone important, while he, on the other hand, had settled his sights on woodworking in the shed of an old white man, a foreigner at that.

"Brewster and Anvil had a nice visit the last time he was in town," Marlenna said.

"Is that right, Brewster?"

"Yes sir. He came out to my place."

Brewster wanted to say, sure, he came out to Ole Summit, looked around and decided the place wasn't fine enough for him. Brewster remembered Anvil's talk the afternoon he had come to Ole Summit. It was talk about how sorry he was that his family hadn't qualified for the Jack and Jill Club, but then there wasn't one in Low Ridge anyway. Membership in Jack and Jill would have assured him an undisputed place in the Alphas at Fisk.

"I had to sweat that one," Anvil had said. He spoke openly about his desire to get into the Boulé or the Guardsmen after he graduated and joined himself with a first-rate law firm. Brewster knew nothing of these organizations except what he saw in an occasional *Jet* or *Ebony* he thumbed through at the barber shop or glanced at when he saw one of these magazines on Mama Tee's dinette. There wasn't anyone in Low Ridge who could even make good conversation about any club outside of the Elks, in which he was sure Albert Mixon and Herman Thomas both maintained memberships.

"It's not too late for you," Anvil had said to Brewster. "You could still go on. Get out of here and go off to a college. You got the money now. You're older than most freshmen, but it doesn't matter. You have time to get your education. You're too bright to stay here."

"What's Anvil going to talk about, Daughter?" Albert Mixon asked, not letting go of conversation about Anvil.

"Segregation and legal challenges," Marlenna said, "and he's just the one to speak on those issues."

"That boy is something," Albert Mixon said. "Daughter, do you remember when you and Anvil found that dog? Herman wouldn't let Anvil keep it, but Helen let you girls keep that puppy in your bedroom."

"Skipper," Marlenna said.

"That's it," Albert Mixon said. "That's what you named it. Anvil taught that little dog all kinds of tricks. You and Anvil took Skipper to County Training School and did a talent show. You remember that?"

"I do," Marlenna said.

"That boy could do anything," Albert Mixon said. "I guess he's still showing us that."

The point has been made, Brewster thought. He rocked in his chair and sipped the sweet tea Marlenna had given him until she announced, "Father, we're going inside. Will you join us?"

"No, I'm going on up to my room. I want to read the paper."

They were about halfway through *Invisible Man*, and the book had gone down paths Brewster had never considered. Dr. Bledsoe, who Brewster envisioned as Albert Mixon—short, rounded belly, balding head, speaking with white folks like he had some real power, but bowing and scraping all the while—had maliciously deceived the college boy in the book. The young man made Brewster think of Anvil, but the young man in the book who was searching for himself was more humble than Anvil had ever been. Why should Anvil be humble? He walked through magnificent corridors, speaking with powerful men, and Brewster could not even imagine the grandeur of that. He laid awake in the darkness at Ole Summit trying to see and feel what Anvil must know, but he could not. Anvil's life was too grand even for Brewster to imagine.

While Marlenna read *Invisible Man* out loud, Brewster ran his tongue on the line that formed the inside of her ear, putting his nose there. Then he kissed the bone of her chin, but she continued to read about the young man exiled from college and sent to New York in search of work. The young man wanted everyone to see him better than he was, not southern, not northern, a man above classification.

> *The counter man came over.*
>
> *"I've got something good for you," he said, placing a glass of water before me. "How about the special?"*
>
> *"What's the special?"*
>
> *"Pork chops, grits, one egg, hot biscuits and coffee!"*
>
> *He leaned over the counter with a look that seemed to say,* There, that ought to excite you, boy. *Could everyone see that I was southern?*
>
> *"I'll have orange juice, toast and coffee," I said coldly.*
>
> *He shook his head. "You fooled me," he said, slamming two pieces of bread into the toaster. "I would have sworn you were a pork chop man. Is that juice a large or small?"*
>
> *"Make it large," I said.*
>
> *I looked silently at the back of his head as he sliced an orange, thinking,* I should order the special and get up and walk out. Who does he think he is?
>
> *A seed floated in the thick layer of pulp that formed at*

*the top of the glass. I fished it out with a spoon and then
downed the acid drink, proud to have resisted the pork chop
and grits. It was an act of discipline, a sign of the change
that was coming over me and which would return me to
college, yet so subtly changed as to intrigue those who had
never been North. It always helped at the college to be a
little different, especially if you wished to play a leading
role.*

"We'll stop here," Marlenna said. "Besides, I can't read with a
nose in my ear."

He kissed her and spoke with his lips brushing hers. "I want to
settle it," he said. "Seal it," he whispered. "We need to do that. This
has been going on too long."

"Not yet a month, Brewster. Not to mention that my father's
upstairs reading the newspaper or listening to the radio and could
come down any time. And we both got work tomorrow." She put her
arm around him and pulled. "All good things in due time," she said.

He stumbled awkwardly to his feet, and she guided him to the door.

Anvil was scheduled to arrive on Friday morning and conduct a
workshop at Limrick Road Baptist the same day. On Friday,
Brewster went to 32 State Street when he left the Three Brothers
shed, thinking he would go with Marlenna to the church. Albert
Mixon met him at the door. "Marlenna's helping your grandmother.
They're cooking supper for Anvil up at the church. He came by here
this afternoon. If you haven't seen him yet, go on to the church."

At Limrick Road Baptist, Anvil stood in the center of the room
beside Matthew, speaking with a group of ladies who had gathered
around him. Mama Tee brought a covered dish from the kitchen and
placed it on the serving table. She spotted Brewster by the door. "I'm
glad you came on. Doesn't he look like something!" Mama Tee tilted
her head in her dainty way and smiled toward Anvil. "Go on over
and talk to him." Brewster did not move toward Anvil but he observed him.

Anvil stood tall and thin. He wore a crisp shirt with maroon
stripes and navy-blue slacks with sharp creases. His tan leather
loafers looked soft as baby skin. Standing in the church annex in the
middle of the heavy-set women in cotton print dresses and flat-soled
shoes, he looked like what he was—an outsider.

"Where's Marlenna?" Brewster asked Mama Tee.

"In the kitchen there. That girl's been working on one thing or another all day."

Marlenna stood at the sink washing dishes when Brewster came into the kitchen. She looked at him over her shoulder. "I'm glad you came, Brewster. You can help me in the kitchen or you can talk to Anvil. You choose." She didn't abandon her job at the sink nor did she dole any work to him. He stood awkwardly while women came and went from the kitchen carrying food.

"You got a couple of butter dishes clean?" Pinky Lancaster asked when she came into the kitchen.

"Here," Marlenna said, "in the rack."

"Let me pour this sugar up, honey, and then I'll get those butter dishes," Pinky said.

"I'll dry them."

"Sweet Johnny!" Pinky Lancaster said. "This is the end of the sugar. We better send somebody up to the Piggly Wiggly."

"Send somebody over to the parsonage. June's probably got some," Mama Tee said.

Marlenna turned to Brewster. "Go on over to the parsonage and see if June has a cup or two of sugar. That would save us a trip to the store."

He went to the parsonage where June James gave him the remainder of a bag of sugar, and when he brought it back into the annex, Anvil saw him and waved. Brewster carried the sugar into the kitchen, gave it to Mrs. Lancaster, and stood again in the doorway.

"Excuse me, honey. You better move on in or out because you're in the line of delivery," Mrs. Lancaster said and patted him on the shoulder when she passed through with the sugar bowl.

He stepped fully into the kitchen and leaned against the counter. Marlenna finished the dishes and untied her apron. "Come on, Brewster. Let's go talk with Anvil."

"Brewster," Anvil extended his right hand and caught Brewster's elbow with his left hand. Anvil smelled of aftershave and looked as if he advertised toothpaste or hair cream in *Jet*. His hair was trimmed close to his head, his face clean shaved, but even more outstanding, he was in command, and this showed in his appearance. "Sit at my table. That'll give us time to catch up on things," Anvil said.

But when they sat to eat, Matthew and Anvil were in conversation about organizing teams to go door to door down Limrick Road on Saturday morning, distributing information about Matthew's Low Ridge Association.

"We've got to identify leaders," Anvil said. "And leaders come from unexpected places, maybe a woman who has raised kids all her life, cooked a thousand meals, taught Sunday school, worked in ten white houses cleaning floors and bathrooms. You'd be surprised that sometimes these kind of people make fantastic leaders. You find skill where you least expect it," Anvil said.

"I've got a few people picked out, folks I think can carry the load," Matthew said.

"Brewster can be one of the team leaders," Anvil said. Marlenna patted Brewster's arm, proud he had been acknowledged, but Brewster saw himself as the outsider, watching the Low Ridge Association develop. There was no reason for his coming to see Marlenna, because she was the designated secretary for Anvil, taking notes for him and writing down ideas offered up by his admirers. Brewster knew he would decline being a team leader because his workload was too heavy at Three Brothers. He had one of the best jobs of any colored man in Low Ridge. He was lifting the black man by the work of his own hands. What more could anyone ask of him?

While Marlenna, Matthew, Anvil, and the canvassing teams went door to door on Saturday morning, Brewster went to the Three Brothers shed. He worked on mahogany chairs for an order in Birmingham. He didn't have to be in the shed this day, but he didn't want to be working with Anvil, running errands for him, taking orders from him, standing and waiting while Anvil visited with this one and that one. He would rather be in the shed where he knew his way around and where he was in control.

In the afternoon, he decided to clean the shed, which he had intended to do for some time, but had not found the opportunity. He restacked lumber and put tools back into their proper locations and swept wood curls from under workbenches and out of forgotten corners. Deak came into the shed, excited to see this activity. Deak got a push broom and the two of them worked themselves into sweat. By late afternoon, the shed took on a clean and organized appearance.

"T'is place look like new shop," Deak said when they swept the last of the wood shavings onto the lip of the dustpan and emptied it into the trash bin. "T'is place even smell good now. We work like termites in ta woodpile on Monday what with t'is shop clean," Deak said. When Brewster left, Deak had a can of 3-In-One, oiling gears on the lathe.

At the Mixon house, Anvil stood in the front parlor, holding a wine glass in his hand—there was no question he felt comfortable.

"Brewster, would you like something to drink?" Anvil asked. "We're just warming up a bit by the fire before we go to the church." Brewster declined the offer because what he wanted was a double shot of whiskey, no ice.

"After Anvil's talk we're going to have supper at the church again tonight," Marlenna said. "You come on back to the kitchen after the talk."

He wanted to speak with Marlenna, but with Anvil present, this was impossible. He wore work brogans, and Anvil stood before the fire in his socks, which were as slick as onionskins. He wore a flannel shirt, and Anvil wore a starched, white shirt with a monogram on the cuff. Anvil stood tall and sleek, with thin shoulders and narrow hips, while Brewster towered with broad shoulders and a thick chest that made him feel like a squared-off block of wood.

"I just stopped by to check on the time for that talk," he said, seeing himself as an oaf in work pants, brogans, and red-plaid flannel. "I'm going out to Ole Summit to change."

"You're fine, Brewster," Anvil said. "Folks will be dressed all kinds of ways. Work clothes are completely acceptable." And when Anvil said this, Brewster would have crawled out to Ole Summit, crawled on all fours if he had to do it in order to change his clothes. Anvil Thomas was not going to place Brewster McAtee at Limrick Road Baptist in a red-flannel shirt while he wore a tailored suit bought in Washington or New York.

Brewster arrived at Limrick Road Baptist before the talk started, but the pews were filled. He squeezed in beside Mama Tee and one of the heavy-set women gave him a look that thrashed him for crowding the pew. Because Marlenna was going to introduce Anvil, she sat up front in one of the chairs generally reserved for ministers. When she saw Brewster, she left the rostrum and came to him.

"I'm glad to see you."

She leaned into the pew, getting her face close to Mama Tee's. "Maybe he's decided to become a member of the Low Ridge Association after all," she cooed.

"We'll put him to the test. Maybe we'll let him in and maybe we won't," Mama Tee teased. The women laughed. Marlenna patted Brewster on his knee and returned to the podium.

Brewster was in no mood to take any pleasure in the meeting, and he was already sizing up the presence of Anvil on the stage. His law degree gave him a stature over and above any Negro in Low Ridge.

Matthew spoke first. He rose and raised his hands, palms open to the crowd, and when the congregation hushed, he began.

"We are here tonight because we want a little taste of the American pie," he said. "We want to be paid a fair and decent wage for our labor, and when we spend our hard-earned dollars, we want the same respect a white man or a white woman or a white child gets. We could be home resting, getting ready to start another week of work, because we all labor to put food on our tables and shoes on our children's feet. But we are here because our hands are ready to do the labor that will bring justice." The audience interrupted him with a chorus of affirmation.

"It is one of our own that has come tonight to tell us about how the sea has parted and we have a path to walk on. It's not the Red Sea; no, it is the law that is opening up, the law that is parting and making a way for us to follow. And follow we will." The crowd rocked and swayed and answered, "Yes," "yes!" Anvil sat on the stage, a smile on his face, looking like a sphinx—wise, young, and satisfied. The congregation sang.

When Israel was in Egypt's land. Let my people go!
Oppressed so hard they could not stand. Let my people go!
Go down, Moses. Way down, Moses. Way down in Egypt's land.
Tell old Pharaoh, Let my people go!

Marlenna rose and the crowd settled. Marlenna said all of the things that made Anvil important—his degrees from the best universities, his honors, his awards, his working in the federal courts, and his loyalty to his family and friends in Low Ridge. Then Anvil rose to thunderous applause.

He spoke about Brown vs. the Board of Education and how separate but equal was no longer acceptable. "The very laws of this land kept us segregated and maintained Jim Crow. Now, separate but equal has been overturned, but the struggle isn't over. Look at what's happening in Little Rock. Governor Orval Faubus has maneuvered in every way known to man, blocking those nine students from attending classes at Central High School, but Thurgood Marshall himself went for a visit in Little Rock and met with Daisy Bates and the students. And this is why we've got to have the Low Ridge Association, because we've got to support each other."

"It's time!" someone shouted.

Anvil continued, "In a recent Gallup Poll, Orval Faubus was voted one of the ten most admired men in the world, along with President Eisenhower, Sir Winston Churchill, Dr. Albert Schweitzer, General Douglas McArthur, and Dr. Jonas Salk."

"No, no, no," voices rose like a chorus, different tones echoing and blending and fading. The audience talked to him, agreeing with him, wailing when he enumerated the injustices with which everyone had ample experience. Marlenna watched and listened.

Brewster thought of Tod Clifton in *Invisible Man,* the king of a man who rallied the crowd, the man who could sell Negro pride like a precious commodity, but he was ultimately reduced to selling red-lipped Sambo dolls on the streets of Harlem.

> *What makes him happy, what makes him dance,*
> *this Sambo, this jambo, this high-stepping joy boy?*
> *He's more than a toy, ladies and gentlemen, he's Sambo,*
> *the dancing doll, the twentieth-century miracle,*
> *look at that rumba, that suzy-q, he's Sambo-Boogie,*
> *Sambo-Woogie.*

Brewster listened to Anvil's words and felt the pain of knowing Anvil spoke the truth, accurately, eloquently, and the people were hungry for his words. But at the same time he wanted to see Anvil Thomas reduced to Tod Clifton selling Sambo dolls, and that thought made Brewster despise himself. People had crowded in the church with the back doors held open by bodies eager to hear even a few words. But Brewster felt the pain of disliking Anvil, disliking him because he spoke the truth, disliking him because he stood tall, commanded attention, and held Marlenna's eyes while he addressed the crowd that wept for love of him.

After the talk there was food, a feast laid on the tables. Brewster watched as Anvil put his arm around Marlenna, keeping her close to him. He watched from the edge of the crowd, eating not one morsel. About ten o'clock, when the first of the crowd began to disperse, he left without speaking a word of farewell to Marlenna or to Mama Tee.

At Ole Summit, he sat on the porch and petted Valiant, who rested with his head on Brewster's knee. About midnight, he went to bed, but woke a little after three and took a blanket to his joiner's chair on the porch. He couldn't get the chill off himself. Valiant whined to go back inside the house, but Brewster endured the cold. He was miserable and he welcomed the cold as punishment for being the thickheaded outsider that he was.

9

Rain came on Sunday, low and heavy clouds bringing sheets of water across Ole Summit. Brewster stayed away from church because Anvil was to deliver the message, and he had enough of watching Anvil stand in the light. He felt dull and ox-like and sat on the porch watching the rain until it soaked him. Valiant whined and paced by the door wanting to go inside, but Brewster sat in his deep green chair, enduring the storm until he was wet and chilled to the bone.

There was lunch for Anvil at Herman Thomas's, and Brewster had been invited in a roundabout way. Marlenna said to Anvil, "Does Brewster know about dinner on Sunday?"

"I'm sorry, Brewster, I forgot to tell you. Come on to the house after church. Mother and Grandmother are making a big dinner and they would like for you to be there."

But he didn't go. At noon he ate tuna fish out of the can, and in the late afternoon, he opened the ironing board in the big room and ironed his shirts. He also finished reading *Invisible Man* and spent some time considering it. The young man in the book had been deceived—lost his dreams, but had not lost his ability to chart some courses for himself. The book was good to ponder on a Sunday afternoon when his mind continued to see Anvil with his arm around Marlenna and her moving with him, sharing the illumination Anvil walked in. Marlenna spoke Anvil's language. She graduated from Shaw. She knew the best and the finest. He envisioned her picture in *Ebony* at high social events—Marlenna and Anvil Thomas, the beautiful and the powerful. He wanted to smash Anvil, to cut him down, but he knew there would be nothing gained; the score would not be even. Anvil Thomas was the man who had it all. *Them that's got shall get. Them that's not shall lose. So the Bible says and it still is news,* he could hear Billie Holiday's saxophone voice, mellow and true.

He wrapped himself in his misery until early evening when he drove to Hurley and played cards in the windowless room behind the grocery store. Jackson Summerall was there. He had been in the same class with Brewster and Anvil, but he left County Training after tenth grade and had never finished school. He had a bullet-shaped head with sweat on his forehead, and his eyes were red because clouds of smoke drifted up from the cigarette he held between his teeth.

Some crazy man was there too, wearing a blue satin suit, a traveling man with a thick scar down his neck. Brewster lost twenty dollars early, and the game got loud and hostile. The blue-suited traveler had a temper honed sharp as a cutting-edge, and he spoke in a high-pitched voice, unsettling Brewster's stomach. A little after nine, Brewster folded and eased out, not making a show of his departure.

When he drove past Marlenna's house, he turned onto Limrick Road, shone his lights into her backyard and looked for her Chevrolet, but it wasn't parked at 32 State Street, and this made him feel more wasted and angry. He thought about driving to the Thomas house to see if Marlenna was there with Anvil, but he decided against it. He maintained his own command, and for this he was proud of himself. He drove out to Ole Summit, but he didn't sleep well because he kept seeing Marlenna looking up at Anvil, his arm around her, their sides joined.

Monday morning brought clear skies because the wind and rain blew every cloud away and ushered in cold, bright air with it. Deak Armbrecht greeted Brewster with more animation than Brewster had seen in the old man since Gretta had taken sick. Evangeline came every day to clean and cook for Gretta Armbrecht, who had not been out of the house in at least a month. The cool air put Deak in a spry mood, and he moved around the shed in quick, small steps, looking like an oversized elf, but Brewster felt dull. He threw the apron string over his neck and hoped his headache would lessen with the steadfast certainty of his work. He gathered several boards that had been cut for chair legs and took these to the short lathe. Deak went to his workbench where he used a spindle gouge to finish chair-rung tenons, and he whistled while he checked the least diameter of each rung with a pair of calipers.

By mid-afternoon Deak had worn himself out. He quit work early and went to his house to sit with Gretta. Brewster worked alone in the shed, finishing his job at the lathe and moving to the drill bench where he screwed the bit into place and clamped a chair arm onto the shelf, making it ready for drilling.

"Seems you left early Saturday night and you decided not to show up at all on Sunday." Marlenna's voice echoed in the shed and rang through his head, startling him. He turned and saw her in the doorway, a cranberry-colored sweater around her shoulders, her arms folded across her chest, not a trace of a smile on her face. He wanted to walk to her, lift her from the ground and pull her to him, but he held back.

"I did," he said, feeling awkward and oaf-like, standing ankle deep in a pile of wood shavings.

"I suppose something was bothering you," Marlenna said.

"Something WAS bothering me." Perspiration popped out on his forehead and spread to his chest. His own image flashed in his head, standing in his canvas apron, his hands on a wood clamp, shavings over his feet, and he knew with certainty that a small-town wood-worker could not compare to an educated, big-city lawyer. The scale would not balance the two, no matter how much hope was added to his side of the dish.

Marlenna caught him off guard when she smiled. "Well, if something is bothering you, why don't you come over to the house when you leave here. Let's see if it can be worked out." She turned and went out the double doors.

Albert Mixon sat at the head of the table, his belly pushing against the edge. "These are some of the leftovers from Saturday night," Marlenna said. "We fed Anvil and the organization committee and we divided what was left."

"This is fine eating," Albert Mixon said, "and Anvil can't eat another bite of it because he's back in Washington." He speared a slice of ham with his fork.

The food looked better to Brewster before he knew it had been prepared for Anvil. He ate sparingly because his heart was not in eating. The conversation was about Marlenna's students, and then it shifted to Albert Mixon and his business.

"I placed three housekeepers this very day," he said proudly and put ham and potato salad in his mouth at the same time. "Henrietta Pugh went with the young Nelson family. Bobby Nelson took his daddy's job running that lumber mill and his wife had a baby. I expect Henrietta's gon' be there a long time." Albert Mixon shoveled in another bite, and Brewster was content to remain out of the conversation unless addressed directly. He was saving his words for when he spoke with Marlenna alone.

When they finished eating and the dishes were cleared, the three of them went into the parlor where Marlenna played the piano for her father. The music soothed Albert Mixon, who rested his feet on the coffee table, and in a short while, a small gravelly snore came with every breath he inhaled. With his eyes closed, his head rested against the back of the chair cushion.

"It's too cold to go outside," Marlenna whispered. "I don't want to wake him. We could go into his office and talk there." Before Brewster could pass judgment on this idea, Marlenna took him by the arm. They went through the kitchen, opened a side door, and stepped down into the office of Mixon Domestics and Laborers. The room was long and narrow, and at the back, close to the door that opened from the kitchen, was a desk with an American flag to the right of it. On the floor was a burgundy and green rug with designs that looked like branches of a tree spreading through it. On one side of the rug was a deep green leather couch and on the other side were two upholstered chairs. Brewster stood behind the sofa, taking the room in, while Marlenna lit the gas heater, which was close to the door that opened to State Street. Then she sat on the couch and motioned for Brewster to sit beside her.

He nearly tripped on the edge of the rug because he was studying the room that was reserved for white folks in Low Ridge. The room was spare and elegant with the leather sofa and two chairs upholstered in flame-stitch. He sat on the couch and heard the leather exhale.

"You have a problem with Anvil, don't you?" Marlenna asked.

"I'm surprised you didn't go back to Washington with Anvil. He kept you tucked under his arm." When he said this, rows furrowed above his brow. "To be friendly with a man is one thing, but Anvil touches and holds you like he's afraid you'll get away."

"He's that way. He draws all the women to him, and with Anvil it doesn't mean a thing."

"It's a wonder some man hasn't cut his hands off by now."

Marlenna opened her own hands and placed them on top of Brewster's. "Anvil is not the man I want. I don't want that kind of life. I would wilt like something out of water, going from city to city, from one meeting to the next, always standing in front of a crowd. I can do it for a while, but I pay a price. I told you I was raised on a good dose of solitude. I don't get it and I'm thrown off center. I didn't sleep last night because I had to figure out who I was all over again."

"He's a lawyer," Brewster said, "a N-e-g-r-o lawyer. Your daddy's right, we're going to be reading about him in the newspaper and everywhere else." Brewster twisted his mouth when images of Anvil in *Jet* or *Ebony* shot through his mind. He could see Anvil in

the society shots, drinking and dining with the powerful. Anvil
would have a smile on his face that said *I'm enjoying life. I have
arrived at the top, the place everyone else is clawing to reach.*

"How did he make it all the way from Low Ridge to Washington,
DC?" Brewster didn't want an answer because his question was a
concession that, in fact, Anvil was a powerful man.

"It wasn't easy. I'm sure of that. When has it ever been easy?
But, Brewster, you've come a great distance on the same hard road."

"I'm a carpenter working wood in a shed. I couldn't go the
places Anvil Thomas goes. Hell, I can't even imagine what he does.
Can't even see it in my head."

"I've been there, Brewster, and I don't want to go back. Anvil's
going to be walking a line with one foot in the white man's world,
and he'll be wobbling and tipping, trying to stay balanced. I've lived
that already. Mother looked out these windows to see what the
neighbors were doing, and when they painted their house, it wasn't
long before we painted ours. If they put a concrete birdbath in the
yard, we went hunting for one. We wanted them to forget we were
the colored family. We stayed in here and peeked out the windows."

Marlenna raised both hands into the air, palms open, "And,
Brewster, I'm tired of hearing this woodworker stuff. If you don't
realize the value of your own labor. . ."

He kissed her, taking her last words into his mouth, pressing her
to him, parting her lips with his. She placed her hands on the back of
his neck, holding him. She kissed him with an open mouth and he
wanted to settle things between them. He wanted to know she loved
him because he had loved her since the day she came into the Three
Brothers shed. His lips felt the smoothness of her skin, and he worked
his way down her shoulders until his mouth opened against the
fullness of her breast while he slipped his hand under the cranberry
sweater, releasing the clasp of her brassiere, pushing the sweater up
and putting his mouth on the wine-purple of her nipple, feeling the
knot at the tip of it with his tongue. She made a groaning sound and
he felt a rush inside himself, her hands working circles on his back,
the pads of her fingers soothing, but the tips of her nails pricking his
skin with urgency that sent another rush through him.

This was Mixon Domestics and Laborers, and he did not want to
release any part of himself here, not in this office, but Marlenna's
fingers loosened the buckle of his belt, and her tongue outlined the rim
of his lips. Her hands moved to the buttons of his shirt while he
eased the cranberry sweater over her head, dropping it on the leather

seat of the couch. They should be in the upstairs room at Ole Summit, the windows opened to the full sky, the stars and the moon providing them light, not here where the room was closed-off and an ancient smell of blight thickened the air. But, with his hand on her back, they slid down onto the burgundy and green rug, and he felt the smallness of her waist, the width of his hand reaching from one side of her to the other. He pressed his nose to her skin and smelled the rosewater, but when he put his tongue against her skin, he tasted a tang that ran contrary to the roses—the rawness of flesh.

She pulled away from him and turned her skirt to the front, unzipped it and slipped it past her legs, and when she removed her hose and panties, she folded them, placing them on the sofa. He saw the nakedness of her body, smooth and firm, but the inside of her thighs were soft to his touch, and he rubbed the palm of his hand there. He removed his pants, putting these on the couch beside her clothes. The rot from mildew somewhere in the room was in his nose, but he pressed his face to the softness at the inside of her thigh, and the taste and smell of Marlenna drove out every odor and vision that was Mixon Domestics and Laborers. She placed her hand on him and he rose to her touch.

Hell could take Mixon Domestics and Laborers. He needed to let loose any cords that held them apart. Heat was on his shoulders, and he ran his lips up her body over the bone that pushed through the front of her hip, over the flatness of her stomach, over the mid-section of her ribs to the center of her breasts, moving out to smother her nipples in open-mouthed kisses, smelling her, filling his nose with the scent of roses, and tasting the sweetness and tang of Marlenna. He put himself inside her, moving up and back over her, up and back, driving out everything that wasn't him and Marlenna, leaving only what was raw and hungry, her fists grasping the skin of his back, clinching, opening and grasping again. Up and back, tasting her body, filling his nose and mouth, his chest and stomach and legs with her. Up and back.

"I love you," she whispered, and when she called his name, he could not hold back from releasing himself and sealing their union.

They lay on the rug, Marlenna on her side, her shoulder under his arm, her head resting on his chest. He was between sleep and wake and was startled when she sprang off him, hands flying toward the cranberry sweater, the black skirt tossed over her head, the hose and panties shoved under the sofa seat.

"Daughter," he heard Albert Mixon call from the house. "Daughter."

Marlenna put one shoe on and stood, wobbling and balancing herself against Brewster's shoulder as she slipped on her other shoe. "Clothes!" she mouthed, but the word was silent. She ran her hands across the front of her hair.

"Father, we're here, in your office." She went to the door, opening it to the kitchen. Brewster pulled his pants on and kicked his shorts under the couch. Marlenna stood in the door, allowing him time to slip his arms into his shirt and sit on the sofa. His shirt was unbuttoned and hung loose over his pants and he curled his feet, which were bare, toward the bottom edge of the couch. His back was to Albert Mixon who stood in the kitchen doorway.

Marlenna stood in the center of the doorway, one hand posted on the door casing, "I wanted to show Brewster your beautiful office." She took a small step backward, allowing Albert Mixon to peer over her shoulder, but she did not surrender her post. Her hand held firmly against the door casing, and he remained at the top of the steps, making no move to enter the office.

"You two stay here as long as you want," he said. "I'm going on up to bed. Don't forget to turn that fire out."

Asking Marlenna to marry him was easy. It was settled on the burgundy and green rug in the office of Mixon Domestics and Laborers.

"The Lord has blessed this family today," Mama Tee said when they told her. She spread her palms wide and raised them above her head. "Thank you, Jesus! Thank you, J-e-s-u-s!" She stood and danced a flat-footed step in her chenille slippers.

When Brewster told Deak Armbrecht, he clapped his hands together. "T'at one fine gal," he said. "You be plenty happy. My son what live in Kansas got no interest in t'is place. We start work on plans t'at make t'is place for you. What we call it? One Brot'er?" he chuckled and went back to sanding the piece of wood in front of him as naturally as if he had not raised the banner of ownership, the possibility that Brewster Thomas McAtee could own Three Brothers, manufacturers of fine, hand-made furniture, some of the best in the Southeast.

"Brewster, I think it would be nice if you talked to my father. We don't need to ask permission, of course, but we should talk to him. I think you should do that," Marlenna said.

The thought of speaking with Albert Mixon positioned a dart above Brewster's head, one that could shake loose and do injury. But he would speak to the devil himself if it pleased Marlenna. He decided to talk with Albert Mixon before supper, because his food would not settle if he had to do that task after eating.

While Marlenna set the table, Brewster went into the parlor and found Albert Mixon sitting on the burgundy settee, his feet propped on the coffee table with the newspaper in front of his face. He would not ask Albert Mixon for permission to marry Marlenna because she had made her own decision. When he sat opposite the old man and was squarely envisioned by the eyes that peered about the reading glasses, he spoke quickly.

"Sir, Marlenna and I would like to get married. We plan to do that and we hope you're happy with it." He realized that what he had said was something between a request and a declaration, but the words were out and they rested in the room, waiting for the old man's response.

Albert Mixon removed his feet from the table and placed them solidly on the floor. He folded the newspaper. He twisted his mouth and ran the palm of his hand over his nose while he inhaled.

"I was afraid of this," he said. "I had hoped she would do better. Shaw is the oldest Negro college in the South. Do you know that?"

Brewster decided not to answer this question. An answer might lead him down roads where he did not want to travel with Albert Mixon, who studied him, taking him in with the thick lenses of his glasses. "Marlenna has a fine education. I wanted better for her," he said. He didn't speak again, but folded his hands, looking down at them. Brewster took this as his dismissal.

"I'll provide well for her," he said. Albert Mixon only sighed, and Brewster slipped out of his chair and went into the kitchen.

"Was Father pleased?" Marlenna asked.

"Reasonably so," he lied, not wanting Marlenna to concern herself about Albert Mixon's opinion of him. They set the wedding day for the Saturday before Easter when Marlenna would have a week off from her teaching.

"You can hold that dress up over there in front of that mirror, but you can't put it on. If we let colored try on clothes, we couldn't sell them." Mama Tee repeated what the sales clerk had said so Brewster could hear it.

"You got to make up your mind, though, because you walk out of here with it, and we don't take it back," Marlenna completed the scene, and her eyes filled with tears.

"Now I know why Mama never bought clothes from Gwin's. She'd drive over to Hurley County where there was a little shop in the back of a house, just a bedroom really, but a Negro woman owned it, and Mama went over there to buy clothes. She made most of her own clothes though, and she made all the clothes that Carmella and I wore."

"Don't worry about it," Mama Tee said. "Usually I can tell if a dress gon' fit by holding it up."

"My wedding dress isn't going to come from sad circumstances," Marlenna said. Brewster listened, but didn't involve himself in wedding plans because he had no experience in these things. He put his arm around Marlenna and he listened to the women. They made the decision that on Saturday, they would drive over to Hurley, pick a pattern from the Butterick book, select a satin for the skirt, and a batiste for the bodice.

Sewing the dress took a solid month, with Mama Tee measuring and cutting, fitting and stitching. Then Marlenna took a needle and thread, and they worked together attaching tiny pearls to the bodice, one pearl at a time. The wedding dress was a three-quarter-length tea-dress with a full skirt and a fabric belt with a rhinestone buckle. For Marlenna's head, a short veil was attached to a cloche covered in seed pearls.

"I love it," Marlenna said.

"Better than anything Gwin's got," Mama Tee said.

Marlenna and Mama Tee left early on a Saturday morning in March and drove back to Hurley County to purchase satin shoes and elbow-length gloves to complete the outfit. In the bedroom store in Hurley, Marlenna bought a pink suit with a straight skirt and a jacket that had three rhinestone buttons. This she planned to wear on their wedding trip.

Brewster didn't see why the wedding had to be so involved. It should have been enough for Matthew to pronounce the vows, Mama Tee to prepare some food for the wedding party, and he and Marlenna to set themselves up at Ole Summit. That was the way he would have planned it, but whatever Marlenna wanted was fine with him because he was getting what he wanted—Marlenna Mixon McAtee.

He had two commitments he set for himself. He wanted Marlenna to pick a ring he would give her on their wedding day and he wanted to complete an ebony high posted bed for her wedding present—tall, oversized, with posts carved in leaf patterns and two tiny gold bands separating the carving from the silky polished ebony of the tops and bottoms of the legs. Deak admired his sketch of the bed and stayed in the shed until well past dark helping Brewster carve the posts.

Marlenna's sister, Carmella, and her husband, Big Ed, and their son, Little Eddie, arrived. Unlike Marlenna, Carmella was heavy-set, large-boned, and taller than Marlenna. She taught voice in Raleigh, and she announced her presence by singing pieces of songs as she went through the rooms at 32 State Street. Her voice zigzagged from jazz to gospel and on to opera, filling rooms with her songs, her bright-colored print dresses, and spicy smelling perfume, but her husband, Big Ed, was slight of build and nervous. When he grew agitated, he sighed through his gold teeth, shaking his head in disgust, and Carmella settled him by rubbing her large hands against his back.

"Don't worry about it, Ed," she cooed when a cup slipped from his hand and broke in the kitchen sink. He squared his lower lip and hissed through his teeth. Big Ed paced through the house in his cream-colored suit with its three-button vest, and his hard-heeled shoes clicked on the wood floors. His fist pounded the table when Little Eddie whined or fussed, and Carmella set herself in motion calming both of them.

Two of Marlenna's friends, Kate and Marion, arrived from Raleigh, and Carmella prepared a celebration supper. Brewster drove his Buick away from 32 State Street after midnight and was back in Low Ridge at the Three Brothers shed before seven on the next morning. While Marlenna was busy with her friends, he was shoring up things in the shed before the wedding, because Marlenna had planned their honeymoon—a trip to New York City.

"This is my gift to you," she told him. "I put my entire month's pay into this trip." He didn't want to go to New York and he didn't like the idea of Marlenna paying. If she wanted to go to New York, he had the money.

"This is my gift to you," she repeated and put her hand over his mouth to end the discussion. He didn't like it, but he reasoned he would have a thousand times to counterbalance her gift, and he would let it ride. Marlenna was strong-minded, but so was Mama Tee. He was not stepping into territory that was foreign to him. He didn't want a woman broken and as weak-willed as a hollow reed. He would not turn Marlenna's gift into a contest between them. He would accept her gift and return it with steady work, a paycheck every Friday, land, and fields of cotton and corn.

Deak hired an extra man for the shop, a young man whose real name was William Smith, but who preferred to be called Skinner. He was wiry, ebony complexioned, and what had impressed Deak was that Skinner came in early and stayed late, but Brewster watched Skinner with a careful eye because his work was not exact. He short-stepped on projects, trying to hurry a job that needed slow-time. Skinner had not completed school, and he had a baby by some girl who came to the shed every afternoon about six o'clock.

"Where you from?" Brewster asked Skinner.

"Lived behind the fillin' station off Limrick and 2nd. There by myself now. Ran mama off. Drunk all the time and putting out for anybody wantin' some."

Skinner stacked three mahogany planks under Brewster's workbench. "Place quiet now," he said. "Still get awake though by some old man wantin' pussy middle of the night. Kicked one down the steps other night." Skinner talked loose, but when Deak was around, he whistled or hummed or bobbed his head to some tune passing between his ears. When Deak called Skinner to carry a load of wood from the truck into the shed, he answered, "Yes, sir, Mr. Deak. I'm coming, sir. On my way."

Skinner was not ready to draft or finish, but he could cut, sand, and do easy joints with supervision, and while Brewster was cautious of Skinner, he was relieved that Deak hired him. Brewster would be in New York for an entire week and Deak needed somebody in the shed.

On Thursday Marlenna's aunts arrived from Hurley County, and Albert Mixon hopped around the house, being certain that every guest was well served. Marlenna was at the point of tears from the exhaustion of entertaining and maneuvering around people who slept in every bedroom and made pallets in the parlors. Brewster knew they should have gotten married quietly, but he didn't say this to Marlenna for fear that a flood of tears would overwhelm her. He tolerated the chaos at 32 State Street, reviewed the status of his work with Deak and Skinner, and made preparations for their trip to New York.

Mama Tee brought two enormous ferns from her backyard and placed these in the front of the church. Several white lilies hung out of long tubes that stood on wrought-iron stands on the floor in front of the altar. When Brewster smelled these, he knew this must be the scent of Heaven. Carmella, Kate, and Marion, dressed in rose-colored satin gowns, stood in front of the mirror in the women's bathroom with the door open, while they worked on their hair and make-up.

Anvil arrived the morning of the wedding to serve as best man, because Marlenna, Mama Tee, and Albert Mixon would have been disappointed if he had not been asked. "It would be a shame not to ask somebody important like that," Albert Mixon said.

"Anvil Thomas adds something special," Mama Tee agreed.

"Anvil would be an excellent choice if you don't have someone else in mind," Marlenna had nudged. And Brewster considered this. He decided he wanted Anvil to see Marlenna walk down the aisle to become Mrs. Brewster Thomas McAtee. After he telephoned Anvil, he allowed Marlenna to ask two of her cousins from Hurley to escort Kate and Marion down the aisle because Brewster told her there was no one else he wanted to ask. TeeBoy was gone, and he hoped that Tom would not come to the wedding at all, and Deak Armbrecht would not fit with the wedding party. He and Marlenna had laughed when they considered this—an old white man, pasty and low-legged, escorting a young black woman down the aisle. It would have been a sight to see, but one that nobody was likely to see in Low Ridge. Albert Mixon's sisters had sons who were eager for the job, and that suited Brewster fine.

"I'm so glad you come all the way from Washington for this wedding," Mama Tee said when she rubbed Anvil's back. "You add class, don't he, Brewster?"

Brewster affirmed Mama Tee, but he thought TeeBoy should be here, his thin, straight body in a dark suit, grinning when the "I do's" were pronounced.

The church was nearly full with the ladies from Mama Tee's Sunday school class, the deacons, members from Limrick Road Baptist, teachers from County Training School, and Albert Mixon's relatives. Anvil escorted Carmella and stood behind Brewster, followed by the cousins with Kate and Marion. When Marlenna walked down the aisle of Limrick Road Baptist, Brewster's eyes took in every detail. Her face had a smile fixed on it and flowers were in her gloved hands, pink roses in the center surrounded by tiny white lilies. Her satin skirt reflected light and flowed from her narrow waist. Her breasts were outlined under a row of tiny pearls on the batiste fabric of the bodice. The wedding dress had cost tears and hours of work, but Brewster thought the way Marlenna looked in it paid the price in full. He met her eyes and guided her down the aisle where he extended his hand and entwined his fingers through hers.

Marrying Marlenna Mixon was beyond what he had imagined, a fate beyond his own dreams. When he thought this, he nearly laughed. Marlenna, seeing him, smiled, and Matthew's lips broke open in joy that circled his face. In the hushed church, Brewster listened to Matthew's words, repeating them when he was told to do so, and he listened to Marlenna's responses, her voice a soft echo against the baptismal font. He drew his focus narrow and he held it there, centered on Marlenna.

After the wedding, the guests trooped back to 32 State Street where the only white faces were those of Deak Armbrecht and several members of the Luce family who had come to the wedding out of respect for Mama Tee. The white guests huddled together at the front door, an ill-at-ease minority. Beads of sweat were across Mama Tee's forehead as she rushed platters of little sandwiches and sweets to the front door, enticing the white guests to step into the parlors. The Luces stayed long enough to take several sips from their punch glasses and they went out the front door headed up State Street, but Deak came into the left parlor, the one with the bean-shaped, wine-colored settee, and he visited with Marlenna.

Brewster was standing in the kitchen talking with one of Albert Mixon's sisters when he heard the commotion at the front door. Tom, dressed in a wrinkled gray-striped jacket, his tie askew, had arrived at the wedding reception and had already gotten into a fray with Big Ed. Before Brewster reached the door, Big Ed laid a solid blow against the side of Tom's face, and Tom folded like a broken stick. The women screamed and Big Ed stood defiant. Mama Tee bent down beside Tom, and she called out for someone to bring her a cold cloth. Brewster slipped his hands under Tom's shoulders while Anvil lifted his feet, and they put him on the couch, leaning his head against the sofa arm. Tom's left arm with his loose hand flopped on the floor; Brewster lifted it and placed it across his father's chest.

"Too bad," Anvil said, and backed away from the sofa, looking at Tom. He put his arm around his own father, and he and Herman Thomas headed for the kitchen.

Deak left quickly. Albert Mixon's sisters gathered in the kitchen, speaking in hushed voices. Kate and Marion put napkins to their faces, attempting to conceal their amusement, and Mama Tee huddled on the couch beside Tom.

"Shit-headed nigger," Big Ed said as Carmella put her arm around him encouraging him up the stairs. "Shit-headed nigger," he repeated, his arms flaying. Carmella backed away from him, but at the same time, she managed to ease him up the stairs with the soothing softness of her voice.

"He needs to go on home, soon as you can get him up." Albert Mixon spoke in the direction of the sofa, not looking at Mama Tee.

At three o'clock with only family and houseguests remaining, Marlenna came down the stairs, wearing the pale pink suit she had purchased in Hurley. She had a pillbox hat on her head and she wore white shoes that had come from the bedroom shop in Hurley. The small group threw rice on the couple as they climbed in the back seat of the Riviera, with Skinner driving them to the Calhoun County train station.

When they reached the Calhoun Depot, Skinner took the suitcases out of the trunk and walked them to the train. "We could get close to the dining car, but we could also have a fight on our hands, and I've had about enough of that for one day," Marlenna said. They boarded the last car, dirty and nearly empty with the exception of a large, middle-aged Negro woman who wore a hat and a mink stole with the heads of the animals still on it. She occupied one seat, and her bags spilled over to the seat beside her. Three Negro soldiers played a loud game of cards in two seats that were turned to face each other.

Marlenna leaned forward and patted the overnight case she had at her feet. "If we get hungry, I have some cakes my aunts packed for us."

She removed her hat, placing it carefully in the hatbox she had brought. When she leaned back in her seat, Brewster put his arm around her, and she rested her head against his shoulder.

"I can't bear to think about Ed and Tom," Marlenna said. "I know Carmella felt awful, but she should have left Ed back in Raleigh, and Tom should have stayed away." Her voice trailed off and Brewster did not step in to fill the silence. He was not going to debate about Tom on his wedding day. He drew Marlenna to him, resting his chin on the top of her head and she settled.

"You'll love New York," she said speaking in a slow voice. "We can go almost anywhere—restaurants, the theater, shopping. You'll know what it feels like to go in places without wondering if you'll be kicked out, without putting your head down, or thinking about every move."

They sat silent, listening to the clanking of the train. He felt Marlenna's body nested in his arms. The miles separating Low Ridge from New York could take their time in passing, because he had what he wanted here, and he could use the time to set his mind on the newness of his status—husband to Marlenna Mixon, Marlenna Mixon McAtee. He began to let all the activity of the previous weeks ease off of him. His body moved with the jostling on the tracks, and he watched the dirty railyards go by. Then there was darkness, and they were in the denseness of thick forests, and they both slept.

10

"Harlem House," Marlenna told the taxi driver, a white man who didn't appear to take offense at driving Negroes across the city.

"This isn't the fanciest place, but I've stayed there before. Everyone is nice." Marlenna talked, but New York subdued Brewster, the vastness of it quashed him into silence, rousing him and suppressing him in the same instant.

At the hotel, a bellman dressed in a long gray coat took their suitcases. "Where's your overcoat, mahn?" he asked in an accent Brewster had never heard before.

"Don't have one."

"From doon south," the bellman said, threw his head back and laughed. "Easter mighty cold. Won't be much Easter stroll today," he said.

Brewster looked at his watch and realized Mama Tee was in her pew at Limrick Road Baptist, and New York City was so different from Low Ridge he might as well be walking on the moon. Marlenna bought a newspaper in the lobby and took it upstairs.

"Too cold for Easter," she said, "but we'll find plenty to do. We won't be bothered by this weather at all."

In their room, neat but barely large enough for the bed and one chair, Marlenna unpacked her clothes, then sat cross-legged on the bed with the newspaper opened in front of her, while Brewster sat in the straight-backed wing-chair, watching her. New York was too big for him and had been hostile to his mother when she had come, hoping to grab a tiny fistful of its wealth. He was uncomfortable in this giant world where he didn't know directions and didn't know the rules, and that left him feeling like he was in deep water, unsure of the depth, not knowing how far he would need to put his feet down to touch bottom. The small room added to his discomfort—closed-up against the rain and the cold. He was ready to go back to Low Ridge where he wasn't suspended, trying to create something to do.

"Oh, Brewster, look at this." Brewster sat beside Marlenna on the bed, and she read where her finger pointed.

Duke Ellington, Ella Fitzgerald, Carnegie Hall. TONIGHT!

134

Marlenna turned toward him, a smile on her face, "That's what we're going to do. This will take the chill off a cold Easter."

She sat in his lap and wrapped her arms around him. Her legs linked tightly around his waist. He held onto Marlenna, bringing her down on top of him, feeling a rushing current run through him, and he was grateful that in this giant city where he didn't know his way around, at least his body was set on automatic. Marlenna raised her head from his chest and began unbuttoning his shirt. He closed his eyes and slipped his hand under her sweater, lifting her brassiere and feeling her breast, finding the tiny mole just past the nipple on her left side, and touching it with the pad of his middle finger. With his eyes still closed, he put his hand in the small of her back and recognized the distance, his hand stretching from one side of her ribs to the other, and when she kissed him, he knew her lips too, by the taste and the feel of them.

His need was urgent and their slow rocking back and forth suspended time in the tiny room with the rain beating down, gray and heavy. There was only the core of himself craving its own release, vital in the up and back, up and back, up and back. She put her lips on his, open to him, and there was nothing but letting loose, freeing him and finding himself again. He had been nearly lost somewhere in the rows of towering buildings and the crowds at the train station who spoke a melody foreign to his ears.

When Marlenna rested her head on his chest, he closed his eyes, and they both slept. When he woke, it was late afternoon and the room was dark except for a crack of light under the bathroom door, behind which he could hear water running in the bathtub.

If New York by day was massive, the city by night was staggering, with towers of windows, illuminated, narrow mountains glowing. With his head cocked back on his neck, looking at the walls rising above him, he ran head on into a man, who cursed him. Marlenna's arm rested in the bend of his elbow, and after his encounter with the angry man, he concentrated on maneuvering through the crowd, using his body to create a path for Marlenna, dividing his attention between the throng of people on the street and the illuminations above him. They took a taxi for some of the distance, and the ride caused him to feel unsteady again, because the driver created a third lane and went past a bus that stopped on the right side of the street. But Marlenna enjoyed it all, naming landmarks as the taxi weaved and jerked. Brewster looked and breathed and listened and drew into himself as much of the city as he could hold, because he would share it with Mama Tee.

When Brewster heard Ella Fitzgerald's voice, he thought of the smoothest horn, crying and laughing with breaks, blending and pulling back into unbroken flows of pure tones. *Ooooooh-da-wah-daaaaaaeeeeee.* Her head back, the microphone at her mouth. Tone-ribbons streamed from the throat and lips of this great woman. Narrow banners drifted into the auditorium—unadulterated, vibrant colors floating toward the audience, wrapping around heads and hearts, tangling on fingers and notching behind ear lobes. The sheer banner that hit Brewster's eyes and floated past his head was gold—gold as honey, warm as sunlight on ageless amber. He knew that, if he died tomorrow, tonight he had sat in Carnegie Hall, more white folks than Negroes, and he heard the great Duke Ellington and Ella Fitzgerald play hot and cool and shower the audience with brilliant, everlasting colors. He took in every bit of it, trying to lock into his memory the rhythm-snapping grunts the horns made, gliding and rolling. He would keep his guard up, but New York was luring, there was no question about that. He would not embrace this city because it was too big to hold on to, but before he left Carnegie Hall, he decided at least to court it. It was fast-and-loose, free-and-easy, and he had never before lingered in such a place of pleasure.

Monday took on a pattern that lasted the week. Rise late. Drink coffee, heavy with hot milk, eat biscuits with jelly already rolled into the center of them. Then they went out into the streets where the Black Muslims sold newspapers on the corner, and the air felt brisk, even though it was laden with smells of food, frying and baking, and of people who got too close and carried musty odors of closed rooms and moth-balled coats, and breath hot and wet in the cold air.

"Pride, baby, pride," the man on the corner, wearing a black suit and a white shirt said when Marlenna bought the Muslim paper.

They took the subway or the bus or an occasional taxi—Lenox or 125th Street, the starting and finishing points. Streets rolled by with numbers instead of names, subway cars passed into and out of darkness, and he didn't have time to sort it all out because one scene changed into another too quickly. He followed Marlenna through the great department stores, Gimbels and Macy's, where he felt ill at ease, but Marlenna wanted him to see the latest New York fashions and the Brooks Brothers suits, flannel and tweed. They could not afford to buy any of this, but Marlenna placed hats on his head, homburgs, Chesterfields, Tyroleans, and she studied him, turning his head at an angle. They did make one purchase for him, a dark gray blazer, very practical. Then he sat in several shoe departments making conversations with the clerks while Marlenna was off looking at women's clothing she described as scooped-necked or nubby-textured. She gathered ideas for outfits that she and Mama Tee would sew when she returned to Low Ridge. In the afternoons, they collapsed in their room, making love and reading newspapers, until the sun slipped behind the tall buildings.

"I would like to hear this man,'" Marlenna said. "Maybe we can get over to the mosque and hear him talk." When she took her bath, Brewster read the article in the Muslim newspaper, *Muhammad Speaks*. This man, Malcolm X, was full of fire, and Brewster wanted Marlenna to take these papers back to Low Ridge and put them on the table in front of the wine-colored, bean-shaped settee for her father to see. How would he respond to this man? *Too much heat for Albert Mixon*, Brewster thought and smiled.

"Be a ticker-tape parade for that mahn won that piano playing over in Russia," the bellman shouted at them as they went through the lobby on Thursday. "Don' miss that."

And they did not miss it. They saw the ticker tape flying as Van Cliburn paraded through the streets of New York, riding on the back seat of a black convertible, draped with an American flag

"I have seen everything now," Brewster said, caught up in the excitement that was New York on this special day. That very after-noon, Marlenna bought Van Cliburn's record; *Tchaikovsky Concerto No. I,* the record jacket read. Brewster laughed because his lips would not say the letters T-C-H together no matter how many times Marlenna said it for him. Marlenna placed the record in the bottom of her suitcase to take it home and play it on the player in the big room at Ole Summit.

On Thursday evening when they ate in the hotel restaurant, Brewster made up his mind to tell Marlenna about her father's refusal to find work for his mother in Low Ridge and how Bess had come to New York, but had been destroyed by what she found here. He had wanted to tell Marlenna about this before, but he had not. Now the distance separating Low Ridge from New York provided him safety from his own dislike of Albert Mixon, and he hoped Marlenna could take a long-view of her father from here.

"When she came back from this place, she was drinking so much shiney until her head never was straight again. She didn't see the New York we've seen," he explained to Marlenna, putting his fork on his plate and watching her face. "She never said what happened, but the situation Bess McAtee found here was not what she had been told." He wanted to say more, to accuse Albert Mixon of fraud, but he was cautious, not wanting to drive a wedge between him and Marlenna. That would make Albert Mixon the victor, and he did not want to loosen the love that he and Marlenna held between them. Marlenna stopped eating and listened to him, her eyes focused on his.

"We found her curled up on the ground like a child put down for a nap. It was in the winter, and she had brought her knees up to her chest to warm herself. She closed her eyes and that's the way we found her."

Marlenna reached across the table and took his hands. "I'm sure my father tried to locate work for her in Low Ridge. He suffered when someone needed a job and he couldn't find it." She withdrew her hands, folding them in front of her, but her eyes remained locked on his. "I'm sorry. I know he felt sadness about what happened."

Brewster made a conscious decision not to argue with Marlenna about Albert Mixon. Instead, he reached across the table and again took her hands into his and continued to hold them even when the waiter came to clear the dishes and left apologetically when he saw their arms circling the plates and their hands together. Marlenna was not her father and he was not his. He loved her in such a way that she completed him, made him more than he was, and he liked the feel of her hands in his, warm and small, and holding tightly to him. He had told her about his mother and about her father, and that part of it was done.

The next morning, Brewster used their breakfast time at the hotel as an opportunity to tell Marlenna about his dream. He was not a lawyer, was not a man who knew the big cities, but he had dreams. As they could afford it, they could add on to the house. He would plant ten acres of corn this spring and lease fifteen acres of land to the paper mill to plant pine seedlings to be raised and harvested for pulp. He wanted to own more land than any Negro in Low Ridge County and he suspected that he had won that honor already. He planned to rival the richest white landowners.

"Nobody can take land from us. We have it to fall back on. Matthew called our place the Garden of Eden. You and Mama Tee can plant whatever flowers you want on it because those sixty acres are yours too. That old crazy coot in that tarpaper shack, I want to buy him out too. But all things in good time."

"I love that land, Brewster. I love the way it smells, fresh and green and easy to breathe, and I have a few ideas for the house. We'll make it our kingdom." Brewster felt almost light-headed when Marlenna said this; she appreciated what he had produced from his work and his shrewdness. He felt the fullness of his manhood, and this filled his thick chest with pride.

When they left the hotel, Marlenna insisted they take the bus past Striver's Row and the Dunbar Apartments. "If your mother worked for a wealthy family, they might have lived here," she said, pointing to the brownstones of Striver's Row. Brewster didn't care where his mother had lived. He cared only that she had been crushed by this massive city and had come back to Low Ridge defeated.

When they came back to the hotel in the late afternoon, the bellman shouted at Marlenna, "Go on doon the block there, you hear Malcolm. He's talking in front of the Hotel Teresa. Go on, if you want to hear something good."

Brewster and Marlenna stood on the edge of the crowd by the curb in front of the Hotel Teresa, but they could see him—a lean, ginger-colored, redheaded black man speaking with passion.

"Don't do what the man wants you to do. The man don't have your interests in his heart. Turn your back on that stuff. Turn off the television. Blondes have more fun," he said, imitating the television commercial. "But when have you ever seen a black woman have more fun with blonde hair? You've seen 'em try. But a black woman got beautiful black hair that jumps back when the water gets on it. A black woman is a queen," he said. "An African queen."

"Un-huh, Malcolm, un-huh," the crowd said. "Tell 'em, Malcolm, yeah man."

"He will be a leader," Marlenna said. "He says what the rest of us feel, but can't articulate."

Brewster made no judgment. He thought the man was a rouser, whipping up the crowd, and he wondered out loud whether Mama Tee would support a leader like Malcolm X.

On Saturday, Brewster and Marlenna checked out of the hotel at five in the morning. The weather had turned cold and rainy again. Marlenna wore thin leather gloves, a pink and green checked coat, a spring coat she called it. Brewster had resisted the temptation to purchase an overcoat, thinking he could not afford the luxury, but his suit jacket was too thin to keep out the chill. When he ducked his head to get into the taxi, rain ran down the back of his collar, making him shiver. The clouds hung low and dark, matching his mood. There would never be another time when he would be on his honeymoon in New York, but Marlenna seemed content enough, although she was quiet.

She had purchased a quantity of books, and on the train she removed her shoes, tucked her legs up under her on the seat, with her coat spreading over her like a tent. She leaned her back against the window, and, to Brewster's annoyance, she read, page after page, moistening her index finger with her tongue, turning pages without looking up.

His suitcoat, still damp, made him feel uncomfortable, but he was too cold to remove it. He wondered if their car was the only one without heat, and he suspected it was, which annoyed him even more. He read a little of *The New York Times* that Marlenna purchased in the lobby just before they left, but he had no interest in the stories, and his hands felt cold and stiff. He folded the paper, and he put both of his hands under him, sitting on them, looking and feeling brittle in his suit with his arms rigid beside him, the palms of his hands holding his butt cheeks.

Marlenna laughed. "Brewster, you look like a penguin. Relax, and read for a while." Her voice was smooth as satin. "On a day like today, hunker down. Keep your mind busy and this bad weather will pass. I learned that a long time ago. Don't fight it," she said and laughed again. Her head came out of the pink and green checked coat like a face on a short totem pole.

"I'm not going to read," he said. "I'm going to think. I'm lining up my work for when I get back. I've got plenty to think about."

With the palm of her hand, she rubbed the side of his face, his hair and the back of his neck, and he felt her hand soothing him like liquor running down the back of his throat, burning and warming.

"I'm hungry," Marlenna said. "When the porter comes through, let's ask him to bring us sandwiches."

He was hungry too. Nearly eleven o'clock, and they had been up since before five without any food. He studied the passing forests, encased in a thick gray mist from the rain and from the spring air that was trying to overtake winter. He checked his watch at regular intervals, waiting for the porter, but when he had not come into the car by eleven thirty, he was at the point of desperation.

"If you can't wait," Marlenna said, "go hunt for him and ask him to bring us sandwiches. Ham for me."

He didn't want to hunt for the porter on the other cars, but he was hungry and ready to do battle, if necessary. He walked onto the platform connecting his car to the next one and nearly slipped down on the wet and cold metal plate, but he caught himself on the pole in the middle of the link. He located the porter when he reached the third car from his own, and he gave the man their order. He walked back through the cars with considerably more confidence than he had when he was searching for the porter. When he reached his own seat, he settled in beside Marlenna, thinking that he was different from the man who had left Low Ridge a week earlier.

He was one of the few Negro men in Low Ridge who had been to New York, had taken a train, and had learned something about negotiating for himself in the biggest of cities. Hell, no! He was one of the few men in Low Ridge, black or white, who had ever been to New York, shopped in some of the finest stores, gone to the theater, rode the subways, and ate in restaurants. He was not the same man who left Low Ridge just a week before, unsure of what stretched before him.

It was early morning when the train pulled into the Calhoun station. Skinner waited with the Buick, but to Brewster's annoyance, he brought his girlfriend, Rozelle.

"Hope you don't mind, I brought Rozelle to keep me company?" Skinner asked, a wide grin on his face.

"Of course not, Skinner," Marlenna answered him.

The fog was so heavy that if he had not spotted the IMPEACH EARL WARREN sign, he would have missed the turn into his own property. He felt good when his wheels rolled on his own land. When he switched on the lights at Ole Summit, the warm gold of his polished floors made him glad to be back in his house, but when he entered the big room, he stopped. Lined-up against the wall were eight mahogany chairs with back slats crossed like cathedral windows.

Skinner doubled his body, laughing. "The boss man surprised you, huh? I had to see this," Skinner said, watching Brewster. "Me and the boss man brought these out yesterday."

Brewster pulled an armchair away from the wall and put it under the center light in the big room. The seat was upholstered in beige needlepoint with strawberries, deep green leaves and vines running through the fabric. Brewster ran his hand over the curves of the slats and felt the satin of the finish while Marlenna sat in one of the chairs.

"Our wedding present," she whispered. They pulled each chair away from the wall examining it individually under the light. Marlenna got down on her knees, looking closely at the needlepoint through which the summer bounty had been hand-rendered. Every chair was the same as the one before it, but they pulled each one out and put it under the light, admiring it.

"Boss man says you got to make yourself a table now. Says he not gon' do that for you. He done his part. So says the boss man." Skinner and Rozelle walked around the eight chairs. "These are fine," Skinner concluded. "I watched the boss man make these myself. Even helped a little."

Skinner carried the suitcases upstairs before he and Rozelle left. With the eight dining chairs in a line in the center of the big room, Brewster and Marlenna went upstairs to rest in their ebony high-posted bed and spend their first full night together at Ole Summit.

11

In June, Brewster took money he earned from leasing his land and bought lumber to build a shed at Ole Summit, a place he could work on Saturdays and Sundays, and where he could build a table to match the cathedral-slated chairs Deak had given them as a wedding present. Brewster drove Deak out to watch the construction, and they ate their lunch, sitting in straight-backed chairs on raw pine floors.

When the workshop was finished, Marlenna and Mama Tee surrounded it with boxwoods, mondo grass, and two laurels, one to the east of the shed and one to the west. This building, which would gray with time, looked softer with trees and shrubs around it. Brewster was glad to have his own place to work on weekends because he did not like Marlenna on the land by herself, even though he hadn't seen Travis Peets come near the spindle-posted porch, and Valiant patrolled the paths. This shed at Ole Summit was his place, his own shop where he could smell the new pine of his walls and floors, and he liked the way the light reflected amber across his work spaces in the late afternoons of Saturdays.

The rhythm of Ole Summit changed in September when Marlenna's two-toned Chevrolet headed toward County Training School, pulling out of the lane ahead of Brewster's Buick. In the afternoons, Marlenna visited her father or Mama Tee after school, and when she came by the shed, they drove to Ole Summit together. This pattern was followed except on Thursdays, when Marlenna cooked supper for her father and attended the Low Ridge Association meeting at Limrick Road Baptist. Brewster was satisfied. At night he slept with his arm wrapped around Marlenna, her body resting in the bends of his own.

But in mid-October their pattern changed when Marlenna arrived at the shed looking ashen, her hands trembling. "I'm not feeling well," she said. "I'm going on home."

Next morning she moved slowly and ate only buttered toast, refusing her coffee. In the afternoon, she didn't visit her father or cook supper for him, and she didn't attend the Low Ridge Association meeting with Mama Tee. On the weekend, she stayed in bed and slept. She didn't attend church on Sunday morning, and by Sunday night Brewster could not sleep because when he closed his eyes, TeeBoy came—hideous, blood pouring from his chest, his feet moving in weighted, slow, and wide steps. This sight propelled Brewster upright in bed, waking Marlenna.

"My chest is tight. I'm going out on the porch for some air." He kissed Marlenna on the side of her face, slipped his shoes on with no socks, and went to his chair on the front porch where a cold breeze sounded in a whistle when it passed through the leaves of his trees. He leaned his head against the back of the chair and dozed, but TeeBoy came again, dancing macabre, and Brewster felt relieved when he saw gray-blue in the sky that soon had some coral color in it.

"You go straight over to Dr. Hamilton's office."

"Let me check in at school, Brewster. I'll go after I get everything started there. Besides, Dr. Hamilton won't be in his office yet."

"Let me know what he says soon as you know something," Brewster said. Marlenna kissed him, and then touched his lips with the tips of her fingers before he closed the door of her Chevrolet.

In the Three Brothers shed, Brewster worked on chairs for the courthouse, an order delivered by the judge personally, and he checked his watch periodically, wondering if Marlenna had seen Dr. Hamilton and when she would come to give him a report. At noon he ate his lunch on his stool in the doorway of the shed and worked a few more words into the crossword puzzle that Deak had given him. He finished his lunch, and he lifted his bench from the doorway into the shed when he heard Marlenna shouting behind him.

"Brewster, I'm fine. I need some rest. I'm going on to Ole Summit. I'll have supper on when you get there." She did not get out of the car and shifted the Chevrolet into reverse.

"What did the doctor say?" He shouted this, thinking Marlenna would park the car and give him a full report, but she did not.

"I'll tell you about it tonight." Marlenna cranked the window up before he reached the car.

When Brewster arrived at Ole Summit, he saw smoke rising from the hearth and lights on in the big room, giving the house an orange glow.

"Brewster, come here and sit with me in front of the fire," Marlenna said, before he could hang his jacket on the rack.

When he sat on the floor beside her, she placed her hands, one on each side of his face, pulling him to her, kissing him, whispering:

> *Little brown baby wif spa'klin' eyes,*
> *Come to yo' pappy an' set on his knee.*
> *What you been doin', suh—makin' san pies?*

Marlenna said this while running the tip of her finger around his mouth. He had grown accustomed to verse flowing out of her, connecting whatever was on the inside of her with what was happening on the outside. He accepted this, and he welcomed her touch because during her sickness there was no touching and no love making, which had left him void. In one motion, he reached to untie her robe, placing his lips on the softness of her shoulder, but again she put both of her hands on the sides of his face, bringing him in front of her eyes. "Brewster, we're going to have a baby."

It took a moment, but when the words landed clearly in his brain, he stood up and clapped his hands. "We're going to have a baby here at Ole Summit? Our baby, here at Ole Summit?"

> *He's pappy's pa'dner an' playmate an' joy.*
> *Come to you' pallet now—go to yo' res';*
> *Wisht you could allus know ease an' cleah skies;*
> *Little brown baby wif spa'klin' eyes!*

Before Marlenna could get the last word fully past her lips, Brewster sat beside her again, placing his hands inside her robe, pulling her to him, feeling the smoothness of her skin, and placing his mouth on the carmine circle of her nipple.

Mama Tee danced when they told her and then she wept, pulling out a handkerchief tucked into the waistband of her dress and rubbing it through the folds under her eyes. Then she embraced them. "A blessed child will come out of this love."

Even Albert Mixon was pleased. "I wish Helen could be here for this baby," he said. "Oh, she would have liked this." He smiled, and Brewster saw a face he had never before seen on the man, a face that softened him.

Marlenna wanted a bedroom for the baby, and Brewster wanted to add the room to the house like a garment on which the seams are natural and almost invisible. He still dreamed of buying Travis Peets' land, but there was no point in worrying about that now. His shed had taken nearly all of his cash reserves, and the addition on the house would drain the remainder, leaving no money even if Peets lowered his price to something reasonable.

Marlenna wanted the baby delivered at Ole Summit, but Dr. Hamilton refused. "I'm too old to go chasing after babies," he told Marlenna. "I don't do home deliveries," he said with his arms locked tightly across himself.

"I don't want my baby to be born in the colored wing," Marlenna said.

Brewster kept quiet. He did not want the baby to be born at Ole Summit because he too was worried about the distance from the hospital, but he would rely on Dr. Hamilton to remain firm, which he appeared to be doing—a solid block of resolve, held tightly by his own thick arms across his chest.

Albert Mixon wanted his daughter to move back to 32 State Street until after the baby's birth. "You need to be close to the hospital," he said. "You don't need to be way out there."

Marlenna found an old midwife who lived off Limrick Road. "She's delivered hundreds of babies. When the time comes, we'll call her. Actually, what we'll do is call her neighbor. She doesn't have a telephone. We'll call Skinner, get him to go get her and bring her out here. It'll all work out," Marlenna said. "I want the baby to be delivered at Ole Summit."

Brewster had never been insistent with Marlenna, but on this issue he held firm. "The baby will not be delivered at Ole Summit," he said on a Saturday night when they sat on the front porch, Marlenna in the new rocking chair he had built for her. "I have made up my mind about that."

"I won't have our son delivered in the colored wing," Marlenna said equally as insistent. "Coming and going through the back door," she added.

"How you know our baby's going to be a boy?"

"I feel him." She watched the bullbats soar above the trees and dart straight down again.

They had not decided on a name for the baby. "Do you want to call him Brewster? A son named after his father would be nice."

"Definitely not. All my life I've grown up with Tom saying 'That gal tricked me. She done name the baby Brewster when I said clear as day, the boy's name is Rooster.' This baby will not be named Brewster," he said, closing the discussion.

"My father wants the baby named after him, Albert Crown Mixon. I know the Crown is a little much, but his mother thought Albert sounded like royalty, so she put the Crown in there for good measure."

"H'mum," Brewster sounded through this nose, not parting his lips. Albert Crown McAtee would be a bad start on life, and if he didn't offer any support for the name, maybe Marlenna would drop it without discussion.

"Well, my father has certainly earned the honor. We could leave off the Crown and call him Albert Mixon McAtee. That has a pretty good sound."

"H'mum," he let out through his nose again, wishing he could come up with a name, but his mind didn't work well on those kinds of things. The job of naming the baby would belong to Marlenna.

On a Sunday evening, Brewster and Marlenna watched the sun going down, a big rose-colored ball that decorated the sky with pink, purple, blue, and yellow strokes landing on the laurels Mama Tee and Marlenna had planted. The trees had a magic appearance in the vari-colored show of sunset. When the sun dipped several degrees lower, and the sky was streaked with merely two shades of pink and purple, Marlenna spoke.

"I know his name." Her face was on the fine mist of colors the sun continued spraying. "His name is Laurel. Albert Laurel McAtee. We'll call him Laurel, but putting Albert first will please Father."

From that moment, there was never a doubt that the baby's name would be Albert Laurel McAtee. If the baby happened to surprise them and be a girl, Marlenna had settled that too. Her name would be Helen Teelda McAtee and they would call her Tee. Mama Tee strutted when they told her, and old Albert Mixon nearly popped a chest button when he heard the name Albert Laurel McAtee.

The settling on one issue speeded the decision about another. The baby would be born at Our Savior's Home in Calhoun County, which Brewster didn't like, but at least Marlenna had dropped the business about the baby's being born by some half-blind midwife driven to Ole Summit by Skinner. Dr. Hamilton wouldn't deliver the baby because he would not drive the fifty miles to Calhoun, and besides, he said openly he didn't like the head nun who ran Our Savior's Home. "Hard headed" was the way Dr. Hamilton described her, and

Brewster concluded she didn't kowtow to him, nor did he to her, and it was best that they not get into each other's paths.

Marlenna made all the arrangements, and on a Friday in late May, they drove to Calhoun for Marlenna's final check-up by the woman doctor, a Negro nun named Sister Francesca. Our Savior's Home was a full hour's drive from Ole Summit, and Brewster thought the place was eerie. In the middle of Platt's Row, the Negro section in Calhoun, down a narrow street with three or four lean-tos on a single lot, rose Our Savior's Home, a large white granite building that sparkled in the afternoon sun. The place had an unearthly appearance. Adding to the supernatural effect of glittering whiteness at the end of a narrow asphalt lane, the nuns wore long black robes with enormous white hoods like wings perched on their heads. Both Negro and white sisters moved about the place in slow motion, their robes weighting them and trailing behind them as they cared for patients, mostly black with a scattering of elderly white. The infirm sat in wheel chairs on the grounds with statues hovering over them in perpetual meditation.

"Isn't this wonderful!" Marlenna moved her hand in front of her chest with her palm open.

"H'mum," Brewster sounded. He would have preferred the colored wing at Low Ridge County Hospital. At Our Savior's Home, he felt unbalanced, causing him to whisper when he spoke. When he met Sister Francesca, he felt even more off balance. He had never met a Negro woman like this doctor. Sister Francesca had light brown skin and black eyes that looked straight at you when she spoke, and there was no softness in her voice, no easy words. Her questions shot from her mouth—short, crisp—and she commanded those around her to do this or do that. She was not from Alabama and that was obvious.

"Isn't she wonderful?" Marlenna said again, not waiting for an answer. "This is where Albert Laurel should be born."

When Marlenna went in the room for her check-up, Brewster sat outside on a concrete bench beside a gray stone statue of a man in a long robe holding a bowl that had been filled with birdseed. He sat away from any of the patients and the nuns with their white-winged heads. He watched a squirrel perched on the side of the bowl, holding a large seed, cracking it in the corner of its mouth. This place had a beauty to it, there was no question about that, but at the end of the asphalt drive, he could hear sounds of Platt's Row—a baby crying and the talk of men sitting near the street, idle on a Friday afternoon. Platt's Row was not unlike Limrick Road. Before sunset the men would pass around a bottle, if it had not already started its rotation. After a while they would stumble home to be mean drunks or passed-out drunks. He knew the story well, because he had seen it repeated and repeated and repeated on Limrick Road. Ole Summit set him apart and would separate his child from idleness, liquor, and afternoon dice. Our Savior's Home was no more than an ordered stronghold in the midst of this chaos, but he would not want to be here at night with the granite building rising like something from another world, and the statues lurking faceless in the dark.

A light breeze moved the May heat, and Brewster let his mind drift to Ole Summit where the nursery was finished. Marlenna had insisted that the room have light, "lots of light," she had said. He put four full-length windows in the room, two on the south, facing the front of the house and two on the east to catch the morning sun. On the outside, he put deep green shutters echoing the windows below them and when he pulled onto the lane, he was pleased that the second story addition more nearly balanced the house against the wide porches that wrapped around the front and the east side.

When he brought home the cradle, a dark oak basket resting on scroll feet with its only decoration being semi-circular rays on both the headboard and the footboard, Marlenna said, "This is perfect. This will be passed down to generations of Laurel's children." She walked around the cradle rubbing her fingers along the rays, and he thought he should have put more time into a piece that would be passed to generations of McAtees.

Marlenna had convinced herself, and Mama Tee too, that Albert Laurel was an inspired name. "The laurel tree is a native of North Africa. Heroes and scholars were crowned with the laurel," she said. "It has sweet bay leaves, flowers, and black berries, something for every season," she told Mama Tee.

Mama Tee crossed her arms over her large breasts. "Umm'huh. God gave you that name. When the right thing pops into your head like that, you know you heard something outside yourself speaking."

Brewster sat, thinking these easy thoughts, until Marlenna came behind him and playfully grabbed his shoulders, making him jump straight up, like a cat surprised by a sudden noise. Marlenna laughed, and the sound blended with those at the end of the asphalt drive.

Marlenna woke him. "Honey, my water broke. I expect we need to go on pretty soon."

The bed was wet beside him. He shot up like cannon fire, opening the drawer for his undershirt and reaching for his socks at the same time. Then he hopped across the floor dangling a dark sock on his raised foot while Marlenna slipped a loose dress over her head.

"Brewster, honey, will you come around and put my shoes on? If I lean over, Albert Laurel will start kicking."

With the water having already broken, Brewster wondered how much time he had before the baby tried to bring itself into the world, but when he knelt in front of Marlenna to slip her shoes on her feet, she was in no hurry. She stroked his hair. "I love you, Brewster. We'll never be exactly like we are now." She said this slowly as if she wanted to think about it, as if they were sitting on the front porch and had a whole evening ahead of them instead of an hour's drive, trying to make it to Our Savior's Home before a small head pushed itself between her legs. He eased his arm under her back, lifting her out of the chair.

The moon was out and the stars visible. Even Travis Peets' blighted property appeared benign in the soft light of an early summer full moon. Low Ridge rested quietly as they pulled through town past Albert Mixon's house, past Limrick Road, past County Training School, and past dense woods.

"I'm a little nervous," Marlenna said, and Brewster reached across the seat, taking her hand.

"Isn't it beautiful tonight? Albert Laurel McAtee will be born when the stars and the moon are out. Born on a clear night."

She thrust her leg hard against the floorboard, drawing a sharp breath, and Brewster accelerated, pushing the speedometer up a full five miles. They entered the row of neat small houses that lined the central street in Calhoun and he slowed, turning off the main street into Platt's Row. The Buick rushed down the narrow streets with lean-tos perched by the road. Three men sat on the grass by the road, drinking beer from squat bottles, and they waved at the Buick as if the time were noon and they were flagging a visitor. When Brewster and Marlenna reached the asphalt lane, Our Savior's Home rose before them, majestic in the moonlight, the white granite sparkling and the lawn illuminated by the full moon. Brewster parked and circled the car to the passenger side. He put his arm around Marlenna, and they walked to the concrete porch and through the double glass doors where a nun sat behind an enormous desk raised two feet in the air on a black marble platform.

"You're here for delivery?" she asked, coming down two steps from the tall desk and rolling a wheel chair toward them. "Sit here," she said in a voice that sounded like silk and didn't fit the plainness of her bulbous face, pressed forward by the tight hood encircling it. She walked back to her desk and placed a telephone call. All her movements were slow, deliberate, not matching the urgency of a baby pushing, insisting on entering the world, not waiting for a sign that all was ready. Marlenna held Brewster's hand, squeezing and releasing it, and squeezing again.

"I've called Sister Francesca," the nun said to Brewster. "I'll take Mrs. McAtee down the hall, then you and I will complete the paper-work."

Brewster bent beside Marlenna, "I'll be beside you as soon as they let me," he whispered and kissed the edge of her ear, which felt hot to his lips.

"Enough of that now," the nun said and pushed the chair down the hall and around the corner.

After Brewster completed the papers, the nun escorted him down the same hall where she had pushed Marlenna. They entered a small waiting room. "We'll let you know when we have ourselves a baby," she said.

A man, a woman, and a teenage girl huddled in the corner of the waiting room where the man sat on a couch, the woman in a chair, and the girl on a hassock. The girl leaned close and spoke in hushed tones with the woman, whose hair was oiled but stood out from her head like feathers on some wild bird. The man acknowledged Brewster's presence with a nod, but the woman and the girl only looked at him. Brewster walked directly to the dark window and stared across the yard where he could see the statues highlighted by moonlight. He thought about taking his baby home to Ole Summit, and how the child would put deeper roots into the place, a second generation on his land.

"Watcha here for?" the man broke the silence in the room with his raspy voice.

"Have a baby," Brewster answered. "My wife is in labor now."

The man wiped the corners of his lips with the side of his hand. "Daughter's here," he said, his mouth turning like he was rotating balls in it and when he moved his lower jaw, his tongue floated in his mouth. "She gon' have a baby too. No daddy," the man said, air coming out of his mouth, flat, but rapid. "This is my wife and my other girl," the man said, and both the mother and daughter glared at Brewster.

"Come on, take a seat. Could be long night." The man slapped the couch seat with his open palm.

"Don't think I can sit," Brewster said.

The man laughed. "You from 'round here?"

"Low Ridge."

"You got a hospital over there. Why you come here?"

"My wife. She wanted the baby to be born here."

"Boy done this to my girl not paying a penny," the man said. "That's why we here." He raised his enormous feet and rested them on the table in front of the sofa, and Brewster saw orange clay packed hard on the soles of his brogans. The man rubbed his hands together, filling his time with movement. "That boy could least come on over here," the man said, turning toward the woman and the girl.

"Don't worry about that now," the woman said, heat and anger in her voice.

"That boy could least come on over here," the man said, defiant. "Won't see him now most likely. He could get hisself a job and give this baby a little something every now and 'gain. Won't do that neither."

The girl looked at Brewster. Her eyes were large, and like her mother, her hair oiled and pinned back, but pieces jutted from her head, stiff and matted, and her tongue, deep pink, came out and circled her lips. Brewster nodded his head, acknowledging the man, then turned back to the window.

"Done told you I'm gon' get another house," the woman said, spitting the words. "I know a woman wants Tuesday and Thursday." The man didn't say a word, but air rushed out of his nose and he threw his hands in the air letting them drop loudly on his thighs.

"You got a baby girl," the nun said when she came in and spoke to the family.

The man clapped his hands. "Didn't want to start raising no boy at my age," he said. "If we got to have another 'en, least it's a girl."

"You can come on back and see the baby," the nun said.

"Guess we might as well," the man said. He walked over to the window and slapped Brewster on the shoulder before he left the room. "Your'n be here soon," he said.

Brewster was sorry he had shared space on this night with this family. He would tend his baby, looking for the favor he knew he would see in his child. He sat on the couch at the opposite end from where the man had sat, not wanting to feel the man's warmth still in the sofa. He leaned his head back on the cushion and dozed.

"Your baby is here," the nun said. A smile fixed on her face. "It's a boy. You can come on back."

Brewster followed the black-robed, white-winged nun down the still hallway, her feet clicking on the tile. Albert Laurel McAtee, wrapped tightly in a blue blanket, slept in a crib close to the viewing window. Brewster's knees almost buckled. He wanted this moment in time frozen long enough for him to do all the right things—call Mama Tee, call Carmella, even call old Albert Mixon, and the moment should remain fixed while he had time to study every detail of the baby behind the glass window, wrapped snugly in his blanket. He watched Albert Laurel's chest move up and down in small regular shifts.

"What's his name?" the nun asked.

But Brewster did not answer for fear of giving himself away. He had never wept in the presence of anyone, and he would not do that here in this strange building with a winged woman watching him. Little Albert Laurel's lower lip trembled, his mouth opened in an almost perfect circle, and he let out a quivering, raw sound, which woke the other two babies, and they joined him.

"It's my son," he said. The word *son* sounded good to him. It felt good coming out of his mouth. "My son," he repeated. "He's the leader of the pack."

"Would you like to see your wife now?" The sister walked with Brewster down the long hallway, and they entered Marlenna's room through a muted-green door. When Marlenna saw him, she raised both of her arms. He lowered his face to her, kissing the warmth of her neck.

"Did you see our son?"

"He's beautiful," Brewster answered with a voice that broke.

"He was born at sunrise," Marlenna said. "Just as the sun rose."

12

Mama Tee came to Ole Summit to care for Albert Laurel, and company came too. Albert Mixon came carrying a large white box with a blue ribbon. "Told the clerk at Gwin's to fill it up with things for a boy," he said when he handed the present to Mama Tee. "Then I said, wrap it all up and I'll come back. I don't know what's in it."

When Marlenna and Mama Tee opened the box, they found a pair of baby shoes, a hat, a white and blue gown, a blanket, and a rattle. Albert Mixon grinned as each item was taken from the box and placed on the kitchen table.

"Hold him, Father," Marlenna said, extending the baby toward him.

"Noooo, no," he shook his head. "I don't know one thing about holding a baby." But when he put his face close to Marlenna's, he clacked his tongue and touched the blanket wrapped around Albert Laurel.

Tom came with Trumpet Eyes Sam. Marlenna was surprised to see them standing in the big room at Ole Summit because Tom had never come to Brewster's land. The two men stood, out of place in the big room, with their thin cotton shirts loose around their hips and their khaki pants baggy in the knees and long at the ankles. They brought an undershirt for the baby, rolled in a brown paper bag, twisted at the neck. Tom extended his right arm with the bag held in his fist.

"The baby needs this undershirt," Marlenna told them.

Tom smiled, exposing a gaping space to the right side of his two front teeth, and his eyes, more pink than white, watered. When they leaned forward to see the baby, Albert Laurel wailed, his mouth round, his lips trembling. The men laughed, covering their lips so their breath did not touch Albert Laurel McAtee. Before they left, Mama Tee fed them, seated at the kitchen table.

"You should have gotten them out of here," Brewster said to Marlenna. "Lucky I wasn't home. I don't want Tom on this property."

"Mama Tee wanted them to eat, Brewster. A baby brings people together. They came with the right spirit."

"Sweet Jesus!" Brewster hissed.

Carmella came with Little Eddie. "I've left Big Ed," she said. "He doesn't know it yet, but I'm gone. That man was mean when he got mad. Ran off with one of his singers. I'll have my divorce if he doesn't come back for six months." Carmella laughed. "Thinks he left me, but I left him, and he doesn't know where to find me." She sang the last words.

"I've been thinking of coming home," she said. "Setting me up a studio. Teaching voice. Got to stay in Raleigh until I get that divorce. I want to be rid of Ed."

She sang to the baby, soft and low, resting his head against her breasts, *Lo lea lo, baby. Lo lea lo. Rest your head, baby. Rest your head and sleep.* She sang for Marlenna and she sang on the porch at night, the sound levitating at the edge of the woods. When she left to return to Raleigh, Marlenna wept.

Church folks came, bringing food and eating at the kitchen table with Mama Tee. On a Sunday afternoon, Deak Armbrecht arrived, wearing a white shirt and a baggy gray suit. He held his hat in his hand, and he ate coconut cake while he sat on the porch and commented on how Brewster's workshop fitted into the place with the plants snug around it. His wife, Gretta, had cancer, and the weight of that bore down heavy on his shoulders, causing him to drag his left foot when he walked.

Laurel turned six months old on December 2, and everyone had settled into a comfortable schedule with Marlenna back to her teaching and Mama Tee established at Ole Summit. In the Three Brothers shed, an accountant named Harry Dunn began assessing the value of Three Brothers so Brewster would have a figure to take to the bank when he sought a loan.

"We got to get Skinner trained," Deak said. "You gonna need t'at boy. When I sell t'is place I may go off to ta islands." He did not specify any particular island and Brewster took his words as idle chatter. Deak did establish Skinner at a workbench, and both he and Brewster began to train him. The shed had never been so lively because, unlike Deak and Brewster, Skinner did not like the feel of silence.

"Real name's William," he said, "but my old man would shoot something and send me out to skin it. Must have been six when I skinned my first squirrel. Vomited all over that thing and he made me skin it, vomit and all. After that he gave me everything there was to

155

skin and dress. Didn' call me by my name, just yelled, 'Skinner,' and I'd come running." Despite Skinner's talk, he was learning to use the lathe, and Brewster planned to start him in the finishing room.

Before Christmas, Harry Dunn brought Deak a final report containing a list of all the assets of Three Brothers, the shed, the equipment, the inventory, the jobs already on the books. "T'is what you need take to t'at bank," Deak said when he gave Brewster a copy of the accountant's report.

Brewster took the papers home and reviewed them with Marlenna. Deak had put a fair value on everything. On several items, Deak had struck through the appraisal and had hand-written his own estimate—in every case, lower than Harry Dunn's.

While he worked on the bank forms at the kitchen table, Marlenna kissed him on the side of his face. "I'm proud of you."

"We don't have the money for Three Brothers," he reminded her, "and we may not be able to get a loan."

"You have a record, a solid record. You've never missed a note on this land," and she rubbed his shoulders with her thumbs pressing circles against his muscles.

When he took the forms to the bank, he left them with a loan officer, who looked like he should be in high school, not in the bank making decisions about whether or not a man could own a business. "Jimmy Jackson," he said when he introduced himself. "We'll be back with you," he said when Brewster gave him the papers and left.

For a solid month, Brewster did not hear one word from Jimmy Jackson. At Ole Summit, he sorted the mail everyday looking for a bank envelope. He watched the double-doors at the shed to see if Jimmy Jackson would walk down the block and tell him personally about the loan. When the telephone rang and Deak answered it, Brewster listened to see if the message was from Jimmy Jackson. At night he thought about what would happen if he could not secure a loan and if someone else bought Three Brothers—where would he go and what would he do? He would go from being a man with a job and land, to being a man totally dependent on his wife's labor and on whatever he could earn from his sixty acres.

Halfway into the second month, Brewster walked down State Street to the bank and waited to speak with Jimmy Jackson about his loan. "I have your file here," Jimmy said. "We've studied it carefully. You need more insurance. Mr. Armbrecht doesn't have nearly the insurance on that place that he needs. Get more insurance and come back. I'll keep your file active," he said.

Brewster wondered why the man had not called to tell him this or had not sent him a letter, but getting insurance was an easy hurdle to jump if that was all it took.

When the insurance policy was written, Brewster returned to the Bank of Low Ridge. "You need more collateral," Jimmy Jackson said.

"The assets of Three Brothers serve as their own collateral," Brewster said.

"Don't work that way," Jimmy Jackson said. With the knuckles of his right hand, Jimmy rubbed his pale chin and Brewster could not see even a hint of whiskers there. "The assets of Three Brothers would cover some of the loan, but what would happen if you didn't get work? We'd have to have us a liquidation sale and that kind of thing never generates all of the loan value. You got some property out Ole Summit Highway, and we gonna need that as collateral to underscore this loan." He gave Brewster some more forms.

"T'is not right," Deak said and shook his head. "We got plenty work. I go t'ere tomorrow. We get t'is mess right."

Brewster did not want to use Ole Summit as collateral. Not that he thought Three Brothers would fail, but his acres were what separated him, set him apart from Limrick Road, and the rest of Low Ridge too, for that matter. He wanted to add land to his holdings, and he didn't want to take even the slightest chance of losing Ole Summit.

"Don't worry. That young man at the bank is showing himself. Let Deak Armbrecht handle him." Marlenna rubbed the back of Brewster's shoulders, and he thought she must be right.

But the next day, Deak returned to the shed with certainty that the bank would not approve the loan without Ole Summit as collateral. "T'ey got to have t'at place as backup," Deak said.

Brewster resigned himself to listing Ole Summit as collateral. He assured himself he was strong and Three Brothers had plenty of work. He had leased twenty acres to a farmer who lived near Bulah, and that money would come in next summer. Everything would be fine. He had to do whatever was required to own Three Brothers. Brewster completed the papers listing Ole Summit as collateral and left them on Jimmy Jackson's desk the next morning. This put a dark cloud at the back of his head, but Marlenna was brooding about other matters. Through Matthew and the Low Ridge Association, she had information about what was happening in Nashville where college students had decided to desegregate the downtown.

One NAACP member in Nashville had telephoned another, who had called another, and another, and prayer requests had crossed the state line and had come down into Alabama, traveling all the way to Limrick Road Baptist where twenty or thirty people gathered to get a report and to pray for the young people who sat down at the Woolworth lunch counter and refused to leave unless they were served.

"Take Laurel on home," Marlenna whispered to Brewster when he entered Limrick Road Baptist after work. "Mama Tee and I are going to stay a little longer."

Matthew James paced in front of the first pews. "Our young folks occupied every seat at the diner, and a group of white hoodlums came into the restaurant, started beating them, and putting lighted cigarettes down their backs. The last word I received is that the police arrested the young folks at the counter."

"Did they arrest the white ones that's doing this?" Mama Tee asked.

"No," Matthew said. "Not that I have heard."

"Lord, take care of those children," Mama Tee said, her voice pleading.

"Lord don't, we will," one man said.

"No," Matthew said. "That's not the way."

Brewster took Laurel from Marlenna, and the baby twisted and squirmed in his father's arms. "You come on before long," Brewster whispered to Marlenna. "I don't like you driving out to Ole Summit after dark, especially not with all this going on."

He had warned her about Travis Peets, but Peets kept to himself and even Brewster had decided that he was a pitiful old man, poor and ignorant, who was more a nuisance than an actual threat, and Brewster thought the sheriff continued to ride close rein on him. But on Friday and Saturday afternoons there were cars parked on Ole Summit Highway and on the hard-packed dirt that came up to Peets' ramshackle house. Slim Tate had told Matthew he suspected Peets was hosting cock fighting in the woods and he would investigate when he had the time, but the time had not come. Brewster knew the cars would be there when he drove home this evening.

"You come on now, soon," he whispered.

Marlenna nodded her head and motioned for him to take Laurel out of the church. The baby had twisted around in his father's arms and had managed to grab a hymnal with his balled fist.

"I won't be long," Marlenna whispered.

Brewster left the church quickly because Laurel let out a screech when his father put the hymnal back in its rack, and his loud lament echoed through the sanctuary.

While Brewster did not want Marlenna and Mama Tee to be on the highway after dark, he was content to leave the women in prayer for the young people in Nashville. He followed the stories in the newspaper and he listened to Marlenna when she told him what was happening, but he could not involve himself beyond that point because he had plenty to occupy him in the Three Brothers shed without taking on anymore problems.

At Ole Summit, he fed Laurel, gave him a bath, and put him down for the night. Then he put on his heavy jacket and stood on the front porch watching for Marlenna and Mama Tee. It was nine o'clock, and later than Brewster thought they should be out, but Marlenna was a woman who heeded her own advice. She would drive home when she got ready, and not one minute before.

When the cold air drove him inside, he hung his coat on the rack, put another log on the fire, and sat on the couch in the big room, waiting for the sound of Marlenna's Chevrolet to echo on the lane. He leaned his head against the back of the couch and closed his eyes, and when he woke, he looked at his watch. Eleven o'clock. He rubbed his fist over his eyes, reading the hands of his watch again. He went into the kitchen, turned on the lamp above the stove and put his watch under the light. Eleven o'clock. Had they come in and not awakened him? He went up the stairs, looked in his own room, and then looked in Laurel's room where Mama Tee slept. He bounded down the stairs, put his jacket on and went outside, walking nearly the full length of the lane, his heart pounding. *Keep balanced*, he said to himself—*don't tilt this way or that. It would be foolish to get worked up for no reason.* He walked back to the house to telephone Matthew.

"Meeting's been over since a little before nine. They left after the meeting. I know, because I spoke with Marlenna before she pulled away from the curb."

"I'll call the Sheriff."

"Don't do that yet. I'll tell you what we'll do," Matthew said. "You leave from there headed back to Low Ridge and I'll leave from here headed out Ole Summit. We'll meet midway. We'll find them. Maybe they had a little car trouble, or maybe Marlenna and Mama Tee stopped by one of the ladies' houses. You know how women are about that. I'm going on out to the car now."

Brewster knew Marlenna had not stopped anywhere and he knew Matthew knew this too. He went up the stairs two at a time, wrapped Laurel in a blanket, and walked down the stairs slowly, not wanting to wake the baby. He placed Laurel on the front seat of the car, still sleeping. Brewster's head turned left and then right, studying both sides of the lane before he pulled out onto Ole Summit Highway where he cruised slowly, looking at the sides of the road and into the edges of thick woods, There were no cars in front of Travis Peets' place. There were no gullies, no ravines along Ole Summit where a car could have run off the road. The land was flat and the woods thick, growing almost onto the highway. He didn't encounter another car until he met Matthew's old battered Cadillac about midway back to Low Ridge. They pulled to the edge of the road, and Matthew walked to Brewster's Buick.

"No sign of her?" Brewster asked.

"No sign coming this way. Let's go on back to your place. If she's not there, we'll call the Sheriff. Soon as the sun comes up, I'll call some members of the church and we'll search these woods round 'bout here."

Laurel screamed in a piercing howl, ripping through the darkness, making Brewster's heart pound harder and causing Matthew to jump backwards with his hand cutting a clean line to his heart. "I forgot you had that baby," he said, gulping air.

Brewster stretched across the seat and patted the blanket that was over Laurel. The baby put his thumb in his mouth, sucking loudly.

"I'll follow you on back home."

Brewster drove to Ole Summit, leaning forward against the steering wheel, straining to see deeply into the woods, and listening to the sounds Laurel made, drawing hard against his thumb. He pulled his Buick almost to the house before he saw Marlenna's Chevrolet, and parked beside it was another car.

Marlenna came out of the house with her arms out in front of her. "We just got here. We drove all the way to Bulah because two men were following us."

"That wasn't the half of it!" Mama Tee shouted from the porch. "They was right beside us, and we couldn't even see this lane let alone turn onto it."

A tall elderly Negro man came down the steps, extending his hand. "This is Reverend Singleton," Marlenna said.

"Thank God for Reverend Singleton!" Mama Tee said from the porch.

"He followed me back home tonight," Marlenna said. "I was afraid to come on by myself."

160

They went inside and gathered around the table. "We were nearly home when a car came racing up behind me. I didn't see the car in my rearview mirror, but suddenly it was there. I thought, was that car coming fast and it caught up with me? Then I thought the car must have been parked along the road or in the woods and we hadn't seen it. Maybe it was behind me all the way from Low Ridge and didn't have any lights on. That car came from nowhere and was almost on my bumper. The driver turned his lights on bright, blinding me every time I looked into the rearview mirror."

"They was so close, I thought they was gon' ram right into us," Mama Tee said.

"I speeded up to nearly 60, but that car stayed on my bumper. I slowed some and the car slowed. I knew I had to go on to Bulah," Marlenna said, "I couldn't turn around."

"Mighty fortunate they come and got me," Clifton Singleton said. "Then again, I guess we mighty fortunate we made it back here."

"About halfway between here and Bulah, that car pulled around me and I saw two men in the front. They pulled around me and slowed down. Then I didn't know what I was going to do, because if that car stopped in front of me, there was no place to turn. One car did pass on the other side of the road, going toward Low Ridge, and I tooted the horn, but the driver didn't slow down, and the other car stayed in front of us creeping along for miles." Marlenna shuddered, and Brewster put his arm around her.

"'Lord,' I said, 'You got to take care of us because we can't do it now,'" Mama Tee said.

"After a while the other car speeded up and I thought they were gone, but they pulled off the road ahead of us and got behind us again and stayed there. Okay, I said to myself, I'm going to fight. I'm going to crash our car into somebody's bedroom if I have to. I put my foot on the gas pedal and didn't take it off. That car stayed behind me all the way into Bulah."

"I learned something tonight. If I'm ever in trouble, I want to be with this girl," Mama Tee said and took Marlenna's hand.

"When I reached Bulah, the traffic light was yellow," Marlenna said, "and I ran through it and looked in my mirror to see if the men would stop for the red light. They didn't, but they were a little ways behind me. Half a mile and I would be outside Bulah. I was looking left and right, searching for any kind of place that offered some safety. Then I saw a small church down a long drive with a parsonage beside it. I swung the steering wheel a sharp right and bounced down the drive, leaning on my horn with my lights shining directly into the parsonage."

"That's when you came into the picture?" Brewster said, pointing at Clifton Singleton.

"Nope," the reverend said. "That was a white preacher who had the good sense to bring these two to me."

"That preacher came out carrying a gun. 'What's going on here?' he shouted at us. 'What do you think you're doing?' By this time, the car had turned into the driveway, but stopped out by the road. I pointed at the car. 'Two men there, they followed us from Low Ridge. I came on to Bulah for help. May I come in and call my husband?'" Marlenna bit her lip. "'You better go on,' he said. 'Look there, that car's going on. You go on too.'"

"'Please, may I call my husband?' That man told me no." Marlenna rubbed her forehead with the pads of her fingers. "I was afraid to get back on the road. I thought for a moment and then I knew what to ask." Marlenna raised her index finger in the air. "Can you show me to a Negro church?"

"He got in his car and drove ahead of us to Reverend Singleton's church. He stopped at the curve, just long enough for us to know that was the preacher's house and by the time we opened our car doors, he was gone."

"Thank God, Reverend Singleton let us in," Mama Tee said.

"I called here, but didn't get an answer," Marlenna said. "Reverend Singleton followed us back to Ole Summit and we waited for you. I knew you were out looking."

"Not safe to be out after dark right now," Reverend Singleton said. "We should be sure everybody knows about this before night falls again."

Matthew James spread the word up and down Limrick Road and onto the side streets off Limrick. And the word filtered through Bulah, one mouth at a time. Brewster was convinced the car came from Travis Peets' place, and he kept a loaded gun on the top shelf of the closet. At night he drifted into shallow sleep, got up and walked through the house while everyone else slept. He looked out the kitchen window into the woods, but saw only darkness.

"Martin King has been sentenced to four months on a Georgia road gang for sitting down at a lunch counter in Atlanta," Marlenna told Brewster when he came in the door at Ole Summit. Marlenna sat on the sofa watching the six o'clock news with Laurel asleep in her lap. Mama Tee stood behind her with a spatula and a hot pad in her hand. "I can't believe it," Marlenna said. "This is 1960 in the United States of America." She rubbed Laurel's forehead with her slender fingers.

"Jail, no bail, that's what they're saying," Mama Tee said. "And I wish I was young enough to be with them. If I was fifty years younger, I'd go straight on to Nashville or Atlanta. Jail, no bail, I'd say, and they could haul me off. Maybe I'd be in jail with somebody important. Wonder which one of those cities Anvil's in?" Mama Tee asked. "Nashville or Atlanta? You think we'll ever get a group to integrate the Low Ridge Diner?"

"We're probably too small," Marlenna said. "But what happens in the big places will happen here eventually, I guess."

"That word *eventually* sounds like forever and forever," Mama Tee said, and her chenille slippers made a scraping sound as she went to the stove to serve supper.

Brewster got the call from Jimmy Jackson on the first day of February. "Come on up here. We got this loan ready. Guess you just bought yourself a business." When Brewster went to the bank to sign the loan papers, he felt the excitement of being a Low Ridge businessman, owner of a storefront on State Street, even if Ole Summit was collateral.

He went to County Training School and waited outside Marlenna's classroom for the bell to ring. She leaned over her desk, scoring papers, and did not see him come in, so he eased behind her and lifted her off the floor. "We own ourselves a business," he said, whispering in her ear. "Three Brothers, manufacturers of the finest handmade furniture in Alabama."

When he put her down, Marlenna turned toward him. "Sweet times," she said. "These are sweet times."

13

His wife Gretta died the same week Deak signed the papers making Brewster the owner of Three Brothers. Deak's son came from Kansas, staying for a few days and caring for his father. Before he left, he established Evangeline as the woman in charge of the house and of the old man. But prodding and encouraging in every way that she knew, Evangeline could not draw Deak from his bedroom where he sat in his recliner with the drapes drawn. Brewster went into the kitchen of Deak's house every morning to get a report.

"Eats a mouthful of this and a mouthful of that and pushes the food away. Says he don't want no more. Sits there in that chair all day, sleepin'. When he opens those old eyes, they all red and watery. You go on up and see what you can do. I can't do a thing with that man," Evangeline said.

Brewster tapped on the door, and when he heard Deak lower the footrest of his recliner, he went into the room, even though he was not bidden to do so. With the bedroom dark, it took some moments for Brewster's eyes to adjust. When they did, he saw Deak sitting in his chair, a red plaid blanket across his lap. Brewster sat on the edge of the bed facing the old man, who opened his eyes, but did not move. Deak's matted hair rested flat against the right side of his scalp, his glasses were on the table beside the chair, and his eyes, weepy and dull, appeared vulnerable, with the skin sagging in folds beneath them. A musty odor filled the room—the scent of sickness and weariness and soiled clothes and unwashed flesh, and the smell made Brewster want to grab Deak and run for sunlight. When he was able to put enough of the stale air into his lungs to speak, he was direct.

"You need to come on out to the shed. We need you there and sitting in here is not going to do you, nor us either, one bit of good."

When Deak opened his mouth, it too looked matted and rimmed with a white powder. "Not going back out t'ere. T'at place belongs to you," he said and pulled the blanket halfway up his chest.

Brewster locked eyes with Deak. "We need you in the shed. You still got a few things to show all of us before you call it quits."

When Deak set his jaw in defiance, turned his head, and lowered his eyes, Brewster surprised himself by reaching across the man's lap and putting his hand on top of the pale hands that held the blanket in knotted knuckles. "We miss you. The place's not the same without you at your workbench, and I got my plate more than full trying to train Skinner. I sure could use you."

Deak brought his eyes back around, and Brewster kept his own hand over Deak's thin, cool hands that held tightly to the red plaid blanket. Deak's head shook a slow affirmation. "I come back for little while," he said with the white powder wet and stringing between his lips.

Brewster patted Deak's hand. "We'll see you tomorrow," he said. "Tomorrow morning," and he left quickly before Deak had time for rejoinder.

"Going to be a man what not work by t'at clock," Deak Armbrecht said when he came into the shed midmorning of the next day. "T'is man not going to look at t'at clock." And true to his word, Deak napped at noon and sat on his bench in the middle of the double doors whenever he chose.

Brewster rose refreshed in the mornings, ready to come to his business, and he stayed after everyone had gone home, walking the length and breadth of his holdings. He rubbed his hands over the furniture in the showroom, and in the shed he walked past every workbench, feeling pride in his ownership. He stood in the middle of the shed and closed his eyes, smelling the fragrance of raw wood. Three Brothers was everything a man could ask for, satisfying work and plenty of it, and he, the master of his own shop. He held Three Brothers and Ole Summit; he held them and they held him. They could sustain him and his family for generations. He had come from nothing and he had acquired all that he held by his own work. He had every right to feel pride.

"Don't get proud," he said out loud. He grinned and breathed deeply, filling his lungs with the spice of his wood. He had a presence on State Street that remained visible twenty-four hours a day.

After sending Skinner out to make a delivery, both Brewster and Deak were pleased to have the place quiet for a while, and Deak took the newspaper, settling himself in the breeze between the double doors. "What man you going to vote for in t'is special election?" Deak asked when Brewster walked past the doors.

"Don't vote," Brewster said. "Never have."

Deak put his hands on his bony hips and studied Brewster. "You need to vote," he said. "T'at is ta American way."

"Can't get registered," Brewster said and walked to his work-bench.

Deak climbed off his stool and went to where Brewster worked. He leaned his hand against the edge of the wooden shelf. "One of ta boys what registers ta voters, he teaches ta Sunday school. You go t'ere with me. I tell him you want ta vote in t'is election." Deak turned to walk away as if the issue were settled. "We do t'at tomorrow," he said over his shoulder.

As far as Brewster knew, the only Negro who voted in Low Ridge was Herman Thomas, and he voted because he was better educated than most whites in Low Ridge, because he came from New York City, because he was light-skinned, and because he was the principal of the Negro high school. County records needed to show at least one colored voter and Herman Thomas filled that spot. Matthew's Low Ridge Association was organizing some voter registration, but they anticipated considerable resistance. Brewster knew this from Marlenna, who planned to go to the courthouse with Matthew's group. But if Deak's Sunday school teacher worked in the registrar's office, and if Deak stood with him, surely he could register, and then there would be two Negroes on the Low Ridge voter roster. He liked the thought of voting. It was the kind of activity a businessman should do.

"Deak wants me to get registered to vote," he told Marlenna when they sat at the supper table.

"We're making a list of people who want to go to the registrar next week. I'll add your name to the list."

"Deak says he knows one of the registrars. It's his Sunday school teacher, and he'll go with me tomorrow."

Marlenna clapped her hands. "Wait. Let me get this straight. Deak knows the registrar and he's willing to go with you?"

"That's what he says."

"This could be the open door. I'll call Matthew and tell him."

"Wait a minute," Brewster said, and he had the uneasy sense of losing control. "I'm not sure this is what I need to be doing. I'm thinking about it."

Marlenna rose to clear the dishes from the table and remained quiet while she washed them at the sink. Brewster knew what Marlenna wanted, but he had a family to consider and a business to build and good relations to maintain on State Street. But, on the other hand, if Deak was willing to go with him. . . . "You think I should do this?" he asked when he took a dish towel from the drawer and began drying a plate.

"I do. This is the first time we've had any white person willing to go with us. In fact, I want to go with you and get myself registered before next week."

He was quiet while he dried the dishes and put them into the cabinets. Why shouldn't he vote? He paid for a business license and had his shop on the main street in town. He read the paper and knew what was happening. He should vote. There wasn't even a question about that. He settled the issue with himself, and before they went to bed, Marlenna laid out her clothes for the next day, not her usual white blouse and dark skirt, but a navy-blue suit. "It's going to be a special day and I want to remember every detail, even what I was wearing," she said, and Brewster was glad he had made his decision.

When Marlenna entered the shed, Brewster was in good spirits because he had a well-respected backer going to the courthouse with him, and in a short while he would hold a new title, registered voter. When Deak came out the back door of his house, wearing his white shirt, baggy wool pants, and carrying his gray felt hat, the three walked to the courthouse.

"Howdy do," Deak Armbrecht said and extended his hand to Blake Sanders, who was much younger than Brewster had imagined. He had reddish-blond hair, blue eyes, and clear, white skin. He wore a short-sleeved shirt with a dark tie. Sanders rose from his desk, a wide grin on his face, and he extended his hand to Deak, clasping his left hand on Deak's shoulder.

"What brings you here, Mr. Armbrecht?"

"T'is is Mr. Brewster McAtee and his wife Missus Marlenna. Mr. Brewster is ta owner of T'ree Brothers now. T'ey are here to get registered for ta voting."

Brewster noticed pink rising from Blake Sanders' collar, creeping up his cheeks. "I'll have to check a couple of things," he said. He dropped into his seat and began to shuffle papers on his desk. "I need to check the deadline," he said. "We may be past the deadline for voter registration."

"No, we're not," Marlenna said. "We've got another week according to yesterday's newspaper."

"Okay. Just sit over there. I've got to get the papers that we need." The pink color had turned to a red and had advanced all the way to Blake Sanders' forehead. Brewster sat with Marlenna and

Deak in a row of chairs against the wall, and Blake Sanders went into a side room.

"I wonder what he's going to do now?" Marlenna whispered.

"He's got something up his sleeve," Brewster answered under his breath, but he felt some satisfaction that Deak was still confident in the procedure. Deak had picked up a magazine on the table in front of him and was thumbing through it. When Blake Sanders returned, he handed Brewster and Marlenna a set of papers.

"I'll take you to a side room," Sanders said. "These are tests you'll have to pass to register."

Deak took the papers from Marlenna's hand. "Let me see t'is," he said. He lowered his chin, dropped his glasses to the tip of his nose, and read the first page with his eyes focused above his glasses. "I did not take t'is test for ta voting," he said, in a mutter, speaking and reading at the same time.

"It's new policy," Blake Sanders said, his face looking like he had some awful affliction.

Brewster looked at some of the questions on the test. Who was the tenth president of the United States? What is the sixth Amendment to the U.S. Constitution? Who was president during the Spanish-American War?

Deak held Marlenna's test, and while he continued to question Blake Sanders about it, a thin, wiry, white man came in wearing overalls over a faded blue shirt, and sporting a Reese-Feed cap, set at an angle on his head.

"I'm here to register," the man said when Blake Sanders turned his head toward him.

"This is not a good time." Blake Sanders said. "You need to come back tomorrow."

"Hell!" the man said. "That's not what the newspaper said. Newspaper said I could come in here anytime from ten in the morning until three in the afternoon. The time's one-thirty. I intend to get registered and I don't have time to waste neither."

"T'is test gonna take all afternoon," Deak said, turning to the man.

"Test?" the man said. "What test? Newspaper didn't have one word about no test."

The red on Blake Sanders face had pooled into little uneven blobs, raised and welt-like. "It's a new policy, a voter test," he stammered.

"Hell," the man said. "I ain't gonna take no test. Newspaper did not say one word about no test."

"I need to speak with my supervisor," Blake Sanders said. He walked to a side room, looked back at the would-be voters before he closed the door behind him.

Brewster read more questions: Who was James Madison's vice president? In what year did the United States enter the First World War? Who is the current attorney general for the state of Alabama? Name three members of the State Board of Education. How many counties are there in Alabama? Who was the state's first governor?

Brewster knew that he could answer some of the questions, but he didn't know if he could answer enough to pass the test, and he wondered if he and Marlenna should leave before they engaged in this humiliating process. If they took the test and failed it, Blake Sanders could say that he tried to register them, but they failed the voter test, and they were not qualified for full citizenship.

In a few minutes, Sanders emerged from the side room with a middle-aged man in a light blue shirt with his long sleeves rolled up to his elbows. "Jim Stevenson. I'm Blake's supervisor," he said, extending his hand first to Deak, then to the man in the overalls, and finally to Brewster. He nodded toward Marlenna. "There's been some confusion here," he said, looking at Blake. "The voting commission has been considering giving a test for voter registration, but it hasn't been approved. We failed to tell Blake here that the test wasn't approved yet."

"T'at mean my friends not have to take t'is test?"

"That's right," Jim Stevenson said. He stepped back to Blake Sanders' desk, picking up a stack of short cards. He shuffled three off the top. "Sit down at that table over there and fill out these cards." He dealt one to the man in the overalls, one to Marlenna, and one to Brewster. Within the span of only several minutes, Brewster and Marlenna became the second and third black citizens of Low Ridge, Alabama to be registered voters.

Deak, Brewster, and Marlenna walked calmly back to the shed, but once they were inside the doors, Marlenna grabbed Deak, nearly lifting him from the floor. "Thank you," she said.

Deak grinned. "We caught t'at rat and we tossed him by ta tail," he said. "I can't believe t'at boy would go along with such as t'at. I know his mama and I know his papa. T'at boy should be ashamed of what he is doing. I gonna sit on ta front row at t'at class on Sunday, and he will turn red all over again."

There was celebration at Ole Summit on Sunday with food in abundance. Matthew was there and Deak came for a short while.

Some of the twenty who planned to go to the courthouse on Tuesday stopped by to eat and sit on the front porch, visiting about the positive changes they saw coming to Low Ridge. Mama Tee was proud and let everyone know it. "I've 'bout decided Brewster McAtee can do anything," she said. And Brewster avoided being near her because she was impossible to control and it was embarrassing to hear her brag.

The *Low Ridge Gazette* wanted to run an article about Brewster and Marlenna registering to vote. Brewster was reluctant. "Do it," Matthew said. "When the other black folks see that you went in there and got registered, they're not going to be scared. When the white folks see that the colored folks who are registering have got something to contribute to this community, they won't be scared either," he said.

The reporter came out to Ole Summit on Tuesday, the same afternoon twenty other Negroes attempted to register. On Wednesday, the front page of the *Low Ridge Gazette* covered the story with pictures of the twenty black citizens at the courthouse, and in the center of the page was a large picture of Brewster and Marlenna with an article about their registration the week before. The reporter made much of the fact that Brewster and Marlenna were only the second and third Negro voters in Low Ridge and that Brewster was the new owner of Three Brothers, one of the most prominent storefronts on State Street. The reporter also interviewed Deak Armbrecht, who spoke of his pride in having been with these two fine citizens when they registered.

Only five of the twenty Negroes who waited at the courthouse were allowed to register. The registrar found some technicality with the applications of the other fifteen. Marlenna gave Brewster a full report. "'You're not playing fair,' Jim Stevenson told Matthew. 'You should bring only one person at a time. We can't handle a crowd like this.' 'We're willing to wait,' Matthew told him. 'We don't want to rush you.' 'Well,' Jim Stevenson told him. 'You bring one person at a time and we may get that man or woman registered. Don't you come in here with twenty ever again.'"

Marlenna paused for breath and took Brewster's hand. "But Brewster, they may not be able to register voters fast, but they sure could turn us down fast. They had all twenty of us in and out within an hour."

On Sunday when Marlenna and Matthew stood by the doors of Limrick Road Baptist and talked after the church service, Matthew spoke of his disappointment in the progress of voter registration in Low Ridge. "We haven't come as far as I thought we had."

"Yes, we have," Marlenna countered him. "Two weeks ago we had only one black voter in Low Ridge, and now we have eight. That's an eight hundred percent increase in less than two weeks."

Matthew's laugh came from his chest and circled his face. "That's right," he said. "That's exactly right."

The following week, attention turned from voter registration to the Freedom Riders trying to make their way down the length of Alabama and over to New Orleans. At noon Brewster sat in the middle of the double doors reading about the thirteen riders on the Greyhound bus, and in the evenings, Marlenna and Mama Tee followed the story by watching Walter Cronkite on television in the big room at Ole Summit. The trip stalled in Anniston when the Greyhound was bombed, but there was a miracle—no one was killed.

"We done seen a sign," Mama Tee said. "It's a marvel those riders got out of that bus alive. That whole thing was on fire."

Newspaper pictures of the bombed bus sent little spikes popping up under Brewster's skin. Students, black and white, their heads held in their hands, sat on a grassy berm with the bus in the background, smoke billowing from the opened door. The riders hoped to be in New Orleans by the weekend for a rally there. The bus would pass only thirty miles to the west of Low Ridge, and some of the members at Limrick Road Baptist wanted to go to the highway to watch it, but Matthew spoke against this, arguing that the smaller the crowds, the better, and that prayer was more important than witnessing the bus. Brewster felt agitation in his stomach when he read about the abuse the riders withstood in Birmingham, and he knew he made the right decision when he registered to vote.

"This world may end right here in nineteen-hundred and sixty-one," Mama Tee said. "Calamities come in the last days. These are calamitous times," she insisted.

Even Laurel, usually in constant motion, sat stock-still with his nose almost touching the TV screen. He studied the pictures of the bus with black clouds pouring out the front door, and he went with Mama Tee and Marlenna when they prayed at Limrick Road Baptist.

Travis Peets added a Confederate Battle flag to his house, draping it across the rail of his front porch and allowing it to flap down, with its lower edge almost in the dirt. This amused Brewster more than angered him. "That man is so lazy," he told Marlenna, "he doesn't hang that damn flag, he throws it over the porch."

"He's speaking with that flag, Brewster, and I hate driving past it. You need to talk to Slim Tate again about buying him out."

"We don't have the cash for what he's asking," Brewster said.

"When the money comes in on that land you leased, see what you can do then."

"It'll take a while. We got two mortgages—one on this place and one on Three Brothers. We are mortgage poor."

It woke him from solid sleep, but he could not tell what it was. He sat up in bed, trying to clear his head.

"It's the phone. Brewster, THE PHONE, answer it," Marlenna said. "ANSWER IT." She reached across him trying to get to the telephone.

Brewster managed to put the speaker to his ear, but before he could say a word, a thick voice said slowly.

"You're b-u-r-n-i-n-g. Can you feel it? You're b-u-r-n-i-n-g, nigger."

"What? WHAT?"

The man's voice said the same words again, slowly and clearly, deep and resonant. "You're b-u-r-n-i-n-g. Can you feel it? You're b-u-r-n-i-n-g, nigger." Then there was a click.

Awake now, he rushed to the window, looking toward the lane. Was Ole Summit on fire? The house? The woods? He ran downstairs, smelling the air. He shouted the message to Marlenna, behind him on the steps. He glanced into the rooms downstairs and went out on the porch, looking down the lane. The phone rang again, and Brewster bounded to the kitchen.

"What? What? I'll be there," he said. "I'll be right there."

"Deak," he shouted at Marlenna. "Three Brothers is on fire."

"I'm going too."

"No, stay here with Laurel and Mama Tee."

"We need to be together." In the bedroom, she threw a dress over her head and bent to slip her shoes over the heels of her feet. Mama Tee came to the door.

"Three Brothers is on fire," Brewster said in Mama Tee's direction, and she fell backwards, her shoulders hitting the doorframe.

"Sweet Jesus!" she said. "Sweet Jesus!"

"Call Matthew and let him know. Tell him you and Laurel are here alone," Brewster said. "There's a shotgun, loaded in the closet here." Brewster and Marlenna took the steps two at a time, headed toward the car.

He had never imagined flames like these—orange tongues leaping from the Three Brothers shed. The showroom had been consumed and now smoldered, red hot. Searing flames shot from the roof of the shed, while firemen sprayed them. A crowd had gathered and Brewster saw Deak, his hands in his pockets, his thin shoulders sagging, standing in the middle of the street, watching the fire consume Three Brothers.

"Won't be one t'ing left," Deak said when Brewster stood beside him. "Not one t'ing." Deak wiped his cheeks and his forehead with the back of his hand. The west wall collapsed and flames thrust out the side windows, lapping past the roof.

The firemen doused Deak's house, which had not caught fire because they had kept a wall of water between the shed and the house and rotated between wetting the house and fighting the blaze. Brewster felt heat on his face and on his chest.

"We not leave one t'ing on," Deak muttered. "I check. I get up in ta night and go check on ta shed. We not leave one t'ing on," he repeated.

When the fire had consumed all of Three Brothers, folks headed back to their houses. The fire chief came to where Brewster and Deak stood. "You own this place?" the chief asked, looking at Brewster. "We got it fully contained, nothing left though."

The chief put his arm around Deak Armbrecht, frail and dazed. "Mr. Armbrecht, go get a cup of coffee and close your eyes for a few minutes, if you can. We're going to begin our investigation as soon as everything cools down. I'm going to walk you on home," he said and nudged Deak in the direction of his house.

"I'll be on over soon," Brewster said. "I'm going to walk Marlenna to her father's."

Deak looked up at Brewster, shook his head, and toddled off with the fire chief's arm still around his bony shoulders.

Matthew and Albert Mixon stood beside Marlenna. When Brewster approached them, Albert Mixon reached out his hand and patted Brewster's back. No words were exchanged, but the gesture on the part of his father-in-law was not lost on Brewster.

"I need to speak with you, Matthew," Brewster said. "I'm going to walk with Marlenna to her father's and call Mama Tee, then I'll come on to the parsonage."

14

In the kitchen at the parsonage, Matthew poured Brewster a cup of strong, black coffee. "Tell me again, what did he say?"

"You're burning. Can you feel it? You're burning, nigger."

"Who do we tell and how do we go about telling them? I'm going to call Ed Bell. We need one more head in on this thing."

In minutes, Ed Bell from the AME church down the street was at the table with a cup in his hands. Ed Bell, in his sixties, with patches of gray mixed amply in his short-cropped hair, was known for his thick black-framed glasses and his slow, calm speech. After Matthew told the story, Ed Bell leaned his chair back on two legs, crossed his arms over his chest, and uttered one long "hummmmm."

"Well, do we go together to the sheriff, or do we let Brewster go by himself?"

"If he goes on by himself," Ed Bell said, "the sheriff won't know that we know. If we go with him, then the sheriff knows that we know, and we are at liberty to tell the community. We can help the sheriff keep things under control because we are free to tell those that need to know."

"Well, let's do it," Matthew said, "if that's what Brewster wants."

"I haven't told Deak about that call," Brewster said. "I want to tell him, then I'll meet you back here and we'll go see Slim Tate."

"He's in the livin' room, there," Evangeline nodded when Brewster went to the front door, avoiding the charred remains of Three Brothers at the back of the house. Deak sat in a green damask chair with his hands folded in his lap. He did not acknowledge Brewster when he came in. Brewster sat in the chair beside him, but Deak did not focus on him.

"I can shed some light on that fire. We didn't leave anything on. I got a telephone call that tells what happened." When Brewster repeated the message, the most awful expression came over the old man's face. His mouth stretched into a thin and purple-lipped oval, the tip of his nose turned red, and his eyes had water in them. "Three Brothers was burned most likely because we registered to vote."

Deak raised his right palm waving it in a gesture signaling he could not speak, but he understood what Brewster told him.

"I'm going on to the sheriff now. Matthew James is going with me. I didn't want to go before I told you." When Brewster stood, Deak stood with him, and the two walked toward the front door with Deak's feet scraping on the floor.

"T'at was my life," Deak said, "and t'at place belonged to you now." Before Brewster could turn to go down the steps, Deak threw his arms out and embraced him without saying a word. In the brief locking of chests, Brewster felt the thin body and bones of Deak Armbrecht.

"Tell me again, exactly what did that voice say?" Slim Tate asked.

"You're burning. Can you feel it? You're burning, nigger."

"You certain, that's what you heard?"

"Certain."

"What time was it?"

"About four. I didn't look at the clock then, but when I got to town, it was nearly twenty minutes past."

The sheriff rubbed his chin. "You recognize the voice?"

"Wasn't long enough. He said just those words. It was a man's voice, a young man, I would judge."

"I don't want trouble," Slim Tate said. "I won't have trouble around here."

"We already got trouble," Matthew spoke for the first time. "Brewster here lost his livelihood. He's got no work to go back to. We got big trouble."

Matthew James' words hit Brewster like a fist to his chest, almost knocking the air from him. He had insurance, but he didn't know whether it would replace what he had lost.

"I'm going to see what the fire chief found," Slim Tate said and stood. "I don't think we need to tell anybody about this until we get ourselves a report. Even then, we don't need to be telling everybody."

"I differ with you on that," Matthew said. "We need to let the black community know if they are in danger. And Brewster here, what's he going to do to protect himself?"

The sheriff dropped into his chair. "We can't have any trouble. You know Low Ridge's been a fine community, a good place for us all to live. We don't want to get the colored community all stirred up."

"Nor do we," Matthew said. His words snapped, crisp and direct. "But we can't have our livelihoods and possibly our lives taken."

"Look," the sheriff said. "I'm going to have a talk with the fire chief. I'll get to the bottom of this thing. You all hold tight and I'll be back with you. You go on to the parsonage, Reverend. I'll let you know something quick as I can. Then we are all going to keep our heads and not let this thing get out of control."

"What's going to happen to the folks that done this?" Reverend Bell asked.

"Whoa now! We going too fast," Slim Tate said. He rose from his chair. "Let me figure out what's happened first. No need to jump to any conclusions. Stay cool." The sheriff turned to the hat tree where his pistol and holster hung.

Only one partial wall remained of the showroom, and it jutted up, charred and ragged. Brewster placed his foot into the black ash, and water oozed around it. He walked in the ash and water to the place where his workbench had been, longing for the old shed with its familiarity, for the smells of wood spinning in the lathe and for the cloudy windows that looked out on State Street. He knew the way sunlight traveled across the aged wood floors at four o'clock when the autumn sunrays cut a wicked path through the shed and he worked at the lathe or the hardware bench or in the finishing room until the sharp rays were below eye level. He longed for all of this just the way it had been.

He squatted to examine the charred remains for any pieces of his previous life and found the severed head of a hammer, the partially melted blade of a saw, a blackened pull that was to be used on an oak highboy, and some nails that had survived the heat, virtually un-scathed. He gathered these, placing them in a plastic tub he had found by the side of Deak's back steps. When he filled the little plastic tub, he took it to Deak's porch, tapped on the door and removed his shoes, covered in black, wet ash. Brewster and Deak sat at the kitchen table, lifting each object from the tub, wiping each piece with a rag Evangeline gave them, and placing it on a clean dishtowel as a prize from their past life.

Word spread through the black community, and at five-thirty a prayer meeting convened at Limrick Road Baptist. Before he spoke about the trouble in Low Ridge, Matthew James reported on the Freedom Riders, who made it to Montgomery, but the protection had gone back to Birmingham. When the riders got off the bus, they were beaten by an angry mob; even the reporters were beaten.

"I have grave fear for the people on those buses, young and old," Matthew said, "black and white. The bus was bombed in Anniston and they went on. They have been beaten in Birmingham and in Montgomery, and they still plan to go on. While we pray about our situation here, let's pray for those there who are faced with clubs and baseball bats and hate." Matthew's voice had a weary sound.

I don't want to be here, Brewster thought, and he began making lists in his mind while the others prayed. He needed to look at his insurance policy. How much was covered? When could he get a check? Since the fire was deliberately started, would the insurance company delay payment? How many accounts could he and Deak remember? Could he begin anew on the work that had been in the shed?

He leaned over to Marlenna, "I'm going on to Ole Summit. Come on when you're done. I've got to go over that insurance policy." He left quickly before Marlenna had time to reply. She would be angry, and he knew this. He would have to soothe her later, but for now he had to get out. As his Buick pulled away from the church, he could hear prayers for the Freedom Riders in Montgomery, and he would be next. The prayers would be for him, but he could not wait.

At Ole Summit, he got a piece of paper and jotted down what he considered to be the important parts of the policy to study these in detail. He would drive to Hurley tomorrow to meet with the insurance man. After he put the policy aside, he began making a list of all the projects in the shed and the names and telephone numbers he could remember. He would call these people and tell them he was rebuilding everything, showroom and shed. "Don't worry," he would say, "your order will be completed in record time. We've had a set back, but we'll be as good as ever in no time."

Then he made a list of supplies he would need—woods, drills, sanders, hardware, a long lathe. He would buy the minimum and hope he had credit sufficient to get going again. He telephoned Skinner and told him to be at Ole Summit at seven—seven sharp! They would work in the Ole Summit shed.

Marlenna came in with Mama Tee and Laurel. When Mama Tee saw him, she put her index finger in the air. *"Fret not about the wicked,"* her voice raised in volume. *"Be not envious of the wrongdoers! For they are gonna fade like the grass, and wither like the herb."* She rubbed Brewster's shoulder. She took Laurel's hand and went up the stairs.

Now, he had to deal with Marlenna, and he decided to open in penance. "I'm sorry for easing out of the church like that. . . ."

"Ease out! You didn't ease out, you ran out. You flew!"

"I couldn't sit there thinking about all I have to do. I have to be ready to face tomorrow because it's coming, and I needed to prepare for it." He picked up the stack of papers on the kitchen table. "I've been going over this insurance policy, and making lists of the jobs we were doing in the shed and the supplies I'm going to need. Brewster McAtee and Three Brothers are starting work at seven tomorrow morning. You and Mama Tee were there to represent this family, and I needed to be here."

She came to him and put her arms around him and pressed her head to his chest. "I love you," she said. Marlenna sat at the table, and he told her about his time spent with Matthew, Ed Bell, Sheriff Tate, the fire chief, and Deak Armbrecht. Then he laid out his plan for the morning, his trip to the insurance company in Hurley, his gathering of wood for his shop at Ole Summit, his telephone calls to customers whose pieces had been destroyed in the fire. He put before her the steps he would walk to rebuild Three Brothers. She listened and then she told him how so many people had come to her and pressed her hand and pledged support. Brewster and Marlenna talked until after midnight, and then he slept in a chair by the front door with his shotgun by his side.

It was two days after the blaze before the *Low Ridge Gazette* published an article stating the fire might have been deliberately started. It was several more days after that when the sheriff called Brewster and asked him to come to Matthew's office.

When Brewster arrived, he saw the sheriff's car parked in the red clay beside the church. He climbed the metal steps rising along the outside wall, and on the metal platform, he found the door to Matthew's office open. Slim Tate sat in the brocade chair and Matthew leaned against his desk. Brewster sat beside Matthew on the corner of the desk.

"I got a report," Slim Tate said. "We got good news. You can tell all your folks 'round here they don't have no more problems. That fire wasn't started; it was a wiring problem in the shed—frayed wire. Must of sparked and set all those wood chips on fire and then set the place a-blazing."

"Sheriff, are you telling me that fire wasn't started deliberately?" Matthew asked.

"Exactly right."

"What about the call to Brewster?"

"I can't tell you one thing about the call Brewster here says he got, but I can tell you what the fire chief says, and he says it was started by a faulty wire. He's going to write the report that way. Brewster, you're going to be mighty pleased about that because you can get that insurance money a whole lot quicker."

Brewster knew that was right because he had talked to the insurance man in Hurley. A criminal investigation would put a hold on his money. Brewster folded his arms across his chest. He would remain silent. A long drawn-out process would kill any hope of rebuilding Three Brothers. Outside of the insurance money, he had no other resources. He had a loan to pay off at the bank; he would lose Ole Summit if that was not paid. No point in hurting himself any worse. He needed to move forward.

"What are we going to do about the problems in this community? A man gets a call that his place is on fire and his business burns to the ground. What are we going to do about that?" Matthew asked, his eyes round, glaring at the sheriff.

Slim Tate ran his cupped hand over his mouth and smoothed his mustache. "You know I don't allow problems in this community. If there ever was a problem, there AIN'T no problem now. If there was a problem, it's GONE from this town now."

"Are you telling me that whoever started that fire has left this community and will not be prosecuted?" Matthew asked, with anger sounding in his voice.

"I'm not saying NOTHING like that. I told you, the fire chief said that blaze was started by a faulty wire. A spark landed in some wood chips, most likely. But what I also told you is if this community had a problem, we don't have it anymore." The sheriff spoke slowly, deliberately and raised his volume when he continued. "I said, WE DON'T HAVE NO MORE PROBLEM. You folks don't need to worry. Everything can settle on down."

Matthew wanted to go to the newspaper, and he wanted to bring in a legal team from Atlanta, but Brewster wanted to put his time into rebuilding. Marlenna wanted to call Anvil Thomas, but that was the last thing Brewster wanted. If he had done what he wanted to do, he would have lifted Slim Tate by the collar, and he and Matthew both would have had a go at him. He imagined what it would feel like to slam his fists into Slim Tate's ribs, but he didn't have that luxury. He had Marlenna and Laurel to consider, and he had to do whatever was necessary to protect Ole Summit and to rebuild Three Brothers. He didn't have time to drag ass around Anvil or Atlanta lawyers. Besides, there was no good that would come from any more investigation. The sheriff had driven the guilty party or parties out of town, and Brewster knew this because Slim Tate ran Low Ridge with an iron fist. Brewster knew too, that if he made an issue of it, there would be nothing to prosecute, no evidence. There would be a court battle, and Brewster McAtee would lose everything.

"I don't like to lie down and play dead," Marlenna said when Brewster told her.

"We're not. We're very much alive. In fact, we're trying to figure out how to stay alive." With that, Marlenna didn't argue, but Matthew could not convince another soul to visit the voter registrar at the courthouse.

Deak didn't come to Ole Summit to work. He rarely went outside his living room, where he sat with his hands in his lap, not appearing to look at anything in particular. When he walked he grasped the furniture with a claw fist, steadying himself. When Brewster sat at Deak's kitchen table reviewing the projects they had worked on in the shed, Deak could recall some customer names, but could not remember any telephone numbers. His red and watery eyes had a blank look to them, and he rested his forehead on his cupped hands.

"You young," Deak said. "You build t'at place back."

The insurance company processed the paperwork, but the money was not sufficient to cover rebuilding the shed and the showroom and supplying it with furniture. Brewster had worked through this in his head every night since the fire, every night before he fell into sleep. The bank had already sent a letter, which Jimmy Jackson personally delivered to Ole Summit. Brewster memorized the important line: "Please come to the bank no later than June 30." Pay up, in less than plain English. The insurance money would pay most of the loan on Three Brothers, but there was still a mortgage on Ole Summit, and there was no money left to rebuild. He needed tools and wood and supplies and everything from paper to a full-sized lathe, none of which he had at his Ole Summit shed. He drove sixty miles to purchase an old lathe that he cleaned up and made do. At night, with the lights out, he worked through the numbers until he fell into the pit that was sleep. The sun coming in the east window woke him in the mornings, as tired as when he landed in bed the night before, but he rose with the sun and started.

Part Two

The Sum of Augusts

15

He came into town early to speak with the judge about a table he had ordered for the courthouse. Customers did not like to drive outside of town to place an order or to discuss it, so Brewster drove to them. He needed the work and he would drive to wherever he could find it. The judge wanted to meet early, so Brewster parked his car at the courthouse at seven-thirty. The judge held a cup of coffee in his hand, but he did not offer one to Brewster. They worked through decisions on the dimensions, the width, the length, the height of the table, the kind of wood, and the finish, but when Brewster asked what kind of legs the judge wanted on his table, he said, "Damn, Brewster, I didn't know there were so many decisions to be made on a table. What kind of choices do I have on the legs?" Brewster sketched out several options, and the judge studied them. "Fat legs," the judge said. "I want these fat legs on my table, and these curved feet." He tapped the paper on which Brewster rendered his drawings, and Brewster scribbled a note about cabriole legs.

When Brewster left the courthouse, he went to Deak Armbrecht's to see if Deak felt well enough to go out to Ole Summit for the day. The old man could sit in the rocking chair by the stove, and maybe he could sketch a draft of the judge's table. This would not tire him, and there was no one better at sketching a piece than Deak Armbrecht.

Evangeline, her hands deep in the pockets of her apron, came to the porch when Brewster pulled his car in the yard. "I can't wake him," she said before Brewster reached the first step. "I called him, but he won't get up. You come on in and see what you can do."

Brewster took the stairs two at a time. His heart raced, but when he saw Deak, he calmed. The old man rested, his soft white hair matted to his forehead. His head lay in the middle of the pillow, his hands folded on his chest with his fingers wrapped around his wire-framed glasses. Brewster sat on the bed beside Deak and touched his hands, and there was no warmth in them.

"You woke him up yet?" Evangeline shouted from below. "You get him up? That man sleeps sounder than any man I ever seen before. You two come on down here, and I'll fix you some breakfast."

Brewster rubbed the hands where the fingers held the glasses, and he took note of the brownness of his own against the blue-veined paleness. He grasped firmly on the hands and held them, and when he did this he used this moment to say his goodbye because he knew he would not have another time when it was just the two of them. "It was a long run, old man," he said. "You set the pace and maybe I'll even pass it if I can."

"Come on now!" Evangeline shouted.

Brewster released his grasp and tapped Deak's hands lightly with the pads of his fingers. He placed his palm one more time on the hands that held the glasses—his final goodbye. He rose from the bed and stepped to the hall door, which he closed behind him. He went down the steps with no rush. Evangeline stood at the foot of the stairs, her hands balled in fists in the pockets of her apron.

"He's at peace," Brewster said.

"Lord! Lord have mercy! Lord have mercy! That old man done died! Oh Lord! Oh Lord!" Evangeline brought her hands to her face, and her voice rang in Brewster's ears.

Brewster took her hands, holding them. "We need to call his doctor," Brewster said. "The doctor will know what to do. We need to call his son after the doctor gets here." Evangeline poured Brewster a cup of coffee, and they began the process of caring for the dead.

"That was the finest white man I've ever known," Mama Tee said. She eased herself into her chair. "Sweet Jesus, what a day don't bring."

Deak's son came from Kansas City, and he asked Brewster to serve as a pallbearer. Brewster was the last pallbearer, sitting on the first pew, at the end of the row closest to the window. He knew if he had come on a Sunday morning, he would have been turned away from worship service, but even in death, Deak Armbrecht extended one more passage, and Brewster McAtee sat here at the front of Low Ridge Christian Church. Marlenna and Mama Tee and Skinner came for the funeral too. They sat, side by side, on the last pew.

At dusk, Brewster went alone to the cemetery—the tent was gone, but a long spray of white roses covered the spot where Deak was put in the ground. The sun had not yet set, but the moon was visible in the clear sky. Brewster circled the flowers one time and stood in front of the grave. "You rest. Three Brothers will be Three

Brothers again, standing on that very spot. I'm going to take care of that. Those that did this will not have the last say."

He took one step back and stood in front of the grave a full minute, observing the spot where the old man rested beside his wife, Gretta. He turned and walked with heavy steps toward the street. He carried the weight of rebuilding on his shoulders and in his legs, but he was young, and he knew he had the backbone to lift Three Brothers, raising it from the fire.

In the midst of worry over rebuilding Three Brothers, a beautiful buff-colored, squared envelope with an embossed gold seal over the back flap arrived in the mail at Ole Summit. Anvil was getting married. He invited Brewster and Marlenna to the wedding, which was to be held in some church in Washington, DC, and they were invited to the reception too, which was to be held at a club just outside the capital. Brewster twisted his mouth when he read it. He could barely afford gas to drive his Buick over to Bulah, let alone driving to Washington. Marlenna went to Gwin's, purchased a silver tray, had it wrapped in thick white paper, and she included a card, which she had Brewster sign. She wrote a personal note to Anvil and mailed the package to his apartment. The wedding invitation calmed Brewster in an odd way, because it reminded him that somewhere life unfolded itself in normal patterns, somewhere, but here at Ole Summit there was only work, labor serving as a bond, holding him in place.

Deak's old house had a FOR SALE sign in front of it for over a year before Brewster convinced Deak's son, Malcolm, to sell for four thousand, six hundred. It was less than he wanted. He asked seven, but when it didn't sell, he went down to six, and when the house still did not sell, Brewster offered four, six. Malcolm called from Kansas City to say he would take that amount, and Brewster went to the bank to add more mortgage on Ole Summit.

He played his game with everything on the table. One misstep and he would lose all—the bank would own Three Brothers and Ole Summit. He cleared the last of his timber, over twenty acres, sold the wood and leased the land to a local farmer who grew feed corn. With the money he earned from his timber and his land lease, he bought the tools and supplies he needed for his shed, and he paid Skinner. There was no cash left to pay himself. They lived on money that Marlenna brought home from her teaching, but jobs were coming in steadily at Three Brothers.

He could not afford to rebuild on the site of the old Three Brothers shed, but he would have a showroom in Deak's house and Three Brothers would again have a presence on State Street. He had cleared all the charred debris from the lot in front of the house and this was done slowly on Sunday afternoons with a rake in his hands, or a sledgehammer to knock down the partial wall that stubbornly remained and the pipes that stuck up like vipers, twisted to distortion. He and Skinner resurrected Brewster's old truck for the clean up.

"You can't drive that thing," Marlenna had said.

"I can and I will," he told her.

He cut it loose from the weeds and briars that hemmed it into its resting place in an open field surrounded by scrub oaks. He banged and hit on the frame until the field poachers abandoned their property and fled back into the woods. Skinner made it run again and had done it all on Sundays, not charging a dime.

Brewster had come every Sunday afternoon to the charred lot where Three Brothers had been. He spread his tarpaulin on the ground, filled it, dumped the load in the bed of his truck, and when the truck was full, he had taken the blackened load to the dump, and had come back for more, and more. Matthew wanted to help, but Brewster said, "No." He hadn't given a reason, he simply said, "No." He carried every bit of the blackened debris with his own shoulders. Now he could come to the back door of Deak's old house and see State Street with no charred remains to mar his view. Everything at the Ole Summit shed and at Deak's house had been done in small steps because he was doing it by himself, but in just a little over two years, he had turned Ole Summit into a real carpentry shop, and had secured orders from as far north as Birmingham and as far south as Mobile. He had cleared the lot in front of Deak's old house, and he would have a showroom again. He had done all this using only himself—his legs, his arms, his shoulders, his back. He had gone to bed late, woke in the middle of the night, his mind overwrought, and he had risen early to move forward one small step, followed by one small step, followed by one more.

Matthew had asked Slim Tate to talk to Travis Peets again so that Brewster could be done with Peets' rubble, his battle flag, and his IMPEACH EARL WARREN sign that had faded to near invisibility in the direct sunlight on Ole Summit Highway. The two-by-fours holding the sign had loosened in the soft dirt and leaned with the sign about to fall from its own weight. Brewster knew when it did fall, he could not remove it because it was on Peets' property. He would have to wait for Travis Peets to clear the remnants, and that could take years.

When Slim Tate finally came out Ole Summit Highway to speak to Travis Peets, it was late on a Saturday afternoon in April when Mama Tee and Laurel had gone with Paulette into Low Ridge to have supper at Paulette's Café. After he spoke with Peets, he swung his Ford with the gold-lettered Low Ridge Sheriff's Department insignia onto Brewster's lane and brought his report. "Peets went down on his asking price," Slim Tate said. "He'll take eight thousand, nine hundred. He's got a son down in Florida somewhere, and he's thinking about going down there and setting himself up in a brand new house trailer. Says he can't do it for less than eight, nine, though."

"Still high."

"Well, we got him down some. You can wait and he may come on down some more. If you worried about him having something to do with that fire, you can relax. That old man didn't have one thing to do with that. He's old and he's crazy, but he didn't have nothing to do with that business." He placed his hat on his head and started down the steps.

"This sure is a beautiful spot," he said when he stepped off the front porch and opened the door of his patrol car. Brewster and Marlenna stood on the porch and watched him leave.

"We don't have the money to buy Peets' place anyway," Brewster told Marlenna. "I've scratched up every dime I can find or borrow. We'll have some more when we collect on our land, but his price is still high."

"I dream of owning those three acres," Marlenna said. "I want him gone. Maybe we can cut back more. Start saving a little." Brewster circled her with his arms and drew her to him.

"We got this place to ourselves for a while," he said, "and the moon is showing itself. Let's turn all the lights out and go up to that ebony bed. See how the moon shines through the window. I'd like to see what you feel like in the moonlight."

"Same as I feel in the light from that bulb," Marlenna said and pointed to the light in the front hall.

"No," Brewster said, his nose in her hair. "I think you feel different in the moonlight." He lifted her, with her legs dangling at his calves, and carried her to the door.

Laurel was nearly four-years-old, and in the two years since Three Brothers burned, Brewster had almost no time to give his son. He had projects waiting for him in the shed, and every day he made at least two trips into Low Ridge, sometimes three. There was not enough time in one day to come close to completing everything he scribbled on the list he kept in the right front pocket of his shirt.

"Dad, you throw me some balls?" Laurel asked, holding his short bat and tiny mitt, and squinting his eyes in the morning sun.

"Can't do it now," Brewster said. "Give Dad some time to get things settled down. Then we can play ball."

"Let's play a little before Skinner gets here."

"He'll be pulling up any minute," Brewster said. "Give Dad time and I'll get things under control. We'll have lots of days for ball then." He said this with confidence, but in truth, he could not imagine when he would have time to play ball. Skinner would bring his son, David, who was a year older than Laurel, and the boys would play. At noon, Skinner would get out and throw the ball with them, whoop and holler and run until Brewster had to call him in, just like a child. It may be better to be Skinner, Brewster thought. He comes to work, does what he's told to do, and doesn't have a thing to worry about, at least he doesn't worry about one thing, even if he should. But despite Skinner's easy ways, David was a fine boy.

"That's a man child," Mama Tee had said. "Thank the Lord, Skinner's got somebody to take care of him."

"I'm gon' have David with me today," Skinner said the first time he had brought his son to Ole Summit for the day. "Rozelle done run off." He shifted weight on his feet. "I run her off. She hanging out with some ole man, and I know she gon' be gone soon. I told her, go ahead on. Leave. But the boy, he stays. That's what I told her, and she wants to make a big case of it. Got my knife, and she knows my name and all. The boy stays with me, I told her. Get on out. She goes on and I got the boy, and he's here with me 'til I decide what I'm gon' do with him." And with that, Skinner put the sleeping boy down in the corner on the floor of the shed at Ole Summit. Brewster knew David was a permanent fixture because Skinner would not work out any other arrangements.

"He'll be good company for Laurel," Mama Tee told Skinner.

"He'll start to school in a little over a year, and he won't be no problem then," Skinner said. Brewster accepted the situation because he needed Skinner. He was over a barrel—no, not a barrel, a pit, so murky and dark, he couldn't even begin to guess the depth.

Skinner's car pulled onto the lane, and Laurel ran to meet it. Mama Tee heard the car and shuffled to the front porch, sliding on the backs of her chenille slippers with her apron around her neck, untied and lapping over itself in the front. "You had breakfast, boy?" she shouted at David.

"Yessum."

"I fed him today, Miss Teelda," Skinner said.

"You doing good," Mama Tee said. She chuckled and worked her lips together and out, studying Laurel and David, who ran to the field, followed by Valiant, close on their heels. Mama Tee went inside the screened door, and Brewster heard her feet sliding along the floor.

Brewster had planned his day. He would get Skinner started in the shed, and he would go into Low Ridge because he had some men working in Deak's old house. The old windows would be removed and wide plate glass picture windows would be added on both sides of what was the old back door. A small porch would be added because the house had good concrete banisters to support it. A person walking up State Street at night could come on the porch and admire the furniture through the lighted windows. Eventually, he would build ornate benches to go in the lot where the old shed and showroom had been, and he would grass the area because he could not see the day when he could build again, but Three Brothers showroom would be on State Street, set back, and in Deak's old house, at that. He worked with the men until nearly ten and was about to leave when Albert Mixon came to the back door, his hat in his hand.

"Can I speak with you, son?" He had never called Brewster *son* and had never requested a time to speak. The word *son* stood large in Brewster's mind. On the back porch Albert Mixon sat on one banister and Brewster sat across from him on the opposite slab of concrete.

"You're walking down a hard path now, and I want to be of some help. I have a little money saved you can use. I also have time." He ran his fingers around the band of his hat. "Mixon Domestics and Laborers isn't doing nearly the business it used to do. I still got a few in the community who come to me, but mostly the young ones are getting their own jobs. Times are changing," he said, looking down at the brim of his hat.

"Thank you for your offer," Brewster said, "but I believe I've got

enough to cover things." While he was not at all sure he had enough
to cover the expenses of getting Three Brothers going again, he did
not want to accept money from his father-in-law. That would be bad
policy.

"I could be of some help to you," Albert Mixon said. "Feel free
to use my experience as you see fit. I don't expect to be paid."

Brewster extended his hand to his father-in-law. "Let me put
some thought to it," he said. "I do need help. Lots of it."

"Who's going to manage the showroom?" Marlenna asked,
gratified that her father had come offering money and service. "My
father would be wonderful at that. He's established himself in the
white community, and he's comfortable talking with just about
anybody."

Brewster had already thought of these things. He knew almost no
one in the white community, and he would be uncomfortable speaking with the white customers, showing his furniture and trying to sell
it. What if he rebuilt the showroom, stocked it with some of the
finest furniture to be had in Low Ridge or anywhere in the surrounding communities, and no one, with the exception of a few Negroes
off Limrick Road, came to look or to buy.

"I'm going to think some more," he told Marlenna, not wanting
to commit himself to Albert Mixon without working through all the
details.

After Sunday dinner, at which all the talk had been about Anvil
who spoke that morning at Limrick Road Baptist about the trouble in
Birmingham—fire hoses opened on marchers and bombs exploding
in Negro sections of that city—Brewster went back into Low Ridge
to visit with Albert Mixon. He had decided to ask his father-in-law to
manage the new Three Brothers showroom.

"You will be paid," Brewster said, "but that won't be much for a
while, because there isn't any money." When he said this, he felt
young again, standing by Albert Mixon's back porch, looking up at
the man sitting in his rocking chair.

"I'm not worried about money now. If I can make Three Brothers profitable, we can settle on a figure that will make my work
worthwhile." They agreed on a small partnership for Albert Mixon, if
he managed the showroom to profitability. They shook hands, and
Brewster went to Deak's old house and did some trim work there
until well after dark. Laurel was asleep when he got back to Ole

Summit, and Marlenna was in bed. Most nights Laurel was sleeping when Brewster came into the house, and in the mornings there was too much driving him, too much pushing him, to sit on the porch at Ole Summit and talk with Laurel. The men who started the fire had robbed him, robbed him not just of the furniture, the shed, the tools, the property, but robbed him of his previous life, a life in which there had been time for some leisure, time for thinking, time for family, and time to take care of Ole Summit.

16

When Three Brothers showroom opened in June, Brewster sweated as he paced inside the shop in his dark suit, white shirt, and tie. Albert Mixon stood outside the store on the sidewalk, tying balloons on short sticks to give to children who came to the showroom or passed on the street. He arranged for a Coca-Cola stand to be set up on the curb, and Brewster watched his father-in-law, a broad grin on his face, wave at passing cars.

Potential customers did come, not to make purchases, but to drink a free Coca-Cola and to look at the merchandise, and Albert Mixon greeted each one of them. After a while, Brewster slipped out the door and went to Ole Summit to work in his shed.

On a wet and unusually cool evening in early June, Marlenna came to the shed beside the house at Ole Summit where Brewster worked on bedroom furniture for the showroom. She sat in the rocking chair close to the stove, but there was no fire in it.

"You could almost use some heat tonight. The rain's given the air a little chill," she said.

"It's relief, if you ask me," Brewster said, not turning toward her. "Laurel's in bed."

"I know. It's late, but I wanted to work a little more."

"I didn't come to hurry you." She sat, rocking gently with her head leaning against the tall back slats of the chair, her feet pushing slowly against the raw pine floor. "Brewster, I went to the doctor yesterday. We're going to have a baby. Another baby."

Brewster turned to her and saw her hands outstretched toward him. He pulled her up and wrapped his arms around her, feeling the warmth of her body, the thinness of her shoulders, her head below his chin. "This will be a December baby," Marlenna said. "Born before Christmas."

She wept with her face pushed against his chest, and he felt the warm water through his shirt. He was uncertain why she wept—happiness, sadness, because the night was wet and cool, because this baby had been created in scraps of time, grabbed at the end of a day worn thin with work and worry. He held her tightly against his chest, resting his chin on the top of her head, and he closed his eyes. He loved Marlenna Mixon McAtee. If certainty existed nowhere else, he knew his love for Marlenna was steadfast. He bent down and lifted Marlenna, carrying her like a baby, with her knees over his right arm and her back braced by his left arm. When Marlenna laughed, Brewster spun around and did a flat-footed dance. He carried her to the front door of the shed and gently placed her feet on the floor. He switched off the lights, and they huddled together running through the rain to the front porch of the house.

On Sunday Marlenna cooked a special meal and baked a coconut cake to celebrate Mama Tee's eighty-third birthday. Mama Tee had thinned considerably, the ligaments in her neck showed, thick and stringy, but her silver hair crimped beautifully around her face and rested in a knot at the back of her head. Still a proud woman, she dressed for church, wore belts around her waist and shoes with hard soles, but in the car, on the way home, she tucked the belts in her pocketbook and eased the shoes off her feet, replacing them with her chenille slippers.

Mama Tee pushed the food around on her plate, eating little of it. She rubbed her stomach and put her head in her hands. "I don't know what's wrong with me. My stomach's been aching me for days. Days!" She slapped her hand against the table.

"I'm getting you to the doctor tomorrow," Marlenna said.

"Guess I got indigestion," Mama Tee said. "I'm not hungry anyway."

While Mama Tee's stomach was unsettled by sickness, Marlenna's stomach was delicate too, especially in the mornings. If she moved too quickly, she was in the bathroom with her head over the toilet bowl. If she smelled coffee brewing in the house, she had dry heaves for half an hour. Brewster connected two extension cords to the coffeepot, ran the cords across the kitchen floor, and out the front door where he brewed his coffee on the porch.

In the afternoons both Mama Tee and Marlenna rested in the big room, but they rallied when they turned on the television in late August to see Martin Luther King speak to over 250,000 who gathered on the Mall in Washington, DC. Brewster and Skinner came in from the shed and pulled two chairs from the kitchen, placing these to the left side of the TV to watch the speech with the women, who sat on the couch, leaning forward to be close to every word Martin King uttered. Laurel and David sat on the floor with their noses almost touching the screen. Mama Tee spoke out, encouraging and supporting Reverend King as if he stood in front of her at Limrick Road Baptist.

The power and beauty of his words touched each of them. For the next several days after the speech, they all walked in the triumph of Martin King's majestic phrases, remembering them, uttering them, passing the sounds through their heads—*heat of oppression . . . transformed into an oasis of freedom and justice . . . I have a dream . . . I have a dream . . . I have a dream.* But on Sunday morning, September 15, eighteen days after Martin King's triumphant speech in Washington, Sunday school had just ended in churches all over Alabama. At Limrick Road Baptist, Mama Tee sat with her friends in the Sunday school classroom and waited for Marlenna to come and walk with her to the sanctuary. And in Birmingham, four little girls, who had just finished Sunday school, went to the basement of the Sixteenth Street Baptist Church to put on their choir robes in preparation for the worship service. Calamity crept behind them, lurking, unexpected, driven on a wild and evil wind. Sixteen sticks of dynamite exploded, blowing the church apart and killing Denise, Carole, Addie, and Cynthia. Within sight of the church, a man named Robert Edward Chambliss, also known as Dynamite Bob, a Birmingham Klan member in the Eastview 13 Klavern, stood on the street corner.

Marlenna wept. Mama Tee stretched herself on the couch and remained there for two days. She rose only to bake a peach pie that Brewster would take to Limrick Road Baptist Church because Anvil's mother died in her bed in Low Ridge the same day the four little girls died in the Baptist Church in Birmingham. Food would be served in the fellowship hall after the funeral of Anvil's mother on Wednesday.

When Brewster delivered the pie to the church, he cut through the sanctuary headed toward the back door that led to the fellowship hall. He froze midway down the center aisle when he spotted Matthew sitting by himself about seven rows from the front. Matthew wore a short-sleeved plaid shirt, and when he turned toward Brewster, tears streamed down his face from his eyes to his chin. The sight of Matthew sitting in the church alone, weeping, struck Brewster like a blow.

"I'm sorry, Matthew. I was taking this pie to the basement."

Matthew wiped his face with his handkerchief. "I wish everybody who comes to this church would sit in this sanctuary, sit alone and talk to Jesus. It's beautiful in here." He took in a deep breath and let it out. "I guess I wasn't talking, I was slap boxing. We were slapping it out over what happened in Birmingham."

"Who's winning?"

"We got a few more rounds to go, but He's put a few things before my eyes in a different way. I had to sit here until I knew for sure He was weeping too. We were wailing together. He's as upset about what's happened over in Birmingham as I am." Matthew wiped his face again with his handkerchief, and he stood up.

"You walk up and down Limrick Road and you can almost hear a pin drop. Pain has shut lips. We've turned inside ourselves, and we're all going to explode if we can't let some of this pressure go. I need to know what to say on Sunday to ease some of the pain we all feel. I want to open us up and let a little of that pressure ease out."

"I'm sorry," Brewster repeated, holding the pie like an offering before the altar.

"No, that's fine. I did about as much as I could do. I'll come back into the ring later and we'll have another round." Matthew wiped his face again and tucked the handkerchief in his back pocket. "You going to be here for the funeral?"

"I'll try," Brewster said, and walked toward the basement door behind the sanctuary.

"Anvil won't be staying after the funeral," Matthew said to Brewster's back. "He'll be going over to Birmingham for the funerals there."

Marlenna cooked soft foods for Mama Tee—grits, mashed potatoes, corn bread mixed into tall glasses of milk—but the pain did not leave. Dr. Hamilton prescribed stronger medicine that put Mama Tee to sleep, but when she woke, the pain woke too. The church ladies came to nurse her because she had nursed more than her share of folks over time.

"Don't worry," Matthew told Brewster. "We'll keep somebody with her. You got enough to worry about, and I expect one more thing will tip the seesaw out of balance. Marlenna doesn't look good. Circles under her eyes. Got a little ash in her color. You take care of her and we'll take care of Mama Tee."

The descent came swiftly once Dr. Hamilton told them. The cancer in Mama Tee had spread to nearly every organ. "No point in probing and poking and peeking inside her," Dr. Hamilton said. "It's best to give her some peace."

"That's what we'll pray for—peace," Matthew said. "If we are at peace, we hold all the riches of this world in our grasp."

"I feel like Old Man Time is running close on my heels, but I'm not going to let him catch me, not yet," Mama Tee said. Her long gray hair, pulled to the side of her face, had a rubber band wrapped around it. "I've got a baby to see. I'll have to get out of this bed when Marlenna brings that baby home. Who's going to help Marlenna take care of it?"

But on Friday, November 22, the day an assassin's bullet ripped through the head of President John Kennedy in Dallas, Mama Tee went to bed and did not get up. "It's better to sleep this year out," she said. "God Almighty! Can another thing happen?" On her fingers, she counted the days remaining in 1963. "Thirty-nine more days," she said. "I think it would be good if we all went to bed. The government should order us all to get in our beds and pull the covers over our heads and hibernate until next year. Maybe we'll all have some sense in nineteen-hundred and sixty-four." Marlenna brought her warm chicken broth, and she sipped a few swallows before she put the cup on the nightstand.

"I don't want anything big," Marlenna said. "You two cut a small tree. Don't you come back here with a big tree because I'm going to send you back out if you do." With these instructions, Brewster and Laurel went in the woods, off the lane, looking for a spruce or a fir. Marlenna wanted to have the tree in place and decorated because she thought Christmas would be here before she could get home with the new baby.

Brewster and Marlenna worked the weekend decorating the tree and caring for Mama Tee. They made a trip into Low Ridge to purchase a new bat and mitt for Laurel, a new sweater for him, some games, and Christmas candy. These things they hid as presents for his Christmas.

Monday night they drove to Our Savior's Home, but unlike the starry night when Laurel made his arrival, this was a night of a new moon, and a mist fell, thick and heavy. The white granite of Our Savior's Home didn't sparkle, but had only form and rough denseness in the dark of the cloudy night. Helen Teelda McAtee arrived on Tuesday morning, December 24, 1963.

"You could do yourself a favor by staying here another day," Sister Francesca told Marlenna on Wednesday morning. "Tomorrow would be every bit as good as today for taking that baby home."

"It's Christmas. I want to go home."

"Hard headed," the nun teased her.

"I am," Marlenna affirmed.

"Go on then! No walking. No climbing stairs. Lots of rest."

Sister Francesca herself pushed Marlenna's chair down the hall. Another sister followed, holding Helen Teelda in the bend of her wide-robed arm. The squeaking of the wheelchair echoed against the walls of the somber halls, because anyone who could be home for Christmas was at home. When they reached the front door, Sister Francesca helped Marlenna into the seat of Brewster's Buick, placing little Helen Teelda in her arms. She stood by the door, lifted her black-robed arm, and waved at them as they pulled away. Brewster watched her in the rearview mirror, a tiny, solitary, dark figure, standing in the doorway of Our Savior's Home, looking toward Platt's Row, her hands joined and resting in the center of her body.

"I want Mama Tee to hold Helen Teelda," Marlenna said when Brewster pulled the Buick to the porch at Ole Summit.

"No stairs," Brewster reminded her.

"I can make it, if you help me."

Paulette, who was sitting with Mama Tee, braced Marlenna on her left side and Brewster put his right arm around Marlenna's waist. He cradled the baby in his left arm as they eased Marlenna up the stairs, slowly, one step, then resting, and one more, until they were at the second story landing.

"Open the shade," Marlenna said when they entered the dark room. "I want Mama Tee to see the baby."

Marlenna sat on the edge of the bed and Brewster stood behind her. She rubbed the side of Mama Tee's face, taking the baby from Brewster and holding her in front of Mama Tee. "This is Helen Teelda. I want you to hold her." Mama Tee gave no sign she heard Marlenna. She breathed shallow and her eyes, circled by the bones of her brows and cheeks, remained closed. Brewster stepped in front of Marlenna and squatted with his weight on his ankles. He rubbed Mama Tee's forehead, but still she did not open her eyes. "Mama Tee," Marlenna whispered again. "Brewster, ease her up on the pillow."

When Brewster did this, Mama Tee opened her eyes. "This is

Helen Teelda," Marlenna said. "We're going to call her Tee," and she put the baby near Mama Tee's chest.

"Hold that baby," Mama Tee said in mouthed words, barely a whisper.

Marlenna lifted Mama Tee's arms, establishing them on the spread over her stomach, and she eased Helen Teelda McAtee into the waiting embrace.

"Helen Teelda," Mama Tee's lips formed the words. "My baby. God blessed me," she whispered.

Five days after Christmas they buried Mama Tee in old Hope Hill. She rested between Daddy Divine and TeeBoy. Bess lay at her feet. Tom came to the church in a thin yellow shirt, no jacket. He smelled foul, and he wept like a baby, his shoulders shaking, wiping mucus from his nose with the back of his hand. Marlenna gave him a handkerchief, and both she and Matthew comforted him. Tom's appearance annoyed Brewster. Tom had not come to see Mama Tee in her final hours, even though she had asked for him. Brewster had gone in search of Tom, but could not find him. With Mama Tee too weak to open her eyes, Brewster had lied to her—told her Tom stood beside her bed. He had taken Mama Tee's hand in his own, allowing Mama Tee to think she held Tom's hand. Now, too late, Tom wept like a Pharisee in a show of sorrow. Brewster wanted the service to be over; he planned to come to Hope Hill late in the afternoon by himself. He would stand alone in this spot where Mama Tee, Daddy Divine, Bess, and TeeBoy rested. He would say his farewells by himself.

17

In the early months of 1964, Marlenna persuaded Paulette to stay
at Ole Summit and care for Laurel and baby Tee. "I'm done at that
café anyway," Paulette said, "If I stay in town, my girls will have me
cooking in that kitchen. I want to be in the country, so this suits me
fine." And in late spring, Carmella returned to 32 State Street,
bringing Little Eddie with her and posting signs on telephone poles
on Limrick Road and all the side streets off Limrick.

CARMELLA MIXON HAS ESTABLISHED A VOICE STUDIO
AT 32 STATE STREET
CARMELLA STUDIED VOICE AT SHAW UNIVERSITY
SHE OFFERS PROFESSIONAL INSTRUCTION
CALL FOR AN APPOINTMENT

She brought her own piano from North Carolina and positioned
it in the corner across from the wine-colored settee, sending the old
upright out to Ole Summit to be lovingly installed in the big room,
where it was decorated on top with a scarf and a small varicolored
vase that had belonged to Marlenna's mother.

Several students did call Carmella, and by the end of the month,
she had three students taking lessons in her new studio, but that was
not enough business to sustain her and Little Eddie, and keep her
clothed in the beautiful floral silks and linens she liked to wear. She
went to work for her father at the Three Brothers showroom where
she used her voice training to great advantage.

Brewster watched her at work with customers. "This is high
quality," she said, confidently. "It will look good ten years from
now." She cooed and coaxed and assured her customers by pleas-
antly affirming their choices. "Oooooh, the color is happy. This will
make you feel good," and she sang a snippet from some opera or
other, and the customer laughed and attributed the good feeling to the
couch or the chair, and signed the papers for monthly payments.

Carmella's return, which renewed activity in the house at 32
State Street, took years off of Albert Mixon, who rose early, dressed

himself in his pin-striped suit and fresh shirt, and strutted down State Street, tapping his gold-tipped cane, stopping to visit with anyone he met. At Three Brothers, he unlocked the door, turned on the lights, dusted, swept the floors, and arranged displays, until the shop opened at ten.

Brewster too experienced a new vision, which came unexpectedly from Carmella's return. She brought with her a magazine from one of the historical associations in North Carolina and gave it to Brewster, because in it was an article about a furniture maker named Thomas Day, a free Negro living and working in North Carolina during slavery—one of the best-known and most respected furniture makers of his day. Brewster studied the photographs of Tom Day's work: African masks carved into the side rails of a mahogany mantel, the eyes large and piercing below furrowed brows, the carved flesh under the eyes and down to the chin signaling distress, fear, doubt, the mouth tight and somber. But above the face rose a jester's cap and below the face hung a ruffled collar, and the mahogany shone with a luster, giving warmth to the wood.

Another picture showed a staircase newel post in the shape of an African warrior, and another photograph displayed a beautiful mahogany post with a snake curled at the foot, its head stretching up the post. The lines and patterns revealed Tom Day's imagination and evoked emotion from the wood. Brewster studied these pictures and began working on a sideboard for which he carefully selected the finest mahogany boards with grains showing luster and movement.

He decided to carve African-style masks into the front panels of the sideboard, identical masks, one on each of the large squared, thigh-portions of the sideboard legs, and he knew the face he wanted to carve into his sideboard was that of his mother, Bess. At night he went through photographs in several old shoeboxes where Mama Tee had kept family treasures. He found yellowed and torn photographs and buttons from garments of long deceased relatives, buttons only Mama Tee could have identified by owner. He found his old report cards from County Training School and some letters from Mama Tee's brother who had lived in Birmingham. He found three pictures of Bess, but not one of them showed her face in any detail. There was not one portrait of his mother, not one close picture showing her face.

At night, Brewster's last thoughts before lapsing into sleep were of Bess's face. He tried to cement a picture of Bess in his head that would not slip away when his hands met the nothingness of the mahogany, because he needed to transform the picture in his mind into the smooth wood. One night he woke to see TeeBoy standing in the corner of the room, arms folded over his chest, quiet and peaceful—unlike TeeBoy who usually came with a dance, his arms spread wide, showing his wounds.

Brewster rose from bed, put on a light jacket, went down the stairs and out on the porch. He sat in his deep green joiner's chair and closed his eyes. Sometime between night and sunrise, between sleep and wake, the image came to him. He saw Bess's face in the window of the Greyhound bus as the bus pulled out of Low Ridge headed for New York City.

The image was clear—fixed. It could not be lost in the jumble of all the other images and lists of tasks that rambled in his head. Bess's face pressed to the window, and her eyes held Brewster's eyes as the bus pulled away from the Low Ridge station headed for New York. In those eyes Brewster saw his mother's love, his mother's fear, and her burden. The image of Bess that came to him as he dozed on the porch at Ole Summit was better than a portrait; the image was not posed but was a living image fixed in his heart's eye, and he was ready to begin carving the mahogany—purple and amber.

Brewster was glad he had his sideboard to work on. Marlenna and Matthew made a four-hour drive west to Mississippi to meet workers in Neshoba County who organized voter registration. Matthew wanted to learn more about what was happening there so he could apply some new strategies in Low Ridge. But Brewster wouldn't allow himself to be pulled off his center, because he had plenty to keep himself busy here in his own shed. He enjoyed the smoothness of the mahogany in the palms of his hands, and he rubbed his fingers at the lines of his mother's lips, checking to be certain all roughness was gone—the wood as smooth as satin.

In the late afternoons, he worked on the top of the sideboard. One-and-one-half inches from the top edge, he tapped into place and glued a one-quarter-inch ebony band that fit so snug his fingers could not feel any rises. Just ahead of the ebony band, he fitted a thin, one-inch veneer of white ash. The white ash would turn rich amber under the varnish and its grain would resemble an open fan, reflecting high and low lights in a rhythmic pattern. The mahogany with the amber ash and the tiny ebony bands appeared to be a continuous piece of wood grown in a miracle of nature.

Albert Mixon first saw the piece when he, Carmella, and Little Eddie came to Ole Summit for Sunday dinner. "I want to display this piece in the front window for a few days, then we'll get it out of the sun, but we'll keep it there on the floor for a while."

"That piece is going right here in the big room," Marlenna said. "I've already picked the spot for it," and she pointed her hand toward the north wall.

"Daughter, this is a work of such quality, we need to display it for a while. You'll get it back, but we need it in the showroom for a few weeks."

Carmella ran her hands over the top of the sideboard and bent to study the masks carved on the front legs. "We got to have this in the showroom," she said. "This will draw them in and I can sell. I mean I can SELL," she said. "This will start the conversation, and then they'll have to have something new for the living room or the dining room. You know how these white folks think. They'll be some that will want to buy this piece. I can sell it, if you're interested."

"Not interested," Brewster said.

But to Brewster's surprise, it was this piece that created a name for him from Mobile to Birmingham, and it established Three Brothers as a place to come and see what was in the little house converted to a showroom. A reporter for the *Low Ridge Gazette* came to sit and eat his lunch in one of the ornate benches Brewster put in the open lot where the Three Brothers shed once stood. Before the reporter could even sit down and unwrap his sandwich from the wax paper rolled snug around it, he saw the eyes of Bess glaring at him, following him, peering out the window beside the back porch of Deak Armbrecht's old house. The eyes watched him as he walked to the window for a closer look. Then the reporter opened the door and went inside. That was when he met Carmella, who could make a good story even better with the drama embedded in her voice. She told Brewster and Marlenna about her conversation with the reporter and demonstrated how the reporter had knelt in front of the piece, studying the masks, and how he walked around the sideboard watching Bess's eyes.

Carmella told the reporter about the work of Thomas Day, the free Negro who had lived and worked in his own carpentry shop in Milton, North Carolina in the mid-1800s. She told him how Brewster had seen pictures of Thomas Day's work, and how Brewster had constructed the sideboard with the face of his mother, Bess McAtee, carved into the flat, front legs. The drama grew richer when Carmella told the reporter how Thomas Day eventually went bankrupt because no laws in North Carolina forced white people to pay free blacks for their labor. So Thomas Day had put everything up for sale, his tools, his land, his horses, his shop, and his slaves.

"Yep, he had slaves," Carmella had explained to the reporter. "And he sold all his furniture too, just before the Civil War erupted. He died before the War began." Her eyes were wide with drama when she continued. "In fact, they think he died the very year the war opened, and he's supposed to be buried somewhere there in Milton." She performed the drama for Brewster and Marlenna, taking her own part as well as that of the reporter.

The reporter went back to the *Gazette* without ever having removed the waxed paper from his sandwich. He wrote the story as Carmella had told it to him, and he telephoned the shed at Ole Summit and arranged an interview with Brewster. After the reporter's piece appeared in the *Low Ridge Gazette* with pictures of Brewster and of the sideboard, some fellow called from the *Birmingham Post Herald* and he came, took pictures, and wrote a story about Brewster and his work. Then a woman called from the Women's Pages at the Mobile newspaper, and they ran a story too.

"They're not walking in," Carmella told Brewster, "they're driving in. They're coming from Mobile and Fairhope and Monroeville, and a man came in the door from Huntsville the other day. You build something else special like this," Carmella told him. "Something I can sell."

Brewster began work on a mahogany four-poster bed with curved posts that straightened to fluted and reeded columns, and he began work on a pair of carved newell posts with snakes coiled and grasping the banister rails in the firm grip of their opened mouths. In a little over a month's time, the shed picked up three special orders: one from Mountain Brook, just outside Birmingham, another from the Springhill area of Mobile, and one from Brewster's lumber supplier who lived outside Brewton.

Carmella sold furniture in the showroom almost as fast as Brewster and Skinner could make it. Albert Mixon was riding high too, because he had been invited to several women's clubs—one in Monroeville and one in Winston County—to talk about the Three Brothers furniture collection. He took photographs of Brewster's sideboard and of his four-poster bed and of some of the newer pieces in the showroom. Albert Mixon spoke to the ladies about Brewster's designs and about the heritage Brewster had found in the work of Thomas Day.

Brewster had been invited to speak at these meetings and

Marlenna said she would go with him, but he turned down these offers. He knew he would be nervous and he would regret it as soon as he accepted. And besides, driving around to meetings would take him away from his work. Albert Mixon took Carmella with him, and they entertained the ladies with his speeches. Then Carmella sang for them. It was quite a show, according to the two of them. Not many sales came from these events, but Albert Mixon had a good time and Carmella drew some pleasure from her performances.

In early July, Brewster collected money from the lease of his land, and with good sales at Three Brothers, he paid down most of his loans. Matthew went with him to visit Travis Peets, because once again he was ready to buy him out. Marlenna's birthday was in late July, and he wanted to hand her the deed to Peets' place; he would put it on a silver platter and give it to her like the defeated head of a vanquished foe.

Peets sat on his porch when they pulled Brewster's Buick onto the hard-packed red clay of his driveway. Peets lowered his eyes and watched them get out of the car. "We've come to talk to you about buying this place," Matthew shouted as soon as his head came past the rail of the car door. Brewster and Matthew stood at the foot of the steps and looked up at Peets on the porch. A young girl, six or seven years old, sat in the chair beside him, and she watched them.

"Don't want to sell my land no more," Peets said. "My son's not in Florida now. Went up north to work. Detroit City. We got his girl, Ruby, here with us. Don't want to go to Florida now. Land's not for sale."

"We can negotiate," Matthew said.

"No," Peets said. "Land's not for sale."

"You sure, Mr. Peets?" Matthew asked one last time.

"Sure," the old man said, but Brewster did not want to leave. This was not the way he had worked things out in his head. This time he had come prepared to pay Peets' price. He had the money and was ready to spend it.

"I'll pay your asking price," Brewster told the old man who wore only his undershirt beneath the galluses of his overalls. Brewster had money and this should buy him what he wanted and he wanted these miserable three acres. Peets rose and the little blonde-headed girl walked with him to the porch rail.

"Don't want to sell," Peets said, his face red, but slack, showing no expression—detached and distant. "Don't have no place to go. My son went north. Go on now," he said. The little girl took her grandfather's hand and watched them.

Matthew got in the car, but Brewster continued to stand in front of the Buick, not willing to give up, because he wanted the deed on the silver platter for Marlenna.

"Go on," Peets said, but this time the words came sharp with a rasp, a raking sound crossing his teeth.

Matthew put his head above the door rail. "Come on, Brewster. Mr. Peets don't want to sell."

Brewster got in the car, but he was not ready to leave. He wanted this land. He wanted it for Marlenna and he wanted it for himself and this was not the way his negotiation was supposed to end. But Matthew cranked the engine, circled on the hard-packed dirt, and turned left on Ole Summit toward Brewster's own lane.

When Brewster could not purchase Travis Peets' land, he paid out his bank loans and purchased fifteen acres across the highway. Land on his side of the road was not for sale, but he negotiated a good deal on the land opposite his curved lane, and it was this deed that he put on a silver platter and gave to Marlenna on her birthday.

"I want you to clear that land," she said, "and I want you to plow it. I'm going to sit here on the porch with a glass of tea in my hand and watch you drive a tractor on my new fields." He laughed when she said this, and that was exactly what he intended to do.

18

In September, on the day school started, Brewster dried the cast-iron skillet with the dishtowel and put the pan under the stove. He hummed the old "Crossroad Blues" he remembered from Club Troubadour when the High Steps played.

The morning air had turned cool, invigorating him, and beams of light filtered into the kitchen. "I'll be on the porch," he shouted up the stairs when he went outside. He wanted to watch Marlenna and Laurel pull out of the lane.

Laurel came to the porch, his shirt crisp and tucked into his pants, with his tie adding to his orderly appearance. He sat in the rocking chair beside his father, and Brewster studied him. This was indeed a child who would walk through life in good favor—hand-some and smart. Never had there been a boy who would have more backing from his father. Tom had been a weight riding on his back, but he would carry Laurel, he would watch him, waiting for him to show his skills, and he would help Laurel climb to the top.

When Marlenna stepped onto the porch, she wore a straight skirt, navy blue with a white blouse, but around her neck was a scarf emblazoned with navy, lavender, and yellow flowers, and she carried with her the unmistakable fragrance of rosewater. She held her purse and two books in her hands.

"This is an exciting day. Won't ever be another first day in first grade." She put the books in her left hand and patted Laurel's head with her free hand.

Paulette came to the porch holding hands with Tee, who toddled beside her. "I've got to see this boy leave for school," and she bent to straighten Laurel's tie.

Marlenna and Laurel went down the steps and got into the Chevrolet. Brewster and Paulette stood on the porch and watched until the car turned onto Ole Summit Highway.

"This is a good day," Paulette said. "I remember when every one of my four started to school. A day like this is a milk and honey day."

As the fall season progressed, Marlenna came home with reports about Laurel in the Hummingbird Readers, and these were the best readers. Although Marlenna taught in the high school, she had opportunity to observe Laurel, and what she saw pleased her. He wanted to play ball in the weed lot after school, and Marlenna brought home reports about this too. She allowed him to play while she graded papers and prepared her lessons for the next day, but he was never ready to leave when she waved her hand and called to him.

Marlenna also brought home reports of Carmella's son, Little Eddie, four grades ahead of Laurel. In October, he got into some trouble at County Training, and Carmella was called to Herman Thomas's office on two occasions, the last time, when Eddie got into a fight with a boy and put his fist into the boy's eye.

"Herman Thomas is getting old," Carmella said to Brewster and Skinner when they took a cabinet by the showroom for display. "Do you think he could be picking on Little Ed?"

"A blacked and swelled eye is a blacked and swelled eye," Skinner said. "Did the boy have a swelled eye?"

"He did." Carmella's lips pressed together and she folded her arms under her breasts.

"Well, I expect old man Thomas got to call somebody when one boy swells the eye of another."

"I guess so," Carmella said and looked so defeated, Brewster felt sorry for her.

"Probably boys horsing around," Brewster said, trying to ease her worry.

"That's what I told her," Albert Mixon said. "I don't know the first thing about raising boys. I just had my two girls and mostly Helen did the raising of them. But I told Carmella, it's probably not anything to worry about."

But Brewster thought trouble came with Limrick Road, and he was glad he had his acres off Ole Summit Highway. Trouble was too easy to find in a place where men lounged under trees in the afternoon, drank whiskey, and played cards on plywood boards spread across the frames of old chrome dinette chairs. Men sat on cinderblock steps at Happy Landing smoking reefers wrapped in brown paper, and the sound of pistol fire was not uncommon there. TeeBoy had been pulled into all that was Limrick Road, and it had destroyed him. Carmella had better watch Little Eddie or he would walk down one of the roads that led to trouble, but Brewster's sixty acres would protect Laurel and would keep him separated from the vice Limrick Road nurtured.

From the big front window of his shed, Brewster saw the old Desoto pull up the lane, and he watched it. When it slowed in front of the shed, he recognized Trumpet Eyes. Trumpet Eyes stepped out, and Brewster saw he was thin as a stalk, the stubble on his face had grayed, skin hung loose off the edge of his face, and his arms were as spare as a child's. He opened the shed door, and Brewster continued his work, pretending he had not seen him come up the lane. Trumpet Eyes came through the door, removed his cap, and held it in his right hand. A large gap in the front of his mouth caused a whistling sound when he spoke.

"Your daddy's dying. Better come on and see him. He won't make it long."

Brewster didn't answer.

"Laying up there at his house. Doctor says everything's gone down. Liver's 'bout stopped, heart's not strong—that's as I understand it. Doctor says his kidneys don't work right most of the time, and he's swole-up big in his feet."

"How long has he been down?"

"Flat in the bed two weeks. Needs to go on to the hospital, but I can't make him. He don't have no money to go with noway."

"I'll be on this afternoon," Brewster said.

With that, Trumpet Eyes put his cap on his head and left.

Marlenna went with Brewster to the old house at 20 Perry Street. Happy Landing, across the street from his father's house, was more run down than ever, and four men sat on the steps. When Brewster and Marlenna entered the house, the sight of it sent a wave of dread through Brewster. He wanted to turn around, go out the door, and not be bothered with what he knew he would face. Newspapers, dirty clothes, remnants of food, glasses and plates, candy wrappers, and beer cans cluttered the chairs and the sofa. In the bedroom, Trumpet Eyes read a newspaper by the light from the window, and Tom rested in bed, a small mound under an old quilt. He held almost no weight on his bones. He opened his eyes when Brewster spoke to him, but he did not speak in return.

"We've got to get him to the hospital," Marlenna whispered. She hunted for a washcloth in the bathroom, but could find nothing but a dirty towel which she moistened to wipe Tom's face. Brewster called Our Savior's Home, then he stood by the bed, but he did not touch his father. Through half-opened and matted eyes, Tom watched like a hurt animal, his dark eyes following every movement. Brewster folded the quilt back, exposing his father's tee-strapped undershirt, thin undershorts, and reed-like legs.

"This is all I can find." Marlenna handed Brewster a pair of dirty khaki pants and a crumpled shirt. The clothes smelled musty with food odors and body sweat. Brewster put the shirt around Tom's shoulders and helped his father slip his twisted left hand through the armhole. He slid the pants over Tom's swollen feet and pulled them up Tom's raised legs. Tom lifted himself slightly, and Brewster pulled the pants up to his waist. Tom fumbled and labored with the zipper and the snap until Trumpet Eyes stepped forward and finished the job.

"Can you walk, Tom?" Brewster asked his father. Tom closed his eyes and appeared to sleep.

Brewster put his arm under his father's back, sitting him upright, and he moved his father's legs and feet to the edge of the bed. He lifted him and carried him out of 20 Perry Street. He used to dream of lifting Tom and throwing him into the ditch at the road, but now he carried him toward the back seat of his Buick, holding him like a baby.

At Our Savior's Home, two orderlies placed Tom on a gurney, and he opened his eyes only long enough to see the place where he rested and closed his eyes again. His body trembled, his jaws knocked up and back, his teeth chattering like thin ice hitting the sides of a glass. Brewster and Marlenna completed the paperwork while the sisters covered Tom with blankets and wheeled him down the long green corridor.

When Brewster and Matthew came the following day, Trumpet Eyes stood close to the bed with his back resting against the wall. Although there was a chair in the room, Brewster did not sit; he too leaned his back against the wall, not far from Trumpet Eyes. Matthew walked to the bed and held Tom's hand.

"Started in the potato sheds," Trumpet Eyes said. "That's how long me and your daddy knowd each other." He said this as if Brewster was interested in knowing the history of their friendship.

"We was young and we started working in those potato sheds. Wanted to work our way up to counter and timekeeper. The good jobs. You know those jobs, preacher?"

"I do." Matthew turned to face Trumpet Eyes. "Count the sacks and sign off on the time for everybody. I've spent my days in the corn and the potato sheds too, and might spend some more before I'm done."

"After a while we knowd we was not gon' make it. Some got to be timekeeper, but they was the old ones, old men and a few old women. Young ones like us not gon' make timekeeper 'til our shoulders slump."

Tom listened and wiped the edge of his mouth with his bent wrist. "Never was," Tom whispered, and the words sounded heavy.

"Shiney, we made our money on shiney. Drunk a good bit of that too," Trumpet Eyes grinned exposing his yellowed teeth. "Guess that what gon' kill us now."

"Thought I had time," Tom whispered. He opened his eyes. "Gone now."

Trumpet Eyes stepped close to the bed, and Matthew relinquished his spot, stepping back, leaning against the wall with Brewster. "We hung together. We wasn't worth a lot. Had to stick together and maybe add up."

Sister Francesca herself called at four-thirty in the morning. "Better come on," she said. "The signs are not good."

When Brewster drove to the parsonage, Matthew stood in the doorway with a coffee cup in his hand. "You want some?" he said and pointed to his cup.

"No," Brewster said. "We better go on."

In the hospital room, dim and shadowy, the sound of Tom's pulling for air filled the dusky spaces. Matthew walked directly to the bed and took Tom's hand, although it had a tube attached to a vein on the front surface.

Tom did not open his eyes, but muttered something, struggling to give the words air. Brewster fitted the words into meaning—"S-h-o-u-l-d d-o-n-e b-e-t-t-e-r."

"We all should do better," Matthew said.

"P-r-a-y," Tom said, and the word was no more than a moist stream of air, the p, a long but impotent explosion at his lips. "P-ray."

Matthew motioned for Brewster to get out of his chair and take Tom's hand, and when Brewster took the hand that Matthew had been holding, he felt the calluses in Tom's palm, the skin rough and worn coarse. He felt the bones in Tom's fingers and the coolness of Tom's hand. He did not remember another time in his life when he had held his father's good hand. Matthew closed his eyes and prayed in a normal sounding voice, not in a whisper, and not loud, but the words sounded in a regular pattern, not like last tidings uttered at bedside of a dying man.

"Tom is a man who could have done better, Lord, but we all could have done better. You are a God who is not waiting to get us, not wanting to trap us, to catch us, not desiring to punish us harshly, but waiting to take us if we come home. Tom wants to come home. Tom has his arms out asking for forgiveness. Is that right, Tom?"

Matthew opened his eyes and looked at Tom whose eyes were closed and whose chest heaved in little lifts trying to gather air. Tom did not open his eyes, but he shifted his head up and down in an affirmation, and Brewster saw tears run down Tom's cheeks and onto his pillow.

"Tom is a man who is asking forgiveness and who wants to come home. We know that, even on his deathbed, if a man sees the error of his ways and asks forgiveness, he will be received in the kingdom of heaven. Tom is the prodigal son who has come home. If he repents his sins and you see that, then all is forgiven. You will be waiting to receive him like the father of the prodigal. You will be there when he steps from this life into the next."

Tom coughed and gasped for air. He doubled up, with his head and knees almost meeting. Brewster released his father's hand, and Matthew hurried to the door and called the nun, stationed at a desk down the hallway.

"You men need to step out for a while," the nun said. "Go down the hall to the waiting room. We'll come for you." Brewster turned and looked once more at his father who grabbed short breaths in fierce, shallow gulps, trying desperately to shove it down to his lungs.

"How you doing?" Matthew asked when they entered the small green waiting room. Neither man sat.

"I saw him beat TeeBoy 'til blood ran," Brewster said.

"He was knocked down himself," Matthew said. "Don't explain everything, but some parts of his life are standing in clearer light."

"We all been knocked down," Brewster said.

"Fear and anger, and most of us start kicking somebody."

"I'm letting it go," Brewster said. He put his hands with his fingers spread wide in front of him. "I've opened up these hands and I've let it go. He brought down Bess and TeeBoy. All I can do is open these hands and let it go. If I hold on to this grievance, I'll have to carry it, and I don't want to haul that load."

Matthew cuffed Brewster on the back of his neck. Both men stepped to the window and looked out over the grounds. A mist united with the morning air, locking a thick, damp calmness over the place.

"It has its own beauty here," Matthew said.

"You could almost forget at the end of that driveway there's every kind of madness and meanness. You could almost stand here and forget that."

"That's the way of grace," Matthew said. "It's that lightsome that comes right in the middle of all the chaos."

"He's gone," the nun said when she came into the waiting room. Behind her stood Trumpet Eyes, dressed in a ragged tee-shirt, faded green work pants, and rubbersoled brogans.

"I want to go back in the room by myself," Trumpet Eyes said. He followed the sister down the hall, and after a while Matthew went into the room and came out with his arm around Trumpet Eyes.

When Brewster went to 20 Perry Street the next day to tell Trumpet Eyes about the funeral, the house was empty. Brewster walked across the street to Happy Landing and asked the men who sat on the cinder-block steps if anyone there had seen Trumpet Eyes, but no one had seen him.

At the grave, Matthew read scripture. He read the verses from the fifteenth chapter of Luke:

> *I will get up and go to my father and I will say to him,*
> *"Father, I have sinned against heaven and before*
> *you; I am no longer worthy to be called your son;*
> *treat me like one of your hired hands." So he set off*
> *and went to his father. But while he was still far off,*
> *his father saw him and was filled with compassion;*
> *he ran and put his arms around him and kissed him.*
> *Then the son said to him, "Father I have sinned*
> *against heaven and before you; I am no longer*
> *worthy to be called your son." But the father said to*
> *his servants, "Quickly, bring out a robe—the best*
> *one—and put a ring on his finger and sandals on his*
> *feet. And get the fatted calf and kill it, and let us eat*
> *and celebrate; for this son of mine was dead and is*
> *alive again; he was lost and is found!" And they*
> *began to celebrate.*

When Tom was lowered into the ground at old Hope Hill Cemetery at the feet of Mama Tee and to the left of Bess, Matthew read from the third chapter of John:

> *Indeed, God did not send the Son into the world to*
> *condemn the world but in order that the world might*
> *be saved through him.*

"It's closed," Brewster said to Marlenna. "No father, no mother, no brother, no grandparents. When I go, I carry with me all of what happened on 20 Perry Street. The record will be closed."

And just outside the white wrought-iron arch that said Hope Hill Cemetery, Brewster put his arm around Matthew. "When we walked together with Tom this last distance, you became father, brother, and always friend." Matthew did not answer. He put his hand in the middle of Brewster's back, and they walked to the oyster-shell driveway.

19

Late on a Saturday afternoon in early January, Matthew's car rumbled to the porch. When he came up the steps, Tee went to him, and he hoisted her on his shoulders. Brewster joined Matthew, and they went into the big room with Matthew still carrying Tee on his back. "I've been to Selma today. They've got all kinds of things going on over there. I wish we could get some action here in Low Ridge."

Matthew circled around the big room with Helen Teelda on his shoulders, and then he stood in front of Brewster. "Since this time last year, we got five new voters here, that's all we been able to get to the registrar. Folks say, yes sir, yes sir, I'm going on down there to get myself registered, but they don't. They're too afraid." Matthew bent his knees down and up, giving Tee a bumpy ride. She squealed and laughed. "Martin King is over there in Selma now, and he plans to get voters registered. The vote is the prize," Matthew said. "Every man holds equal power when he goes to the ballot box. We got to put that prize in black hands, but the whites got a tight fist on it and they won't let go."

He put his hands over his head and brought Tee in front of him, kneeling and placing her feet on the floor. "This is one sweet baby," Matthew said. "As God is my witness, I want to give this child something to grow up proud and happy about. But don't seem like it's going to happen."

On Thursday, Matthew went to Selma to march. Marlenna wanted to go too, but could not because of her teaching. Brewster was relieved. When Malcolm X spoke at Brown's chapel there, Brewster thought the whole place would come apart—Selma would splinter and float in a million little pieces all the way over to Low Ridge. But Malcolm spoke and left town, and Martin King was released after the *New York Times* printed his letter from jail, yet Sheriff Jim Clark claimed black folks came, protesting, into the courthouse and urinated on the desks and threw books on the floor.

"Everybody's got to know that's a lie," Matthew told Brewster. "They arrested me too, and when they took me in that courthouse, I couldn't have drawn a drop of water if I'd tried. Wasn't nobody peeing on any desks."

Matthew drove back and forth to Selma and brought reports to his congregation. He drove to nearby Marion where he marched in an evening rally and was hit on the head with the handle of an ax. A bandage covered the left side of his head when he spoke in church with the corner of his lip broken and swollen.

"I went to Marion," he said, "and I have never seen such carnage. When Reverend James Dobynes knelt down to pray, the police started beating him right there in front of our eyes. They beat him on the head and on his back and the man still on his knees before God. They drug him by his feet to jail. I was lucky," Matthew said and pointed to his face and head.

From the march in Marion, Brewster learned one other important piece of information. A reporter from NBC News named Richard Valeriani was in Marion on the night of the march, and he gave a report from the streets and pictures flashed on the TV screen. Marlenna screamed when she saw Travis Peets in the crowd, his hand raised, a whip held high.

"I saw him Brewster! I know it was him. In front of the camera, flailing like a mad man."

"He won't leave Low Ridge," Brewster said. "He's not the only one. Crazy men are everywhere, and I guess we got one close here on Ole Summit. We'll watch ourselves. That's all we can do anywhere." Marlenna put her head on Brewster's chest, wrapped her arms around him, and held him in a tight lock.

Three days after the night of brutality in Marion, Malcolm X was assassinated in Harlem. "I heard his words in his own voice, and for that I'm grateful. I sat in Brown's chapel over in Selma and heard the man," Matthew said.

"We heard him too. You remember, Brewster? We heard him in New York in front of the Hotel Theresa. That was a hundred years ago," Marlenna said.

On Saturday when Brewster looked out the window of his shed, he saw a curly blonde-headed girl standing beside Laurel. He went out the door and saw it was little Ruby, Travis Peets' granddaughter. "Your folks know you're over here?" Brewster shouted at the girl. She turned to him, startled, and he saw her face, round and full, and her gray-blue eyes.

"I come to play."

"We gon' play some ball," Laurel said.

"You're not going to play at all," Marlenna said from the porch. "You've got to go home. Go on back the way you came. Your folks will be looking for you." Marlenna came off the porch and took Ruby by the arm. "Come on." She walked with the girl down the lane to the nearest path. "Did you come this way?"

"No ma'am. I come from over there," the girl said.

"Come on then," Marlenna said and walked to the path halfway down the lane. Brewster joined Marlenna, and the two of them stood at the path and watched Ruby go into the mottled light of the woods. "We don't need that kind of trouble."

Laurel came over to where they stood. "We were going to play ball."

"Has that little girl ever come over here before?" Marlenna asked him.

"No, ma'am," he said. "I was looking at my baseball cards on the porch, and when I looked up I saw her walking toward the steps. She hadn't been here but a few minutes when Daddy came out of the shed, and then you ran her off."

"That girl can't come over here," Marlenna said.

"Son, that's a bad situation," Brewster said. "Her grandfather could be a dangerous man. If that girl comes over here again, you come and get me."

March roared in with strong winds and heavy rain, and on Sunday morning when Brewster stepped outside to start the car for the drive to church, he spotted a gray heap on the lane. It didn't look like a tree limb. When he walked toward it, he saw the trail of blood on the ground before he reached Valiant. When he lifted Valiant's head, he saw the bullet wound.

"God Almighty!" Marlenna said. Laurel buried his face in his mother's waist and cried. Tee put her arms in the air, and Marlenna held her.

"I'm going to put him in the ground before we go on to church. I don't want to face this when I come home." Brewster walked toward the shed to get his shovel, with Marlenna and Laurel one step behind him.

"How could Valiant get shot, Daddy?"

"Mr. Travis Peets," Marlenna said. "Brewster, you need to go to the sheriff."

"Let's get the dog in the ground and we'll go on to church. I'll get Matthew to come out this afternoon, and we'll go ask Travis Peets what he knows about this."

"You two shouldn't go over there."

"If Peets is going to stay, I need to talk to him about this. If he didn't do it, I guess we got ourselves an even bigger problem."

Matthew, who had spent his week on the road marching from Selma to Montgomery, was already well into the service when Brewster, Marlenna, Laurel and Tee arrived. He spoke to the crowd and they spoke back to him.

"Only two percent of the Negroes in Selma are registered to vote. You know the name of the sheriff over there—Jim Clark."

Jim Clark, echoed again and again through the church. *Jim Clark, Jim Clark, J-i-m C-l-a-r-k*—and the name faded through the congregation.

"And he told the black folks coming to the courthouse to go on home. There wouldn't be any voter registration that day. But the problem has been that no day is a good day for registering Negroes in Selma. We've been back time and time again, and Sheriff Clark says go on home."

"You go home, Mr. Clark," a woman's voice spoke.

"But the people didn't go home. They went to the churches, and we got so many people in Selma who want to vote, that the law enforcement had to direct traffic around the churches. People sat in the windows and stood outside because there were so many people inside, they couldn't get through the doors."

"And we said if we can't get to vote, we're going to march to Montgomery and tell the world we can't register in Selma. And you know how hard it's been to get out of Selma, how hard they've made it to cross the Edmund Pettus Bridge. They wouldn't let us. They drove us back with clubs and dogs and firearms."

The voices rose to such volume, Matthew had to stop, and he waited for silence. When quiet descended, he cleared his throat.

"But last Sunday was a day that will be marked in the history books, because on Sunday, over three thousand of us left Brown's Chapel, and we finally crossed the Pettus Bridge, and we set out on

Route 80 headed for Montgomery. I'm here to tell you it was a grand day. I was there. We couldn't all be there, and I was marching for every one of you here at Limrick Road Baptist. I looked out and I saw a sea of humanity, white faces and black, young and old, from north and from south. It was like Ghandi's march to the sea, but we were going to the state capitol. Going to Montgomery.

"People in cars came by and shouted all manner of profanity, and some old farmers along the way watched in silence, but they held up signs that called us every bad name you can imagine and some you probably can't bring to your mind, but it didn't matter because we were headed north on the highway. Headed toward Montgomery. We were out of Selma and nothing was going to stop us. We were going to tell the world that we wanted to vote in Alabama. As we headed north on the highway, we sang this song, *Pick 'em up and put 'em down, pick 'em up and put 'em down, marching on to Montgomery town.*"

Matthew got into the rhythm of marching feet. He stepped away from the podium, and his feet moved as he sang in his rough and uneven voice, "*Pick 'em up and put 'em down, pick 'em up and put 'em down, marching on to Montgomery town.*"

Some in the congregation joined him. "*Pick 'em up and put 'em down, pick 'em up and put 'em down, marching on to Montgomery town.*" More and more joined and the entire congregation swayed, lifting their feet up and down, even though they sat in the pews. They raised their feet and rocked with the rhythm of their words, "*Pick 'em up and put 'em down, pick 'em up and put 'em down, marching on to Montgomery town.*"

Old Aunt Laney hobbled to the front, and Matthew met her at the steps, took her hand, and escorted her up the stairs. She put her arm through the bend of Matthew's elbow, and they marched across the platform, arm in arm, moving to the rhythm of the congregation. Aunt Laney's feet lifted so high, she appeared to be strutting. "*Pick 'em up and put 'em down, pick 'em up and put 'em down, marching on to Montgomery town.*" Matthew marched with Aunt Laney down the steps of the platform into the middle aisle of the church, and they marched with locked arms to the back door—"*Pick 'em up and put 'em down, pick 'em up and put 'em down, marching on to Montgomery town.*"—and turned marching to the front again where Aunt Laney slipped back into her pew. Matthew returned to the lectern, wiped his face with his handkerchief, raised his hands for silence, and when the congregation settled, he continued. "We made it to

Montgomery!" and he raised his open palms in victory. The congregation erupted—applauding and stamping their feet.

"Let me tell you what Martin King said when we got there. Here are his words and I bring them to you today. He stood there on the steps of the capitol and he said, 'One day white faces and black faces will walk beside each other, up these steps.' He turned and he pointed to that capital dome. 'They will sit together here in the cradle of the Confederacy.'"

Late in the afternoon Matthew drove out to Ole Summit and went with Brewster to Travis Peets' place. Brewster hated this business of confronting Travis Peets, but it had to be done and he was ready. They got out of the car, walked up on the porch, and Matthew knocked on the grayed wooden frame of the screened door. Travis Peets came, one strap of his overalls down and loose across his chest. He opened the screen and stepped out to the porch. His eyes narrowed when he looked at them, and he did not speak.

Matthew and Brewster both took a step back. "Mr. Peets," Matthew said. "Brewster's dog was shot late last night or early this morning. Do you know anything about that?"

Peets looked at each man, and he worked his mouth into a tight twist. Then he shook his head in affirmation. "I got birds in the back. That dog was in my pen."

"That dog was so old and arthritic, he couldn't have chased a chicken or a rooster if the bird stood in front of him," Brewster said.

"That dog was in my bird pen. A man got every right to shoot a dog that gets in his animal pen. You go on and ask the sheriff." Peets spit tobacco over the porch rail. "He'll tell you the same thing. A man got every right to do that."

"We may have to go on to the sheriff," Matthew said.

"Go on then."

"My son loved that old dog." Brewster looked directly into the eyes of the short, nearly bald man standing in front of him, and at the same time he smelled the odor of food coming through the screened door—fried food, stale and heavy with oil.

Peets looked at them and circled his lower jaw around the wad of tobacco, moving it from one side of his mouth to the other, then he twisted his lips into a tight lock.

"Come on, Brewster," Matthew said, and the two turned and left Travis Peets standing on his porch.

They did not go to see Slim Tate because, in the county, a man had every right to shoot a dog on his property.

"I want to go over there and grab that old man by his throat," Marlenna said.

"Then what would you do with him?" Matthew asked.

"I don't know."

"I'd take him and I'd throw him in the dump," Laurel said, and they all laughed, and the laughter coming through Brewster's throat felt good.

"Peets trash to the dump," and Brewster pretended to drag his feet, hauling a heavy croaker sack on his back, which caused Laurel to nearly double with laughter. "Wonder if they'd charge us extra for a foul load like that?" Brewster knew he needed this laughter, because Travis Peets was a solid ball of annoyance lodged in his stomach. He had to watch himself, steady himself, or he would do something he regretted. He did not tell Marlenna nor Matthew how he felt because it was best to shove that ball tight into himself. Swallow and hold it, shielding it from daylight.

20

"Harlem in '64, Watts in '65, and Detroit City in '67," Eddie said when Carmella brought him out to the shed to help on weekends. "Those brothers up north know what they're doing. It's not this roll over and play dead stuff."

"Black folks in the south don't roll over and play dead either," Marlenna said. "Some of the most courageous folks I've ever seen have stood up right here in Alabama and over in Mississippi. You enjoy some of the rights they stood for and got knocked in the head for and some lost their lives for."

"Matthew can tell you all about that," Brewster said.

"The brothers up north are taking charge. They're running the show," Eddie said. "Saying they're in charge. Not going to be rolled over again," and he extended his arm in front of him, pretending he held a firearm and he pumped off three shots.

The riots started on Sunday, July 23, 1967. Police, state troopers, and the national guard were called into Detroit to settle the situation. By the time the riots ended, forty-one were dead, over three hundred injured, more than four thousand arrested, and over six hundred buildings destroyed or damaged by fire. Property loss was estimated at over $45 million.

"President Johnson, bless his heart," Matthew said on Friday night in late July. He and June had come out to Ole Summit for supper, and afterwards they sat on the porch while they swung and rocked and allowed their food to settle. "Says he's going to be the president who finishes what Lincoln started, and I do believe the man has a good spirit, but not much has changed. We're still poor, and you can walk on Limrick Road there and see that a good many of us don't have jobs and what we do have is using the bones and muscles in our backs and legs and shoulders, hauling and lifting, digging and trudging. Most folks right there at Limrick Road Baptist don't know the first thing about good education because they can't see it. Most don't vote so they don't know politics. This is still the white man's America."

He sipped his coffee and took a forkful of the coconut cake that Paulette had brought to the porch. He looked across Brewster's woods and fields, illuminated in the light of a big amber moon. "President Johnson's appointed an eleven-man commission to answer some questions about why black communities explode. Just blow apart sometimes," Matthew shook his head. "I don't have much hope this commission's going to come up with anything, but I guess it won't do no harm to have one more group look at us. Do you think they can tell us something we don't already know about ourselves?" he asked, and then he laughed and slapped Brewster on the back.

In the fall of Laurel's fourth year in school, Brewster was at the Three Brothers showroom when Herman Thomas called Carmella to tell her the Low Ridge School Board would be hiring a part-time music teacher at County Training School and she should apply. But Carmella wasn't called to the school board for an interview, and in several weeks Marlenna stopped by the showroom after school to tell Carmella the position had been filled by a white woman, Miss LuLu Mae Kahalley, who came every Tuesday to lead the singing.

"Miss who?" Carmella asked.

"LuLu Mae Kahalley," Marlenna told her again.

Every time Brewster stopped by the showroom at Three Brothers, he listened to Carmella tell the story of the lost job from the vantage where she observed life. He could almost taste her disappointment, and it made his own mouth dry and salty.

"Just the time you think you may be pulling ahead, there's a slight of hand, and some white woman winds up with your job, and at County Training of all places. No white woman would have wanted that job unless a black woman applied for it. That black woman was me. Here I'm selling furniture, and she in the black school singing."

"This must be what integration means," Albert Mixon said. "Fewer black teachers get to teach. White teachers take the jobs in the black schools."

"Brewster, you won't believe what happened today," Marlenna said as they sat at the dinner table. "I want Laurel to hear this. I was proud of him."

Laurel rolled his eyes and looked at his father in a bond of manhood.

"At the end of music class today when the students were leaving the gym, I heard the piano. I didn't look because I watched the students leave, and I thought Miss LuLu Mae played a piece as a marching tune for the children, the very same piece she taught in class. But when I turned my head, Brewster, it was Laurel at the piano. Laurel played the music. I went up there and told Laurel I was ashamed of him for playing the piano when he knows students are never allowed to touch the instrument. Too much teacher in me, I guess. I hadn't fully realized how amazing it was." Marlenna smiled in Laurel's direction.

"'This youngster has wonderful ears. Let him play,' Miss LuLu Mae told me. 'He has a lot of music in his head,' she said. Can you believe that, Brewster? Laurel was playing the piano."

Laurel could not hold his grin when Brewster looked at him. His mouth opened in a proud smile. Brewster spoke to Marlenna, but wrapped his arm around Laurel's shoulder. "Look at Carmella. You said your mother used to play. You can play piano yourself. And TeeBoy. He never had any kind of instrument, but he could dance— was dancing the night he died. Laurel inherited music from both sides. It's a gift." He patted the top of Laurel's head.

"I traded a Joe DiMaggio for a new Hank Aaron today, Dad," Laurel said.

"That boy chews enough bubble gum to rot all his teeth. Spends every nickel he gets on buying gum for those cards."

"That's okay," Brewster said, and again he tapped Laurel on the head in a gesture of anointment.

As the fall season deepened, Marlenna came home with news that Miss LuLu Mae had assigned Laurel as her assistant, and while she played the piano, Laurel began each song on pitch, and then the other students joined him.

"Great," Brewster said. "That's great." He put his hand on Laurel's shoulder and felt the small curve of his son's shoulderblade.

At the Christmas program Laurel's class sang carols and even Carmella came to hear them. Tee sat in her father's lap as Miss LuLu Mae called Laurel to the front and introduced him as her assistant, and with his back to the audience, he led the songs as Miss LuLu Mae played piano. Brewster loved seeing his son standing in the center of the stage, publicly acknowledged as a leader. He and Tee both feasted on Laurel in the spotlight.

"That's my name sake," Albert Mixon whispered to Marlenna. "That boy's going to make something of himself," he concluded at the end of the program, and he strutted out of the auditorium in search of Laurel, his gold-tipped cane lightly touching the tile floor as he nodded at those around him.

"I'm going to ask Miss LuLu Mae to give Laurel piano lessons," Marlenna told Brewster during Christmas break. "Of course, I won't do it until I ask Carmella because that job should have been hers and I know it. Carmella can teach Laurel voice, but even she admits she's not a trained pianist, and Miss LuLu Mae has studied piano at Oberlin. I haven't made up my mind for sure, but I think I may ask her. What do you think, Brewster?"

"Probably turn us down," Brewster said without taking his eyes off the paper where he calculated the quantity of wood he needed to build a table with an extension leaf for a customer in Montevallo.

"It'll be 1968 in a few days, Brewster. Some people have changed a little. Besides, she's fond of Laurel, and she's the one who said Laurel has talent."

"We got two women at church giving piano lessons."

"There's Grandmother Scott, but Brewster, she must be at least seventy-five. There's Elvina Banks, but she's not formally trained. If Laurel is going to study, seems to me he should have someone trained." She stressed the last word, narrowing the focus to Miss LuLu Mae.

"I don't know what all this trained business is about. Plenty of black musicians have done more than fine without being taught in some white woman's house. Duke Ellington for one and Satchmo Armstrong for two."

"But Brewster, you remember back when that man from Texas, that Van Cliburn, went to Russia and won that competition. We saw him in New York when they gave him a ticker-tape parade. I'll never forget that parade and that man riding in the open car, walls of paper floating down on him, and on us. Everywhere he was in all the newspapers. Laurel has talent, and why shouldn't he have the best education? He can do what he wants to do with it, but he should have a chance."

Brewster remembered seeing the redheaded young man with the curly hair sitting on top of the back seat of the black convertible. For a solid year after they got back from New York, Marlenna had played Van Cliburn's record as she cleaned house at Ole Summit.

"You can ask that Miss LuLu or whatever her name is, but I bet you a hundred dollars that woman never gave a colored boy lessons. Probably has no intention of doing it now." He looked squarely at Marlenna.

Marlenna tucked her lips together and pushed air slowly out her nose as she considered this, but Brewster could tell the idea continued to play in her head. "I should go ahead and ask Elvina Banks," Marlenna said, and her voice had an edge of anger in it.

"Today settled it," Marlenna said when school started again after Christmas. Marlenna's hands were on both of Laurel's shoulders as he stood in front of her in the kitchen. "Miss LuLu Mae called this boy up in front of the class and he took requests—piano requests, Brewster. He played 'God Bless America' and a little of 'Yankee Doodle,' and he played a song one of the boys hummed. He was amazing. I've made up my mind I'm going to ask her. I'll talk to Carmella tomorrow, and if my asking Miss LuLu Mae doesn't hurt her, then I'm going forward. This is for Laurel. He needs a trained teacher."

Brewster and Skinner were in the break room at Three Brothers when Marlenna stopped by after school the next day. "What difference does it make?" Carmella asked. "I didn't get that job and I won't get it now. Go ahead and ask her to teach Laurel. This is a new world. No reason a white woman shouldn't teach Laurel."

Marlenna did ask Miss LuLu Mae, who said she would check her schedule to see if she could make room for one new student in her studio, and in the week Miss LuLu Mae considered her decision, Brewster helped Marlenna sort through all her mother's old music books. She kept out the easiest pieces for Laurel. She called a piano tuner, who got the old upright in good pitch, and she polished the cabinet with a rich oil Brewster brought her from the shed. All the while, Laurel insisted he wanted to play baseball, not piano, but Marlenna reminded him he had a gift, which was also a burden— God-given talent to be tended, nurtured, and developed.

After a solid week's consideration, Miss LuLu Mae added Laurel McAtee as a member of her studio—the last lesson of the day, Tuesday afternoons at six-thirty.

All the news on Laurel's advances at the piano came to Brewster second hand, generally at the dinner table where on Tuesdays, Marlenna told every detail of the piano lesson. "I sit there in Miss LuLu Mae's living room and, Brewster, that's a sweet time. He can play!" she cooed.

"May I go on up to my room?" Laurel asked.

"If you're finished eating," Marlenna said and reached to rub the side of Laurel's face, but he shot under her arm and went up the stairs to his room.

Marlenna put Laurel on a strict schedule, and Brewster observed, not involving himself in the piano lessons. Marlenna was the educator, not him, and Brewster thought a mother should set the course for a child. He observed in silence while Laurel practiced one hour a day, every day. Laurel fussed about it. He didn't want to do it, but Marlenna stood behind him and made him work; she made him go over each part of his lesson as Miss LuLu Mae had outlined it. Every week he practiced three pieces, and he read music from a book that had soldiers marching across the lines like musical notes; he repeated scales and arpeggios, and practiced holding his hands like tents above the keys; he sat at the kitchen table and filled in the blanks on mimeographed worksheets that smelled of chemical fluids and purple jelly. By Saturday evening, his purple sheets were completed and placed in a buff-colored manila folder ready for his lesson on Tuesday. Laurel wanted to play ball with the boys in the weed lot across from County Training School, but Marlenna made him sit at the piano and practice his three pieces one hour each evening and two hours on Saturday, and Albert Laurel McAtee became a serious musician despite himself.

Skinner pleaded with Brewster to let Laurel stay in Low Ridge and play ball because he had a mixed team. "This is history," Skinner said. "We got black boys and white boys playing together for the first time. Laurel don't want to miss a thing like this. I'll take good care of the boy. Look at David, I take good care of him, or he takes good care of me, one or the other, but we do fine. Let the boy stay in town."

Brewster thought about it and decided his son needed to be in the company of other men. He needed to feel his manhood, the full strength and power of it. He persuaded Marlenna to allow Laurel to stay four nights at his grandfather's house when Skinner's team played a triple-header. Marlenna argued against it, saying he needed to do his schoolwork and practice his piano, but Brewster told her a man should spend some time outdoors, especially in the spring of the year. "The black man has a big history in the ballpark," Brewster argued. "Goes all the way back to the colored teams," he explained to her.

On the fourth night of Laurel's stay in Low Ridge, the telephone jangled into Brewster's sleep, waking him with an awful start.

"Brewster, the Sheriff's got the boys. They slipped out. Stole cigarettes at the Pak-N-Sav. Come on into town. We got to go get them," Carmella's voice broke in a sob. He had her repeat the words, tell him again the message he did not want to hear, and then he dressed and left Marlenna in the kitchen, a cup of coffee in her right hand and tissues wadded in her left.

When Brewster and Carmella arrived at the Sheriff's Office, Brewster was pleased Slim Tate was not on duty. An officer brought both boys out. Neither boy wore cuffs, and for this Brewster was also grateful. Laurel came to him, wrapped his arms around Brewster's waist and placed his head over Brewster's heart.

"This one took the cigarettes," the officer said and pointed to Little Eddie. "This one was in on it, but he waited outside."

"Last time he's ever gon' do something like this," Carmella said, and she snatched at Little Eddie's arm, pulling him toward her.

Carmella agreed on a time when Little Eddie would return and speak with a judge, and the officer turned to Laurel, pointing his finger in the boy's face, "You got lucky. Next time you'll be in the same situation."

"Won't be a next time," Brewster said, and the officer looked at him but said nothing.

"You ever gon' learn?" Carmella asked when they were in the car.

"Had a little fun," Eddie said. "We didn't mean no harm. Happens that way sometimes."

"Get your head busted," Carmella said, anger in her voice.

"Not that bad," Eddie said, and he placed his hand on Carmella's back. She turned to him and slapped his hand in midair.

Brewster kept quiet. He would speak with Laurel on the drive out to Ole Summit. He knew already the boy meant no harm. He wanted to keep up with Eddie, but he had made a misjudgment and for that he could have paid serious consequences. He would explain all this to Laurel, but this was a reminder to him too, a lesson—a warning. Keep the boy close, don't let him find trouble on Limrick Road as TeeBoy had done. He would shield him on his sixty acres, safeguard him there, and on the drive back out to Ole Summit he also prepared himself to talk to Marlenna, the lioness protecting her cub, who would look at Brewster with an accusing eye—*The fullness of his manhood, huh?*

When summer came, Brewster bought more land, property on the north side of Peets' three acres, and now he had the man surrounded—it was only a matter of time before Peets would sell, simply a matter of time. He planted cotton in his new fields, which he tilled with Laurel beside him on the tractor, and he hired a man to help them. Travis Peets came to the edge of his land, put his hands on his hips, and watched them, but Brewster ignored him.

Laurel fussed about not spending more time in Low Ridge with David and Eddie, but Brewster and Marlenna kept him busy with plowing, helping in the shed, and practicing his music. In the evenings, Brewster sat beside Laurel on the piano bench and fingered some of the tunes he remembered from the honky tonks around Low Ridge, old stuff—blues from Charlie Patton, Robert Johnson, and Muddy Waters.

"This is the Negroes' music," Brewster said. "Comes from the heart."

"And from the field," Marlenna cut him short.

"From the dirt-poor farmers tilling the soil. That's what we're doing this summer. Right son?"

"Yeah," Laurel said and fingered some new chords for the melody Brewster found with his index finger. Laurel didn't need any music for these pieces. He added chords and held the notes an extended time, making his own statements.

"This is the black man's classics," Brewster said, and Laurel grinned at his father.

Helen Teelda came into the big room, sat on the floor, and watched them. When she started school, she would take her lessons from Elvina Banks at church. She had her first *Big Note Easy Reader*, and occasionally she attempted to pick out a few notes on the keys. She would not be the fast study her brother had always been, but she tapped her feet and listened to her daddy and Laurel play.

21

April 4, 1968, when Brewster came through the doors and walked into the passage at Ole Summit, he saw Marlenna, Laurel, Paulette, and Tee in front of the television, handkerchiefs in their hands, tears on their faces. "What's wrong? What's happened?"

"I can't say it," Marlenna answered, her voice raw and hoarse from her weeping. "You tell him, Paulette."

Before Paulette could speak, Tee came to her father, put her arms around his legs, and he lifted her. She rested her damp cheek on his shoulder. Paulette told him what had happened at six o'clock on the second floor balcony of the Lorraine Motel in Memphis, Tennessee. The unthinkable. Martin Luther King shot in the neck by an assassin. Martin Luther King dead at the age of thirty-nine. *Too young. Too young,* Brewster thought.

The TV played his speeches, and they echoed in Brewster's head.

> *I don't know what will happen now. But it doesn't really matter with me because I've been to the mountaintop. Like anybody, I would like to live a long life. But I'm not concerned about that now. I want to do God's will. And He's allowed me to go up to the mountain. And I've looked over. And I've seen the promised land. I may not get there with you, but we as a people will get to the promised land. I'm not worried about anything. I'm not fearing any man. Mine eyes have seen the glory of the coming of the Lord.*

In the stillest part of night, the weight was heavy on Brewster's chest, and he could not sleep. He went to the porch and sat in his deep green chair, and then he rose and walked to the end of his lane, trying to understand what had happened, trying to see the world in the light of a clear, full moon, but what happened on this old floating sphere, set in the middle of God's creation, didn't make sense. The voice of a good man silenced; the peacemaker gunned down; thirty-nine, thirty-nine years old. He walked back to his porch, turned again and walked down the lane all the way to Ole Summit Highway, looking at his land, looking across the street at his plowed fields, looking at the paths that came into his property from the woods, and he could not make any sense of it. He looked up at the stars and felt as small as an ant, and he felt kicked by a giant toe connected to a cruel and uncaring force. Martin King, DEAD.

If any of you are around when I have to meet my day, I don't want a long funeral. And if you get somebody to deliver the eulogy, tell them not to talk too long. Every now and then I wonder what I want them to say. Tell them not to mention that I have a Nobel Prize, that isn't important. Tell them not to mention that I have three or four hundred other awards, that's not important. Tell them not to mention where I went to school. I'd like somebody to mention that day, that Martin Luther King, Jr., tried to give his life serving others. I'd like for somebody to say that day, that Martin Luther King, Jr., tried to love somebody.

"My heart is aching so much today, I can hardly get air inside my chest," Matthew said from the podium on Sunday. "If I can get the breath, I want to give you some of Martin's last words. That's what I can do. I can give you some of his last words, and I can tell you what the Christian has to do at a time like this. I can't do very much to seal the wound you've got opening your own hearts today, but I can do these two things—tell you what Martin said, and tell you what I know the Christian should do."

Matthew paused and appeared to struggle for air, and Brewster watched him. Brewster could not get enough breath in his own lungs, and he knew the weight was pressing on Matthew's heart. Matthew wiped his eyes with his handkerchief and studied the faces of his congregation. "Here is what he said: It's all right for us to talk about long white robes over yonder, but ultimately people want some suits and dresses and shoes to wear down here. It's all right to talk about the streets flowing with milk and honey, but God has commanded us to be concerned about the slums down here and his children who can't eat three squares a day. It's all right to talk about the New Jerusalem, but one day, God's people must talk about the new New

York, the new Atlanta, the new Philadelphia, the new Los Angeles, the new Memphis, Tennessee and, I'm going to add, the new Low Ridge.

"And Martin King said this. He said, 'I won't have any money to leave behind. I won't have the fine and luxurious things of life to leave behind. But I want to leave behind a committed life.' That's what Martin King said."

Matthew paused and pulled out a small glass of water from under the lectern. He drank a swallow while the congregation spoke back to him in the space he left open. He wiped his face and continued. "And what is the response of the Christian? It is not to give evil for evil, not give violence for violence, a tooth for a tooth. It is our job to live that committed life. Do good wherever we find ourselves, reach a hand out to those in need, lift ourselves up, hold on, have faith, put one foot in front of the other, and march on. Those are our jobs now. That is Martin King's legacy. God give us the grace to walk through these days and nights of darkness." And Matthew invited prayer, prayer from any mouth that wanted a voice before the Almighty, and the church became alive with the sounds of intercession, beseeching peace for themselves and for a grieving nation. Laurel put his hand in the hand of his father, and Brewster held it, placing his left hand on top of it, feeling the warmth of Laurel's hand in his own.

Laurel was into his second year of piano study, and, by Brewster's observation, he seemed to realize some joys from his music study—at least he didn't grumble about it anymore. He sat at the piano bench, and Marlenna no longer stood behind him. He struck notes falteringly at first, and then he began to play the melody line, keeping his eyes on the page of music.

"He's doing well," Marlenna said. "Miss LuLu Mae tries to find places in the music Laurel might not have considered. Rests that break the patterns and long notes that hold the beat, but Laurel generally finds them all before she has to show him. I'm proud of him."

Laurel spent long hours in his room or at the piano bench—always alone. There were no other boys at Ole Summit for him to play with. Ruby Peets ran across the property occasionally, and Marlenna stood on the porch and watched her until she left, walking or running down one of the paths on which she had appeared. Skinner's son, David, didn't come out because he played ball on the mixed team in Low Ridge. Laurel wanted to be in town, but Brewster would not allow it—the boy had been misled once, and Brewster determined this would not happen again. He had nearly followed Eddie into havoc, but had been spared injury. A second time and he may not be so fortunate. Brewster would keep Laurel on his own land—no harm would come to him there.

In his third year of music study, Miss LuLu Mae declared Laurel to be the best student in her studio, advancing faster than any student she had ever instructed. He played edited versions of the European composers—Bach, Beethoven, Chopin. But he also picked up the sounds of Muddy Waters and W.C. Handy, and he could play his own rendition of "The Memphis Blues," the notes floating in his head and transported to the pads of his fingers.

In the evenings, Brewster and Marlenna listened to him play— sometimes they sat in the big room and watched his hands drift over the keys forming arpeggios and blocked chords in one hand while the melody played from swift fingers in the other hand. Some evenings they listened from the kitchen while they cleared the dishes and put them in the sink, and Paulette and Tee danced around the kitchen table, moving to Laurel's music, holding hands and twirling. On Friday nights, they listened on the porch, if the night air was warm enough. If there was a chill, they started a fire in the hearth and sat in the big room to hear him and watch him play.

At church, Matthew asked Laurel to play something nearly every Sunday. He played pieces from memory for the offertory, his own versions of the old spirituals. Some Sundays he played Beethoven or Chopin for the final number while the congregation filed out of the sanctuary, ready for their Sunday dinners. Brewster and Marlenna remained seated on the second row from the front and watched Laurel's fingers on the keys.

Laurel received praise from everyone with the exception of Mrs. Banks, who said not one word about his accomplishments. It was obvious to Brewster and Marlenna that Elvina Banks thought they had stepped out of their place, courting the white man's music and worst of all, shunning her, she who had provided piano lessons to Negro children in Low Ridge for over thirty-five years, she who gave lessons to little Tee, but not to this gifted one—Albert Laurel McAtee. But Matthew came forward with praise in abundance. "Laurel has been blessed," he said, "and we can all enjoy this blessing."

Skinner had begun attending Low Ridge Baptist with David, who had transformed his father into a first-rate citizen. David was acknowledged as an outstanding student at County Training School, and Skinner was as surprised as was anyone else that his son had been marked with all the signs of the high-minded—anointed from birth with a keen intelligence and an affable spirit.

"Not done one thing to deserve this," Skinner said. "This is a blessing from somebody." Skinner purchased a navy-blue suit, white shirt, and red tie, and he sat on the second row from the front with Brewster and Marlenna. Matthew often asked David to read scripture while Skinner watched his son with a look of satisfied disbelief on his face—this was his son, smart and talented. How had this happened? But Skinner himself had earned a favorable reputation in the white community, as well as in the black community, because he coached the mixed ball team, which was on its way to a state championship. If Brewster had guessed ten years earlier how life was going to meander, he never would have imagined Skinner would enjoy this position, balanced comfortably with white and black admirers.

Laurel regretted not being on Skinner's ball team, but Skinner spoke words of encouragement to Laurel. "Don't you worry about that," he said. "You got your hands busy with that piano. One pair of hands can only handle just so much. We need folks to watch just like we need folks to play. God blesses the watchers as well as the players." And Skinner withheld no praise, "That boy's good at whatever he tries. Can't hardly wait to see him on the big stage."

In the spring of 1971, Marlenna convinced herself and Brewster too that Laurel would get a superior education at Low Ridge Junior High School because the buildings and facilities were new and because all the white schools enjoyed the favor of the county school board. She also believed he needed to learn from an early age to compete with white youngsters in the classroom because that would be the avenue to advancement. Skinner decided David would go to the new school too, Matthew enrolled his middle son Bo, and a few other youngsters from Limrick Road Baptist signed up.

The bus carrying students to Low Ridge Junior High School picked up kids from Bulah and came out Ole Summit Highway, headed to town. Laurel wanted to ride the bus because David would get on at one of the first stops in Low Ridge, and that gave the boys time to visit before school started. On the first day of classes, Brewster walked down the lane to the road with Laurel. He stood beside him while they waited for the bus. Ruby Peets stood at the end of her driveway, not more than fifty yards away from them, and she waved. Brewster put his hand in the air in a short salute, but turned immediately to face his son and to look at his own plowed fields across the road, his back to Ruby.

When the bus driver pulled to the shoulder of the road and opened the door, he pointed to Ruby. "Either you got to go that-a-way or she's got to come this-a-way. I'm not going to make but one stop." Laurel got on the bus, and Brewster heard the driver repeat the same message to Ruby when he stopped for her.

"How's school?" Marlenna asked Laurel at the supper table after his first day.

"Good," he said.

"Just good?"

"It's okay."

"Did you learn something today?"

"Not much. First day and all."

"It's beautiful, though," Marlenna said. "You're in that brand new building."

"It's okay." He pushed his food around on his plate, ate a little, and announced in a tired voice he needed to go to his room to start his homework. Neither Brewster nor Marlenna disagreed with him, and he left the table and went up the stairs.

When Brewster and Marlenna washed the supper dishes at the sink, Brewster offered his own interpretation of what he had heard. "I think it's his age. I don't think he's going to be forthcoming with much information."

Marlenna put the plate she rinsed on the drain board, put her damp hands on her hips, and looked at Brewster. "That was obvious," she said. "Clear and obvious!" For a split second, Brewster saw the firm-set jaw of his father-in-law imprinted on Marlenna's face, she removed her apron, threw it on the counter, and went up the stairs.

Paulette laughed. "I think she was looking for a little more on the interpretation end." She took Marlenna's place at the sink and handed Brewster a dripping plate. "Truth is, she's worried about him being one of the few black boys at that new school, and she's worried because Laurel's so tight-lipped. When a mother's worried about one of her babies, she's going to be short with everybody."

On the second day of school, Brewster again walked with Laurel to the end of the lane and stood beside him on Ole Summit Highway. "We better move to just about the middle," Laurel said. "That driver's not going to make two stops."

Several minutes after Brewster and Laurel assumed their new positions on the soft shoulder of Ole Summit Highway, Ruby Peets came to the end of her driveway. She also moved closer to the mid-point between the two properties, but she kept her distance, a full fifteen feet away. When she saw the bus, she moved in Laurel's direction. Brewster stood back several paces, watching Ruby and then Laurel get on the bus. He couldn't see Laurel because he had taken his seat on the opposite side of the bus, but Ruby sat in a window seat almost in front of where Brewster stood, and she turned and glanced at him before the bus exhaled heavy exhaust out its rear pipes and eased onto the asphalt of Ole Summit Highway.

On the third day, Brewster again walked to the end of the lane with Laurel, and they stood on the shoulder of the highway between the two properties. When Ruby came to the same spot where she stood the day before, Brewster observed her in quick glances, a heavy-set girl, with broad shoulders and thick legs, and her short, curly blonde hair was held off her face with a headband. She wore a dark skirt and a cream-colored blouse, and carried her books in the bend of her right arm. Laurel did not look in her direction, but looked north on the highway in the direction from which the bus would come, and he made small talk with his father about Skinner's ball team which had taken second place in the state competition. After the bus had pulled away, Brewster stood and watched it until it entered a curve down the road and was out of sight. Brewster walked back to the shed wondering if he and Marlenna had made the right decision to send Laurel to Low Ridge Junior High School. Laurel was quiet and sullen in the evenings, but Marlenna attributed this to his age.

"I raised four," Paulette said, "and I can tell you, every child starts to change some at about thirteen. I think they're beginning to become more like themselves. Meeting themselves and finding out who they are. Takes a whole lot of energy to meet yourself, and they stop talking for a while. They must be talking inside themselves all the time and they don't want to spend that much time talking outside themselves. Laurel's fine."

Brewster thought Paulette was right—it was partially his age. But he also knew Laurel had a cast-iron will, and that suited Brewster fine because that strong will would make him successful.

Every man needed that—Laurel's unbending, his unwillingness to engage in easy conversation did not disturb Brewster as it did Marlenna.

When Brewster went out the door with his son on the fourth day, Laurel turned to him. "Dad, how many days you going to walk down the lane with me? I think three days is about enough."

"I want to be sure everything is okay," Brewster said. "I can drive you into Low Ridge if I need to."

"The bus comes right here," Laurel said. "No need to drive. Besides, you got work."

"You right about that," Brewster said.

"You worried about Ruby Peets? 'Cause if you are, you can stop worrying about that. We don't even look at each other, let alone speak. She stays toward her place and I stay toward mine until we see the bus. She gets on the bus and sits with her friends, and I sit by myself until David gets on and he sits with me. Everything's fine, Dad. I feel kind of funny about you going down there and standing with me."

On the fifth day, Brewster waited on the porch and watched Laurel walk down the lane, and he moved to the far end of the porch to see him turn onto the shoulder of Ole Summit Highway. He did not go to the shed until he saw the yellow-orange of the bus pass the lane, braking to a stop, and he still stood, leaning over the banister, trying to glimpse the bus until he heard the door pulled into the side of the bus and the exhaust exhaled out the rear pipes.

22

Jake Warner, owner of Warner Timber, had a six-columned house at the south end of State Street. Several accidents occurred every year in front of the property because the place, set back on at least three acres of green carpet grass with a white picket fence around all three acres, distracted drivers. Drivers would look toward the grandeur and forget to navigate the bend in the road and run head-on into the telephone pole in the curve. Lack of speed saved the drivers and the passengers because the turn had already slowed them down to a crawl, and the house, rising like a cathedral out of a green sea, brought them to a near stop before they drifted into the pole in front of them.

Jake Warner, whose daughter took lessons from Miss LuLu Mae, planned a recital in his home, and Marlenna reported to Brewster that a note had been posted about the recital on the front door of Miss LuLu Mae's house

"Laurel knows his music," Marlenna said. "He's got plenty of pieces to play. But he needs a new suit. You're in charge of that, Brewster. Navy blue would be nice with a new tie, and be sure the tie has a little burgundy color in it. I always like that combination, navy with burgundy."

"You sure Laurel's going to play?" Brewster asked, and Laurel shrugged his shoulders.

"We're in her studio, Brewster. Laurel's Miss LuLu Mae's best student. It's not as if we're going to sleep over at the Warner place. Miss LuLu Mae will want to show him off." She rose, taking her dinner plate to the sink.

On Saturday, Miss LuLu Mae telephoned to request that Brewster, Helen Teelda, and Paulette come with Laurel and Marlenna to the next lesson. "He has plenty of pieces to perform, and we shouldn't let those go to waste. He has quite a repertoire and plays them all splendidly," Marlenna said, relaying the call from Miss LuLu Mae.

"She probably wants us to help her decide which piece he should play on the recital," Marlenna said. "He could give the whole program." She patted Laurel on his shoulder on her way to sweep the front porch, Tchaikovsky's *Concerto No. 1* playing in the big room.

On Tuesday, the day of Laurel's lesson at Miss LuLu Mae's house, Paulette prepared a special dinner: fried chicken keeping warm in the oven, potato salad in the refrigerator with lots of chopped olives and diced onions, green beans on the stove, and apple cobbler, ready to go into the oven as soon as they walked into the house after Laurel's lesson. Paulette wore a church dress, but without her hat. Tee wore a pink dress with white lace around the collar, and satin ribbons held the ends of her braided hair. At Marlenna's insistence, Brewster put on a fresh white shirt and his tweed jacket.

At Miss LuLu Mae's house, Paulette sat in the chair to the left of the piano, while Marlenna and Brewster sat on the sofa. Tee sat in a small rocking chair behind Laurel, and Miss LuLu Mae positioned herself across the room, next to a side table. Miss LuLu Mae had mimeographed a program in purple-jelly on plain white paper that listed the pieces Laurel would play, although she didn't need to do this for Brewster or Marlenna because they knew, by heart, the name of each piece.

Brewster thought Laurel's first piece, Edna Mae Burnham's "From a Lighthouse Window," was powerful. It had big sounds, big chords, and Laurel used his upper body to create the storm raging in the ocean outside the tiny lighthouse that stood on narrow legs in the tumultuous waves. To Brewster, this piece was the story of a lone man who survived a potent storm in the dark of night, a great-hearted man who held on through the wind and the darkness.

In Chopin's "Raindrop Prelude," Brewster saw colored drops of water descending—pink and blue, yellow and lavender, lime green and pale orange—tiny dots like confetti that flexed and wobbled when they fell and broke into millions of colored shimmering slivers when they landed and splashed. Beethoven's "Moonlight Sonata," was a blue moon piece—deep blue night with an enormous yellow-orange moon.

The sheet music for each of these pieces said "Easy Edition," but Brewster knew there was nothing easy about this music his son played. After each selection, Laurel bowed as Miss LuLu Mae had taught him to do. After the slow, plodding sounds of the "Moonlight Sonata", he proceeded to a breathless rendering of the "Minute Waltz"—tiny ballerinas on top of a music box, dancers no bigger than the smallest finger on Brewster's hand, twirling, dipping, and spinning, standing on tip-toed feet, moving so fast they created streaks of light that trailed iridescent stardust behind them.

The music was indeed beautiful, and Brewster watched Paulette wipe tears from the rims of her eyes with a filmy white handkerchief when Laurel played his last piece. Tee sat transfixed, watching her brother in the parlor of this white piano teacher. Brewster scratched his neck because his shirt had too much starch around the collar and was about to rub his neck raw. He was uncomfortable in the house of this old white woman who sat in the chair against the wall and looked to him every bit like an old crow, except her gray hair and pale white skin broke the pattern. She nodded her head to the beat in the music and smiled when Laurel finished each piece, like he needed her approval to proceed to his next selection.

Brewster wouldn't have been here if Marlenna had not insisted he come. Laurel played well, certainly, but Brewster could sit on his own porch in the cool of the evening, sipping iced tea and enjoying his son playing the piano. He could look out over his fields and his deep green woods, and enjoy the sweetness of Laurel's sounds floating over his acres. And when the boy was done with his practice, Brewster could go inside and jam with him, both of them sitting at the piano bench, Brewster pecking some of the melody with his index finger while Laurel supplied the rest of the melody, the chords and arpeggios. Laurel took old pieces and made them new, adding his own syncopated rhythms, adding parts of his own self that came through his arms and down past his elbows to the tips of his fingers. Brewster saw no point in being here this day, sitting uncomfortably on the hard couch with his starched Sunday shirt rubbing a red circle around his neck. As Laurel played Mendelssohn's "Preludium," Brewster thought of the fried chicken, the potato salad, and the apple cobbler waiting for them at Ole Summit, and he was ready for this event to be over.

He would not spoil this day for his son, so Brewster rubbed his neck with the cooling palm of his own hand, and he smiled politely at Miss LuLu Mae. After Laurel played his last piece and stood beside the piano, bowing deeply at the waist, receiving applause from his teacher and his family, Miss LuLu Mae went into the kitchen and brought out a plate of little cookies and passed them around. She handed out small paper napkins and brought out a teapot, placing it on the dining room table, offering tea to Marlenna, Brewster, and Paulette, and Kool-Aid to Laurel and Helen Teelda.

Brewster declined the tea and would not have touched one of the little hard cookies, but Marlenna cut her eyes at him and let him know—do not scorn the hospitality extended by Miss LuLu Mae! Brewster ate two of the tough little cakes, and when the plate was passed before Laurel, he looked at his father before he also took two of the round doughy balls. Laurel nibbled a small bite out of the first one and left the second one on his plate, but Brewster ate his cookies and regretted each bite he swallowed, because it cut into his appetite for fried chicken and Paulette's potato salad and her famous green beans with bacon and peppers, the same recipe she had cooked at her café for nearly thirty years.

Marlenna sipped her hot tea and ate the little hard cookies as if they were as worthy as the warm apple cobbler waiting at Ole Summit. On the drive home, Marlenna and Paulette chatted about the brilliant performance they had heard and about the warm hospitality of Miss LuLu Mae. Brewster, Laurel, and Tee sat quietly, listening to the women.

On the following Tuesday, Marlenna came through the doors at Ole Summit with a tissue at her eyes, "Miss LuLu Mae called Laurel's lesson his recital. She says Jake Warner invited only some of the students to play because the recital is private. PRIVATE." She sniffed and blew her nose. "I know Laurel's not going to play because he's the only black youngster in her studio."

Laurel stood behind his mother, taller than she. "I'm kind of glad I'm not going to play."

"I am too," Brewster said. "Now I don't have to put on one of those stiff-haired shirts and I don't have to put that noose around my neck." He raised his hands and pretended to knot a necktie.

"When I asked her what piece Laurel was going to play, that's when she told me he had given his recital at her house. Her skin turned white-hot with little red blotches floating on her cheeks, and her eyes, Brewster, her eyes froze when she looked at me—ice blue."

Marlenna went to bed, refusing to eat supper, but Laurel sat with the family at the dinner table. Paulette amused them, telling stories about the people who came and went from her café years earlier when her place was the only business in Low Ridge where a black man or woman could buy a hot meal. The evening passed with the day's disappointment settling in the rafters until they all went to bed.

While the disappointment remained sealed in the rooms at Ole Summit, the family got back to its routines and went through the week in regular patterns. On Sunday after the family returned from church and began setting the table for a late lunch, Miss LuLu Mae telephoned. Brewster answered and handed the phone to Marlenna. The rest of the family, including Paulette, stood in the big room watching and listening to Marlenna. When she put the phone back on the receiver, she announced that Miss LuLu Mae said Laurel was invited to perform in the program. He would be the last student. In fact, he could play two pieces, the Preludium and a really jazzy piece, "a honky tonk piece" Miss LuLu Mae had called it. It could be a piece he played with his father.

"He can play the liveliest piece he knows," Marlenna reported and looked at them.

She's got to make a special case of Laurel, Brewster thought, but he did not say it. *That's why she wants him to play honky tonk. Let everybody know he plays the Negroes' music.* That was fine with Brewster. Let him play the music of the field and of the heart, the music of experience and hurt and joy and pain. Fine, fine because his son could play the old white man's European music, yes, and he could play the black man's music too. Black as the earth from which every man came and returned. Brewster wanted to say all of this, but he held his words, wanting Laurel to make his own decisions about what he would play and when he would play. These would be Laurel's choices. Brewster maintained his own silence in favor of his son.

At the supper table, opinions bounced like tennis balls at a match, with each family member having the opportunity to hit.

"Miss LuLu Mae told me the program's printed," Marlenna said. "Says Laurel's name's already on it."

"He has his suit," Brewster said. "We took care of that last Saturday."

"I know my music," Laurel said.

"The boy will knock the socks off those white folks," Paulette said.

"I want to see what that big house looks like," Tee said.

"Well, I guess he won't ever have to do it again, unless he wants to," Brewster said.

"Oh, he'll play again, and it'll be in much grander places than this," Marlenna said. "This is only the start," and Laurel grinned.

On Saturday evening, Laurel wore his new navy-blue suit, his Sunday shirt, and his tie with a navy and burgundy pattern woven into the silk. Both Marlenna and Paulette wore their best church

241

dresses, and Tee wore a new dress made of mint-green batiste, with tiny tucks in the skirt and silk ribbon woven through the edge of the white linen collar. Brewster wore his suit, his starched shirt, and a tie around his neck. The women rode in the back seat. Paulette got in first and adjusted her skirt so no wrinkles would crease into it. Tee sat in the middle, and Paulette smoothed Tee's dress into a silky flow before Marlenna got into her place. The women allowed Laurel to sit up front with his father. Brewster glanced in the rearview mirror at the women, who sat stiffly in the back seat, not wanting to be in the least bit of disarray when they arrived at the columned house set deep on the green carpet grass.

Brewster pulled his old Buick through the large white gate and drove slowly up the drive that circled in front of the tall porch. Three large globes hung between the columns, and gas-flared lights illumined circles on the outside walls of the house and on the asphalt of the circular drive. Every light in the mansion appeared to be on and the entire place glittered, drawing the guests inside.

When they entered the foyer, Brewster saw Tee take the whole place in, turning her head to see both parlors on either side of the entry and wrapping her arm around the rose-colored fabric of Marlenna's belt, steadying herself while she gazed at the intricate work on the chandeliered ceiling. Folding chairs were set in an enormous parlor to the left of the tall foyer that had floating stairs ascending to a second level. Laurel stood straight, but stiff, beside his father, and the five of them froze in a huddle until a teenage boy, dressed in a dark suit and serving as an usher, stepped forward. "I'll show you to seats," he said. The boy turned and walked to the left parlor. Marlenna pushed Tee in front of her and motioned for Paulette to follow. Marlenna fell in line next and then Laurel, followed by Brewster. The teenage boy who led them stopped at the last line of chairs and extended his arm for Tee to enter the row. The boy counted out three programs and handed them to Brewster. Brewster kept one and sent two down the line toward Paulette.

"We don't each get one," Brewster whispered. "Share," a message intended for Tee.

"Back seat," Paulette hissed, and Marlenna cut her eyes at Paulette, who responded by tilting her head up and raising the point of her chin.

The grand piano, with its satin black finish, rested on a raised platform in the front of the large gallery, and it reflected a sheen from a series of spotlights above it. The windows in the room extended from floor to ceiling, and the glass twinkled with dots of light from candles on stands that had been placed in the center of each window. The younger performers sat in a line of front-row chairs, and Miss LuLu Mae, wearing a black silk dress with tiny pink rosebuds screened into the fabric, walked in front of them, whispering final instructions.

The lights dimmed in the parlor, causing the platform with the piano to appear to be an island, elevated and formidable. Brewster studied his own children. Tee sat on the edge of her chair, leaning forward, more standing than sitting, watching the makeshift stage. Laurel sat rigid, holding his hands, looking down at his thumbs.

The first child, a little girl in a white satin and lace dress, played "Mary Had a Little Lamb" with one hand, and when she was finished, the audience sounded a collective "aaahhhh" and applauded loudly. For over an hour Brewster endured the fumbling of the white youngsters who sat on the front row, or near the front, and they rose when Miss LuLu Mae called their names. They grinned at the audience, and most of them missed notes or played off rhythm or had to stop and start their pieces again, though several played with steady beat and studied control. It was a long hour. It rolled past the minutes—slowly, slowly, and Brewster felt his hips growing weary, pressed against the hard metal of his folding chair. And then it was Laurel's time to play.

Miss LuLu Mae stepped to the stage. "Ladies and gentlemen," she said. "Our last performer is Laurel McAtee. He's naturally musical, as you may well guess. He will now play Mendelssohn's 'Preludium,' and then he'll play a little surprise piece, a little honky tonk." She put one hand at her waist, put her other hand in the air, palm open, and she swung her hips. The audience laughed at her joke.

Laurel stood. Brewster watched him, and at the same time, he reached for Marlenna, putting his arm around her, and her body eased into the bend of his shoulder. Locked together, they watched Laurel, they feasted on him. He stood beside the piano, tall and straight, in his new blue suit, and he bowed, elegantly. When he began the Mendelssohn piece, he played with uncommon presence, his notes clean and distinct, filling the room with joyful sound.

The piece sounded like marchers, strutters, straight and tall, each one standing well over six feet; the marching notes made clean strides through the room, stepping in controlled patterns, in union, each note connected properly to the one before it. When Laurel finished, the audience applauded, but Laurel remained at the bench. His hands hovered above the keys, and the audience hushed. He started with a little sprinkle of playful notes, just enough to tease a melody, soft and low. Then he repeated the theme more boldly, stated it directly, and the audience listened. And then the music laughed at itself and took off on a wild ride, the theme going in five different directions, rolling chords in the right hand and the melody pounding in the left, the rhythm syncopated, breathing like a jazz musician who knows exactly how to pull the listeners into the musical narration. Brewster knew this piece, at least he knew the opening notes; he had heard it in a joint over in Hurley County twenty years earlier, had played the notes for Laurel, and the boy had taken it from there, adding, building the piece, changing rhythms, varying the message ten different ways. This was Laurel's own piece now, something he created from a fistful of sounds Brewster had placed on the keys.

The white audience began to clap with the music because they thought they understood the rhythm, but then it shifted again, and they kept on clapping for some long seconds until they realized Laurel had left them behind. Brewster did not know how the boy continued to play. *Bong, bong, be-bop, bop, bong, bop bong, bop bong.* Chords rolled in the left and then those same chords rolled backwards. The audience laughed, and one man shouted "whooooo" because the ride on this piece of music was thrilling—Laurel drove and he took a sudden turn changing directions, up a hill, down into a valley, turning a corner. Hold on now, Brewster thought. Place those hands on the safety bar because Laurel McAtee is at the keys, driving and taking this white audience on a ride where only he knows the route, but they can see the scenery. Hold on. Hold on tight. Tight. And then the notes rolled in both hands, the pace fast, fast, racing, then it slowed to little sounds, and some woman sang through the keys, soft and low, her voice smooth as whiskey, then she laughed, hit a final note like a little female giggle, and the audience exploded. Laurel stood and bowed, with the audience erupting in applause. Before Brewster had time to realize what was happening, the audience members were on their feet, and Laurel bowed a second and a third time. He left the elevated island and weaved his way through the chairs and came back to stand beside his father, while the audience still applauded and turned toward the back of the room to face Laurel. He stayed near Brewster's right elbow as a sea of white faces turned to congratulate him.

Mr. Jake Warner himself came to where Brewster and Laurel stood, and he escorted the family to the foyer where refreshments were arranged on a round table in the middle of the entry room. A black woman carrying a silver platter that held little cups of punch walked toward them extending the tray. They each reached for the handle of a small cup filled with a pink frothy drink.

"This boy can play!" Jake Warner said to Brewster. "I have to tell you, I wasn't expecting any of the youngsters to play like this. That last piece was a nice break from all that other stuff." Then Jake Warner moved away from them with his hand on the back of the black woman who held the tray. The woman turned, extending the pink drinks toward the other guests.

"Help yourselves to the food," Jake Warner smiled over his shoulder.

Brewster was glad Laurel had made the decision to play, because now Laurel knew his music commanded attention; when he sat before the black and white keys, he was master. He had created sounds that floated like ribbons around the room, and other sounds that jerked heads like strings on a puppet. Laurel was prince at the keyboard and tonight he had to know it. He stood beside his father, tall, lean, and elegant, a glass of pink punch in his hand, and he accepted words of praise from the white people who came to him and courted him. The family ate cheese breads and white-iced cakes, and Laurel shook hands and smiled at every guest who rendered greetings and compliments. On the way out the door, Tee grabbed one last handful of pink-iced cookies to eat in the car on the drive out Ole Summit Highway.

23

When Laurel played for an evening program at school, he asked if the family could give Ruby Peets a ride. "She won't have a way to get there if we don't take her. Her grandparents won't go out at night unless they have to. They're old, I guess."

"We can't take that girl," Marlenna said. "Now if her grandmother called and asked if we could give Ruby a ride, that would be a different story."

"She won't have any other way to get there," Laurel protested.

"Your mother's right," Brewster said. "When they want us to give that girl a ride somewhere, they'll ask us."

"I know you wait for the bus with Ruby every morning, but you keep to yourself," Marlenna said.

"I speak to her," Laurel said. "We don't talk much. I feel sorry for her because a lot of kids make fun of her. Her house and all, " Laurel said to clarify himself. "I know she wants to come to the program tonight."

It was strange, Brewster thought, to hear his son plead a ride for this white girl. What would Travis Peets have thought if he had heard Laurel? And Brewster thought too that the old man was now a neutralized force. With the white schools having been integrated, he could not broadcast his segregationist venom as far or wide or deep as he once could, and this thought satisfied him.

At the end of school term, when class officers were elected for the coming year, Laurel ran for president of his class and much to Brewster's surprise, he was elected. The *Low Ridge Gazette* carried an article about how well integration had worked in Low Ridge. Smaller pieces were carried in the *Mobile Register,* and *The Tuscaloosa News.* He knew this because friends at Limrick Road Baptist gave him copies of these other papers. Somehow Anvil Thomas saw the Low Ridge article, which included a picture of Laurel, and he sent a letter of congratulations to the boy, handwritten on hotel stationery. Albert Mixon cut the article from the *Gazette* and taped it to the front window of Three Brothers showroom, and Matthew held the article in front of him as he stood at the pulpit on

Sunday. The congregation erupted in applause, and Laurel dropped his head, studying his thumbs. Brewster knew Marlenna was right about their son and about his name. Laurel was a crowning glory on the heads of his father and his mother, the best fruit of the vine.

Skinner's son David had a good year too and played on the school ball team. Matthew's son, Bo, was shy and didn't stand in as much light as did Laurel or David, but he had done fine and Matthew's oldest son, Jason, who studied at the University of Alabama, did well in his studies and came home for the summer to work in the corn and potato sheds, sorting and grading the produce.

"I think the 1970s may be better than the 1950s or the 1960s," Matthew said. "This may be a whole decade of peace and prosperity."

"That would be nice," Brewster said. "That would be nice," and he laughed from the thought of it.

It was twenty minutes after two in the afternoon when Carmella telephoned Brewster in the shed at Ole Summit. "Eddie cut a boy at County Training. He's at the sheriff's office. Come on and help me."

Brewster went with Carmella to the sheriff's office, but there wasn't much he could do. Eddie was taken to the county youth center sixty miles away. He had gotten in a fight with an older boy at school and pulled a knife to even the difference in their age and height. The boy he cut had a slice in his chest two inches long and a quarter-inch deep, but Eddie got lucky because the cut missed vital organs and was stitched-up with no permanent harm.

"Eddie doesn't have his mind on school," Marlenna said. "He's there only because Carmella makes him go. Soon as the bell rings, he's down Limrick Road somewhere, hanging out with a bad crowd."

When the case came to hearing, Eddie was sent to state school at the youth center. "This may be what he needs to teach him a good lesson," Carmella said to Brewster and Marlenna. "He's in those teen years now. I don't have many more years to influence him."

Carmella drove to the state reform school one evening a week to have supper with Eddie, and she went again on Saturday to spend time with him. He would be in the reformatory only one semester, but Carmella expressed her hope that the impact would be permanent.

"You see the trouble a boy can get himself into?" Marlenna asked Laurel. "Staying busy keeps a boy out of trouble and, Laurel, there's a whole world out there. So much to see and do, but you need to be prepared. Keep on studying and when opportunity comes, Albert Laurel McAtee will be ready."

"Eddie's okay," Laurel said. "You're focusing on his bad points and Eddie has lots of good points."

"I'm glad Eddie's gone for a while," Marlenna told Brewster. "I'm not saying I'm glad the boy got into trouble. I'm not saying that at all. What I am saying is that Laurel is in junior-high school, and he doesn't need a negative influence so close to him. Maybe Eddie will finally see what happens when you get yourself into trouble."

When Eddie came back to Low Ridge, he got an afternoon job in the potato sheds where new machinery sorted and cleaned the potatoes and rolled them down to the burlap sacks. Eddie carried the sacks to the warehouse or to the trucks for shipment out of Low Ridge.

"He's so tired when he comes home, there's not much energy left for trouble," Carmella said. "I believe he finally learned his lesson. Maybe he's going to make something of his life now."

Marlenna gave up her routine of sitting in Miss LuLu Mae's front room and listening to Laurel's piano lesson. She made the decision herself not to go inside the piano teacher's house. She told Brewster she no longer enjoyed watching Miss LuLu Mae give Laurel his instructions because the conflict over whether or not he should have been included in the recital at Jake Warner's house spoiled the pleasure she took in observing his lesson. "Besides, he's a teenager," Marlenna told Brewster, "and he doesn't like his mother staying so close to his side." She established a new routine. She parked in front of Miss LuLu Mae's front door, let Laurel out of the car, and she and Tee drove to Three Brothers where they drank Coca-Colas and visited with Carmella.

On Tuesdays, Brewster and Skinner knocked off early in the shed, and they used these afternoons to bring furniture to the Three Brothers showroom. Paulette came too, for a visit with her daughters at the café, riding in the cab of the truck, sitting between Brewster and Skinner. Albert Mixon made Tuesdays special by paying for the Coca-Colas that rolled down the chute of the machine in the break room, handing them personally to everyone—Brewster and Skinner, Marlenna and Carmella, and Tee, and to any customers who happened to be browsing in the store. Marlenna and Carmella sat on the couch and put their feet on the table in front of the sofa, and the men hung back by the door, at the periphery of the merriment—close enough to be joint owners and contributors of any joke that made the round, but far enough away to avoid the appearance of loafing or of intruding into the company of women.

"The girls remind me of my Helen," Albert Mixon said. "I enjoy hearing my daughters laugh," he said and leaned his back against the doorframe, close to the Coca-Cola machine.

But when Carmella spoke about Eddie, the conversation grew somber. As soon as Eddie turned sixteen, he dropped out of school, gave up his job in the potato sheds, and could be found sitting on the cinder-block steps of Happy Landing, smoking marijuana and hanging out with a rough crowd.

"I've told the boy a thousand times you can't keep company with the devil and not feel fire. He's responsible for fifty pounds on me. I eat when I worry," Carmella said, and she patted her belly, round and jouncy.

Brewster knew for a fact that Eddie had stolen money from Albert Mixon and that his grandfather, on more than one occasion, had asked him to leave the house at 32 State Street. For months, Carmella had spoken openly about her worry that Eddie would get pulled into some business that would send the whole Happy Landing crowd to the state penitentiary.

"Hell," she said. "He may be the ringleader for all I know." For his part, Brewster wanted the boy to stay out of trouble because he did not want to negotiate with Slim Tate over any business whatsoever, but he knew Carmella would call on him to intercede with the sheriff if Eddie got himself into big trouble. He knew too that Marlenna worried about Laurel being sucked into Eddie's trouble—unwittingly becoming a part of it or trying in some way to help Eddie—and being caught in the middle of the Happy Landing crowd.

After Laurel's lessons on Tuesdays, they all went to Paulette's Café and ate supper. Skinner and David joined the crowd, and sometimes Matthew and June came with Bo and their youngest child, Divinia.

On a Tuesday in early December, Miss LuLu Mae waved at Marlenna when she parked the car at the curb to let Laurel out. She came off her porch and walked to Marlenna's car. "When you come back to get Laurel, come on into the house. I want to talk to you," Miss LuLu Mae said.

Sitting on the couch in the break room at Three Brothers, Marlenna wondered out loud what Miss LuLu Mae wanted to say. "It makes me nervous waiting to go see her," Marlenna said as she slipped her shoes off and put her feet on the coffee table in front of her.

"Probably going to retire," Carmella said. "Old enough, that's for sure."

"Naw, she's gon' tell you Laurel's gon' play piano at some big, fancy place," Skinner said. But Brewster also had some concern about what Miss LuLu Mae wanted to discuss, and when it was time to go, he went with Marlenna to speak with the piano teacher.

When they entered Miss LuLu Mae's parlor and sat on her couch., Laurel continued to sit on the piano bench, but he turned to face his parents. Miss LuLu Mae positioned her chair so she faced Brewster and Marlenna.

"I've come to a difficult decision," Miss LuLu Mae said. "I've given Laurel all I can give him. The greatest gift a teacher can give is to let a student go when he's received the bounty of her knowledge. And that's the situation I find myself in with Laurel. It's time to let him move on."

Brewster did not know what this meant. Was Miss LuLu Mae refusing to teach Laurel any longer? Was this Laurel's last lesson?

"There is a teacher, a black man, at Beaumont State. He served on the faculty at Rutgers University and has returned to Alabama to be close to his family. I met him at the state piano teachers' convention. Laurel needs that level of instruction."

Laurel sat listening and watching. Marlenna leaned forward with her elbows resting on her knees.

"I've taken the liberty of speaking with Professor Rimes about Laurel, but you need to call him personally and set an audition time," Miss LuLu Mae said. "December is the last month of the year. That's why I've made my decision now. So Laurel can begin a new year with a new teacher, a new season in his preparatory study." She handed Marlenna a sheet of stationery on which she had written in even and light-handed script, *Professor Cecil Rimes, Beaumont State College, 435-2906.*

Marlenna thanked her and folded the paper. "Laurel has a bright future," Miss LuLu Mae said. "I'm glad I've had the opportunity to give him his early start. I plan to see him perform in some grand halls before I die," she said.

Marlenna surprised Brewster by leaning toward Miss LuLu Mae and kissing her lightly on the cheek when they stood on the porch saying their goodbyes. With Marlenna's misgivings about Laurel nearly missing the opportunity to perform at Jake Warner's, Brewster thought he would never have witnessed even a quick brush of affection from Marlenna toward Miss LuLu Mae.

The first week of January in the new year of 1974, Brewster, Marlenna, and Laurel drove the seventy miles to Beaumont State to audition before Professor Cecil Rimes. Tee wanted to go with them, but Brewster and Marlenna made her stay at Ole Summit with Paulette because this was Laurel's day, and he did not need any distractions.

Beaumont State, a historical Negro college established by northern Presbyterians during reconstruction, was a full sixty miles from Low Ridge. Brewster had always intended to drive to the campus to look around. In fact, he had considered enrolling there as a young man when he still owned the possibility of going to college, but he had never done this, never set foot on the campus of Beaumont State. He thought it was like so many things close at hand, a person doesn't see them, or merely accepts them and ignores them, but this particular January afternoon the college took on great importance as an avenue opening to his son.

They drove on a county highway, with dense pinewoods and thicket on both sides of the road. They passed a lumber mill on the left, and Brewster slowed his old Buick for two trucks that turned into the mill, both loaded with long narrow pine logs, the bark still on them, red flags tied to the longest protrusion. They passed a cement plant where the dust from the manufacturing covered the woods and the highway with a light gray powder. As they came closer to the college, the small homes of black families became more numerous—runty country houses with narrow front porches and with cows or chickens rambling in the side yards or near fields. A few folks sat on their porches with their jackets zipped to their throats. One old man threw up his hand in unspoken salutation as Brewster, Marlenna, and Laurel made their way down the highway to Beaumont State.

Near the entrance to the college, the houses bunched together, ten or fifteen houses long and narrow as arrows, close-fitted on small lots. Brewster thought these must be the houses of the cooks or the maintenance workers, because they could have been taken from Limrick Road or from Platt's Row in Calhoun County: Negro houses, scrimpy and spare, creating a colored section, but not in a city or town, a Negro section on the open road, close to the asphalt on the county highway.

Brewster made a right hand turn and drove under an old wrought-iron arch with letters welded below metal oak leaves, *Beaumont State*. The iron arch was a little rusty, in need of fresh black paint, but immediately the road in front of Brewster turned into a wide divided avenue with giant oaks on both sides. Brewster slowed the Buick to a near stop because the view nearly took his breath away. At the end of the avenue stood a three-storied red brick building with eighteen or twenty concrete steps leading to a landing with six huge, dark-oak doors. Brewster eased down the lane in the direction of this central building that dominated like a refuge for the lost and weary.

Classroom buildings were on either side of the wide avenue; neat, boxy structures also blocked out of old, red brick. One of the buildings had vaulted metal stairs curving above the first story, opening to a wrought-iron landing on the second level. Another building had a cupola, supported by four short columns, and inside the dome a large bronze bell hung. Students walked between the buildings on the boulevard, and the bell sounded, striking the five o'clock hour.

"This is beautiful," Marlenna said, turning her head to the left and the right.

"This is some place," Laurel said.

The black enamel sign in front of the large building at the end of the avenue had gold letters, reading Administration Building. Brewster parked the car and stepped out, thinking he would walk up the wide-spread stairs, enter the building and get directions, but a male student walked past the car, and Brewster asked him for the studio of Professor Cecil Rimes.

"Over there," the young man said and pointed to the building with the stairs that swept over the first floor in a semi-circular span. "First floor. Go through the double doors, and his studio is on the left. First door on the left," the young man said, and he grinned. Brewster thought the young man smiled because he was happy, and who would not be happy in this place, almost bewildering in its symmetry and charm.

Brewster got back in the car and headed in the opposite direction on the avenue, parking in front of the building in which Cecil Rimes had his studio.

"Ah, man. I wasn't nervous 'til I saw this place," Laurel said when he got out of the car and stepped up on the sidewalk. "Now I don't know if I remember my music."

"Laurel, don't you let this place or anybody or anything cause you to doubt your music. You go in there and you play. You play just like you were in Miss LuLu Mae's parlor."

"But Mom. . . ," Laurel started his sentence when a tall gray-haired man came through the dark wood door.

"Are you the McAtees?"

"We are," Brewster said and extended his hand.

"I'm Cecil Rimes. I was watching for you through my windows there." He put his hand out to Marlenna and then to Brewster and to Laurel. He opened the door and stood back, allowing each of them to walk ahead of him through the opening. "This way. This way," he said and stepped ahead of them, turning left and opening the door.

Professor Rimes' studio was large, but two grand pianos consumed the space. Late afternoon sunlight pierced the room through four full-length French doors, which faced the wide avenue; the streaks of low, January light cut beams across the hardwood floor. "This is my studio," he said. "Let me take your coats."

He put their coats on a rack that stood beside the door. "Sit down," he said, and he pointed to a couch and two chairs grouped behind the pianos. A small oriental rug and a low table separated the sofa from the chairs. Professor Rimes took one of the chairs and Laurel sat in the other one. Brewster and Marlenna sat on the sofa.

"Tell me about your piano study," he asked, and Laurel told Professor Rimes about his lessons with Miss LuLu Mae. He told him about the music he played and how he went about his practice. Professor Rimes listened with what seemed to be keen interest. He leaned toward Laurel. He shook his head, acknowledging what Laurel told him, and he asked questions in a deep, soft voice. Already Brewster liked this man, tall and broad shouldered, his face the tan of fine leather shoes. His thick silver hair swept away from his forehead in full waves, his nose long and broad, and his lips full. When he smiled his face carried on it what could have been a century of compassion, wisdom, and plain good humor.

"Well, I guess we should hear you play," he said. "I think you will like best the piano on your left. Most students do. The one on the right is a little difficult to control. Extremely quick action."

Laurel handed Professor Rimes the music books he had brought and seated himself at the piano on the left. He stood again and bent at his knees adjusting the bench.

"Begin anytime you're ready," Cecil Rimes said.

Brewster did not know the names of the music Laurel played, nor did he know the names of the composers, but he closed his eyes and listened to the music that filled the spaces in Professor Rimes' studio. The music spun out like a winding road that looped through mountain vistas with snow in valleys below, clean and unblemished. Brewster kept his eyes closed, and Laurel took him up and down curvy hills that almost made Brewster dizzy, but made him grin too, because the ride was airy and thrilling. Then the notes Laurel played took him to a wide open place, a place almost lonesome because he stood on a mountaintop. He could see seven states, and he knew how alone he was and how small he was up there, but Brewster still kept his eyes closed. Laurel drove him down the winding road—down, down, but it was good, and the air was clean, and his heart was bigger for having been on the mountaintop. Brewster opened his eyes and watched Laurel end on an enormous note that floated in the room until it hooked itself on a low beam of light and hung there for a long minute.

Professor Rimes watched Laurel. "Beautiful," he said, "beautiful."

"Do you want me to go on?" Laurel asked.

"Go on," Professor Rimes said.

Laurel turned and began playing a piece that sounded like a thousand marching soldiers, the sound slamming into the room in rhythm—steady, proud, majestic. Happy soldiers. Triumphant soldiers. Warriors who won the battle and marched home, victors to be embraced, to have rose petals laid under the worn leather of their thrashing boots, and to be fed grapes, abundant on thick, woody stems. No letting up, these soldiers marched home, home, home, home, home—conquerors, heroes—until the last note sounded loud and proud, sharp and defiant.

"Bravo!" Professor Rimes said, and Brewster laughed. "This boy can play," he said. "Do you have any more? My, this is certainly grand."

"I have two more pieces," Laurel said.

"Well," the professor said. "Most of my college students don't come through these doors this well prepared. Proceed," he said, smiling.

Brewster thought the room needed to be swept with some sort of magical music sweeper, because the last piece had left parts of itself standing boldly, defiantly anchored in the room. But Laurel proceeded to play something very different, a piece Brewster thought of as a parlor piece, light and pleasant sounding. This music made Brewster think of afternoon tea served in parlors of old white women. Then the notes stepped quick and light, and Brewster saw May ribbons, bright colors wrapped around poles by little girls in toe-shoes and those filmy skirts floating up and down, up and down.

But the girls around this pole were not black girls, they were wispy white girls, bleached-out in the afternoon sun, parading around the pole, lacing colored ribbons in and out, in and out. *That's well-behaved music*, Brewster thought, when Laurel finished the piece—*gentlemanly music*, he concluded.

And before Professor Rimes spoke again, Laurel proceeded to a piece, down and dirty, and Brewster laughed out loud. Marlenna nudged him with the tip of her elbow, a reminder to be quiet.

Brewster recognized this piece. It was Laurel's own version of an old honky-tonk number Brewster had hummed for him, one of the old Delta blues with some sounds from Muddy Waters added to the mix and some long riff-sounding stuff from Chuck Berry, and some sounds from before either of those two were even born. All the sounds had come through Laurel into some new creation, black as ebony, black as the polished satin finish on the grand piano Laurel played. Professor Rimes clapped his hands on the off-beat, and Brewster joined in. When Laurel finished, Professor Rimes applauded and laughed.

He stood and grasped Laurel on the shoulder. "This is the newest student in Cecil Rimes' studio," he said. "And I think I had better hold on for the ride. We're going to have some fun," he said. Laurel stood and they shook hands.

"Let's go to the cafeteria," he said. "I'm buying supper tonight because I've just received a free concert. We'll talk about lesson times and procedures over dinner," he said, and the four of them went out the door and strolled across an open quadrangle to a crowded dining hall full of students and faculty and a few townspeople.

In celebration of the new piano teacher, and in sober recognition that his old Buick was not reliable transportation for the weekly trips to Beaumont State, Brewster went to Big Eddie's Motors, taking Laurel with him, to purchase a used car. Ernie Ladd no longer worked at Big Eddie's, and Eddie McGhee no longer owned the dealership, but the new owner had kept the same name and the same logo—a big cartoon man driving a small car with his head out the window, a thick, red heart around the miniature car with the words above it—Big Eddie Loves You!

The parking spaces were loaded with good-looking used cars. Brewster and Laurel walked the length and breadth of the lot looking at every vehicle, afraid they would miss a good one. They drove a '71 blue Barracuda and a '73 beige Chevy Nova, and they even took a spin in a little yellow Beetle, knowing full well the car was too small. But they were spending their money and they had every right to envision themselves in all manner of transportation before they locked themselves into one specific car that they were likely to drive for at least a decade.

They finally settled on a '73 Chevelle Malibu, long hood and long rear, solid looking. The car, nearly new and a super sport model, had SS in bold letters on the front fender. Brewster's new car was gold-toned with lighter gold interior, and he thought it looked rich and smelled of new car. Laurel walked around the car, admiring it. "I'll be driving this before long," he said.

"Not yet," Brewster said. "Not quite yet." He laughed, and he put his arm around Laurel. But he knew Laurel was right.

"He's growing up fast—too fast," Marlenna whispered when they admired him at church on Sunday, sitting at the piano bench, accompanying the choir.

But Brewster did not feel the same way. He liked having a son who could go with him to Big Eddie's Motors, and he liked having a son sitting beside him in the front seat of the car driving out Ole Summit Highway, discussing the news and sports or whatever came to their minds. He held Laurel on a loose rein a short distance from manhood, but he would hold on for as long as he could before his son turned into a man—tall, broad-shouldered, thoughtful, and smart. Laurel sat at the kitchen table every night reading the newspaper. He didn't bring many friends home and wasn't asked to go home with friends either, but he came to life at the piano bench, and that was fine with Brewster. His son carried with him an abundance of talent. Brewster knew Laurel would take him down roads he never imagined traveling. This was a new world, a New South, and Laurel McAtee would be one of the players, arriving at manhood ready to step into the opportunities opening before him.

By spring they had all adjusted to Laurel's schedule, which claimed their Saturdays. They were on the road headed to Beaumont State before ten o'clock, and they were in Professor Rimes' studio by a little after eleven. Sometimes Tee went with them, and Professor Rimes invited all of them to sit on the couch and watch Laurel's lesson. "Make a day of it," he said. "You have to drive the boy over here, and you might as well enjoy this beautiful campus."

Enjoy Saturdays is what they did. After Laurel's lesson, they ate lunch in the cafeteria. Sometimes Professor Rimes joined them and they sat at a round table by a large window, overlooking the wide avenue that ran through the center of campus. "When school starts in the fall," Professor Rimes said, "I want to enter him in some of the state competitions. That way, we'll let other people see what a talent we have here."

Laurel smiled when Professor Rimes said this. Lessons with the new piano professor had intensified his love of music and his fascination with creating distinct sounds—Laurel-McAtee sounds that belonged to him. In the afternoons, after he ate a snack at the table, he went to the piano bench and remained there until nearly supper time. Professor Rimes gave him new music, composers he had never played before, had never heard of before. The professor handed him a book, gave him a page number, and told him about the composer, and Laurel went home and began learning this new music. But Laurel had not given up on his own music, combining one sound with another, a little Beethoven marching sound, with a little Mississippi Delta blues, then to a sweet section with wide spaces between the notes, and on to a little gospel for the close. Marlenna crossed her arms and watched him, but Brewster went into the big room and sat in the chair closest to the piano. This boy was going to make something special of himself, and Brewster thought it might well be by combining all these different sounds into something that had Albert Laurel McAtee stamped all over it.

Tee's lessons with Mrs. Banks were going well too, but she didn't have the quick and natural facility at the keys Laurel had. She seemed to enjoy her lessons almost as much as her brother, and she didn't appear to begrudge him any of the accolades that so naturally came to him. She sat on the floor listening to him at the piano, clapping her hands or closing her eyes and moving her arms, elbows out, as if she could fly.

Brewster and Marlenna both observed that Tee was good-natured, comfortable with herself. At school she was an average student; at school performances, she sat in the middle of the group, which made her difficult to see and easy to overlook, if it were not for her smile, a big, easy beam lighting her face. She would be starting junior-high school in the fall, but had begged Brewster and Marlenna to allow her to stay at Country Training School, because she did not want to go to the mostly white Low Ridge Junior High. Marlenna had been offered a teaching position at the white school, but she had turned it down, deciding that both she and Tee would remain at County Training.

"I think I can do more there," Marlenna told Brewster one evening when they dried dishes at the kitchen sink. "Besides, Tee doesn't want to transfer. Herman Thomas is getting on past seventy. He'll be retiring before many years, and I want to stay on with him. When Herman retires, I'll transfer over to Low Ridge High School." She put her hands in the pockets of her apron that was tied around her waist and waited for Brewster to rinse the pot he held. "One day someone will write a book about Herman Thomas," she said. "He's seen everything, all the changes that have come. He's been an eyewitness to the development of nearly every youngster born and raised in this county over the last thirty years."

Brewster thought about Herman Thomas being an eyewitness to all the changes that had taken place in Low Ridge. Black youngsters going to the white schools, black people voting, and now a black man from Cincinnati managing the A & P and Mrs. Dawson from the church working at a window in the Bank of Low Ridge. And he thought too about Herman's son Anvil. He had not seen Anvil in several years, but he had read about him in the newspaper, married and then divorced, and still working as an attorney for the NAACP.

On a Sunday afternoon in May, Brewster was in his shed doing some easy work on the face of a buffet. He had gone to church, eaten his lunch with the family, and he had come to his shed to enjoy some time in the quiet of his workshop. He brought the Sunday paper with him, tucked under his arm, and he put it on the floor near his rocking chair. He planned to sit in the chair, which was close to the stove in the middle of the room, and he would read the Sunday paper, taking all the leisure time he wanted. But before he settled into his chair, he stood at his workbench in front of one of his long windows, and he sanded the middle drawer-face of the pecan buffet and felt for any ridges in the wood.

When he looked up, he saw the old man come down the lane, a cane in his hand, his shoulders bent, looking older and more worn than when Brewster had last seen him, but it was Travis Peets, nonetheless, wearing a thin-lipped and down-turned expression. The old man was about to step up onto the porch when Brewster came out of his shed. Marlenna must have seen him too, because she opened the front door and stood on the porch with her arms crossed and folded under her breasts.

Travis Peets began speaking in excited and short-breathed words before Brewster reached the front porch. "That son of yours come up to my place. Brought Ruby's book. What was he doing with Ruby's book?"

Laurel opened the front door and stepped out on the porch, standing beside his mother.

"What were you doing with Ruby's book?" Travis Peets demanded in bursts of air propelled by the heat of accusation.

"I told you when I brought the book. Ruby dropped it on the bus. I could of left it there, but I didn't want anybody to take it. I wanted to get it back to Ruby."

There was a momentary pause—a few seconds, heavy, gravid, waiting for delivery of the next words, which would establish the melody to which they all would dance. In this space, waiting for the tune to sound, Brewster studied the old man's hands, gnarled hands, both of them holding to his cane, the fingers bent at an odd angle.

"You sure that's what took place?" Travis Peets asked. His words riding a little more solidly on a cushion of sustained air.

"Laurel told you Ruby dropped her book on the bus. He brought it to your house thinking he was doing Ruby a favor. Next time, he'll leave it on the bus." Brewster turned from the old man and looked at Laurel.

"You hear me, son. If Ruby drops her book on the bus again, you leave it there. Don't make any effort to take it to her."

Laurel, who stood on the porch with his legs in a wide stance, folded his arms across his chest, closing himself, securing himself. He looked from Travis Peets to his father. "Yes, sir," he said.

With that, old Travis Peets breathed a quick and grievous shot of air through his wide-spread nostrils and turned to leave. With his back to Brewster, Marlenna, and Laurel, he heaved words over his shoulder as he limped toward the woods. "We don't want no favors and we don't want you on our land."

Brewster watched him leave, his old shoulders bony and rounded forward, the sun reflecting off his tan-colored shirt, tight across the hump of his back.

"That man is twisted part with age and part with hate," Marlenna said. "I wonder if he loves anybody? Does that old man love anybody?" she mused.

"Son, don't you go on that man's land again. If that girl leaves her book, you let it lay."

"Yes, sir," Laurel answered, still looking in the direction where Travis Peets had entered the woods.

"He could be dangerous," Marlenna said.

"He's an old man, Mom. Just a crazy old man."

"Steer clear around him," Brewster said, and when he uttered the words, he heard the echo of Mama Tee speaking to TeeBoy.

24

In the fall of 1975, Professor Rimes entered Laurel in his first piano competition. Brewster and Marlenna would go with him as would Albert Mixon and Tee. Laurel's grandfather drove his 1970 Deville out to Ole Summit. His head barely showed above the steering column, and what could be seen of him leaned to the right. He parked the giant turquoise-blue car on the grass in the yard, and Marlenna and Brewster stood on the front porch watching him. Marlenna fussed because he crushed the thick lawn near the house with the Cadillac's heavy wheels, but Brewster reminded her it was better for her father to park there than to drive too close to the porch. "We may have that Cadillac sitting in the big room if he comes too near the house."

"He'd at least bump into the porch," Laurel said, watching his grandfather, who got out of the car wearing his best navy-blue pin-striped suit, with his white shirt crisp and tight around his neck. He grinned and waved.

"He needs something smaller, something he can maneuver a little better," Marlenna said. "That Cadillac is as big as a boat."

Albert Mixon continued waving at them as he walked to the porch. Brewster studied him, thinking the old man was spry for his years. "Doing all right?" Brewster asked when Albert Mixon was in easy speaking range.

"Fine. As fine as an old man can be," he said and stepped heavily up onto the porch.

"Old man?" Brewster questioned. "You don't look like an old man. Probably outlive most of us." With that Albert Mixon slapped Brewster on the back with his left hand and extended a brown paper bag toward him with his right hand.

"Snacks," Albert Mixon said. "'I love to eat a few snacks when I drive. And I do love a good drive too. Fine day for a drive," he said, surveying the sky. Brewster opened the bag and saw it was filled with peanuts, Tootsie Rolls, peppermints, butterscotch candies, and several small bags of fried pork rinds. He handed the bag to Marlenna.

"We're only going to be gone for the day," she said to her father, "not for a week." Albert Mixon was already talking to Laurel, and he ignored her.

Their drive was sixty-five miles south and slightly west to a small Methodist college that prided itself on music education. Marlenna sat in the back of the Malibu with her father, and Tee sat between them. Laurel requested the privilege of sitting up front, and since he was the performer and this was his day, Marlenna granted it to him. The family was not ten miles down the road before Albert Mixon opened his brown bag, and he and Tee began shelling peanuts, throwing the hulls out the open window, but dropping chaff in the car. The litter annoyed Brewster, but he kept his mouth shut. When he got home, he would take the whiskbroom and sweep the back seat and the floor. He would need to pull the seat out to clean the shells and skins that had fallen back behind it. When Tee and her grandfather had eaten their fill of peanuts, they started on butterscotch candy. Both Albert Mixon and Tee were delighted to be included in Laurel's big day and were determined to enjoy it. Laurel sat beside his father with his music open across his knees, fingering the notes on the page as if his hands were positioned on piano keys.

Even before they turned onto campus, signs reading SONATA COMPETITION, pointed to the music building. When they parked and went inside the building, Professor Rimes waited for them in the lobby. After speaking to each one of the family members individually, and meeting Albert Mixon for the first time, he turned to Laurel.

"You may want to go over a few spots in your music before you play. May want to warm your hands a little and get the notes down to your fingertips. If you do, there are practice rooms in the basement."

Laurel did want to strike some of the notes on the piano keys before he played, and Professor Rimes escorted him downstairs to a practice room. Brewster and Marlenna went outside the building and stood on the porch with the morning sun bright in their eyes. Albert Mixon and Tee decided to take a short walk on the campus. Brewster looked across the college and saw that several of the buildings on the grounds were newer than the buildings at Beaumont State, and they had fancy names on them—MicroBiology and Earth Science.

"Let's sit here," Marlenna said, and they positioned themselves on the top steps of the music building, to the far side so they would not hinder the path of anyone who might want to come or go. They sat close and the sides of their legs touched. Marlenna reached over and took Brewster's hand, holding it and placing her other hand on

top of his. "There's not one place I would rather be than here, sitting
on this step with you, waiting for our son to play piano."

Brewster looked at her. She was beautiful, a little fuller around
the chest and waist, but her face had become even softer than when
they married, more relaxed, more understanding, and almost always
smiling. In the eighteen years of their marriage there had never been
one minute when he had not loved Marlenna, not one minute.

"There's not one place I would rather be either," he said. "I hope
this is a good day for Laurel." Marlenna smiled and said nothing.

They watched people come and go from the music building,
young men and young women in Sunday clothes who came and went
with their parents, chatting about all manner of things, but while they
sat on the steps, they did not see one other black youngster, male or
female, enter the building.

Brewster looked across the campus and saw Albert Mixon and
Tee returning, strutting almost in unison and engaged in lively
conversation. He acknowledged, at least in his own mind, that
Marlenna had been right about her father. He was a bright man, a
man who had made his way in the white man's world. He had turned
Three Brothers showroom into a profitable business and had won the
honor of being the first black man invited to membership in the Low
Ridge Chamber of Commerce. He had been a good father-in-law too,
helping where he could, and always looking with adoring eyes on
Laurel and Tee. Brewster thought about how a man had to continu-
ally step back and reevaluate, and he had done that with Albert
Mixon without ever saying a word about it. There was no need to say
what he thought and felt, he needed only to live what was in his head
and heart. He respected the old man and he showed it. That was
sufficient for both of them.

Professor Rimes came out the door of the music building, and
Brewster and Marlenna stood. "You can come on with me. Laurel is
contestant number five. Let's go in and get our spots in the auditorium." Tee and her grandfather joined them, and they went inside,
with Albert Mixon walking beside Cecil Rimes.

"Let's go on down to the front," Albert Mixon protested when
the professor pointed to a row of seats in the back of the auditorium
on the left side so they could see Laurel's hands on the keys.

"I think we'll enjoy it a little more from this distance," Cecil
Rimes said. "Besides, we don't want to be close enough to distract
Laurel in any way."

With that, Albert Mixon filed between the seats, followed by

Cecil Rimes. Tee entered the row and then Marlenna, with Brewster on the end. Brewster heard Albert Mixon say, "If this was not my grandson who was going to play, I would be home in front of my TV set watching the Series."

"I would be in the very same spot in front of mine," Cecil Rimes said.

"Sixth game," Albert Mixon said. "Fenway Park will be packed." And then the two old men began discussing the players, and Brewster heard the names—Cooper, Doyle, Fisk, Petrocelli, Rose, Bench, Concepcion. And while he listened with one ear to the discussion of baseball, he looked around the auditorium and saw the hall filling, no other black faces among the parents and the guests, and he knew Laurel would be the only black student to perform. He wondered if this made his son nervous, to be the only black player in front of an all-white audience, if he carried the burden of his race as had Joe Lewis and Jackie Robinson, if he carried the burden into this new age in this new arena, in front of black and white piano keys, at a white Methodist college in middle Alabama.

Contestant number one walked on stage, a tall, wispy girl with thin legs and long blonde hair that hung down her back. She sat at the piano and began playing something that sounded breathless and rushed. She leaned forward toward the keys and attacked the instrument with a ferocious demeanor. Professor Rimes pursed his lips and shook his head in a slight negative while the girl played. One note hurried into another, the notes colliding and knocking each other out, flat and dead, before they had time to beguile the listener. Brewster wondered how she could even breathe in the position she had assumed, bent almost at a right angle over the keys. She raced on, and then she missed some notes and went flying back to retrieve them. But she couldn't get her hands on the lost notes, and she waved her fingers above the keys, like birds hovering and fluttering before landing. The tips of her fingers swooped down and grabbed a palm full of notes, but they were the wrong tones. She dropped them at once and her fingers again floated above the keys, and then swooped down again and still she could not locate the missing notes and she viciously assaulted the keys, pouncing on them again and again, listening, but when she could not locate the sounds she sought, she abandoned this section of music entirely and proceeded to another passage at the other end of the keyboard.

When the girl was done with her music, Brewster was relieved. He had never seen such a tortuous rendering of something that was supposed to come from the heart. He took a deep breath, allowing the air to enter his nostrils slowly, and he cycled the oxygen all the way down to his toes. While the girl raced and searched for notes, Brewster had almost forgotten to breathe, and now he felt like he had surfaced above the water and he needed to fill his lungs with air.

The second contestant was a young man, broad shouldered, but not as tall as Laurel. He smiled at the audience, adjusted the bench, seated himself and began to play, much more relaxed than the girl who preceded him, yet he played stiff and studied. He took the notes slowly, almost allowing his fingers to levitate above the keys before playing them. His sound wasn't bad though. He struck the notes, and he made his way around the keyboard fairly comfortably, Brewster thought—slowly and easily.

The third student performed and the fourth, and Brewster could feel the electricity inside himself, energized, waiting. He glanced down the row and saw on the faces of Cecil Rimes, Albert Mixon, Tee, and Marlenna that each one of them knew Laurel was next to play, and each of them was balanced at the point of unknowing: Would Jackie Robinson hit a homerun or a fielder, steal home plate and score, would Joe Lewis knock out the bushy-browed German, Max Schmeling, and save his people from humiliation, would Laurel McAtee outperform, outplay, these white youngsters who already owned a piece of the world by virtue of their skin?

Laurel walked on stage, tall, erect. He placed his right hand behind him on the curve of the piano, and he bowed to the audience members, who applauded politely. He cranked on the knobs of the piano bench, lowering it and sliding it back from the keyboard because, like his father, his long legs needed room. He sat on the bench and placed his hands in his lap for a long moment, then he raised them and positioned them carefully over the keys.

In his mind, Brewster could hear all the instructions Cecil Rimes had given Laurel while Laurel sat at the ebony piano in the studio that had the outside stairs gracefully arched above it. "Take your time. Don't think about one thing but your music. Hear it in your head before you strike the first note. Hum it in your head, the whole first score or two, before you play that first note."

Laurel's head moved slightly, and Brewster knew the music flowed through his mind before he touched the keys. When the first notes sounded, Laurel owned the tones.

"Beethoven," Marlenna had told him before they went inside the music building. "Laurel will be playing a Beethoven sonata." She told him the number of the sonata too, but Brewster had forgotten that. All he knew was, when Laurel began playing, he liked the music Laurel created. The first movement swelled full and easy, rich sounding, light and airy. But the second movement had a marching sound, not a heavy thumping, but a light sound, a joyful sound, not soldiers marching, but heavenly hosts strutting in glory. Black saints, poor old souls who had come from shacks and shanties without sheetrock on their walls, now marched across the stage draped in luminescent robes—soft-footed marchers, maintaining even steps, their robes flowing like flames behind them, halos brilliant in soft blue-green light. These saints didn't look at the audience; they marched lightly, with heads erect, their feet barely touching the stage, their bodies as buoyant as air.

There was Aunt Laney and old Mrs. Shulman, Bess, Daddy Divine, and Brewster nearly laughed out loud when he saw Mama Tee, followed by Deak Armbrecht. Mama Tee strutted across the stage in a soft orange-blue flame, and she looked directly at Brewster, an enormous grin on her face. Deak looked neither left nor right, but was a good soldier, lifting his old feet high, marching like a young man in his old body, lifting his feet, his shoulders held back proudly. And last was TeeBoy, but he did not look at Brewster either. He marched straight-faced, looking ahead. He was the drum major, but he was in the back of the band. He had responsibility for keeping all the saints in line, and Mama Tee was unruly, flaunting her orange-blue robes outside the crisp line of the marchers. TeeBoy flashed his dazzling baton down the line, and it shot a blue flame past Deak, past Mama Tee, past Bess, past Daddy Divine and Mrs. Shulman. But Mama Tee could not be contained; she let her light shine bigger and brighter than all the marchers, because the straightness of the line meant nothing to her.

TeeBoy continued lifting clean and easy steps, lighter than air, his steps as flawless as polished glass. Then, in one quick movement, his gleaming scepter flashed past Deak, tapping Mama Tee gently on her flaming shoulder, and she eased back in line with the other marchers. They paraded respectfully, elegantly around the stage, and their glow faded slowly as the last notes of the movement filtered out to the sides and the back of the auditorium, and eased down—down, down slowly.

In the moments of silence, Brewster breathed deeply and shifted his feet on the floor. Then he was still, not wanting to move at all while his son played. Laurel started the final movement, and it was

different from this beautiful march of the saints. It was the heart
open, showing its love, the blood-red heart of Jesus Christ, exposed.
It was the love Brewster had for Marlenna and Tee and for his son on
the stage, playing for this white audience. This piece was about the
love, bigger than a man's own heart, and the purity of that love
almost broke Brewster open, the notes lonesome and expressing truth
so deep it was holy truth, truth reserved for judgment or for this
moment when Laurel McAtee played. Truth, clearly expressed,
without apology, with head high, shoulders back, truth in the music
that went directly to the open heart. And when Laurel eased the last
notes off the pads of his fingers, the audience did not move but was
encased in silence as thick as water. Laurel held the tips of his
fingers on the keys until the notes eased away, descending off stage,
through the hall, and out the back doors. Movement would have been
too painful until the notes loosened their grip from around the heart.
When Laurel put his hands in his lap, the audience breathed.

"Beautiful," Professor Rimes whispered, and Albert Mixon
removed his handkerchief from his hip pocket, wiping dampness
from under his eyes.

Three more players performed. Brewster thought they were
good, but he thought they did not hypnotize the audience as had
Laurel; they did not cast a spell or snare the audience on the
sharp-edged ecstasy of the notes. After all of the performers had
played, the audience filed outside the auditorium while the judges
made their decision. When Laurel joined his family, Cecil Rimes was
first to speak. "Splendid," he said. "More than splendid," he added.
"Splendid, splendid, splendid," and they all laughed.

The second performer, the broad-shouldered young man, came to
Laurel. "You were awesome, man, awesome," he said.

"You were good too," Laurel said.

"How long you been playing?" the young man asked.

"Since I was about eight or nine," Laurel said.

"I started at five," the young man said, "and I can't do some of
the stuff you do." The two exchanged names, and they shook hands.
Then the young man excused himself and went to stand with his
mother and father.

Professor Rimes drew the family around him and spoke in a
hushed voice. "Laurel played extremely well. His performance was
accurate, and it would be difficult to play with more articulation and
expression than Laurel, but you never know what the judges will do.
I've seen hundreds of surprises. Remember this," he said to Laurel,

and he raised his index finger. "You are always the one who has to judge your own performance. No one else, not even these judges, has the power to tell you how you play. You always hold that power inside yourself unless you surrender it to somebody else, and you're not going to do that. Laurel played well and we know that, regardless of what this decision may be."

"I think he'll come out number one," Albert Mixon said, a little louder than Brewster would have liked.

"Well, he may. He should," Cecil Rimes said. "But I'm telling you that you never know what the judges will do."

Then the family spread apart, and Laurel stood beside his father. Brewster put his arm around Laurel's shoulder and realized Laurel was as tall as he was. "I'm proud of you, son."

"Thanks, Dad. I feel good about it. I played well."

"You did," Brewster said, but he did not tell Laurel that he played so well he had brought out the saints, strutting and marching across the stage, and that he had laid open the essence of love, so pure, so rare, the audience could hardly breathe in its presence.

When the audience filed back inside for the announcement of the winning performance, the contestants were called to the stage for one more round of applause. They lined up in the order in which they had played, walked to the center of the stage, and bowed as a group. Each contestant was presented a certificate for participation in the competition. Laurel stood in the middle, taller than the others, and his features looked even darker, standing in the middle of these white faces. Then the contestants were told to sit in the front row for the announcements, and when they were all seated, the chairman of the competition moved to the lectern and began calling names. Marlenna put her hand in Brewster's hand, and he held it close to his chest.

"Honorable mention," the chairman said, and he called the name of contestant number two, the young man who had walked over to speak with Laurel.

The third place winner was contestant number six, and the second place winner was player number three. Brewster knew that Laurel would either receive first place or he would get no recognition at all, and he squeezed Marlenna's hand, placing it over his heart, which was beating so loudly he could hear the echo whomping in his ears. Brewster glanced down the row, and he saw Professor Rimes had clasped his hands tight-fisted in front of him, one hand holding the other so snugly, the knuckles were ashen.

"Our 1975 first place winner is contestant number five, Albert Laurel McAtee."

Albert Mixon let out a noise that sounded like the hoot of an owl, Tee clapped her hands together, and Brewster felt a quick slice of pain cut across his chest as the blood raced through the tight vessels in his heart. He put Marlenna's hand to his lips and kissed it, as Laurel walked to the stage to receive a trophy.

"As you know, there is also a check for our winner," the chairman said, and he handed the white envelope to Laurel.

"There's nothing like having a namesake who's going to make something of himself," Albert Mixon said when they were outside.

"Congratulations,'" Cecil Rimes said, and he drew Laurel to him in a hearty hug, with Laurel standing taller than his teacher.

On the drive back to Low Ridge, Albert Mixon replayed the event ten different ways, and the whole time he talked, he shelled peanuts, letting the chaff blow through the car. Between rounds of peanuts, he consumed several Tootsie Rolls, and he offered the contents of the large sack to everyone in the car. Again, Laurel sat up front on the drive home, and he laughed at the way his grandfather recounted the day's events. He cut his eyes at his father, and they united as conspirators, partners allowing the old man to have his day, to bask in his pride because this was his grandson in whom he was well pleased.

25

At the close of his first year of high school, Laurel won the state music festival, and he played for the piano teachers' convention in Birmingham. When he got his driver's license, he began driving the family to church. He drove himself to his piano lessons too, with Brewster going along for the ride in the passenger seat beside him, down the winding county highway, past the lumber mill, past the cement plant, past the rows of Negro houses on the highway with vegetable gardens in side yards.

In the summer, he worked with Brewster in the shed. Skinner's son, David, came too, and they labored together, fathers and sons. At noon they carried their stools outside, put them in a circle, and ate the lunch Paulette brought them, hot from the kitchen. They teased and laughed and enjoyed the broad days of hot sun. And in the afternoons, Laurel practiced long hours with the musical works of European white men sounding through the rafters, floating out to the shed, and off into the woods. In the evenings, Laurel listened to recordings of Magic Sam, Otis Rush, and the blues of Eric Clapton. Then he played his music late into the night, combining all the different sounds on the piano, creating dramatic stops, shifting chords, and holding them long seconds. He created melodies plaintive, then shouting, then weeping and laughing.

Laurel brought the blues records out to the shed and played them on an old cardboard phonograph as the four men worked. While the music sounded, Skinner didn't walk around the shed, he danced across the bare wood floors doing strange cross-legged steps, dipping his head, his elbows wide, balancing himself. Brewster, Laurel, and David laughed and clapped their hands when Skinner danced. Skinner, acknowledging his audience, did back steps, dragging-the-foot steps, and high-knee steps. This was a summer that could never end, as far as Brewster was concerned. He had work and plenty of it, and his son labored with him, shoulder to shoulder, and there was always a good time, joking, laughing about one thing or another.

David had given up baseball for football. He played running-back for Low Ridge High School, and in August when football practice began, three white boys in an old blue and white convertible pulled down the lane every afternoon about three o'clock. David hopped in the back seat, and the boys turned around in the yard, drove down the lane, turned onto Ole Summit, and headed toward Low Ridge High School. Laurel waved to them, and then he went in the house to begin his music practice. Brewster wondered if Laurel missed being with the other boys. Maybe he should have gone out for sports instead of spending so much time alone in front of the piano keys. But Brewster dismissed the idea as soon as he heard the beautiful melodies float out of the house, drift across the porch, and come through the open windows of the shed. He stopped his work, leaned against his workbench, and listened.

When school started in the fall, Professor Rimes entered Laurel in three competitions. He won another first place over in Mississippi and took a second and a third place in two competitions in Birmingham. He was a fine student too, doing well in all his courses, but he did not participate in activities after school, except to stay and watch David practice football. Then he came home and he practiced his music. Laurel was Cecil Rimes' star student, and the good professor was never shy about saying it.

Brewster sat on the couch reading his newspaper, and Marlenna helped Paulette in the kitchen. A medium-sized spruce tree stood erect on a wooden stand in the big room, but no decorations were on it. Tee stretched on the floor opening a box of Christmas ornaments, and Laurel sat at the piano practicing some pieces for a recital at church. Brewster folded the newspaper and began reading a story about Joe Namath and the Sunday match-up between the Jets and the Colts when he heard a knock on the door. A visitor at the front door was cause for the entire family to stop their individual activities, because they received little company, and they were not expecting any visitors this day.

Laurel bounced off the piano bench when he heard the knock. "I got it," he said. "I know who it is. It's Ruby. She doesn't have all her notes for the science exam. I'm going to let her borrow mine for a day or two."

Brewster was surprised when he saw Laurel had the science notes beside him at the piano. He realized Laurel knew Ruby was coming, but he continued to read his newspaper and said nothing.

"Come on in," Laurel said when he opened the door. "I have the class notes in here."

Brewster heard Ruby speak to Laurel, and he heard her step into the passage. "What'cha doing?" she asked.

"Playing the piano. Practicing some stuff for Sunday night. I'm going to play on a Christmas program at church."

"Can I hear some of that?" she asked.

"Sure," Laurel said, and he led the way into the big room with Ruby following closely behind him. When she came in, she walked in front of Brewster and sat on the opposite end of the couch.

"Good evening," Ruby said, and Brewster responded, as did Tee. Marlenna removed her apron and came into the big room, sitting in the chair at the end of the sofa, watching Ruby.

"This church stuff is easy," Laurel said. "Let me play you something I'm working on for my piano professor."

"Sure," Ruby said.

Laurel turned to face the piano, and he played something mellow, something that drove in a steady forward motion, but Brewster did not concentrate on the notes, he folded his newspaper and divided his attention between Ruby and Laurel. Ruby wore blue jeans and a University of Alabama tee shirt with a red elephant kicking up dust as it ran under a football goalpost. Ruby smiled at Brewster, and he studied her. She was heavy-set, with thick shoulders, immense breasts, and broad hips. She had blonde hair that fell in abundant curlicues to her shoulders; her hair flared out and made her face appear wide, her blue eyes set in ample flesh.

"That was good," she said. "But I really wanted to hear a Christmas carol. I love the carols. I'm a simple person," she said. "Just play for me one of the good ole carols."

"Any requests?" Laurel asked.

"You pick."

Laurel sat at the bench, turned toward the keys, and he played "Silent Night," but it was his own version, with rolling chords in the left hand and the melody sounding soft and tender in the right hand. Between the first and second stanza, Laurel played a cadenza, a brilliant solo with runs and chords and the sounds coming in waves, then fading slowly to single notes of the melody, joined by mild, almost bell-like sounds of broken chords.

"Wow," Ruby said when Laurel finished. "He is sooooo good. Everybody at school knows it. Everybody says he's going to be famous someday."

"Want me to play one more?" Laurel asked.

"Gosh, yes. I could sit here and listen to you all night."

"Do your grandparents know you're over here?" Marlenna asked.

"No," Ruby said. "Granddaddy's asleep in the recliner and Grandma's cutting zzzs on the couch. They sleep for a couple of hours with the TV on after supper, and then they get up and go on to bed. They say they're watching TV, but they are both snoring so loud, I have to go in my room and close the door." She laughed and Tee did too.

"Well, it's getting dark, and I think you had better start back because you won't be able to see that path through the woods in a few more minutes." Marlenna turned and fluffed the throw pillow behind her in the chair as if her comment was casual, uttered in half-thought while she occupied herself.

Ruby put her elbow on the arm of the sofa, eased her buttocks off the cushions, and extended her neck, looking out the wide window on the east side of the hearth. "Guess you're right," she said, and she stood. They all stood but Tee. Ruby and Laurel walked to the front door, Brewster sat down again on the couch, taking his newspaper off the table in front of him, Tee gently unpacked an ornament, placing it on the floor, under the tree, and Marlenna went into the kitchen where Paulette stood beside the stove watching all of them. When Laurel came back into the big room and sat at the piano, Brewster wondered if Marlenna would come into the room and question Laurel about Ruby, but she did not.

It was after ten o'clock when Marlenna eased into bed beside Brewster, before she mentioned Ruby. "He knew that girl was coming over here."

"Uh huh."

"I think he knows her better than he makes out."

"Maybe."

"You're not worried about that?"

"I've been thinking about it. Maybe they do talk at school. Hell, maybe they meet and talk out there in the woods for all I know. It's got to be okay. That old coot of a grandfather can like it or not. We sent him to that white school and he's going to meet white folks and this is a new age in the South. That's the way it is," Brewster said. He rolled on his side and put his hand on Marlenna's waist.

"But good God, Brewster, if he's going to be talking to the white girls can't it be some girl not carrying around twenty pounds of saddle on her hips, enough fat to fill ten lard cans?"

Brewster laughed at this. He drew Marlenna to him and kissed her lips. "Laurel's got less than two more years at home. Then he'll

be off at college, and we won't have any say about who he talks to."
Brewster put his hand on the side of Marlenna's face, kissing her
again. He turned off the light and eased the straps of her gown over
her thin shoulders.

In the spring of Laurel's junior year, he received the Low Ridge
County Honor Student Award given by the Chamber of Commerce.
There was a big dinner in an old historic home on State Street, and
Marlenna and Brewster were invited. Albert Mixon sat at the table
with them, but he was on his feet much of the time, greeting guests
and talking with the other businessmen and women. Laurel received
a cash prize of five hundred dollars, which was designated as a
scholarship that he could use for tuition or books at any college.
Laurel was the first Negro student to win the award and much was
made of this fact. The *Low Ridge Gazette* took his picture standing
between Brewster and Marlenna, and the reporter interviewed him
for a story.

When the article appeared in the *Gazette* on the following
Thursday, the reporter referred to Laurel as a major talent. "This is a
young man who could put Low Ridge on the national map," the
article stated. The reporter listed Laurel's awards, his piano honors,
and his accomplishments at Low Ridge High School. The picture of
Laurel standing between his father and mother dominated the
Gazette's social page. By Friday, Albert Mixon had the photograph
framed and hanging on the wall at Three Brothers, and he had
another copy on the wall of his kitchen at 32 State Street. Marlenna
had ten copies of the newspaper stacked on the kitchen table, and she
was still gathering more from friends. Brewster did not know what
she intended to do with so many copies, but for himself, he had kept
his regimen simple. He went to Gwin's Department Store and
purchased two frames. He hung one copy of the article on the wall of
his shed and the other one he placed on the dresser in the bedroom.

He had also tucked a reminder in the back of his head to tell
Laurel that he thought he would never live to see the day when a
black boy and his mother and father would be smiling while standing
in the center of the *Low Ridge Gazette* social pages. That was an
accomplishment indeed, and Laurel should know the ground he had
broken and should know his father's pride. "You are my son, and I
am very proud of that," he would say.

Laurel won awards at every piano competition in the state and even brought home trophies, metals, certificates, and cash from performances in Mississippi and Georgia. For the big room, Brewster built a glass-fronted mahogany cabinet with an arched bonnet top sporting a twenty-ray fan in the center block. This cabinet housed the bounty of awards Laurel delivered, symbols of his achievements.

As Laurel completed his junior year of high school, Professor Rimes outlined a practice schedule for Laurel's summer. "We're going to get our audition program ready," he told Laurel. "At the tag-end of fall or early winter, we're going to be traveling to several universities. By spring of next year, you need to know where you're going to college. We want your audition program memorized and resting comfortably in your head. I want you to have a good time when we travel and not worry one bit about your music. If we start working on it this summer, it'll be in your head and in your fingers by the fall."

The University of Michigan was on the schedule. "I know some of the faculty there,'" Professor Rimes said. "They have a big, new performance hall called the Power Center. It has giant glass walls that jut out to the street. When they turn on the lights in that place the whole block glows. If you're performing there, you know all those lights are burning for you," he told Laurel. "Besides, it'd be good for you to get away, experience a new part of the country, feel a little cold air," he said.

"You're going to audition there, and I haven't decided the other places yet. We've got a big summer in store." He patted Laurel on the shoulder. "And then, we're got an even bigger year when the fall comes, your senior year."

Laurel took the music Professor Rimes gave him, and he placed it on the piano. Brewster knew Laurel would spend his summer reading through it, repeating small sections of it over and over again until the notes were in his fingers, but for now his attention was on the junior/senior prom. Brewster went with Laurel when he rented a tuxedo with a white collar that stood up around his neck like a priest's neck band. and the suit had a black bow tie that clipped around Laurel's neck. Several days before the prom, Laurel put the whole outfit on and stood in front of the mirror admiring himself.

"Look at these shoes, Dad. You ever seen a shine like that?"

"Keep that get-up on until I can take your picture," Brewster said, and he went to get his camera out of the drawer in the kitchen.

"You could wait until the night of the dance," Marlenna said.

"We'll take a picture now and another one on Saturday night,"

Brewster said, and Laurel posed himself like a muscle man in a tuxedo. Tee laughed and got in the shot with him, reaching up and holding onto his outstretched arm as if Laurel was lifting her by his flexed muscle.

"I still wish you would ask a girl to go with you to the prom," Marlenna said when they had stopped clowning and Brewster put the camera away.

"I told you Mom, all the girls I could ask are taken already. Besides a lot of the guys are going by themselves. Most of the dances, everybody gets out on the floor and everybody dances with everybody. It doesn't matter. There're a few slow dances, and I probably won't get out on the floor for those."

"You could ask Divinia," Marlenna said. "Matthew said she was going."

"David's done beat me to that," Laurel said. "He asked her about two weeks ago."

"What about Carol Lewis?" Marlenna asked.

"She's going with somebody too. Look, Mom, all the black girls have been asked already, except for Clarissa Jones, and I'm not going to ask her. I'm going by myself, but I'm going to give David and Divinia a ride. I've got everything worked out.

"I wish you had asked a girl earlier. Next year I want you to plan a little better."

"Leave the boy alone," Brewster said. "Sounds to me like he's got everything worked out. We don't need to be rushing him into female company."

With this Marlenna put her hands in the air in a gesture of surrender and went to the kitchen to help Paulette cook supper.

On Saturday night Laurel looked elegant in his black tuxedo and shiny shoes. At dusk, he drove into Low Ridge, picked up Matthew's daughter, Divinia, and David and brought them out to Ole Summit so that Brewster could take pictures of the three students standing before the hearth and next to the piano. But before Brewster clicked the first shot, Marlenna took a small florist box out of the refrigerator.

"A girl's supposed to give you one of these, but since you don't have a girl to take, I guess your mother can give you one." She stood on the tips of her toes pressing the point of the pin through the green florist tape wrapped around the stem of the white rose.

David and Divinia had not wanted to come out to Ole Summit before the dance, but Marlenna enticed them by having Paulette prepare a light supper for them, dishes they requested—little sausages wrapped in pastry, and macaroni and cheese. After the photographs, Laurel, Tee, David, and Divinia sat at the table and the adults served them, hovering over them like eager waiters.

"The year after you graduate," Tee said, "I'm going to start high school, and I can't wait until I have my first dance. I know what I want my formal to look like already, and if nobody asks me, I'm going to ask somebody because I'm not going to the prom by myself."

Laurel cuffed her lightly on the head. "Don't get Mama started."

By the front door, Brewster took one last picture of the three young people in their prom finery and they went out to the Malibu—Laurel up front, David and Divinia in the backseat.

"Don't drive fast," Brewster shouted, "and don't forget whose car you're driving."

"When's the dance over?" Marlenna shouted.

"Midnight," all three young people yelled at the same time, then they laughed.

"Be home by twelve-thirty," Marlenna called as Laurel started the engine.

Laurel turned the car around and waved out the open window before he headed down the lane. Brewster and Marlenna stood on the front porch and watched the taillights of the Malibu until they disappeared on Ole Summit Highway.

"Let's sit on the porch for a while," Marlenna said. "We haven't done that in a long while." Marlenna sat in the swing and Brewster sat beside her.

Paulette and Tee came out and sat in the green joiner's chairs. "It's nice out tonight," Paulette said. "You can feel that warm summer air coming on.

"This will be Laurel's last real summer at home," Marlenna said. "Next summer he'll have college on his mind, and he'll feel like a grownup."

"Don't start thinking about that," Paulette said. "You'll make yourself sad. It's better to sit here and enjoy the sounds of the night birds and not think about much at all."

"I know one thing," Marlenna said. "This summer and all of next year, I'm going to sit down in the big room and listen when Laurel plays the piano because I want to store up a lot of his sounds right here," and she tapped lightly at her heart.

"Ahhh, Mama," Tee said. "You're so sentimental."

Brewster put his arm around Marlenna and drew her close to his side with her shoulder resting under the bend of his arm. He put his other arm across her chest, and he held her in the pocket his arms created.

Brewster, Marlenna, Tee, and Paulette sat on the front porch talking and listening to the cicadas and the night birds until Paulette challenged Tee to a game of Scrabble and the two went inside to the kitchen table. Brewster and Marlenna sat on the porch for a long while, sometimes swinging in silence and other times engaging in easy talk about several of the pieces Brewster was constructing in the shed and about the summer garden Marlenna wanted to plant in the side yard. After Brewster turned the soil for the garden, she wanted two new rose bushes planted close to the house. She had already selected the varieties from the gardening catalogue that came in the mail. "I want a Crimson Glory, a bright red climber," Marlenna said, "and a pink rambler. I saw one with a white eye in the middle of pink petals. That's what I want." She settled her head against Brewster's shoulder.

A little before nine Brewster and Marlenna went inside, and before ten o'clock Marlenna went up to take a shower and get ready for bed. Brewster poured himself a glass of milk and sat backwards, straddle-legged, across the seat of a kitchen chair with the back slats up to his chest, watching Tee and Paulette play the last rounds of Scrabble. When Tee finally won, the two players went to bed. Brewster switched off most of the lights, leaving on the light above the stove and the one in the front hallway for Laurel. Marlenna was still reading when Brewster made his way upstairs, but after he prepared for bed, Marlenna turned off her bedside lamp.

Brewster was in bed, resting in an easy darkness, halfway between sleep and wake when he heard someone talking—a faint sound, but unmistakably someone speaking. He sat up on his elbow to listen.

Marlenna raised her head. "What's that?" she whispered.

The sounds came from the window above the front porch, which had been left open to let in the cool and gentle spring air. Brewster put his finger to her lips to hush her, and he listened. Someone spoke on the porch or in the front yard, that was for sure, but he couldn't make out any of the words, which were soft, almost whispers.

Brewster pulled the covers back, freeing his legs. He put his feet on the floor and walked to the window, looking across the yard and down the lane. He came back to the bed and whispered to Marlenna. "Laurel's home. The car's parked down the lane."

"Who's he talking to?" Marlenna whispered.

"He must have brought David back with him," Brewster said. He went to the closet, found his bathrobe, slipped his arms into it, tied it at his waist, and went down the stairs with Marlenna close behind him. They stepped quietly into the passage, walked to the front door, and peeked out, with Marlenna's head at the rim of the door just below Brewster's. The porch light was on, but they could see no one because the angle of their view was not great enough. The chains of the swing rattled and a girl giggled; unmistakably, it was a girl. They eased away from the door glass in unison, like two pantomime dancers, and they looked at each other.

"Who's that?" Marlenna whispered.

Brewster was having no more of this charade. He opened the door boldly and went out on the porch where Laurel sat on the swing with Ruby Peets in his lap.

"What's going on here, son?" Brewster asked.

Ruby eased herself out of Laurel's lap, slipping down heavily on the slats of the swing.

"We left the dance a little early. It was kind of boring. I gave Ruby a ride home, since we both live right here."

"Ruby didn't have a date either?" Marlenna asked.

"No, ma'am, I didn't. I was going to have to find somebody to bring me home. So I was lucky Laurel was coming straight on back out here."

"Why didn't Ruby get off at her house?" Brewster asked.

"It wasn't nearly midnight," Laurel answered. "We thought we would talk for a little, and I'd get her on home before midnight."

Marlenna folded her arms under her breasts. "It's close enough to midnight. You need to take Ruby on home and get to bed yourself."

"We didn't mean to cause problems," Ruby said. "We thought we would sit here on the porch and enjoy the nighttime a little."

Marlenna didn't respond to Ruby. With her legs splayed wide under her bathrobe and her arms tucked under her breasts, she looked as solid as a sailor, and in the dim porch light, she locked eyes with Laurel. "It's time to take Ruby home," she said.

"Yes, ma'am," Laurel said, and he placed his hand in the middle of Ruby's back, nudging her gently. They stood, and with Laurel's hand still on Ruby's spine, they walked silently past Brewster and Marlenna, went down the steps and to the Malibu.

"Come back immediately," Marlenna shouted.

Laurel did not respond. He cranked the engine, turned the car around, and headed down the lane.

Words shot from Marlenna's mouth like an explosion. "That

girl's going to get Laurel in trouble. Big as a cow. That dress two sizes too small for her. Those hips about to pop the seams. Her breasts pushed up and pinched so tight, it's a wonder she can breathe. When he gets back here, I'm going to give him a word or two." Then Marlenna charged to the swing, sat down, put her head between her hands, and wept. Brewster sat beside her and put his arm around her.

"Laurel has everything, Brewster. That boy has it all. He's smart and good looking and he has talent dripping out his pores, and I'll be damned if I'm going to let Ruby Peets ruin it for him."

"Maybe we should sleep tonight and talk to him tomorrow," Brewster said. "I think we may say too much if we try to talk now. We're tired," and when he said this, he rubbed his hand between the blades of Marlenna's shoulders.

Marlenna took in a long, slow breath. "You're right. If I start on him tonight, I may not stop."

"Laurel's tired too. He's likely to say things he doesn't mean. He'll see the world differently tomorrow." Brewster brought both his hands up and massaged the nape of Marlenna's neck when he said this.

"You're right, Brewster. Absolutely right. I'm going on up to bed because I don't want to see him anymore tonight."

Brewster followed Marlenna. They went up the stairs, into their bedroom, removed their robes, and got into bed. He listened for the sound of the Malibu coming up the lane to the porch. He rested quietly so that he would not disturb Marlenna, but he cut his eyes toward the clock, reading the illuminated face. He lay so still his bones felt heavy as concrete settling densely into the mattress and his joints ached from maintaining his rigidity. After a solid thirty minutes, he still had not heard the car, and he turned to face the clock.

"He hasn't come back yet," Marlenna said. "God, please don't tell me they're over at her house."

"We'll give him another thirty minutes," Brewster said. "If he isn't home by then, I'll get in the truck and go looking for him." Brewster lay on his back, wide-eyed, listening for each second to click on the round-faced clock, and he knew Marlenna's eyes were open too and that she heard every notch as the sweep hand circled the numbers. He took her hand and held it against his chest.

Thirty minutes, nearly two thousand clicks. A long test of patience and endurance. No Malibu. No Laurel. Brewster's body ached from the slow torture of each tick.

"I've been praying," Marlenna whispered.

"Well," Brewster said. "He's been gone nearly an hour. I'm going to look for him."

Marlenna went downstairs to put on a pot of coffee, and Brewster took his time dressing. He was in no rush because he had to decide what he was going to do, what he was going to say when he found Laurel. He was not sure Laurel had taken Ruby home, and if he had not, Brewster did not know where to look for them. He would start at Travis Peets' house. He wouldn't pull into Peets' driveway; he would stop his truck shy of the drive and shine his lights toward the house to see if the Malibu was parked there. If Laurel was not at Travis Peets' house, he would go on into Low Ridge, because he didn't know where else to go.

Where would he go in Low Ridge? He would check at 32 State Street and see if the Malibu was parked there. After that he didn't know where he would look. He would go to the parsonage, wake Matthew, and get Matthew's good counsel. They would search together, wherever Matthew thought they should look was where they would go.

When he came down the stairs and into the kitchen, Marlenna handed him a cup of coffee. "Do you want to take this with you?"

"Let me take a few sips and I'll leave it here. I don't have a place to put it in the truck." He sat at the table holding the coffee cup in both his hands, taking his time because he still did not know where he would search for Laurel or what he would say when he found him.

"I'm going to go first to Travis Peets'. If Laurel's not there, I'll go on to Low Ridge and check at your father's house. If he's not there, I'll go to Matthew's and see what he suggests."

"Do you want me to go with you? Let me change my clothes and I'll go too."

"No," Brewster said. "You stay here. Try to rest a little if you can."

"I'm going to be right here in this kitchen, Brewster. I'm going to be here nursing a cup of black coffee until both you and Laurel get home. I couldn't rest. You know that," and Brewster saw the agitation drawn tight in her lower jaw.

Brewster patted Marlenna on the shoulder, put his cup beside the kitchen sink, and Marlenna followed him to the front door. "If you have to go all the way to Matthew's to find Laurel, you call me from there. Okay?" Marlenna stepped out on the porch with Brewster. "Don't make me wait."

"I'll call," he said. He crossed the yard, opened the door of his

281

truck and slid into the front seat. He felt the burden of an awful mission, searching for his son in the middle of the night. He was afraid of what he may find. If he found Laurel, the boy may refuse to come home. Laurel and Ruby might have run off for all he knew. He had shared none of these concerns with Marlenna, and if he had to voice them, he would save them for Matthew.

He started the engine, turned on the lights, and eased the truck to the lane when he saw car lights turn off of Ole Summit. Laurel had come home. He would have a brief word with the boy tonight, and then they would all go to bed. Tomorrow, with steadier heads, they would bring Laurel to his senses. He turned, looking over his shoulder, and backed his truck to the shed. When he faced the lane again, he saw this was not the Malibu but the sheriff's car pulling close to the porch. He saw Slim Tate open the door and step out of the driver's side, and Matthew stood by the passenger door. It was in that very moment that his brain froze. It froze and he simply could not think, could not imagine what had brought them here. Some men boast they are lionhearted even at the moment of cataclysm, but years from this night, looking back on it, he would know he did not have the lion's heart. He had a man's heart—a breakable heart—and his brain tried mightily to assist his heart, to protect it, so it froze entirely; it refused to speculate; it refused to even think.

He did not ask them why they had come. He did not remember walking toward them, but he did remember lifting his feet at the steps, walking to Marlenna, taking her in his arms, and pulling her to him because he knew they were in a firestorm—he and Marlenna were at Armageddon, and he knew this. He pulled her to his chest, and he placed his large hands over her ears before Slim Tate began speaking because he did not want Marlenna to endure the message the sheriff came to deliver. But she pulled his hands away. She turned her back to him and faced Slim Tate directly.

"Your son's been shot at Mr. G's Social Club. Travis Peets followed them there. Shot him in the parking lot."

Brewster remembered Marlenna's knees buckled, and he caught her with one arm under her breasts, and Matthew was on the porch with his arms around both of them.

"How badly is he hurt?" Brewster asked, and he would not remember how the question sounded, but he would remember the sound of Slim Tate's answer.

"Don't know. The ambulance was there, and they took him on to the hospital. Went by and got your preacher. Thought you'd want him. I came on to get you. I'm gon' take you to the hospital, quick as you ready."

Paulette and Tee were on the porch, and Brewster did not remember seeing them come out, but he did remember Paulette's scream, "Oh Jesus! Oh Jesus! Oh J-e-s-u-s!"

An agreement was struck, but Brewster didn't remember entering into it. Matthew was negotiating, and that was fine because Brewster's brain was frozen and he didn't want it to thaw. Marlenna went upstairs to change her clothes. That was part of the deal. Paulette would help her, another part of the deal. Brewster, Matthew, and Marlenna would drive to the hospital with Slim Tate, and the sheriff would send another car for Paulette and Tee. All part of the deal that Matthew organized.

Slim Tate did not come inside. He sat in a rocking chair on the front porch and waited. Brewster and Matthew sat at the kitchen table. Brewster folded his hands in front of him, and Matthew spoke directly into his face. "Travis Peets followed Laurel's car into town, Followed him to Mr. G's. Laurel got out of the car, went around, and opened the door for Ruby. That's when Travis Peets shot him. Eddie was there. Guess that's why Laurel went, because he knew Eddie was there, and he knew Eddie was a big man at Mr. G's." Matthew pulled his face away and sat deep into his chair, looking to Brewster like he was spent, exhausted from giving out these words, but he continued speaking with the air heavy in his chest. "Not big enough though to stop a crazy fool with a malignant heart and a pistol in his hand."

"Matthew, Laurel's not hurt bad is he?" and when he asked this, he wanted all the right words to be in the answer. He wanted Matthew's assurance, the bullet glanced off, or Travis Peets had bad eyes, or his old hand was unsteady. That was what he needed to hear.

"I don't know how bad he's hurt, Brewster. Eddie rode in the ambulance with Laurel, so Laurel wasn't alone. Eddie was with him."

Looking back on this night, Brewster would not remember getting into Slim Tate's car, but he would remember Marlenna beside him, so small, sitting close enough to be a part of him, melting the heat of her hand to his, and weeping. Slim Tate drove fast, very fast, and the blue light of the patrol car flashed through the thick woods of Ole Summit Highway, but the Sheriff did not sound the siren, and Brewster was grateful for that.

At Low Ridge Hospital, a nurse and a doctor in a white coat met them and escorted them into a small room where they sat in light blue plastic chairs. Matthew sat beside Marlenna, and Slim Tate waited outside the door, leaning against the doorframe, his hat in his hand. The doctor, a young white man, pulled his chair directly in front of Marlenna, and he leaned forward resting his elbows on his knees. He was suffering, there was no question about that. This young white doctor did not want to say what he had to say. Brewster was sure of that because his face had no color in it and his jaws were slack. But he had been given this task, and he leaned forward on his elbows, looking Marlenna in the eyes, and his voice was soft, distant, way off somewhere, but he said the words. "I am so sorry to tell you, so sorry. The doctors did everything they could. The heart was shattered. A direct hit to the chest."

Marlenna whimpered like a weight crushed her.

"This-could-not-be-so," she said in short bursts of air that popped in and out through her throat. "This-could-not. . . ," and Brewster held her tightly across her shoulders to stabilize her air. *"This-could-not. . . . Could-not. Could-not."* She chanted and Matthew held her hand.

SHATTERED HEART. SHATTERED HEART. SHATTERED HEART—Brewster would always remember those words. Laurel's precious heart in smithereens, the heart of his son, burst, fragmented into blood red slivers. He wanted to run—run where? He wanted to hit, to lash, to hew, to maul, leave nothing standing, not whip the money lenders and overturn their tables, not drive them out with knotted whips as Jesus Christ Himself had done. No, he wanted to shake the very foundations of the temple, bring it down, destroy this doctor and every mouth that spoke of shattered hearts—Laurel's priceless heart, Laurel's irreplaceable heart. He rose to bring them down, bring them all down who uttered those words. *SHATTERED HEART.* Matthew held him around his chest, pushed him against the wall, and pinned him there. That was when he thawed, and the water rose so high it nearly drowned him.

The doctor stood. "He's upstairs. We're going to take you there, and you can stay with him as long as you like. Nobody's going to hurry you."

A nurse brought a wheelchair for Marlenna because the doctor said she could not trust her knees, and Brewster leaned against the handles of it and pushed it on the elevator, up to the third floor, to a small room. When they opened the door, Eddie was there standing beside the bed, and so were Carmella and Albert Mixon, who sat in a chair, his head in his hands. Matthew came into the room with Brewster and Marlenna, but Slim Tate waited in the hall. Eddie and

Carmella stepped away from the bed, and Albert Mixon slid his chair back, making a place for them beside their son. Marlenna put her hands on the arms of the chair and pushed herself up. Brewster took her hand, and they walked to the bed. Brewster saw himself do this, like he was a camera above himself, recording his life, not like he was the man living it. Laurel wore a green hospital gown and had several sheets wound tightly around his chest, almost up to his neck. His arms rested on the outside of the sheet, and blood was visible under his left arm.

"You're going to want to keep the sheets around him," the nurse said. "We're outside. Call us for anything you need. Anything," she repeated.

Laurel's eyes were closed, and his countenance was that of the young, the innocent—the skin under his eyes, smooth and supple, his cheeks showing new hair of budding manhood. With the palm of her hand, Marlenna rubbed Laurel's forehead.

"My baby, my sweet baby." She dropped her head down beside Laurel's ear. "My sweet, sweet baby."

Matthew put a box of tissues on the bed beside Laurel and Brewster grabbed a fistful of them. He had thawed, and water poured down the mountain.

Marlenna rubbed Laurel's hands that rested on the folded sheet. "Hands of great art. Special hands." She leaned forward and rubbed them against her face.

Brewster grabbed another fistful of tissues because he was drowning in the flood that closed his throat and blinded his eyes.

"So much promise. So much hope," Marlenna whispered, but Brewster could not speak because Laurel's heart was shattered, and his own was open like the throbbing, red heart of Jesus Christ, exposed, bringing forth blood and water that would surely drown him. Never, never had there been despair so deep. Brewster's body filled with nothingness, beyond hopelessness. Nothing. Nothing. He put his arm around Marlenna, maybe he could save her, because he could not save himself.

Paulette and Tee came into the room, and Brewster knew what he should do. He stepped forward and put his arm around Tee's shoulder. He would save her too, before she was consumed by nothingness. She looked down at her brother and sobbed in the agony of total loss, the anguish of abject sorrow.

Eddie wept, his whole body convulsing, his teeth rattling. Carmella had her arm around Marlenna, and both women held tissues to their faces, filling the cottony fibers with the waters of death. Albert Mixon bowed his head and sat like a man broken in spirit, a man who could not rise above the abyss in which he found himself. The family spoke, one and then another, in partial sentences. One hand touching Laurel's face, another brushing lightly against his hands. They wailed and they whispered and they gathered around the bed, a family seeing its beloved into the dark, uncharted passage of death.

Matthew stepped forward. "Let us hold hands and pray," he said. Brewster had one arm around Tee, and with his other hand he grasped Marlenna and drew her hand to his chest. Albert Mixon stood up and placed his hand on top of Brewster's hand that rested on Tee's shoulder.

"Our Lord and our God, who understands the grieving heart, give Brewster and Marlenna the strength to get through these next days." Matthew breathed deep and prayed on.

"Our sweet Jesus, who knows the suffering of the cross, be with Brewster and Marlenna, Tee, and every family member in this room who feels the sharp, sharp pangs of suffering. Stand beside us all and let us feel your love," and he intoned the name of every person in the room asking for mercy and grace. "This is what we ask for," Matthew said, "mercy, grace, and the strength to get us through the coming days."

The rest of it Brewster marched through like a soldier, simply because it had to be done. It was the responsibility of the living to care for the dead. He marched for Laurel because even in death he had to care for his son, his only son. Matthew took Brewster and Marlenna to Keese Funeral Home where they selected the coffin. Marlenna wanted a blue satin lining because Laurel was her baby boy.

There was the wake at which Brewster thought nearly every person in Low Ridge, black and white, came to hold his hand and utter words that were distant, words that did not begin to touch his misery, his hopelessness, his desperation.

"I'm so sorry for your loss."

"This never should have happened."

"I'm sorry." "I'm sorry." "I'm sorry."

And others collapsed in his arms, wept on his shoulder. He held them and nodded his head in affirmation. The whole time he stood in that line, holding the hands and bodies of all these people, he wanted to take Laurel and run, tuck Laurel under his arm, shield him, protect him, and when it came into Brewster's head that running was too late, Laurel's heart was shattered, Brewster split wide open to nothingness, a vortex of nothing. Down. Down. Down into darkness. Yet, he stood, held hands, and comforted like there was some substance to him, but there was nothing. Nothing.

Cecil Rimes came, and Brewster saw that he too had been sucked into the whirlpool of nothing. His shoulders dropped. His jacket hung on him loose and baggy, like a coat on a skeleton. He pulled a chair close to the coffin, and he sat there beside Laurel. He sat for hours, a large white handkerchief in his lap. Three times Brewster saw him rise and touch Laurel's hands and then, he sat again, bringing the handkerchief to his eyes and nose.

"I will not come for the funeral," he said when he stood. "I cannot bear it. I lost a child. Years ago. And I cannot bear to see another son put in the ground." He did not say *I'm sorry* as so many others had done, and Brewster thought it was unnecessary.

"This is the lost talent," Cecil Rimes said. "Stolen by hate. In two hundred years, how much talent has been taken?" He asked and Brewster did not answer. The old professor sat beside the body again. Before he left, he stood and touched Laurel's long and beautiful fingers one last time.

"I will come," he said, "after the funeral. After some days have passed."

Anvil Thomas was out of the country, but he sent an enormous wreath of white lilies that were as fragrant as the flowers in the church the day Brewster married Marlenna. Brewster stood beside the circle of white trumpets, smelling them, and he wanted to be small enough to crawl inside these little tunnels that carried the scent of purity and peace and pleasure.

At the funeral there were so many cars that Slim Tate himself directed traffic in front of Limrick Road Baptist. The high school let out at noon so all the young people could attend. The doors of Limrick Road Baptist were propped open for the over-flow crowd that stood on the steps and in the yard and out on Limrick Road to hear Matthew speak about Laurel and about the hate that had shattered Laurel's heart.

"We are fragile," Matthew said. "We break when battered by the crushing force of evil. But the evil one will not have the last say, the evil one will be brought down by his own wrath. Jesus Christ Himself will come to stand beside us, comfort us. He is already routing the evil one. He has summoned the Comforter to come to us, to enter our hearts. We know Laurel, our sweet boy, is ministered to by angels, his heart healed, his eyes open. Do not worry, mother; do not worry, father; your precious son is with God."

Mrs. Banks played the piano, the choir sang, and four young people from Low Ridge High School spoke—two white and two black. And there was the burial in Hope Hill Cemetery, with Laurel resting to the left of Mama Tee. Brewster would always remember the angle of the light that cast a beam across old Hope Hill that afternoon, an odd ray, wide and iridescent, shooting through two enormous swelling and rolling clouds. He felt the light shimmer across the ground where Laurel would rest, and it spun across the laps and chests of the mourners in the front row, mother-of-pearl colored, and Brewster wanted the deep, dark brown coffin to be put in the ground while the radiant beam graced the earth.

Then there was the night, and the day, and the long, long darkness.

25

Brewster did not know how many days passed before he looked into a mirror. Surely he saw himself when he dressed for the wake, when he dressed for the funeral, but if he had, he could not remember looking, and when he did take stock of himself on the third day after Laurel was put in the ground, he could not believe the countenance reflected back at him. The man in the mirror was old. The man in the mirror had turned gray. Brewster brought his right hand to his head and felt his close-cropped, coarse hair. His own movement reflected in the mirror assured him that this was indeed himself. In the passage of this week, he had turned gray, lost his youth. His face was lax, and his nose had no starch in it. It lay flat and soft, a nose rendered malleable by age. He raised his fist and shook it at his image in the mirror, and then he raised his clinched hand heavenward. "Don't matter," he said. "Don't-give-shit. Not another thing you can do to me."

Slim Tate came to Ole Summit and stood on the steps. He leaned against the banister and spoke. "Travis Peets is in jail. Won't get out. Judge won't set bail." He pulled a Marlboro pack from his breast pocket, thumped a cigarette into his palm and lit it, angled his lips, and blew smoke backwards over his shoulder. Brewster watched him, but said nothing. After Laurel died, he made up his mind he would not utter one word to anybody unless he wanted to give it, and he had no interest in giving any of his words to Slim Tate. He watched the sheriff and he rocked in his chair and then he looked over his dense woods as the smoke drifted past Slim Tate's shoulder.

"Justice will be done. Let me tell you that. Whatever consolation it brings." Slim Tate drew long on his cigarette, expanding his chest, allowing the smoke to go deep inside him. He turned his back to Brewster and gazed over the land before he spoke again.

"Justice will be done," he repeated, and he delivered the words like a gift, an offering. "Miz Peets and the girl left town. Went to Detroit City to be with her son. Have the address back at the office. But ole Travis is in jail, and that's where he's gon' stay for whatever comfort that can bring."

Newspapers all over the country carried the story of Albert Laurel McAtee, young and black and talented, standing at the door of manhood that would surely have opened to promises fulfilled, shot by a bigot because he dared to be with a white girl. When friends came to Ole Summit they brought newspapers tucked under their arms, one from Louisville, Kentucky that a relative there had sent, one all the way from San Francisco that a son in the army had mailed home to his mother, one from Pittsburgh that a former school teacher sent to Herman Thomas. Friends came with these newspapers as if the articles about Laurel would explain everything, like the stories would bring peace or understanding, but Brewster took the newspapers and put them in stacks on the kitchen table where Paulette served coffee and coconut cake. Marlenna sat in the big room, extending her hand to each person, speaking in whispers to everyone, but Brewster could not do this. He retreated to his shed. He sat in his rocking chair beside his long windows. He watched the guests come and go, and he felt nothing but the thickness of the blackest night.

Brewster and Marlenna got calls for interviews from newspapers and from television stations, but they turned them down. Marlenna said she was not ready to speak, and Brewster did not want to talk with strangers about his son, because his mind was not yet organized, and he did not want to go on television weeping and holding his head down. Matthew spoke to several reporters, and that was fine with Brewster because Matthew had the words that needed to be spoken and Brewster did not. He had no words to give. He was empty, and what words he did have he saved for Tee and Marlenna. Late at night when Tee could not sleep, she came into their bedroom, sat on their bed, and the three of them spoke of Laurel, talked until Brewster got out of bed and went to the porch to wait for morning. Tee took his place, crawling in bed beside her mother.

Anvil Thomas came to Ole Summit, and he brought with him a new young wife and a baby son who toddled on the porch while Anvil pulled his chair in front of Brewster and spoke earnestly. "I was out of the country when Laurel was shot, but I'm back now and I want to do something. What can I do?"

When Brewster did not speak, Anvil rushed on, and Brewster thought Anvil was afraid of the silence, afraid of what the stillness could bring forth. "I've talked to the D.A. I'm convinced the trial will be fair. We're going to send a couple of attorneys from the NAACP to come watch. I may even come myself. What can I do now? What do you need?"

"I want that land," Brewster said. "I want to tear that house down. Bulldoze everything."

"We'll sue for the land," Anvil said. "I've already thought of that."

"Sue, buy, I don't care. I want that land to tear down everything. Like the walls of Jericho, I want it all down. Haul all the mess off. Bury it all," Brewster said.

"We'll talk to Mrs. Peets right away," Anvil said. "We'll let her know we're going to sue."

"I don't want to wait long," Brewster said.

"I won't keep you waiting," Anvil said. His son toddled to him, extended his arms, and Anvil lifted him, placing the baby in his lap and resting his chin against the boy's head. When the baby boy reached his hand to Anvil's jaw and rubbed his father's cheek, Brewster felt nothing because this was not Laurel, not his son, born just as the sun rose at Our Savior's Home, his very name sounding laud and honor. This boy was not Laurel, and Brewster felt nothing as the tiny hands stroked Anvil's face.

Tall weeds and brush shrubs of summer nearly concealed Travis Peets' house from Ole Summit Highway, and for this Brewster was grateful. He made up his mind that he would not look at Travis Peets' old place when he passed it, but despite his resolve, he was drawn to it. His head turned, studying it. He was certain he would see snakes snarled in trees and bobcats resting between porch posts if he cocked his eyes toward the house. He gazed, and then he cursed himself for looking where hellhounds had dwelled. He wanted everything shattered, demolished, and removed, every board, every stick, every piss pot, every pan, even the tiniest scrap of tarpaper.

The district attorney came to Ole Summit too—a middle-aged white woman named Clara Bettis. She was red-headed, thick through the middle, always dressed in a suit and high-heeled shoes, and she spoke in a voice that said she was weary, too tired to be on her wide feet, but she had a mission, nonetheless, and she was duty-bound to complete it. She looked like a woman who had reached her position in life through battle. She was the general with a weathered face, but it was set forth in red lipstick and large gold earrings that dangled nearly to her throat. She took in a deep breath, sighed, and puffed air out her scarlet lips. "We got a tight case because we got *five* good witnesses." She stressed the number five, and Brewster knew that five must be a good sum.

"Trial date's been set for January, the fourth day of the new year." She breathed deeply again, pushed her lips out and raised her eyebrows. "Everybody in this community's sure hoping nineteen-hundred and seventy-eight's gon' be better than nineteen-hundred and seventy-seven." With these words, she straightened the papers on the kitchen table with the palms of her hands, lifted the sheets with red-nailed fingers, and put the papers back in her leather satchel.

Night was the meanest time. Marlenna kept a book on her nightstand, and she rarely turned off her lamp. She let it burn all night. If Brewster dozed, he woke to find her propped on her pillows, her eyes closed, her book resting open on her stomach, the light reflecting off her face. If sleep caught either of them and settled on them for several hours, they woke abruptly, jumping into the bottom-less reality of loss, and then they turned from back, to side, to back, and to side again. Brewster had finally given up on sleep. He wanted only to see the first signs of light, and most mornings he watched for dawn as he sat in his chair on the porch. Before he could see it, the birds announced sunrise, and when they called out in their shrill whistle-blasts, he stood, walked to the edge of the porch, and watched the eastern sky. Before long he saw a tendril of salmon pink twinge into the morning gray, and day arrived.

He was glad he had his work, because in the shed he found some solace. He shaped a cabriole leg and rubbed his hand along the smooth curve of it. He brought the walnut to his nose and smelled the raw wood. He ran his finger along the perfectly shaped foot. He snugged every dowel to flawless fit. Here in his shed where the afternoon sun shone luminous, pacifying him with shafts of light, here where Skinner whistled and the lathe hummed, here he sat in his rocking chair in the genial comfort of afternoon, and he slept for an hour.

In September, Marlenna went back to her teaching. "I cannot sit here at Ole Summit and dwell on it all," she said. "In the classroom is where I feel comfortable. I know what I'm supposed to do there." She would take some time off second semester because she planned to be in the courthouse seeking justice on Laurel's behalf, seeking a reprieve from her sorrow.

Brewster was also glad when school started for Tee. The summer had been long and quiet at Ole Summit, and she needed to be in the company of young people, teenagers who still laughed and who did not yet know life could turn into the blackness of night from where it was almost impossible to see or to navigate.

In October, Anvil telephoned Brewster in the shed. He was back in Low Ridge and wanted Brewster to come to Matthew's office. When Brewster arrived there and walked up the iron steps to the metal platform, he found the door of Matthew's study standing open and Anvil sitting in the burgundy brocade chair that had rested in the same spot for nearly twenty years and looked weary from age and use. When Brewster entered the small office, Anvil stood and offered the big chair to him, but he declined. Matthew rolled his chair from behind the desk and Brewster sat in it. While Matthew stood, leaning his back against the wall, Anvil spoke.

"That land's yours, Brewster. I met with Mrs. Peets. Told her we would sue for it. She didn't want to go to court. Said she was already going to be in court enough. Said she didn't want the land anyway." He laid a stack of papers on Matthew's desk beside Brewster.

"Here's the deal," he said. "She's deeding the land over. You got to sign these papers. She's coming back two weeks from today and she'll take anything she wants off the place. Then it's yours, clear and free."

"She could take everything," Brewster said. "I'm not going to do one thing with the stuff that's on the place but crush it and haul it off. Tell her to bring a big trailer and take everything. That'd save me time," Brewster said.

"I'll tell her," Anvil said and then he stood over the rolling chair and directed Brewster to all the places marked with an X, all the spots that needed Brewster's signature.

"I'll get you a copy of the deed," Anvil said when Brewster had signed the last paper. "Remember you can't do anything until Mrs. Peets has come and taken everything she wants off the place."

"I won't go on that land until then," Brewster said.

Then Anvil folded the papers and placed them in a small brown-leather pouch. He sat in the brocade chair again, and he tucked the pouch under his arm as if he was ready to go, but he remained seated. "Brewster, I'm worried about Marlenna. I spoke at the high school this morning and saw her. She's not well. She's lost weight, skin and bone, and her eyes look like she hasn't slept since Laurel passed."

Brewster hated that Anvil knew of Marlenna's suffering and knew that Brewster could not help her because he could not help himself. He and Marlenna lay apart in the bed at night, each enduring a torment that neither spoke of, awake for hours, afraid to move for fear of disturbing the other. With time, surely he would be able to make everything right again, at least right in all areas except in those private and special places reserved in their singular hearts for Laurel. It would take a little more time. When he was on solid footing himself, he could help Marlenna and Tee. He could reach out and save them, pull them with him to sure and firm footing. But he could not do that yet.

"She's fine," Brewster said. "Getting better all the time."

"If I can help, let me know. I mean that, Brewster. I've known you and Marlenna since we were all children, and I'm going to stand by you now. You let me know what you need." With that the two men shook hands. Brewster left Matthew and Anvil in the tiny church office, descended the metal steps, and he went over to Three Brothers to speak with his father-in-law.

Brewster did not want to clear the land himself. He would hire a crew with a bulldozer, and he wanted Matthew, Albert Mixon, and Skinner to supervise the job. He would not go on the land until every scrap of evidence was removed that said Travis Peets had lived there, had ever existed. Albert Mixon was excited about the job. "I'll be sure it's all busted up," he said. "I'll be sure everything they ever owned is hauled off. That's something I can do for Laurel," he said, "for you and Marlenna too."

"Oh, boy," Skinner said when Brewster asked him to help supervise the demolition. "I'm taking my ax," he said. "Don't mind if I bring David too, do you? It would do him good to help knock that place down."

Two days after Anvil left town, Brewster went back to Matthew's office. When Brewster reached the metal platform at the top of the landing, Matthew, who was sitting behind his battered old desk reading scripture, looked toward the door. "Well," he said. "Come in, come in. When Brewster Thomas McAtee comes to visit, it's a fine afternoon."

"I don't want to disturb you," Brewster said.

"You're not," Matthew said. "I'm looking over some verses for Sunday." He rose and circled to the front of his desk. "Sit here," he said and pointed to the brocade chair. And before Brewster could protest, Matthew put his hands on Brewster's shoulders and pushed him gently into the soft stuffing of the embroidered fabric where Brewster's hips fit comfortably into the indentions left by Matthew's own body.

Matthew walked back to his desk chair, sat in it, and rolled it around in front of Brewster. "What brings you up those cast-iron steps today?"

"A job. I have a job for you."

"I'm generally available," Matthew said, leaning back in his chair and crossing his arms over his chest.

"The Saturday after Mrs. Peets comes and takes what she wants, I'm going to hire a bulldozer and a man to run it. I want you to supervise tearing that place down. Don't want one fragment left of Travis Peets. Want every corner of that tarpaper gone, every board, every scrap, every trace that says Travis Peets ever lived on that land. I don't want to go on the land until it's all gone. Every bit of anything that was him, gone." Brewster studied Matthew with his hands resting over his large chest, his belly pressing hard against the buttons of his shirt. "Will you do that for me, Matthew?"

"It'll take more than a Saturday."

"I know. We'll keep that bulldozer there for as long as it takes. But when it's done, I want the ground to be clean even of his footprints. We'll scrape the topsoil and haul that to the dump too. I've asked Albert Mixon and Skinner to help, and Skinner's going to bring David. You can bring all the help you want. Anybody who wants to come and clean that land off is invited. You'll be in charge of that, Matthew. I just want the job done, that's all."

Matthew raised his eyebrows and puckered his lips. He was quiet for some seconds. "I'll do it for you, Brewster. I won't work on Sunday though, you know that. Probably take at least a week to clean that place off like you want it done."

"A week's fine. Two week's fine. Just so long as there's nothing left that was Travis Peets."

The two men worked out the final details, and Brewster pushed his hands against the arms of the big chair, lifting himself from the seat. He crossed to the doorway and stepped on the metal platform. Matthew followed him. "I have one more question, Brewster. What you going to do with that land after you get it cleared?"

"Grow laurels," Brewster said. "As many laurels as I want to plant." He went down the stairs and did not look back at Matthew.

In mid-November, Slim Tate drove to Ole Summit to tell Brewster and Marlenna that Mrs. Peets would be in town with her son. They would bring a trailer to the property and take what they wanted. He wanted Brewster to know this so that he could do as he pleased, see her or not see her as was his liking.

Brewster, Marlenna, and Tee decided to drive to Beaumont State the day Mrs. Peets came to Ole Summit Highway. They called Cecil Rimes and arranged lunch with him in the college dining room. Their drive on the county highway felt lonesome to Brewster; there was no purpose in it now that Laurel was gone. The trees shot up their bony arms into the gray sky of November, and cold autumn wind whistled at the car windows. Brewster did not speak of what he felt, but Tee did.

"This is not right," she said, "to be going to Beaumont State without Laurel." Neither Brewster nor Marlenna answered her. Brewster kept his eyes on the county roadway until he turned and drove under the dark wrought-iron arch of the college.

They entered Cecil Rimes' studio, and he embraced them. When he spoke of Laurel, he removed a large white handkerchief from his hip pocket and wiped his tears. His skin was the red of an Indian, the brown of an African, and the peach of a European; under his eyes he carried soft folds, baggage from years of study, close reading, late nights, early mornings, loss and laughter. The moisture of his tears glistened in the baggy creases of his face.

"The music Laurel played is still here," he said. "Little pieces of it are up in the corners, snugged in the bolts of the piano, up under the cushions of the sofa, nested around the windows."

He turned and surveyed his studio. "I sit here sometimes, close my eyes and listen."

Brewster, Marlenna, and Tee walked across campus with Cecil Rimes. They moved slowly, studying the buildings, and Professor Rimes told them the history of the college, a Presbyterian school, one of the first institutions of higher learning for Negroes in Alabama. They stood in silence for a few moments before the chapel, and then they walked to the cafeteria where they sat by a window and enjoyed their lunch and took pleasure in the company of each other on a November afternoon when the sun shone at a low winter angle.

On the Saturday after Mrs. Peets left town, the bulldozer inched its way down Ole Summit Highway and pulled onto the hard, rutted dirt in front of Travis Peets' house. Judging from the sounds that drifted to Brewster on his porch. Matthew must have assembled a multitude. Marlenna came out, and the two of them sat in the swing with heavy jackets zipped to their throats, holding hands, not talking, but listening to the clamor of the deconstruction. Tee sat on the porch rail almost all day, listening, with her knees pulled tightly to her chest and her jacket over her legs.

Late in the afternoon, just as night dropped grayness over the woods and the yard, Matthew pulled down the lane with Albert Mixon in the passenger seat. They both got out of the car, and they indeed looked like two men who had been on a demolition mission. Matthew's shirt was torn at the pocket and both men were dirty, covered with light dust from the powder created when material things, that have form and substance, are crushed.

"Come on in," Marlenna said. "Have supper with us. Tell us what you did. How far along did you get?"

"I can't eat," Matthew said. "June has supper waiting for me."

"I'll eat," Albert Mixon said, "if you'll drive me back into town later."

"I'll do that," Brewster said. Albert Mixon sat in one of the deep green chairs, removed his shoes, which were covered in thick dust, and he placed them on the first porch step before he entered the passage at Ole Summit.

He cleaned himself in the laundry room and sat at the table with Brewster, Marlenna, Tee, and Paulette. "There was a crowd there," he said. "Never have seen so many people want to tear a place down. Some black, some white. They wanted that house gone, but for different reasons, I suspect. Whites wanted to get rid of that place because of the man who lived there and what he did was an embarrassment to them, and blacks wanted to tear it down because it was something they could do for Laurel and for his family. Even Slim Tate came by." Albert Mixon paused to butter his cornbread and fork his roast beef, delivering it to his mouth.

"How far along did you get?" Marlenna asked.

"Well," Albert Mixon said wiping his mouth and chin with his napkin. "First thing, Matthew let anybody who wanted anything take it. There wasn't much to get because the Peets got most everything when they came, but some folks found a thing or two they needed. Palmer Stokes got an old shovel, a few of the women took some plants in tin cans that still looked pretty good, stuff like that. Then we all started putting whatever we could lift in the dump truck. Matthew called Low Ridge Wrecker to haul off two old cars on blocks that were off in the near woods. Folks were throwing everything you can imagine on that dump truck, bricks, boards, tin cans, old clothes, cardboard boxes. Those Peetses left a mess." He paused again, taking two or three bites of his food, holding his cornbread in one hand and his fork in the other.

"There was an old refrigerator, two old washing machines, one was an old wringer-type, and we were about to throw that on the truck when somebody said they wanted it and took it off to their car. We picked up, and we carried, and we tossed stuff until noon, and the Low Ridge Diner sent sandwiches and drinks for everybody. I didn't tell you the *Low Ridge Gazette* was there too, but they were. They took pictures several times during the day. It was something!" Albert Mixon said, and he continued to eat.

"I should have been there," Tee said. "I may go tomorrow."

"No," Brewster said. "We won't go until everything's gone. I want a load or two of new topsoil put down too. Then we'll go."

Tee was silent, and Brewster was glad she did not ask again. He did not want the dust nor the soil from Peets' place on his daughter, and he did not want her hands to touch nor her back to lift what had belonged to Travis Peets.

"Just before dark, the bulldozer took one run at the house," Albert Mixon said. "Knocked part of it loose from the foundation. Some of the men were gathering any lumber they wanted when Matthew and I left. We'll get started again on Monday. Won't be as big a crew then, though. Today was the big day," he said. Then he added, "Can't tell you when I've had a more pleasant day's work," and he reached for the butter with his right hand while his left held tightly to his cornbread.

When Brewster took Albert Mixon home, he did not look in the direction of Travis Peets' old house. He did not want to see the land until everything was gone. He controlled his neck and his head, and he did not look.

Clara Bettis came to Ole Summit two times during the next week. The trial was still scheduled to begin January 4. Brewster and Marlenna and any other family members could sit directly behind her in court, she told them. She suspected that the trial would get some heavy media coverage, and the family should prepare themselves for that. "Mrs. Peets will be there and their son from Detroit, and Ruby will be there too because she'll need to testify. You need to prepare yourselves for all of that," Clara Bettis said.

"I'll be prepared," Marlenna said, "but I need to know that Travis Peets will be convicted. I can't bear it if he's let go."

"I've talked to Ruby two times. Went to Detroit to depose her, and I met with her again when her grandmother came to close their place down here on Ole Summit. Ruby will say what happened. Far as I can tell. She won't speak against her grandfather, but she'll say what happened in that parking lot. We got five other witnesses anyway," the attorney said.

Clara Bettis took a deep breath and twisted her scarlet mouth before she spoke again. "I believe we'll get a conviction, but I can't guarantee it. I'd like to give you a promise that old Travis Peets will sit in Yellow Mama, but I can't issue a warrant of certainty. I'm going to ask for the death penalty."

"The death penalty?" Marlenna asked, and she brought the tips of her fingers to her forehead and rested her head there.

"That's right," Clara Bettis said. "If you have any objections, you got to let me know in one week's time. We need to have everything set for trial before Christmas."

Throughout the week, Brewster could hear the sound of the bulldozer knocking and shoveling, straining its engine when it changed angles to assault the property again, and he could hear voices—shouting, laughing, calling above the noise of the bulldozer. Matthew came at the close of each day to give Brewster a report. "House is down. Cleaning up the rubble. Take us through tomorrow on that."

And Marlenna weighed the trial and its aftermath. "I don't want the death penalty, Brewster. I do want him convicted though. I want him adjudged and found guilty in that courtroom, standing before God and me and you and the world." But Brewster maintained his silence. He wanted Travis Peets to know the hour of his death, just as Laurel had known the certainty of his own final minutes, when the gun was aimed at his chest, and the trigger pulled with an aged and lethal finger, and Laurel's heart was shattered.

"Pillars on which that house stood were knocked down. Going to get those off the place tomorrow. Then we'll scrape the soil like you want. Take the rest of the week, but I think we can finish on Saturday. Fire department came today, and those men helped for several hours. This has been a Low Ridge project," Matthew said. "Tearing this house down has brought this community together."

Just before Christmas, Paulette decided to move back into Low Ridge to live with one of her daughters. Brewster worried about losing Paulette because the only time he heard Tee laugh was when she and Paulette were engaged in a project—baking a pie in the kitchen or sewing a red skirt for the Christmas pageant at County Training School. He did not think he had laughed since Laurel was shot, and he could not even remember the sound of Marlenna's laughter.

Paulette said she was going to live with her daughter because the family did not need her any longer. Tee was old enough and could care for herself, and Paulette had three grandchildren in Low Ridge who needed her now. But Brewster had come into the house at noon one day and heard Paulette talking on the telephone with one of her friends.

"I can't stand the sadness here," she said. "It's going to consume me. Eat me up. Swallow me like Jonah in the belly of the whale. They not moaning and wailing anymore, but they gloomy, heavy-hearted, and it's Christmas. I'm going down. Down if I don't get out of the bowels of this sadness."

On Saturday, when Paulette's daughter came to take her into Low Ridge, Tee stood on the porch and watched the car until it turned on Ole Summit Highway headed toward Low Ridge. Then Tee went to her room and did not come out all day.

Matthew came late in the afternoon. "That place is scraped clean," he said. "Two hauls of new dirt been dumped. We need to spread it. On Monday, I got three men to help me rake it."

Marlenna and Tee went to church on Sunday, but Brewster stayed at Ole Summit where he sat in his rocking chair in his shed, beside his long windows, and he watched his land and his woods. And when Marlenna and Tee returned, he sat at the table with them. He put food in his mouth without tasting it, and he looked at them without seeing them. Marlenna and Tee put a small green tree on the table in the big room, and they wrapped clear white lights around the branches, no color in the lights, and they placed only a few of the glass ornaments on the small, spindly branches.

"We will have some kind of a Christmas," Marlenna said. "Won't be like we've had in the past, but we'll have Christmas for Tee."

On Monday night, Matthew came to report that the land was clean, scraped, with new soil, fresh and raked. "I'll put turf on it too, if you want that," Matthew said.

"That's good," Brewster said. "Sod the place, but leave me some good topsoil in the middle of the land. That's where I want to plant."

On Friday afternoon, Matthew returned with news that grass

was on the land. "Looks like a park," Matthew said. "You won't recognize the place."

"A Christmas present," Marlenna said, and she stepped toward Matthew putting her arms around his chest.

From his green chair on the front porch, Brewster saw the sun come up on Saturday morning. He waited until the day was sufficiently announced before he entered Tee's bedroom to wake her. Then he went to the kitchen where Marlenna sat at the table with a coffee cup in her hand. "Dress," he said. "We're going to that land today. It's time for us to see it."

"No," Marlenna said. "I'm not ready yet. You and Tee go. I'll go before long. I don't want to be over there today."

He did not press Marlenna to go with them, but when Tee came into the kitchen, he was ready to see the new land, to behold what he had wanted for a solid twenty years, view what had been destroyed, and what was being rebuilt in Laurel's name. He watched impatiently as Tee ate a bowl of cereal and washed it down with a glass of milk. When she was ready, he held his daughter's hand, and with Marlenna watching them from the porch, they walked down the lane and crossed into the woods. The forest was dark and colder than the open air of this December morning, and their eyes had to adjust to the dimness. The earth's floor was thick with dead leaves and brush, and the ground jutted forth short spikes of bare branches. Summer's wasted briars caught their legs, snagging open stitch-like trails into the denim fabric of Brewster's pants.

"I think we should have walked out by the road," Tee protested.

"We're almost there," Brewster said, holding her hand and pulling her along through the thick undercover of trees, branches, pine straw, brush, vines, and wild grasses. He could see the two of them, like fairytale people, moving through shadowy wildwood, inching their way toward a new land that would surely save them.

"We should have taken the road," Tee said again when another vine with long thorns caught her pants and cut into her leg.

Brewster stopped and leaned toward her, gently removing the barbs from her clothes. "We're almost there," he encouraged her. He had not wanted to take the road, and he did not want to explain this to Tee. He wanted to cross his own property when he entered Travis Peets' old place. He was the victor coming from his own land to claim that which had belonged to his enemy. He took Tee's hand again and led her on toward the sunlight. Together they ducked under a low-hanging limb, and then they set their feet on their new land. They raised their bodies to full height, and neither of them spoke.

The land was barren and beautiful. The morning sun shone on the new grass, which sparkled with jewel-like beads of dew resting on the yellow-green blades. Where the pitiful tarpaper house once stood was open and the ground was covered in new squares of turf. The open field had a gentle roll to it, and the light wind of December made a whistling sound as it circled through the trees on the periphery of the clearing, and in the middle of the property was a large wide-open space with fresh black soil that smelled raw and rich with possibility. They looked at the property, circling it with their eyes and liking what they saw. Brewster took Tee's hand, and they walked to the sod in the middle where they stood in front of the open black dirt. Brewster squatted, resting his weight on his ankles, and the smell of yellowed, morning-wet, new grass entered Brewster's nose, pleasing him.

Tee began to weep, putting the sleeve of her jacket to her nose as a young child would do. Brewster put his arm around his daughter and drew her near to him, allowing her to sob for both of them, tears of regret and sorrow and thanksgiving, grateful that what had been cursed was now redeemed. When Tee settled, they walked in a wide circle around the property, holding hands, looking at the blue sky and smelling the freshness and newness of this place.

"We're going to plant laurel trees in the middle there," Brewster told Tee. "I want a whole row of laurels."

"We need seven," Tee said. "I don't know why we need seven, but I know we do. Seven laurels in a line," she said.

"Seven it's going to be," he said, privately placing his trust in the restorative power of seven sweet bays.

On Monday, Brewster and Skinner drove to Birmingham and loaded the truck with seven slender sweet bay laurels, their branches encased in plastic mesh. The evergreens had thick, leathery, dark green leaves with their roots bound tight in burlap.

"We got a whole forest back there," Skinner said, and they drove slowly, taking county roads instead of the highway, because they wanted to protect the trees from the wind of a fast ride.

"These the kind of trees you put the leaves in gumbo?" Skinner asked.

"That's right," Brewster said "and they have little yellow-white flowers in the spring and small black berries in the fall. In old times, they twisted the leafy branches and wrapped them around the heads of poets and athletes."

"Poets?" Skinner asked, and he turned to look at the thick-leaf trees blowing gently in the December air as they drove down the densely wooded farm roads.

On Tuesday, they began planting the trees, digging the holes deep to secure the stock of the tree and spacing them to allow each tree to grow wide and strong. By Thursday, Brewster and Skinner had planted all seven of the laurels, standing imperious in a row in the center of the newly redeemed land.

"That's a sight!" Skinner stood back, leaned on his shovel, and admired the line of trees. I'm gon' bring David out to see it, if you don't mind?"

"Fine," Brewster said. "It would do him good to see these laurels standing proud," and while he said this, Skinner began circling the line of trees, looking up at the peak of each one.

"We need to put a bench out here when the weather turns warm," Skinner said. "This could be the thinking spot." Brewster smiled when Skinner said this, and he was proud of what had been achieved on this land that had once been hard, rutted, and stripped of good soil.

On Friday afternoon, Marlenna wanted to see the land where Travis Peets had lived. She refused to enter through the woods, so they walked the short distance on Ole Summit Highway and entered the laurel grove from the road. When Marlenna saw the trees, standing tall and green in the middle of the beautifully grassed and rolling land, she wept. She put her arms around Brewster's chest, put her face over his heart, and wet his shirt with her tears. He kissed the top of her head. Without saying a word, she twined her fingers between his, and they circled the laurels, slowly, hand-in-hand.

Three days before Christmas, in late afternoon, just before night descended, Tee spotted the sheriff's car as soon as it turned on the lane. She shouted from the top of the stairs, "Daddy, sheriff's car is coming to the house."

Marlenna, who was standing by the stove, turned the burner off and walked to the front porch with Brewster. Clara Bettis got out of the passenger side in the same instant as Slim Tate unfolded himself, tall and slender on the driver's side. They came to the porch, and Slim Tate stood to one side allowing the attorney to walk before him. Marlenna led the way, followed by Clara Bettis and Slim Tate, and Brewster followed them into the kitchen where they sat around the table.

Clara Bettis breathed deeply, and Brewster saw her chest rise. "I might as well tell you. I don't want to tell you, but I don't have any choice. Slim brought me out because you need to know Travis Peets is dead. Heart attack. Nobody's fault. Deputy checked on him, came back thirty minutes later with his lunch, and the man was slumped over his bed. Dead already, but they called the ambulance and got him on to the hospital. Not a thing anybody could do."

Marlenna put her head on the table, her forehead resting on the wood. Tee leaned against the wall by the stairs watching them. Slim Tate dropped his eyes, and Clara Bettis reached her arm to Marlenna's back and rubbed her. "I'm sorry," she said.

Marlenna raised her head. "I wanted everybody to know what he did. I wanted it all told in court for everybody to hear. I wanted to see him stand before the bar of justice. I wanted to see him convicted," and with these last words, the tears flowed.

26

On Saturday evening neither Brewster nor Marlenna attended the Christmas Eve service at Low Ridge Baptist. Tee played Mary, mother of the Christ Child, in the church program; and Matthew's son, Bo, drove out to Ole Summit and gave Tee a ride to church. When the program was over, Matthew brought Tee home and he came inside.

"I want to talk a minute," Matthew announced to Brewster and Marlenna as soon as he stepped into the passage.

He sat in the chair in the big room, next to the glassed cabinet Brewster had built to house Laurel's trophies and ribbons and medals and certificates. Brewster and Marlenna sat on the sofa facing him.

"We had a splendid program," Matthew said. "Tee did a fine job. I was hoping you would both be there."

"Travis Peets not standing trial set me back, Matthew. I can't seem to get myself going," Marlenna said. Her voice was soft, low, and sounded weary.

"He's standing at the great throne now, Marlenna. Justice, perfect and pure, will be meted out. *'And I saw the dead, small and great, stand before God; and the books were opened; and another book was opened, which is the book of life and the dead were judged out of those things which were written in the books, according to their works.'* Twentieth chapter of Revelations," Matthew said, and he leaned the top of his head against the back of the chair and closed his eyes.

"And in the 4th chapter of the 1st book of Corinthians we find, *'Judge nothing before the time, until the Lord comes and He will bring to light the hidden things of darkness.'*" Matthew opened his eyes and looked directly at Marlenna. "We can put some things in God's hands. Justice is the providence of God Almighty, and we can trust in that promise.

"You need to be back in church," he said. "Back with those who love you the most and the dearest. You too, Brewster. We want you back."

Brewster had not attended Low Ridge Baptist since the funeral, and in response to Matthew's words, he grunted. Matthew looked at

Brewster but said nothing more. He stood, and the three of them walked to the door and out on the porch. The night air was cold, and Brewster shoved his hands in his pants pockets.

At the edge of the steps, Matthew turned to face Brewster. "I meant what I said. You need to be in God's house. Tomorrow is Christmas Sunday. You and Marlenna come on and celebrate God's greatest gift." The words drifted over Matthew's shoulder as he descended the steps. "The son who walked among us."

Brewster tried to hold his words inside his mouth. He pressed his lips together tightly. He held the air in his chest, but the words exploded. "Where was God when my son's heart was blown into a thousand little pieces? Was he, the great I Am, sitting on some high and mighty throne? Comfortable up there? He fell asleep, I guess. Shit, Matthew, God doesn't give one damn. I've learned that. God does not give one damn." He said the words slowly and loudly, letting them ricochet off Matthew's shoulders.

When the words hit against Matthew's back, he turned to face his assailant. His white shirt glowed an unnatural blue-green in the light from the porch. Matthew paced four steps east in front of the porch, turned sharply and paced four steps west, turned again and paced four steps, turned and paced four steps again. He walked up and back, up and back, and his words, his ammunition, poured forth seeking target.

"This is what I know, Brewster." Matthew turned, paced, turned back. "The son of God died too. At the hands of those misguided. Suffered agony. Human pain." Step, step, step, step, and he turned, "There was weeping and wailing up in the highest. And this I know too. There's weeping and wailing up there now because young Albert Laurel McAtee was murdered, taken from his father, and his mother, and his sister, and his friends, taken from all those who loved him, taken in the midst of great promise, great hope, great expectations. An untimely death." Matthew's hands flashed in front of him, up and back like hatchets cleaving deeply into his words, and Matthew's shirt glowed and shone a blue-green light as he paced. His velocity increased and his shirt flamed like wings, not wings of orange fire, but wings of cool green fire, a pure fire, virescent. Matthew paced and turned, a man in motion with blue-green, flaming wings.

"The angels are weeping because Albert Laurel McAtee was murdered. If I did not know that all the seraphs, archangels, saints, all the heavenly bodies, even God Himself is weeping, I could not stand before you." Pacing in the midst of blue-green flames, Matthew gasped for air, "I could not stand here without that certainty." Up and back Matthew paced, the bluish-green wings nearly consuming him in the cool-colored flames. "I could not have given my life spreading the word if the Almighty is not in mourning. If I did not know the comforter is standing beside you ready to embrace you, I could not give the days of my life for anything less." With these words, Matthew ran dry; the flow of his words ceased. He stopped in the porch light, and his wings fell away. He wore a man's shirt, a blue-green man's shirt that cast an eerie glow.

Marlenna stepped down with her arms outstretched and embraced Matthew. Brewster heard her sobs. She put her arms around Matthew, and they held each other, two figures reconciled and glowing in the incandescent light. But Brewster remained on the porch. He watched them and felt nothing but his own fatigue that resided inside him, a constant presence in his back and shoulders, in his limbs and his neck, in his head and on the bottoms of his feet. When Marlenna and Matthew pulled away from each other, they held hands, forming a union, a circle of two.

"I'll be there tomorrow," Marlenna said.

Brewster sat on the front porch in his heavy black jacket at the dawn of Christmas morning—a salmon-pink filament heralded the new day. His hands were stuffed deep in his coat pockets, and his head rested against the green wood slats of his chair. He closed his eyes and waited for the darkness that was inside him to lift; morning always brought release even if the relief lasted only several hours. Darkness would lift and allow him to breathe easy for an hour or two. The elephant would take a crap, Brewster thought, easing off his chest for a while. He watched the eastern sky and waited.

The pink of morning only teased him, because the clouds came, thick and heavy gray. When he went inside, Marlenna and Tee came down the stairs, turned on the white lights of the Christmas tree, and opened presents. Brewster was handed three gifts wrapped in red and green paper, and he stacked them in the corner, promising to open them later. He gave Marlenna a small diamond heart on a silver chain, and he fastened it, locking the clip around her neck. He gave Tee a silver charm bracelet with one charm on it, the numbers welded together vertically 1-9-7-8. Start new, start fresh in 1978, he wanted to tell Tee, but he let the bracelet with the solitary charm speak for itself.

Marlenna and Tee went upstairs to dress for church. They asked Brewster to go with them, but he refused. While they dressed, he walked through a cold mist to the end of the lane to get the newspaper and he took it into his shed, but he didn't read it. He placed the newspaper on the floor and put three sticks of wood in the stove, surrounding them with two handfuls of chipped kindling. Then he lit the tiny wood strips and sat in his rocking chair looking out his long window into the gray mist that was falling on his trees, his forest, his woods, and he waited for the elephant to ease off his chest. "Go on, you need to crap," he said, twisting his lips and gripping the arms of his chair. "Can't sit all night without unloading your big ole bowel. Come on, now, go on off in the woods." But the heaviness remained on top of his chest. He closed his eyes and rocked in his chair beside the wood-burning stove.

Before Marlenna and Tee left for Limrick Road Baptist, they came into the shed. Tee put her arms around him. "I love you, Daddy. Come on and go with us. We'll wait."

"No," Brewster said, and the sound came from deep inside his chest. He shook his head to confirm his resolve. He did not tell Tee that the elephant would not leave. Maybe the big monster died on his chest and would never lift itself. This idea scared him, and he wrapped his arms tightly around Tee and held her.

"You okay, Daddy?"

"Yeah," Brewster said. "I don't want to go anywhere."

Marlenna came to him and bent down where he sat. "I'm glad I'm going to church today," she said. "Come on and go with us. We're going to see Paulette when we leave and take her a present. Come on."

"No," Brewster said and with his index finger, he touched the diamond heart that rested in the soft indention in Marlenna's neck.

"I didn't cook anything special. I'll bring something from Paulette's, and we'll eat when we get home." She kissed him lightly on his lips. Brewster watched as the car turned in front of the porch and headed down the lane toward Ole Summit Highway.

He paced in his shed trying to shake the elephant loose, but the old thick-skinned pachyderm would not budge. The old boy was holding him down, pushing him into darkness so deep that he could not breathe. The rain came, thick and gray, and then the water changed into mist again, a gray veil over Brewster's kingdom. Night had become day and day was night. Brewster read a little of his newspaper, put the paper down, closed his eyes. After a little while, he lifted the paper, read a little more. He placed the paper beside his chair, stood, and paced to the doorway, looking at the grayness of this Christmas. The darkness would not lift, and his chest was so heavy he struggled to breathe.

A little past three, Marlenna and Tee pulled onto the lane. Brewster was sitting on the porch in his thick, black quilted jacket watching the low gray clouds. Marlenna got out of the car and shouted at him. "This weather's bad, but we had a good time despite it." They came into the house carrying armloads of food, and they went back to the car for more. In a short time, a bounty was laid out on the sideboard, the beautiful mahogany table with the masks of Bess carved into the top flat squares of the legs. Paulette sent a feast—roasted turkey, oyster dressing, gravy, green beans with tiny pearl onions, yellow squash casserole, cabbage rolls stuffed with rice and broccoli, yeast rolls, a peach pie, and half a coconut layer cake. Marlenna and Tee announced each dish as they set it out on the buffet, and they also gave Brewster a report on the Christmas service, who sang, and what Matthew said, and how many people gave them hugs and spoke words "that brought us back into the fellowship," Marlenna said.

Marlenna lit one candle and set it on the serving board. She put two long tapers in brass holders on the table. They sat to eat, and Marlenna said grace over the food, thanking God that Christmas morning came with new hope, a new year on the horizon, and God's great promises still in place despite all that had transpired in the year that would soon pass. She leaned in toward the table and took Tee's hand in her left and Brewster's hand in her right, and she formed a half-circle, which Brewster did not close. He listened and he wanted the words to lighten the load on his chest, to lift the darkness, but the eclipse would not pass, would not let light find him. He wanted to tell them that he sat in darkness, the deepest night, but he would not do this on Christmas Day when the candles were lit and the feast set on the sideboard and good-spirited talk flowed across the table. He would not allow his darkness to cut into their light.

He knew the food that he put in his mouth; he recognized it—turkey, dressing, green beans, but he did not taste it, and he was not hungry for it. He folded his arms and listened to Tee and Marlenna talk about Paulette, how good she looked, how much she loved her grandchildren, how beautiful the church appeared, decorated with spruce and holly. How June and Matthew stood at the front door of the church and spoke personally with each person who came to worship. How Albert Mixon was there and how he and Carmella were considering joining in membership with the congregation. "I want to be there that day," Marlenna said. "I want to live to see my father become a deacon. He will too, because he's a natural leader." Brewster saw in her face the pleasure Marlenna took in her father.

"Maybe I can sing a solo that day," Tee said. And then they discussed the song Tee would sing, and Marlenna said she might even practice the piece and accompany Tee on the piano. And Brewster listened to all this with his arms folded across his chest, waiting for the darkness to lift and the weight to lessen.

After their meal, Marlenna wanted a fire lighted in the hearth in the big room, and Brewster went to the shed to get dry wood and kindling. When the fire glowed warm and bright, Marlenna served the coffee and the coconut cake. Brewster ate it in his darkness. After the cake was eaten, Marlenna and Tee sat at the piano bench looking through the church hymnal, and Brewster put his heavy black jacket on and went to sit on the porch. The rain had stopped, but the clouds were thick and low and swirled ominously over Ole Summit, pushed by a damp, cold wind. Brewster thought about the projects awaiting him in the shed and tried to convince his legs to lift him, carry him to the shed, get started on his work. His shed always felt good with a fire in his stove and the fragrance of new wood in his hands, fresh and unblemished, but he could not compel his legs to hold him. He had no interest in his work, and this fact settled on him heavier still. The weight on him was enormous. He felt the tonnage in his legs, his back, his arms—a monster rested on him and he could not breathe.

He passed the evening between sitting in the cold air on the porch and keeping the fire going in the big room for Marlenna and Tee, but the weight pressing in on him was so heavy, he struggled to move. He would go to the doctor tomorrow. Maybe he was coming down with something, some virus that sapped his strength, absconded with his energy. Surely the doctor would give him something that would bring him back to himself, back to the place where food had taste and the warmth of fire in his own hearth drew him.

Marlenna teased him. "Daddy took Christmas off from shaving," she said to Tee. "It's a holiday, though. He deserves one day without a razor."

Brewster lifted his hand to his face and felt the rough stubble of his beard. Not once in this day had he thought about shaving, not once had the idea entered his head. This was another sign that he was sick. He would go to the doctor first thing in the morning. No need to bother Marlenna and Tee. They were getting back to themselves for the first time since Laurel was laid to rest. He would not interfere with this.

Brewster was glad when Marlenna and Tee tired of trying pieces on the piano and they went up to bed. After a while, he walked to the porch again without his jacket. He stood by the steps, looking down the lane toward Ole Summit Highway, looking at nothing in particular, observing the clouds that hung low and blew past the tops of the trees, and then he went inside and made ready for bed.

He lay on his back in the darkness, but he could not sleep. His body felt like a hundred-ton weight rested on him. He was smashed into the mattress and his joints ached, but he did not want to move for fear of disturbing Marlenna. He eased on his side, but even the weight of his own arm smothered his chest. He rotated quickly to his back. Marlenna stirred.

"Brewster, honey, you okay?"

"May be getting a cold," he said.

Marlenna brushed her palm over his chest. He was glad when she pulled her hand away and turned her back to him. He closed his eyes and his lids stuck to his pupils, feeling like parchment rubbing against parchment. He had not slept well since Laurel was put in the ground, a full eight months back, not one complete night's rest in that time. And the pain of Laurel's absence had been with him all day. No, the pain had been with him months, eight months. His eyes burned, but he lay still, keeping them closed, pressed tightly. Weight was bearing down on him, and the darkness was so dense, it made him pant for air.

He eased out of bed quietly, listening to Marlenna's heavy breathing. He reached under the bed and found his shotgun. He kept it there since Laurel was murdered. He kept it there because he needed protection close at hand, from what, he was not sure because Travis Peets was dead, but he kept his shotgun close to protect his family, although it was too late for Laurel. He slipped the gun out without making a sound, inching it slowly from under the bed, wrapping his fingers around it, and lifting it noiselessly. He held it in his hands, crossed the bedroom, closed the door silently, and went down the stairs. He found his brogans by the front door and his thick black jacket over a kitchen chair. He sat on the hallway steps, three stairs up from the bottom, and he put on his working shoes, then he put his arms into the sleeves of his jacket. He tucked the shotgun under his arm and went out to the porch.

He walked down the lane carrying the shotgun. He would not be able to cross in the woods, not in the darkness of the thick clouds. He walked to Ole Summit Highway, found the yellow line in the middle of the road, and he followed that over to his new land, Travis Peets' old place. *Showdown time*, he thought. *Showdown time*. He would slip his shoes off, put the butt of the gun in the soft dirt, position it under his neck, pull the trigger with his toe. Show down time. He raised the shotgun heavenward.

"Talk if you will," he said. "Talk. *Showdown time*."

The moon appeared between the clouds, and for some seconds the land was illuminated in cool, white light, but the clouds thickened again. Brewster stood still while his eyes adjusted to the darkness that returned. He found his way to the line of seven laurels, and he stood facing them. He placed the butt of the gun on the ground, resting the barrel against one of the laurels. "I'm done," he said in a short blast of air.

"Not one night's rest. Not touched my wife. Empty," Brewster said. "Filled with darkness." He spoke to the trees and he spoke heavenward to the thick clouds that circled over him.

He walked around the giant orb of trees, feeling the mud packed in the grooves of his thick-soled shoes. He listened, waited for a response, but nothing. Nothing as sure as the darkness that filled him. The water came, flooding his eyes. *Nothing. Nothing.*

He would take himself out like a man. Blow his head to smithereens because there was nothing. He would put something where there was nothing. A decisive blow. Cut into the darkness, the void. "I am a man," he said and raised his fist heavenward. "I am a man!" he shouted. "You are nothing. And you speak nothing. Nothing. Nothing!" he shouted.

"Mr. High and Mighty, give me one reason to put the gun under the bed. One reason. One reason. *ONE REASON!*" he shouted. He began to circle the trees a second time, tears flooding his face, running in channels out his nose, in trenches past his lips, dropping off his chin. He wiped the water with the sleeve of his thick, black coat.

"My boy's heart split to smithereens. You do not care," he accused. He raised his fist. A cold wind from the west bowed the tops of the trees. The heaviness inside him pushed him to his knees. He dropped onto his shins, the wetness in the grass soaking his pants. "My boy," he said. "His heart shattered. He was as fine as King David. Played the instruments. Stood tall. Fine head. Plenty brains.

My boy." Timber-sized sobs broke free from his chest and thick water streamed down his chin, passing in quaggy lines to the wet grass. "My boy is gone," he said. "Take *this!*" He slapped his chest with the solid palm of his hand. "This chasm is filled with darkness. Night unending!" he shouted.

Brewster stood and walked again around the trees. When he completed his second trip around the green laurels, he squatted to his knees, then he sat on the wet grass and lay flatback on the cold oozy ground, not caring that icy water soaked his jacket. Mud and water sopped around his neck and into the collar of his coat. He wept with an eruption that shook him, his whole chest rising and falling. He was emptying beyond nothing. Nothing from nothing, a void as enormous as the voice of God.

"ONE REASON!" he shouted. "One reason to put that gun under the bed. One reason to put it under my neck." He breathed now, a deep breath, then closed his eyes. He settled in the wet grass, lying flat on the ground, allowing the cold wind to blow across him. He shivered and embraced the barrel of the gun, which lay across his chest. The leaves of the laurel whooshed, dropping water on his face. If he lay very still, the frigid water warmed inside his clothing. He kept his body still, bent his elbow, brought his hands to his eyes, wiped the water, and felt the stubble on his cheeks. He felt his face, the skin under his whiskers. With his fingertips, he searched for himself, the pads of his fingers stepping over the skin of his cheeks, up the center of his nose, circling the hollows of his eyes, onto his forehead, and back down again—one finger-step at a time—his eyes, his nose, his cheeks, his lips, his chin. Again, and then again, his fingers felt his face. He folded his thick arms over his chest, allowing the barrel of the gun to rest there too. His back was wet to his spine, the water pooled around his neck, sopping into his collar, creeping past the waist of his pants, but if he lay very still, the water would not freeze him, and he could breathe. He breathed deep and stayed in the cold, dark wetness.

He was Jacob in the wilderness, but he had not even a stone on which to rest his head. He lay in the wet grass, which was punishment for all his sins, and he on the sodden ground was a mockery to God—a reasonably good man, brought down to this. Let God laugh, and that was all right, because here he was flat on the ground—proof that he and God both were nothing. God could roar with laughter because he, too, was no more than the nothing of this man stretched, supine on the seething, bitter ground. Brewster rested and let God look at him in this state. He took air, slowly, filling himself, and he closed his eyes.

That was when the ladder descended, not a ladder of fire. No, a soft ladder came down, a stairway of clouds, light, no weight whatsoever. He rested. Water in his brogans, his head in mud, a freezing wind on his face, and he rested. Maybe he slept. He was not sure.

That was when the question came to him, clearly. He heard it echo. "Do you love? Do—you—love?"

The question repeated and repeated and repeated, waiting for an answer. "Do you love? Do you love? Do you love?" He heard the question again and again. *Do you love? Do you love? Do you love?*

He allowed the question to echo through his head, echo in his neck, echo in his chest. *Do you love? Do you love?*

"I love," he said. He whispered the words because he was peaceful. "I love," he repeated, his lips moved, his head affirmed, "I love." He said this, though the water was cold on his neck. "I love Marlenna. I love Tee. I love," he said.

He rested still, his feet numb in the wet cold. A thin finger of icy water clung to his neck, but he rested.

The question. The answer. It came on him. Descended. Filled him. The answer was all over him, in his toes, up his legs, in his stomach, inside his heart, in his ears, throughout his head. "I love," he whispered. "Brewster McAtee loves."

He could not think of one reason to go on living in darkness, but he knew the answer now. Even in darkness, Brewster McAtee loves. "I love," he whispered. A bird, a musician of wind and forests, blasted one single note, and then another bird joined him. They saw morning's approach and they shouted. Brewster could not yet see morning, but he knew it was coming because the birds forecast what they had seen, and in that moment, he knew what he would do.

He had not touched Marlenna, really touched her, since Laurel was struck down. He had not held her as man and woman, husband and wife, lover to lover. He had joined sides with her in bed, and she had turned her back. He had petted her shoulder, and she said, "No, I am not ready." He needed to touch his wife. He had to do this. He had to draw her to him, put himself inside her, be one with Marlenna. He would do this because he loved. Because he was a man and he loved.

He shoved himself up on one elbow. He was light. His legs bent at the knees. He pushed and lifted himself. Water sopped in his shoes, but his feet were quick. They moved, fleet and airy, like the soles of his shoes were cushions of cloud. He put the gun under his arm, felt the water run down his neck onto his back, a cold trickle, vexing him, and he slapped at the channel. He felt the wetness on his back and down his legs.

He walked to Ole Summit Highway, crossed the narrow strip of roadside where Laurel and Ruby had stood, waiting for the school bus. He entered his lane, walked the curved path to his porch with wide, clean steps. He sat in his deep green chair, removed his shoes, and went inside with the gun under the arm of his thick, mud soaked black jacket.

Marlenna was at the kitchen table, a cup of coffee in her hand. "Brewster! Brewster!" she shouted. "Put the gun on the counter! Put the gun on the counter!" She said this again with what Brewster heard as fear and uncertainty. "Put the gun on the counter," she repeated.

He crossed to the counter with the gun held flat, the barrel in one hand and the butt in the other, holding it in both hands like an offering. He placed the shotgun on the kitchen counter, and then he removed his coat. "I'll put this outside," he said and took his wet jacket to the porch.

"Brewster, are you okay?" Marlenna shouted behind him when he opened the door to the porch.

"Fine," Brewster said.

He came back inside, went up the stairs, drew a basin of hot water and studied his face in the mirror. He shaved carefully, feeling his skin, pulling his nose back to shave close on his cheeks, lifting the skin on his neck, delivering the surface to his right hand. After he shaved, he brushed his teeth. He showered, letting the warm water run over his body where the icy-cold fingers had gripped him. He shampooed his hair, letting the soap, pushed by warm sheets of water, run across his face. When he stepped out of the shower, Marlenna stood by the sink, watching him.

"Where have you been with that gun?" she asked, her brows furrowed, her arms locked under her breasts. "You were wet and covered in mud."

Brewster toweled dry and wrapped the terry cloth around his waist, tacking one end under the band that circled his midsection.

"I'll tell you," he said.

With his hand, he took her hand and led her to their bed. They sat on the edge, and he touched his lips to the side of her face, but she drew back.

"No, no," she said.

But he would not stop. He had to go forward or they were both dead, breathing, walking dead. He did not stop. He reached across her and untied her robe and put his hand on her thigh, feeling her thin nightgown, feeling the warmth of her body.

"No, no," she said. "Brewster, I can't do this yet."

He could not turn back. They had to do this because they were alive, and they could not help this. They were alive and they loved. They would have traded places with Laurel, either of them would have done that, but they could not. They were alive, and they had to get past this deadness that wanted to claim them.

He eased her gown up her thigh, past her stomach, her breasts, and over her head. He lifted her, placing her gently on her pillow. "I'm not ready," she whispered, but she did not struggle.

Brewster thought of Laurel on the ground, on the ground in the night air of May, and he wanted to ease off Marlenna, stretch out on the cool sheets, and give up. But he would not choose death and he loved. He knew this.

He had to focus, to focus on the softness of her skin, to focus on the rawness of his desire, nothing else, nothing else, but the feel of her breast, his mouth on her nipple, pulling with his lips. Focus. The powdery skin on the inside of her thigh, the curve at her hips. His fullness against her leg. Marlenna kissed his neck, the inside of it below his chin, and it was sweet, the sweetness of her kiss almost sent sharp tears to his eyes, almost filled his brain with something other than rawness and need.

Focus, focus, focus, feel, focus, and feel. She put her mouth on his and he felt her lips, her mouth open to him. Focus, focus, no thoughts, feel, his hand between her legs, finding the spot, feel, don't think. He was inside. Don't think. Her mouth open to him. Don't think. I love you. Don't think. Don't think. Up and back. Up and back. Up and back. Don't think. I love you. I love you. Don't think. Don't think. Up and back. Up and back. I love you. I love you. I love you. Rising like an explosion. Don't think. Feel, feel, feel. I am alive and I love.

And when it was done, he collapsed his head on her neck, and she wept, big sobs, wet sobs. He put his arm under her neck, pulled her to him, and he kissed her. He wept too, in the softness under her chin. They could not go back to that spot where they had started, but they could begin from here. They were alive, they were not dead.

27

The remaining years of the 1970s unfurled themselves like continuous streamers, twisting and winding, one day into the next, into the next, and the next, uncoiling more and more distance from the awful night in May of 1977. And on into the early 1980s, every day loosening itself a little more from the knot of loss, every morning unrolling and drifting into a new day, and then another—Tee in high school, Marlenna back to her teaching, Brewster and Skinner constructing first masters for a new line of furniture contracted by a North Carolina distributor.

The *Low Ridge Gazette* ran a big story about Brewster's new contract with the Carolina furniture manufacturer, and the reporter wrote that Brewster McAtee was one of the finest craftsmen in the Southeast. Albert Mixon cut the article from the newspaper and posted it in the front window of Three Brothers, and he drove out to Ole Summit with a framed copy for the big room.

In her high school years, Tee found herself and claimed her own person. Brewster observed that she was the image of her grandmother. He heard the wisdom and the good humor of Mama Tee when she spoke, and she cared deeply for others. Why had he not seen this before? Tee had stood in Laurel's shadow and was content to be shielded there, but after Laurel's death, she had come forth and presented her own gifts. She did not push herself forward in a crowd, because she enjoyed being in the middle, but even so, she was elected president of her class at County Training School and was the leader of the Youth group at church. In these roles, she worked diligently organizing a bake sale for the prom at school, and at Low Ridge Baptist, she supervised a monthly dinner for the older church members. She was making something special of herself, Brewster thought, and he took great pride in his daughter.

In Tee's senior year of high school at County Training, a young intern joined Matthew at Low Ridge Baptist, John Henry Harris, a student from the Baptist seminary in Florida. He took a special interest in Tee, and although they did not date, he came to the house for Sunday dinner, and Tee went with him in the church van on Saturdays when he gave the senior citizens rides to the grocery store.

"I'm not like Laurel," Tee said. "I don't want to go way off to college after I graduate. I want to stay close. I'm going to Beaumont State."

"That's fine," Marlenna said. "Nobody ever said you had to go far." Tee made her preparations to move into the women's dorm in the fall, but she was also involved in all the activities that were bringing her senior year to a close.

Carmella came to Ole Summit and helped Marlenna make Tee's dress for the senior prom. Brewster listened to the women while they worked. They called the color of Tee's dress "ice blue." The top of it sparkled a purplish-blue, and the skirt was a stiffer material than the top, but it fluttered when Tee spun around. All of the space in the big room was given to the dressmaking project. The sewing machine was set in the middle of the room, the long mirror positioned to the right of it. Tee tried the dress on at least twenty times, the women pinned and fitted, and Tee studied herself in the mirror. She was larger and taller than Marlenna, full breasted and with ample hips. Her hair was cut close to her face and she wore rose-colored headbands, making her forehead appear wider but adding color to her cheeks. She was darker than Marlenna, closer in complexion to Brewster, and she had deep dimples when she smiled, adding warmth and charm to her face, by her father's evaluation. Brewster enjoyed saying whatever he thought would make her smile, because he never tired of seeing her face dimple, and this drew him to the pleasantness of her features.

Marlenna and Carmella talked and enjoyed the good-hearted fellowship of sisters; they laughed and Carmella sang, with Marlenna occasionally joining in. For several nights Brewster and Tee cooked supper, and they were happy to be a detached part of the genial fellowship of the dressmakers.

"Anvil says he's never seen a kid make such a sharp u-turn like Eddie's done after Laurel was shot," Carmella said. "I want you and Brewster to go with me to Atlanta when he graduates.'"

"We're going to do that," Marlenna said, "and Tee's coming too."

"He's applying to law schools," Carmella said. "Anvil's taking care of all that. Laurel's death opened his eyes, made him think, made him look at his own life. He's got a future now." She threaded a pearl onto the tip of her needle. "More than that," she said, "it's much more than that. He'll do something good. Something good," she repeated. "I can feel it. I know it in my bones."

"I'm proud of Eddie," Marlenna said.

Carmella reached across the skirt of the ice blue dress that was spread over their knees as they sat on the couch, and she took Marlenna's hands. "Honey," she said. "I loved Laurel with all my heart and I wanted everything good for him. I never wanted one hair on his head harmed. I would have laid down my own life for his, but I will tell you this, Laurel is still doing good things for Eddie. The boys loved each other, and Laurel's murder shook Eddie to the core. That was the turning day for Eddie. Laurel may not be here, but he's still doing good things," she said.

"I know he is," Marlenna said. "You wouldn't believe the people who tell me they have been touched by Laurel's music or by his smile. Old Mrs. Sims at church said Laurel came to her the other night. She said she woke in the night and saw him clearly, saw him sitting at the church piano, smiling and playing. She said she lay still in bed for at least half an hour listening to Laurel play. She woke in pain, but after listening to Laurel, she closed her eyes and slept."

"He'll keep on doing good," Carmella said. She placed her open palm on Marlenna's cheek, held it there a moment, and then both women reached toward the open plastic case that held the tiny pearls they were sewing to the overskirt of the blue dress.

Tee wanted to ask the young intern from the church, John Henry Harris, to the dance, but Marlenna wouldn't allow her to do that. "He doesn't go to your school and he's too old."

"I can get special permission to bring him, and besides, he's only four years older," Tee argued.

"No," Marlenna said.

Tee asked one of the boys at church to go with her to the dance, a senior who planned to go the University of Alabama after he graduated.

Late in the afternoon on Saturday, while Tee was upstairs dressing for the prom, Brewster sat in the big room and switched on the TV to watch the news. The lead story made him shift forward to the edge of the couch, leaning toward the TV screen. A young black man, nineteen years old, was found that morning hanging from a tree in downtown Mobile. He had been beaten and his throat slashed. The district attorney said he didn't think the crime was racially motivated, but a black state senator from Mobile named Michael Figures said he believed white extremists were involved.

Brewster pulled a small notebook from his pocket, the one he used to record measurements and to make lists of supplies for the shed. He took his ballpoint pen and he wrote in his pocket notebook: *March 21, 1981, Michael Donald, 19, found lynched in Mobile.* He clicked the remote control before Tee and Marlenna came down the stairs. He did not want them to hear the story tonight, but he would be sitting on the front porch waiting for Tee when her date pulled his car onto the lane after the dance. If she was as much as ten minutes late, he would go searching for her.

After all the pictures were taken of Tee and her date, and the young couple left for the dance, Brewster convinced Marlenna to drive with him into Low Ridge to get a milkshake from the Ice Cream Churn. This kept Marlenna distracted and away from the news. Brewster did not want her to worry, and he did not want her to hear the news about the young black man found lynched in Mobile. While he and Marlenna were out, they drove past County Training School. Brewster saw the flash of strobe lights in the gymnasium, and in some strange way, this made him feel comfortable. Tee was at a dance, a school dance; the lights were flashing and everything would be okay. What had happened to Laurel would not happen to Tee. She was in the gymnasium at County Training, and the strobe lights were flashing, creating a fantasy world that the students strutted in and out of while light burst as bright as the sun.

It was the next morning when Marlenna saw the newspaper and she learned the awful news from the headline in bold black ink sprawled across the middle of the page.

MICHAEL DONALD, YOUNG BLACK MAN, LYNCHED IN MOBILE

"I cannot believe this," Marlenna said. "No," she whispered. "This cannot have happened." She folded the newspaper and held it against her chest. When Marlenna put the paper on the table, Brewster sat down, put a cup of coffee beside the newspaper, and he read every word about the young man and about his death.

Michael Donald had walked to his sister's house two blocks away on Friday night. His mother, Beulah Mae Donald, said she woke at two in the morning, realized her son was not home, called his sister who said he left her house to buy a package of cigarettes at the corner gas station. She thought he had gone home. Mrs. Donald made coffee and waited up all night for her son to return, but instead, his body was found after daybreak on Saturday morning hanging from a tree in the downtown area. The article said Michael Donald worked part-time in the mailroom at the Mobile newspaper, he studied masonry at a local technical college, he dated two or three girls, and he was thinking about joining the Army.

Marlenna wondered out loud if all of Alabama had gone crazy. If she and Brewster and Tee and Carmella and her father should pack up and run for their lives. Brewster held Marlenna in his arms and kissed the top of her head. "Let everything work its course," Brewster told her. "There's no proof of one thing or another. We'll be cautious," he said. While he was saying this, he was already planning precautions he would take—more lights outside, and he would load the shotgun and keep it on the top shelf in the bedroom. He kissed Marlenna again and went to his shed to work on a draft of a dresser to match a new bed he had recently designed.

Matthew came late on Saturday afternoon. "I want Marlenna to go with me to Mobile to meet Michael Donald's mother. I've spoken with several family members there, and his mother wants to talk with Marlenna, you too, Brewster, if you'll go with us. Your son shot by a crazy racist, her son on a tree, his throat slashed. Time to talk," Matthew said.

"No, Matthew," Brewster said. "You and Marlenna go on. It should be one mother to another mother." Brewster did not want to talk to Beulah Mae Donald because he did not want to open his own wound, to stand raw and exposed, to be interviewed by the news media, to relive Laurel's death, and to see the pain of someone else in the hell that he was just beginning to crawl out of. In short, he did not want to put himself in the middle of this awful murder. Marlenna wanted to meet Beulah Mae Donald, and Matthew wanted to take her to Mobile. Brewster would let them go. He decided to wait at Ole Summit and to have his arms open for Marlenna when she returned. At least one of them could stand as a bulwark, steadied and distanced from this awful crime.

On Monday morning, Matthew and Marlenna drove to Mobile, and late in the afternoon when they returned, Marlenna went up to their bedroom, but Matthew sat on the porch with Brewster. "It was a good trip," he said. "One woman comforted the other, but Marlenna's tired. That took something out of her today." The two men watched a hawk circle the trees, looking for prey. The bird soared and swooped closer to the trees, flapped his strong wings and looped around the woods again.

"Mrs. Donald says the police have asked all kinds of questions about her son, whether or not he was involved in drugs or was he dating a married woman, or things such as that. His mother said no to all of those questions and told them she suspects the Klan. She told me she had heard of the Klan stopping cars, asking for money on county roads around Mobile, but she's surprised this thing could happen in the city, the very heart of the city," Matthew said.

Tee graduated from County Training School in May, and the Michael Donald case still had not been solved. Marlenna subscribed to the *Mobile Beacon*, a black-owned and black-run newspaper. The *Mobile Register* had long since retired the story to the B-section, but Michael Donald's lynching was front page in every issue of the *Beacon*. The FBI had been called in and that organization vowed to solve the crime, but there were no breaks in the case. When Tee started to Beaumont State in the fall, Michael Donald's murderer or murderers were still on the loose.

Tee moved into the women's dormitory and made her decision to study early elementary education because she wanted to follow in her mother's footsteps and teach. But by the end of her first semester, she was ready to move home again. "I want to go to college," Tee said, "but I want to live at home. I'll drive to Beaumont State three days a week, take my courses, and then I can help out at church. I don't want to give up my senior-citizen suppers. The old folks at church need me," Tee said.

"That's fine," Marlenna said, and she and Brewster rented a trailer to haul Tee's things back to her room at Ole Summit.

"She's interested in one certain party at Limrick Road Baptist," Matthew said. "And that certain party she's interested in is one of the finest young men I've ever met. I'm doing everything I can do to keep him here in Low Ridge. The senior citizens love him, the young folks love him, and there are about four young women at church who are trying to get his attention. I suspect Tee sees all that," Matthew said, and he laughed. "She wants to come home and stake out her own territory."

In the spring of 1983, it became official that Helen Teelda McAtee and John Henry Harris were dating. John Henry made regular appearances at Ole Summit, and in May, Marlenna and Tee drove to Florida to observe his ordination in his home church. "He's every bit as fine as Matthew says," Marlenna told Brewster. "I met his mother and his father and his three sisters. They're good people. He's a young man with plenty of vision."

Matthew went to the Board of Deacons and received approval to offer John Henry the job of associate pastor at Limrick Road Baptist. He was assigned the job of preaching one service a month and teaching the youth on Sunday mornings and Sunday nights. In the fall Tee helped him establish a daycare at the church.

"Working mothers need daycare," Tee said. "Black women have had to leave their children wherever they could. Many times the children have been left at home to take care of themselves. John Henry wants to end that," she said. "He wants the children in a good and safe place, and he wants me to plan activities for the older ones."

Brewster was delighted and amused at Tee's commitment to the new daycare. He and Skinner built cabinets for the new school, and they assembled box-like cubbyholes for the children to put their belongings in when they came to Limrick Road Baptist Daycare. Tee was busy, and she was happy. When Tee wasn't at Beaumont State, she was at church helping John Henry, and on Tuesdays and Thursdays she worked all day in the Limrick Road Baptist Daycare.

In June of 1983, a little over two years after Michael Donald was murdered in downtown Mobile, the case exploded wide open. One Klan member informed on another. James "Tiger" Knowles and Henry Francis Hays were arrested for murder. Tiger Knowles cooperated with the police and the story unfolded.

On Friday evening, March 20, 1981, Hays and Knowles, members of Klavern 900, the Mobile unit of the United Klan of America, went in search of a black man to murder—any black man would do. They were angry because a jury in Birmingham had failed to convict a black man of killing a white Birmingham police officer. Hays and Knowles wanted to kill a black man in Mobile as retaliation, and they reasoned that the lynching of a black man would show the strength of the Klan in south Alabama.

Nineteen-year-old Michael Donald happened to be walking home from his sister's when the two men spotted him. At gunpoint, they forced him into their car. They drove him to a different location, took him out of the car, beat him with tree branches, slashed his throat, and returned him to downtown Mobile where they hung him from a tree—the grisly scene, visible in the early dawn of Saturday morning, March 21.

After the arrests, Marlenna received a hand-written letter from Beulah Mae Donald: "People were telling me there wasn't no such thing as the Klan. Michael must have been doing something wrong. I'm glad it's all come to light."

Just after Tee started her junior year at Beaumont State, John Henry proposed marriage. The young couple sat at the kitchen table and told Brewster and Marlenna about their dreams and their plans. John Henry would stay in Low Ridge until after Tee earned her degree, and then he would seek a church of his own where he could minister to the people "and serve God as I am led," John Henry said. After their wedding, they would rent a small house off Limrick Road, and they would continue to run the daycare at Limrick Road Baptist. Brewster and Marlenna listened and urged the young couple to live at Ole Summit until they were located at a different church.

"We have plenty of room here," Marlenna said. "We'll let you go when the time comes, but let's be together for as long as we can be."

Later that evening, Marlenna put her head on Brewster's chest as they lay in bed with the moon casting white-blue rays across the cream-colored blanket that covered them. "It will be you and me before long," she said. "Back to where we began. Sometimes I lie awake at night and think about events and moments, and I can see them clearly. I wonder why it is that of all the days and hours of our lives, certain times play before us with every detail as clear as the day the event happened." She brought her hand to his and her fingers clasped his palm.

"I can see Our Savior's Home on the morning Laurel was born, and I know the feel of Laurel when I held him the first time. I put my nose to his mouth before he had any nourishment, before even water entered him, because I wanted to know the smell of life so fresh from heaven. His air was clean and new. I can smell it now, Laurel's unspoiled air."

Brewster brushed her hair off of her neck, and he placed the tips of his fingers against the base of her head, working the pads of his fingers in circles.

"I know the angle of the sunlight when we walked home from the courthouse, the second and third registered voters in Low Ridge.

It was lovely, low-angled winter light, and it reflected off the corner of the flower shop on State Street.

"And when Laurel played the piano, Brewster, those moments were bigger than other moments. They stopped in front of my eyes and allowed me to examine every detail, and I hold all of those times here," and Marlenna put her open palm to her forehead, "and here," and she touched the soft flesh above her heart.

When the Michael Donald case came to trial, Tiger Knowles, who was 17 at the time of the murder and who served as an FBI informant, was given a life sentence; Henry Francis Hays, who was 26 at the time of the murder, was given a death sentence. Another man who supplied the rope for the lynching was given 99 years in prison.

In early 1984, Marlenna received a letter from Beulah Mae Donald. She was suing the United Klan of America and six present members of the Mobile Klavern for their property. She was represented by Civil Rights attorney Morris Dees from Montgomery, and she invited Marlenna to come observe the trial. But Marlenna had her teaching and her students to consider, and she remained in Low Ridge.

In February, Marlenna read in the newspaper that Beulah Mae Donald won her case. An all-white jury assessed $7 million in punitive damages against the United Klan of America and the six individual defendants. Mrs. Donald was to receive a quarter of all wages the six men earned for the rest of their lives. The newspaper said the verdict effectively broke the back of the Klan in south Alabama.

"Hallelujah!" Marlenna said. She and Brewster sat at the kitchen table and wrote a letter to Mrs. Donald. "Congratulations on the victory that you won on behalf of your son Michael. Travis Peets died before he stood at the bar of justice, but the Klan here in Alabama has been brought down by your strong hold around their necks and by your courage. We are happy for you, and we take some solace in this judgment on behalf of our own son, Laurel. Justice was served and for that, we are grateful to you and we congratulate you on your valor!"

In June, Tee and John Henry were married at Limrick Road Baptist, and every seat in the sanctuary was taken. People stood in the back of the church to hear the vows spoken, and the congregation rewarded the young couple by wrapping their arms around them and whispering fond wishes into their ears. And the congregation brought gifts—hand-embroidered pillowcases, crocheted potholders, satin table runners with tatted edges, hand-stitched quilts, and Mr. Sampson Riley, a fine artist, promised to paint a portrait of their first-born child.

In August, Matthew announced he would stay on at Limrick Road until the summer of '85, then he planned to take his retirement and move to the Mississippi Gulf Coast. "June has family there," Matthew said. "I've always promised her we would go back. She's been here with me all these years, and fair is fair. We need to be with her family while we've still got a little life left in us. June's mother is ninety, and we want to be part of her last days."

Matthew put John Henry's name before the Board of Deacons to become the new pastor of Limrick Road Baptist when he retired, and Matthew's recommendation passed unanimously. John Henry accepted the offer and continued working with Matthew, preparing himself for full ministry.

The same month Tee graduated from Beaumont State, she announced that she and John Henry were expecting a child. With no money in the bank and little enough to carry them through each month, they were, nonetheless, happy about their news. They told the senior citizen Sunday school class, and all the women in the class brought them names, handwritten on scraps of paper, folded tightly, or rolled into tiny scrolls.

At Ole Summit, Marlenna and Carmella began sewing for the baby—day gowns, tiny shirts, and receiving blankets in white and yellow. Brewster brought the old cradle from the attic, the one with the fans radiating from a central button, the one he had built for Laurel, the one Laurel and Tee has rested in; he took the cradle to his shed so he and Skinner could refurbish it for the new baby. And he deeded three acres of land to Tee and John Henry, land on the east side of the lane where they could build their house when the time came.

"We don't have the money yet," Tee said. "Besides, we'll need to move into the parsonage for a while, I guess, at least until we can bring the issue up with the Deacons."

"The land is yours," Brewster told them, "whenever you're ready to build on it."

The last of his pastoral duties before leaving for Mississippi was one Matthew never imagined he would be called upon to perform. He was asked to serve as the principal officiate for the funeral of Anvil Thomas, who was killed in an airplane crash near Frankfort, Germany. Anvil was on official business for the NAACP when his plane went down in a storm. Anvil enjoyed a national reputation and people from all over the United States were en route to Low Ridge to be part of the memorial service. Matthew was heartsick over the news. "It's a great loss for all of us," he told Brewster, and he closed himself in his tiny office off the metal platform, up the iron stairs, to ponder and meditate over what he would say.

Brewster called Anvil's young wife to ask her what he could do, and she asked him to speak. She wanted Brewster to tell the story about how Anvil won the Peets' land for him and Marlenna without ever going to court. She wanted Brewster to tell the world how he had cleared the land and how he had planted seven laurels in the center of the land Anvil had won for them—seven sweet bays, ever green, and bringing forth their fruit in season. She wanted Brewster to tell how Anvil had made this possible.

Of all the things Mary Ann Thomas could have asked Brewster to do, the hardest thing was for him to stand in front of a crowd of dignitaries from around the country and speak. He was a man who guarded his silence, a man who stood back and let others talk, but for Anvil, he would do this, and for Mary, his wife, and for their young son, Anvil Jr. He did not know how he would rise, walk to the lectern at Limrick Road Baptist, and speak with the world listening, but he would summon his courage and he would stand and he would tell his story, which was also part of Anvil's story.

He wrote it down, the story of his son, of Laurel's great gifts, of Laurel's promise, and he wrote of Travis Peets who burst his son's heart with a single bullet. Then he wrote about Anvil coming to him and offering to help in any way that he could, he wrote about Anvil speaking with Mrs. Peets and making clear to her that she would be sued in court for the land. He wrote about how the land came to him, but he would not walk on it until every sign was removed that Travis Peets ever lived on the land; he would tell them about having the dirt scraped and new topsoil spread and how he had planted seven laurels in the middle of the land. Now he could look at the land, rescued from the wicked and reclaimed, because Anvil Thomas stood for that which was right. He had come and asked to help, and he had claimed the land for Brewster and Marlenna. They could continue to live on their own land off Ole Summit Highway because Anvil Thomas had helped them annihilate the vestiges of evil there.

Marlenna read what he had written, and she rearranged some of his sentences. She added some of her own thoughts, and when that was done, Brewster practiced his speech with small notecards in his hand. Marlenna listened and Tee listened and Skinner listened, as did Albert Mixon and Carmella. Brewster was a man who loved silence, but now he would rise to speak, standing before television cameras and news reporters who would come to cover the funeral of Anvil Thomas. He would rise and speak.

The day of the funeral, he sat in the church with resolve that went down his back like an iron rod, went down his legs and buttressed him. He would rise and speak and tell the world about Laurel, his heart thundering out of him in tiny crimson shards, and he would tell how Anvil won the land and about the struggle that had oppressed all black men, but Anvil had taken part of the burden of that struggle on his own shoulders and had carried it for them all. He knew that, and he would stand and say it.

When he rose to speak, he felt sweat bullets gather on his forehead, but he walked to the lectern, and he heard the sound of his own voice, strong and steady. He told the story of his only son and of Anvil Thomas who stood for justice and fairness. Both Laurel and Anvil were called too soon, too early—before their full fruit had come to harvest. But the fruit they brought forth was good and beautiful. He breathed deeply, filling his chest with air, and he spoke. Brewster Thomas McAtee stood, and he spoke.

When he sat down, Marlenna twined her fingers between his and pulled his hand into her lap. He looked at Anvil's young son, ten years old now, who sat beside his mother and listened to the tributes uttered in honor of his father. Brewster thought how strange it was that he was a father without a son, and young Anvil Jr., a son without a father.

Brewster was on the evening news, standing behind the lectern at Limrick Road Baptist, telling the story of his son and of Anvil Thomas, but he did not watch the news. He had no interest in seeing himself on television. He had stood and he had spoken, and that was sufficient.

When the time came for her child to be delivered, Tee walked in the front doors of Low Ridge Hospital, not in the side entrance where the old colored wing had been. A young white nurse wheeled her to her room, chewing gum and talking all the while. John Henry Harris Jr. entered the world in the early morning hours of November 14, 1985. A white doctor with a kind face and good humor delivered the child from his mother's womb.

"A baby at Ole Summit," Marlenna said. "A new generation."

"A son," Brewster said. When he held the baby, he looked in Marlenna's eyes, and he brought the baby to his chest. He lowered his face to the baby's mouth and breathed the air above the baby's lips. He too wanted to take into himself the air of heaven.

28

Young John Henry Harris, who was called Jay, brought joy to Ole Summit. He was held and laughed over, nurtured, loved and instructed. Tee and John Henry took great delight in their son and carried him in their arms like a prince on a royal cushion. When he learned to toddle, he followed at Brewster's heels, and when he spoke, he summoned "Big Daddy, Big Daddy," and Brewster came to him.

When Brewster and the hired man planted the field across the lane in cotton, Jay rode on the tractor seat beside his grandfather. Brewster explained every operation to the youngster who listened as they tilled the soil, furrowed the ground, and scattered the seeds. Jay grabbed a fistful of the dark, rich Alabama earth and shoved it in the pocket of his small blue jeans.

"What are you doing?" Brewster asked.

"Putting my dirt in my pocket," Jay said. Brewster laughed and lifted him above his shoulders, lifted him heavenward.

Herman Thomas didn't live a year after Anvil was put in the ground, and when he died, the school board decided to close County Training School and send all the children to what had been predominately white schools. Marlenna decided to retire. "We need to travel," she told Brewster. "We'll make another trip to New York and we'll go see Matthew and June down in Biloxi." And they did these things, but this time when they went to New York, they took the airplane, flew from Birmingham to Atlanta, and from there to New York City, and Brewster saw what the earth looked like from above, how small everything was, how tiny each house was, how insignificant it all looked.

In New York he and Marlenna saw two Broadway plays, ate in fancy restaurants, shopped in expensive stores, and he was ready to come home before their five days were over because he missed Jay and Tee and John Henry, and he even missed Skinner. When they boarded the plane, he wished he could go back home on the train he and Marlenna rode on nearly thirty-five years earlier, the train they had taken on their honeymoon from New York to Low Ridge, but this time they wouldn't sit in the colored car, they would ride up front, and they would eat in the dining car. He would like to do that, but not go back in time because he accepted all that had happened, all the days and hours were a part of him, and he carried all his time, even his minutes and seconds, inside himself. But he would like to ride that train again, eat in the dining car, and let Marlenna sleep on his shoulder. He would wrap his arms around her and let the woods and the railyards and the cities pass by, and she would sleep, contented on his shoulder.

Tee got a job teaching at Low Ridge Elementary, and in the fall of 1992, Jay started first grade at the same school where his mother taught. John Henry and Tee broke ground for their new house on the east acres that Brewster had given them. John Henry had worked with Brewster and Skinner to draw up the plans for their new house. Tee wanted wide porches on the first and second floors of her house, and she wanted French doors that opened onto her porches, and she wanted the outside of her house painted yellow because she loved light and she said yellow was the color of enlightenment. "The older I get," Tee explained, "the more I want to understand, and the longer I work with children the more open my mind grows. Besides all that," she said and wrinkled her nose in an expression that reflected Mama Tee, "yellow is a happy color."

In October, Matthew and June returned to Low Ridge as honored guests to celebrate Founders Day at Limrick Road Baptist. Matthew was serving as minister to a small congregation just outside Biloxi, Mississippi. He was as busy as he had been in Low Ridge—going to the hospital, visiting the elderly at home, preparing his sermons.

"I thought you'd retired," Marlenna teased him.

"I'll be dead when I stop serving the Lord," Matthew said and sounded noble and lofty.

But June brought them all down to earth when she retorted, "The man doesn't know when to stop. He'll drop dead taking some of those old women to the doctor. They think he's a thoroughbred, but he's a draft horse trudging from here to there trying to do something for everybody. Poor man's so tired when he goes to bed at night the lights don't go out before he's snoring."

Brewster put his hand on Matthew's shoulder. "Truth is, June, he'll be serving everybody who needs him until that old draft horse in him won't haul another load. That's Matthew and that will always be Matthew," he said.

June put her arms around her husband. "You're right, Brewster. And I guess I love him for it."

"The old draft horse still got ears," Matthew said and brought his hands up toward his head. They laughed and teased each other in this manner, and sometimes their conversation grew serious.

"I read in the paper over in Mississippi that the state of Alabama will finally execute Henry Francis Hays for the lynching of Michael Donald in Mobile," Matthew said.

"Guess that'll finally close it," Brewster said.

"He was twenty-six when he killed that boy in Mobile, and he'll be nearly forty when the state ends the story. Beulah Mae didn't live to see it, but she didn't want it. What she wanted was her son back. And that was not to be."

"I can tell you about that, Matthew. I know all about wanting that which cannot be and how you let go of it a little at a time, but your fingers still have a hold on the idea, you don't want to grasp it— don't close your fingers on it, don't pull the idea close to you, just let it stay loose in your hand, and you'll be alright. If you pull that idea too close to you, it will suck you into it and you'll be gone. But I keep Laurel held lightly, here, my hands on him," and Brewster held his hands up, his palms open, his fingers spread wide.

"Newspaper said Henry Francis Hays will be the first white man put to death for killing a black man in Alabama since 1913."

"Don't make me feel one bit better," Brewster said.

"Me either," Matthew said.

"But it's closed and done, and the Klan got a whipping. They'll come back though, in one form or another."

"Evil always does," Matthew said. "Earth is the province of good and evil. Every man and woman has an obligation to do good to keep the evil at bay," Matthew said. "At least give the Evil One a run for his money," he added.

"I look back on it all, Matthew, on everything that has happened, and I think of a hundred things I could have done differently. I could have saved Laurel if I had given up this place. Turned and run the first day I saw that old coot come on my land. Tucked my tail and run."

"No point in thinking that way," Matthew said. "How many times has this place saved you? How many times has this place sustained you? Where would you have built your home? What timbers would you have used for the beams and the foundation? Where would you have gone when they burned you down in Low

Ridge? You had your place here, and it sustained you and Laurel too. No reason to surrender your dream to evil. Don't have second thoughts about that," Matthew said.

"It cost me, Matthew."

"The Evil One is everywhere, Brewster, and for no reason that any of us can explain, he slips around and does his meanness. That's the way of the world. Won't change. You did right, Brewster. There was not one thing you did that can be faulted. You had courage and you held the ground that belonged to you. No man can be faulted for that."

"Courage?" Brewster raised his voice in a question. "You and Anvil and Marlenna and a hundred others marched and protested, spoke up and spoke out, when I was silent. I was building Three Brothers and saving Ole Summit, and all of you were out doing my battle."

"Now hold on a minute here, Brewster. You and Marlenna went to the courthouse and got registered to vote before any of the rest of us did. And your shop was burned to the ground because of it. No, I won't let you talk like that. You did more than your part. Who was the first black man to own a store on State Street? Who was the black man who raised a son capable of playing piano in the house of old Jake Warner? Who was the black man who served as a pillar in the community, loving his family, building furniture that is recognized as art, adding stature to the black man by his accomplishments? That's you, Brewster. That's you."

"I look at it all, Matthew, and it doesn't seem enough. I could have done more. I had opportunities."

"What's the day of your birth?" Matthew asked.

"The thirtieth day of August," Brewster answered.

"Well," Matthew said. "Life won't be measured by this August or last August or the one before that or the one in nineteen-hundred and fifty-seven or any other August. It's the sum of them all, Brewster. You got to do the addition—the sum of all the Augusts. That's how you get the final score. All the Augusts added up," he said. "And the score is a big fine number, more than passing."

Brewster laughed when Matthew said this. The men sat in silence listening to the cicadas, and each man enjoyed sitting in the presence of the other.

Tee and John Henry completed their house in early spring, and Brewster gave them a table and eight chairs for their dining room, chairs made of dark-notched pecan with cathedral slats crossed and arched in the back rests. The chairs were elegant with the arches reflecting that which is ancient and time-honored, but the sweep of the arches appeared dramatic and modern.

The forest was cut between the two houses, and the ground laid in sod. "Looks like a grassy knoll," Tee said. "Our own park."

"Or meadow," Marlenna said. "A meadow leading from our house to yours."

On a weekend in early May, Brewster, Skinner, and John Henry laid a stone walkway through the grassy meadow, a direct path from the narrow white house with the wide porches to the tall yellow house with porches top and bottom, and French doors that looked out on Ole Summit Highway.

On a hot Saturday afternoon in late May, young Jay went with his grandfather to check the cotton planted in the field across Ole Summit Highway. They walked the rows up and back, up and back with the sun blazing on their shoulders and the heat passing over them in oppressive waves. Brewster stopped several times to catch his breath. A weight had been on his chest for days. It was the heat, the thick sultry hot of a steamy Alabama summer coming on that weighted him. Short, wiry pains had shot through his chest for several days, and he made a note in his mind to call the doctor on Monday. There was no great rush because the doctor couldn't do one thing about the heat, but maybe he could give him some medicine that would help him take off a pound or two. His belly pushed hard against his belt, and it was time to slim down. He needed to be more active, get more exercise. That was what he needed to do.

"Jay, I'll race you to the porch," Brewster said. "Big Daddy needs to work some of this fat off. Not be quite so big."

They stood on the side of Ole Summit Highway across from the lane, and Brewster allowed Jay to call, "On your mark, READY, SET, GO!"

Brewster and Jay shot across the highway. Brewster worked his legs, lifting high, pulling through the heat, keeping within a neck's distance of Jay, running past the woods, past the stone walkway that led to the yellow house, past Marlenna's car, and on toward the porch, but when Brewster reached the porch, his heart throbbed like an open wound, an enormous red wound slitting wide open. Pain shot across him, doubling him, and he fell on the porch when he reached the top step. The pain took his breath away, and his arms were weak as settled water.

Jay thought he was teasing.

"Okay, you win, Granddaddy. Some people got to play dirty to win. Let's say it was a tie," he said.

Brewster's knees drew to his chest, and when Jay saw his grandfather's face, he shouted for his grandmother who came running. When Marlenna saw Brewster doubled into himself, lying on his side on the green floorboards of the porch, she bent to him, but he did not see her.

Brewster saw TeeBoy dancing in the yard, lifting his legs high, laughing, stepping to a steady rhythm, TeeBoy raised his hand and motioned, *come on, Brewster, come on*, but Brewster heard Laurel playing the piano in the big room, and it was sweet, some of the sweetest notes Brewster ever heard. A fine piece, a marching piece, the notes crisp and sharp, a thousand soldiers in perfect step, and maidens on the side watching, sweet little maidens in filmy skirts, floating to Laurel's music.

Come on, Brewster, come on, TeeBoy motioned, and he danced. *Come on. Come on.*

"Don't you hear Laurel playing the piano? I haven't heard him play in such a long time. It's sweet, TeeBoy. Sweet."

Come on, Brewster. Come on.

Marlenna called the county rescue number and was connected to a small office in the basement of Low Ridge County Hospital. An ambulance was on the way.

Jay ran across the grassy meadow for his mother, but Brewster didn't know any of this. He was listening to Laurel play the piano, the melodies rising and falling, drifting through the air exactly as they had done so many years ago. But TeeBoy's hand pulled through the air. *Come on, Brewster. Come on. Come on.*

I'm coming, TeeBoy. I'm right behind you. I'm coming on. Let Laurel finish this piece, and I'll be right on.

Epilogue

The funeral was one of the biggest Low Ridge had ever seen. The doors were opened at Limrick Road Baptist, and folks stood outside to hear Matthew speak of his friend Brewster Thomas McAtee. The *Low Ridge Gazette* carried a front-page story about Brewster's contributions to the community. After Brewster was laid to rest beside Bess and Laurel in the old Hope Hill Cemetery, folks came to Ole Summit bringing food and sweet messages of love.

Marlenna sat beside Carmella in the big room, and Tee sat with Jay on the front porch. "Your grandfather was a great man," Tee said.

"I know that," Jay said, and he wiped his eyes again with the tissue he held in his small fist.

"He loved you with all of his heart."

"I know that too," Jay said.

"He loved this land. He always wanted to own all the land from Low Ridge out to our place here, but he could never get it all. But what he did get will one day belong to you. Jay. Look down the lane and over to the cotton field, look north and south. It will all belong to you. It will be your job to take care of it. Your granddaddy worked hard to get it for you."

"I'll take care of it," Jay said. "This was Big Daddy's land. One day I'll buy the rest of the land from Low Ridge all the way out to our place." Tee reached across the arm of the chair that Brewster had built years before, and she took Jay's hand in her own. They sat on the porch, watching over the lane until the sun dropped to the edge of the green line of Brewster McAtee's woods, and the night birds called.